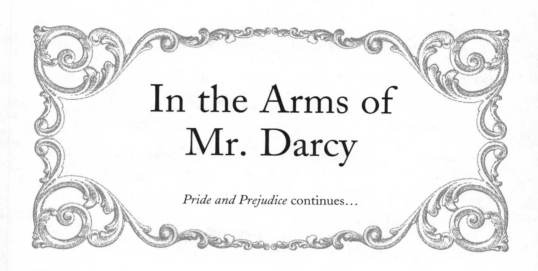

In the Arms of Mr. Darcy

Pride and Prejudice continues…

Sharon Lathan

sourcebooks landmark

Poems quoted by Darcy in Chapter 9:
"The Passionate Shepherd to His Love" by Christopher Marlowe, 1599
"Your Smile Stops the Minutes" by Stephen Lathan, 1986

Published by Sourcebooks Landmark, an imprint of Sourcebooks, Inc.
P.O. Box 4410, Naperville, Illinois 60567-4410
(630) 961-3900
FAX: (630) 961-2168
www.sourcebooks.com

Library of Congress Cataloging-in-Publication Data
Lathan, Sharon.
In the arms of Mr. Darcy : Pride and prejudice continues / Sharon Lathan.
p. cm.
1. Darcy, Fitzwilliam (Fictitious character)--Fiction. 2. Bennet, Elizabeth (Fictitious character)--Fiction. 3. Married people--Fiction. 4. Marriage--Fiction. 5. England--Social life and customs--19th century--Fiction. 6. Domestic fiction. I. Austen, Jane, 1775-1817. Pride and prejudice. II. Title. III. Title: In the arms of Mister Darcy.
PS3612.A869I55 2010
813'.6--dc22
                                    2010018226

Printed and bound in the United States of America
VP 10 9 8 7 6 5 4 3 2 1

The Darcy Saga

BY SHARON LATHAN

This novel is dedicated to my husband, Steve. For over twenty-four years this amazing man has proven to me what romance and true love are. The poem that Mr. Darcy writes and recites to Elizabeth while dancing on Twelfth Night was actually written for me by my husband, at the time my fiancé, and he still quotes it from memory often while gazing into my eyes, just as he did all those years ago. Because of him, my tale of happily-ever-after is possible. Honey, I love you forever! You truly are my soulmate, my blood and bone.

Table of Contents

Cast of Characters

Fitzwilliam Darcy: Master of Pemberley in Derbyshire: 29 years of age, born November 10, 1787; married Elizabeth Bennet on November 28, 1816

Elizabeth Darcy: Mistress of Pemberley: 22 years of age, born May 28, 1795

Alexander Darcy: Heir to Pemberley; born November 27, 1817

Georgiana Darcy: 18 years of age; companion is Mrs. Annesley

Colonel Richard Fitzwilliam: 33 years of age; cousin and dear friend to Mr. Darcy; second son of Lord and Lady Matlock; regiment stationed in London

Lord Matlock: the Earl of Matlock: Darcy's Uncle Malcolm, brother to Lady Anne Darcy; ancestral estate is Rivallain in Matlock, Derbyshire

Lady Matlock: the Countess of Matlock: Darcy's Aunt Madeline, wife to Lord Matlock

Jonathan Fitzwilliam: Heir to the Matlock earldom, eldest Fitzwilliam son; wife is *Priscilla*

Lady Annabella Montgomery: sister of Richard and Jonathan Fitzwilliam

Charles Bingley: Longtime friend of Mr. Darcy; residence Hasberry Hall, Derbyshire; married Jane Bennet on November 28, 1816

Jane Bingley: elder sister of Elizabeth and eldest Bennet daughter; wife of Mr. Bingley

Caroline Bingley: sister of Charles Bingley

Louisa Hurst: married sister of Charles Bingley; husband is *Mr. Arbus Hurst*; residence London

Mr. and Mrs. Bennet: Elizabeth's parents; reside at Longbourn in Hertfordshire with two middle daughters, *Mary* and *Kitty*

Mary Bennet: Elizabeth's sister; middle Bennet daughter

Joshua Daniels: betrothed to *Mary Bennet*; son and partner of Mr. Darcy's London solicitor, *Andrew Daniels*

Katherine (Kitty) Bennet: Elizabeth's sister; fourth Bennet daughter

Lydia Wickham: Elizabeth's sister; youngest Bennet daughter; married to *Lieutenant George Wickham*, stationed in Newcastle

Edward and Violet Gardiner: uncle and aunt of Elizabeth; reside in Cheapside, London

Dr. George Darcy: Mr. Darcy's uncle; brother to James Darcy; resides at Pemberley

Lady Simone Fotherby: widowed Marchioness of Fotherby, Buckinghamshire

Marchioness of Warrow: Darcy's great-aunt; sister to his grandfather

Sebastian Butler: grandson to Lady Warrow; future Earl of Essenton

Lady Catherine de Bourgh: Mr. Darcy's aunt; sister to Lady Anne Darcy; residence Rosings Park, Kent

Anne de Bourgh: daughter of Lady Catherine; Mr. Darcy's cousin

Dr. Raul Penaflor Aleman de Vigo: betrothed to Miss de Bourgh

Stephen Lathrop: Cambridge friend of Mr. Darcy; residence is Stonecrest Hall in Leicestershire; wife is *Amelia*

Henry Vernor: family friend of the Darcys; residence is Sanburl Hall near Lambton, Derbyshire; wife is *Mary*, daughter is *Bertha*

Gerald Vernor: son of Henry Vernor; childhood friend of Mr. Darcy; wife is *Harriet*; residence is Sanburl Hall

Albert Hughes: childhood friend of Mr. Darcy; wife is *Marilyn*; residence is Rymas Park near Baslow

Rory Sitwell: Derbyshire resident and Cambridge friend of Mr. Darcy; wife is *Julia*; residence is Reniswahl Hall near Staveley

George and Alison Fitzherbert: Derbyshire residents and friends; residence is Brashinharm near Barlow

Clifton and Chloe Drury: Derbyshire residents and friends; residence is Locknell Hall near Derby

Charlotte Collins: Longtime friend of Elizabeth's; married to *Rev. William Collins*; resides at Hunsford, rectory of Rosings Park in Kent

Mrs. Reynolds: Pemberley housekeeper
Mr. Taylor: Pemberley butler
Mr. Keith: Mr. Darcy's steward
Samuel Oliver: Mr. Darcy's valet
Marguerite Oliver: Mrs. Darcy's maid
Phillips, Watson, Tillson, Georges, Rothchilde: Pemberley footmen
Mr. Clark: Pemberley head groundskeeper
Mr. Thurber: Pemberley head groomsman
Mrs. Langton: Pemberley cook
Mr. Anders: Pemberley head coachman
Mr. Burr: Pemberley gamekeeper
Mr. Holmes: falconer
Mrs. Smyth: Darcy House housekeeper
Mr. Travers: Darcy House butler
Reverend Bertram: Rector of Pemberley Chapel
Mrs. Hanford: Nanny to Darcy firstborn

CHAPTER ONE

Relative Invasion

ERYTON, LOCATED ROUGHLY ONE hundred fifty miles to the south of Pemberley in Derbyshire and nestled in the pastoral valleys of Hertfordshire, was experiencing an atypical cold spell for this winter of 1817. Snow had not yet fallen and it was warmer than the northern counties, but beyond a doubt, winter had descended with a vengeance not seen in years. Whatever the facts, weather or otherwise, none of the inhabitants of the modest manor known as Longbourn took note. All energies were either focused on preparations for the trip to Pemberley or avoiding said preparations.

Mrs. Bennet had been in a barely controlled dither since her springtime trip to Darcy House in London. She was further incited by Kitty's gushing descriptions of Pemberley, after her daughter's return from visiting there in August. Despite her incessant declarations to anyone listening of the great wealth that her second daughter married into, the woman of humble means had no true concept of such a life. The subdued opulence of Darcy House had amazed her, and based on the picture painted by Kitty, Pemberley promised to be vastly superior. Frankly, she was overwhelmed at the concept and her infamous nerves were on high alert—for justifiable reasons this time.

Between Mary's wedding planning, the Christmas vacation arrangements, and his wife's histrionics, Mr. Bennet found himself retreating to the solitude of his study more and more to evade the frenzy. He merely wanted to see his favored daughter and new grandson, enjoy the pleasure of good company, and lose himself in the library. Inconsequentials, such as fashionable clothing and haircuts, were of no interest.

Transportation to Derbyshire had not actually occurred to him as an issue. His plan was simply to utilize the landau, and if five persons proved a bit snug, all better to maintain warmth! The arrival of the luxurious Darcy coach two days before their scheduled departure, with an obviously carefully worded letter from Lizzy, explaining its purpose with her natural humor, brought a smile to his face. The rationale was of no real importance to the practical gentleman. He instantly recognized the advantage and was pleased, not only for the reasons delineated by his darling daughter, but also for the comfort afforded his old bones. It never crossed his mind to be offended. Besides, Mrs. Bennet's theatrics would have effectively smothered any sensations of insult had they come to mind.

"Such a fine, fine carriage it is!" she gushed. "What a marvelous gentleman he is to be sure! Married our Lizzy when surely no one else would likely have her, always far too independent and sharp-tongued for her own good. Truly a wondrous gentleman, so generous and kind, is he not Mr. Daniels?"

Mr. Daniels's agreeing reply, the hundredth or so such offered since departing Longbourn, was lost in the continuing rambles of his future mother-in-law. Mary's gentle smile and soft eyes met his, giving the flummoxed young man the inner strength necessary to deal with the situation. His weekly visits to Mary since her departure from London had given him the opportunity to become acquainted with his soon-to-be family. As Darcy before him, Mr. Daniels was baffled at how the demure, proper young woman who was his fiancée had arisen from such a family. Mr. Bennet was quieter than his wife, but with a clever wit and penetrating gaze not possessed by his middle daughter. In all ways, Mary was an enigma in the Bennet clan, far more than Lizzy ever had been.

Joshua Daniels counted himself a fortunate man indeed, the antics of the Bennets notwithstanding. His betrothed was a steady young lady, prim, stoic, and fairly humorless; but intelligent, kind, and warm. Since these were character traits identical to Mr. Daniels, the two were well matched. Both approached their union with logic and sensibleness, emotion only a dim part of the decision initially. That there was a physical attraction was obvious to them both, but to say it was a raging passion would be erroneous. Their innocent and balanced natures did not lend well to consideration of such things. However, as the long weeks of their engagement unfolded, both began to sense the stirrings of something stronger; emotions that simmered far under the skin as they gradually took tender liberties with chaste kisses and hand touching. This excursion to Pemberley, as painful as it was for the decorous solicitor to reside as a guest in a client's home, would be an eye-opener. The extended period of time the couple would spend together, often inadvertently alone as people came and went about the enormous manor, as well as witnessing the blatant if constrained demonstrations of affection between their hosts, would enlighten them to the greater riches possibly uncovered in a passionate marriage. Without giving too much away, it is safe to conclude that Mary and Joshua would have a fulfilling marriage in all ways.

This, of course, was in the future. For now, they all persevered for the ride. It rained and snowed intermittently as they traveled, but the sturdily built coach, with thick walls, window shades, rugs, and compartments for heated bricks, made for a fairly comfortable journey. By the afternoon of the second day, as they rumbled through Matlock, the clouds broke and sleety rains ceased. The sun peeked through the gaps, offering no warmth of any significance, but casting eye-blinding tendrils of illumination over the glittering snow blanketing the fields.

It was Kitty who recognized the hamlet of Lambton, familiar from afternoon shopping trips with Georgiana. "Oh! This is Lambton, Papa. It means we are very close! Just a few miles and across the river is Pemberley!"

Lizzy had instructed Mr. Anders to approach from the north rather than the slightly shorter southern avenue veering from Beeley. She would never forget her initial view of Pemberley, as seen from the bridge crossing the River Derwent: the mansion sitting proudly amid the gardens and fountains, ringed to the rear by vast forests, the main façade a breathtaking vision of Darcy heritage and prestige.

The coachman slowed on the bridge, allowing the occupants to gaze lingeringly as well as permitting word of their arrival to reach Mr. Darcy from the unseen sentry he knew was waiting. By the time the carriage drove under the massive stone and vine swathed archway and halted before the portico, the Bennets and Mr. Daniels were silent with awe.

Darcy stood under the entry, commanding and formal, with Dr. George Darcy to his left, wearing a broad, welcoming grin. Georgiana, hair regally arranged and dressed in a lovely gown of pale blue velvet, stood to his right.

Mary and Kitty enthusiastically greeted Georgiana, Darcy's welcoming speech lost in the flurry.

"Mrs. Bennet, how utterly delightful it is to see you again." George approached the spellbound woman, bowing with a roguish flair and offering his arm. "If I may be so bold? I am quite certain there is a lovely young lady lurking in the foyer with an incredibly cute baby in her arms. I had the honor of delivering this infant you know, first to lay eyes on his beauty, as it were. Of course, the real work was accomplished by your daughter, William having some input here and there..."

His voice trailed off as he led the bemused woman into the painted foyer. Darcy looked at Mr. Bennet, smiling faintly at the silently laughing older gentleman. "Mr. Daniels, welcome to Pemberley. Please, gentlemen, let us retire to the parlor where it is warm and refreshments are waiting. I should warn you, Mr. Daniels," he said with a chuckle as the three entered the house, "it is likely you shall discover attention from your fiancée slowly forthcoming for a day or two until female conversation is exhausted. Word of wisdom from an experienced husband given free of charge."

Mr. Bennet laughed aloud, Mr. Daniels blushing.

Lizzy stood at the top of the grand staircase, dressed in a gorgeous gown of brown chenille, a huge smile lighting her entire being, and Alexander nestled in her arms. The proud smile Darcy could in no way prevent lit his face. The two sisters, escorted by Georgiana, were mounting the stairs toward Lizzy. Mrs. Bennet, on the arm of Dr. Darcy, was captivated in open-mouthed scrutiny of the ceiling and carvings abundant in the enormous two-story entryway, momentarily forgetting both daughter and grandson.

The waiting duo disappeared in a mass of flowing skirts and reaching arms, the chatter and exclamations of marvel rising to the rafters. Lizzy's merry laughter lifted above the fray until Mrs. Bennet caught sight of her daughter among the general splendor and her shrill outcry drowned all.

"Oh, Lizzy! How adorable he is! Let me hold my grandson! Hello sweet baby, I am your grandmamma. Well done Lizzy, birthing a male as I recommended. The heir to Pemberley to please Mr. Darcy. And such a healthy boy he is, yes indeed. Someday all this will be yours, you lucky little dear."

Lizzy cringed, glancing into Darcy's pained visage at the bottom of the stairs. "Papa," she spoke firmly to her father, cutting through her mother's proclamations. "Come meet your grandson."

Mr. Bennet had anticipated this moment with moderate enthusiasm. He was happy for Lizzy and her husband, but he had not expected to be unduly moved by a tiny person with presumably no personality or ability to interact.

What a shock it was to the elderly gentleman when his eyes locked with Alexander's! The seventeen-day-old infant was awake and alert. Grandfather and grandson connected gazes, and then Alexander stretched out one wobbly hand as he wiggled and released the newborn version of a giggle.

Mr. Bennet was in love, utterly and completely head over heels. His eyes misted and he gruffly cleared his throat while extending the tip of an index finger to stroke the soft fist. "Handsome chap, Lizzy. Quite attentive and serious, like his father, yet with a hint of humor, like you. Fine addition to the family, I daresay."

Lizzy was beaming, her immeasurable pride in her son now increased by the obvious effect he had on her relatives. She laid her hand on her father's arm, drawing his gaze to her, and lifting to kiss his cheek. "Come inside the parlor, Papa, and relax with a brandy, then you can hold him."

Darcy had observed the unfolding drama with widely divergent emotions. Like his wife, his pride in their son was infinite. He truly considered Alexander the most perfect baby in the entire world and was, therefore, not the least bit surprised at the instantaneous affection. The negative was the epiphany, foolishly not deliberated upon prior, that he would quite probably have to physically evict his child from someone's arms if he wished to hold him! It was not a pleasant idea and the scowl that threatened to overtake his countenance was fought with all the power at his disposal. Plainly put, Darcy was ragingly jealous! An unattractive emotion to be sure, but there it was.

He entered the parlor last, Lizzy already placing Alexander into her father's arms. Mrs. Bennet had moved away without a backward glance and was strolling about the room, examining with a keen, covetous eye. George was positioned near the three younger ladies, charming unabashedly. Mr. Daniels stood apart by the window in an uncomfortable pose familiar to the anti-social Darcy. He approached the poor man with a smile.

"Mr. Daniels, what is your preference? Brandy or whiskey, or perhaps wine?"

"Do not trouble yourself, sir."

"It is no trouble at all," Darcy assured him, motioning to a footman. "I shall have a brandy, as will Mr. Bennet I am certain. A whiskey for Dr. Darcy, and Mr. Daniels…?"

"Whiskey then, with thanks," he said in a small voice, face flushing.

"Excellent! Tell me, Mr. Daniels, how fares your father and brother?" Steering the conversation to general subjects, drinks easing the tension, Mr. Daniels began to calm. Darcy attended to the dialogue while keeping an eye on Mr. Bennet, who was grinning widely as he held Alexander and talked quietly with his daughter. Lizzy glanced to her husband, radiant in her happiness, and blew him a tiny kiss.

Darcy winked, the feelings of jealousy waning gradually in the warmth of Elizabeth's face. His musings were abruptly interrupted by Mrs. Bennet, who he had not noted was nearby.

"Mr. Darcy, Pemberley is magnificent! Surely it must be the finest house in all of Derbyshire? I cannot imagine anything to supplant it. How proud you must be! And to think my little Lizzy is mistress of all this. I would not have thought her capable!"

"I can assure you, madam, that your daughter is eminently capable of handling anything. She is fearless, wise, and extraordinarily accomplished. Far and away the best mistress Pemberley has been blessed with in decades."

Any further rebuttals were halted by a loud infant squeal from the sofa. Lizzy was laughing at the surprised expression on her father's face.

"Am I squeezing him too tightly, Lizzy?"

"No, Papa. Alexander is quite demanding when he requires nourishment. A trait inherited from his father, I do believe." She glanced to Darcy with a grin, her husband crossing to the sofa.

"I would not be too hasty in that assessment, Lizzy, as I recall a young girl who inhaled her food the sooner to return to the play yard or a favored novel."

"Be that as it may, let me take my little wiggler from you before he displays the full lung capacity at his disposal. Come my darling, save your grandpapa's ears and let me feed you."

"Lizzy, can you not have the nanny take him?" Mrs. Bennet asked. "I was hoping for a tour of the house!"

"I am afraid it shall have to wait, Mama, until Alexander is satisfied. Once he is asleep, I will be happy to show you and Papa around."

Mrs. Bennet was staring at her daughter in shock. "Surely you do not…? That is, is there not a wet-nurse for the baby?"

"No, Mama. I prefer to care for our son's sustenance myself. Excuse me, Papa," she kissed her father's cheek, rising with a fussy Alexander sucking on her little finger.

George breezed in airily. "Mrs. Bennet, Mr. Bennet, I would be delighted to escort you both, and the young ladies and Mr. Daniels, on a tour of the manor. If I may be so arrogant, I am quite sure that I am acquainted with the house to a degree surpassing its most superb mistress. After all, I did grow up here and even know the attic corners and hidden passageways."

"Oh, how exciting!" Kitty exclaimed. "Will you show us the secret passages, Dr. Darcy?"

"Alas, my dear Miss Kitty, my decrepit bones would probably break if I attempted to squeeze into narrow confines. Georgiana can don an old dress at a later date and lead you on an adventure."

"Uncle!" Georgiana cried, face rosy. "I have no knowledge of such places!"

"Of course not, my dear, of course not." He winked at Darcy while lending an arm to Mrs. Bennet and Miss Kitty, voice booming in narration as the group filed out. "There is a rather remarkable portrait of my brothers and me, dashing gents all, in the gallery…"

Darcy and Lizzy were left alone with their momentarily placated baby. "William, I am sorry for Mama's words. Are you disturbed?"

Darcy smiled, bending to kiss her lips gently. "It is of no moment, my dearest. Shall I accompany you to the nursery?"

"Thank you, but no. Join our guests, offering your unique perspective on the wonders of Pemberley. Somewhere in the middle, you can divert my father in the library and enjoy a time of well-deserved solitude. I love you, Mr. Darcy."

"I love you, Mrs. Darcy. And you too, my precious little love." He bent to kiss Alexander's cheek, again kissing his wife. Then with a roll of his eyes heavenward, a tug on his jacket, and a theatric sigh, he exited to follow the echoing rumble of George and the giggles of amused women.

With Christmas just over a week and a half away, winter set in with a vengeance and snow blanketed the ground and vegetation, the entire surrounds bathed in glistening crystals. The larger lakes and ponds enriched with fountains provided breaks in the monotony of white, the handful of winter blooms and evergreen trees lending color, and the shoveled drives and pathways provided clarity and contour. The vivid blue of the sky was frequently obscured by clouds, most grey and threatening. The usual hectic movements of wildlife and humans noted throughout the river valley and bordering forests during fairer weather were essentially gone. Naturally, there were still chores to be done by bundled groundsmen, horses to exercise by jacketed grooms, and the few brave winter fowl, deer, and tiny rodents searching for food to disturb the placid winter scenery.

Pemberley was decorated more lavishly than last year, the maids, footmen, groundsmen, and even the senior staff apparently wholly liberated by the joyous atmosphere over the past year. Twelve short months was all that was required to expunge the years of sadness. They had seemingly denuded the forest of holly, mistletoe, pine boughs, and any other greenery remotely Christmassy, draping every balcony, windowsill, banister, fireplace mantel, and alcove. Darcy's jest about mistletoe ornaments proved accurate, with balls at every corridor junction and dangling from each ceiling light and threshold. All the heirloom decorations were in place, as well as a sprinkling of others that had been unearthed while rummaging through the attic for baby furnishings. There were three times as many candles strewn about the manor and grounds with several dozen torches placed throughout the gardens.

One corner of the parlor was cleared and draped with yards of gold and silver edged red velvet, onto which was arranged a plethora of brightly wrapped and ribboned presents. Pine branches decorated with tiny candles further adorned the area. The entire parlor furnishings were shuffled to provide more room, so supplementary sofas and chairs obtained from other chambers could provide more sitting room. Both dining rooms were sumptuously adorned, and the ballroom was polished to gleaming. Instruments were tuned, fireplaces were scrubbed, and chimneys swept, vases of fresh flowers were abundant, lamps were filled, windows were cleaned, patios and walkways were freed of all debris, and scented potpourris were everywhere.

While the servants unleashed their creativity with greenery and ornaments, Lizzy and Mrs. Reynolds had organized the menus and entertainments. The huntsmen, including Darcy a time or two, had provided the main staples for the dietary fare. Desserts of all varieties from basic pies and cakes to elegant pastries and meringues were created. Mrs. Langton and her superb staff could be trusted to whip up an array of tasty dishes and treats to augment the main courses.

The game room was set with extra card tables, a second dart board, Hazard dice, and a domino set of ivory, acquired while in Great Yarmouth, to augment the chess, backgammon, cribbage, and draughts tables already in place. In anticipation that the freeze and snows would escalate, ten pairs of skates were bought and the existing ones sharpened, the curling stones and brooms were brought from storage, and sleds were inspected for safety.

Darcy's prized shovillaborde, a table version of the popular deck game shuffleboard, was polished and placed prominently to the right of the two billiard tables in the billiard room. Two years prior, Darcy had discovered the table in an auction house, thrilled beyond belief and paying an outrageous sum for the one-hundred-year-old relic fashioned after the boards favored by King Henry VIII.

An enormous, wooden floored room on the northern wing near the conservatory was dedicated to various indoor sports. The room had evolved over the decades, from what was originally designed as a smaller ballroom into a second game room. It did not have an actual name, usually being referred to as The Court due to the enormous netted court for tennis and the area by one wall for racquets. The floor was polished and new equipment purchased, including battledores and shuttlecocks for the game of the same name raging through London. The sunny chamber with wide curtain-less windows and a ceiling partially of glass additionally boasted a ninepin alley, shuffleboard deck, a miniature putting green with five holes, a quoits pin, and hopscotch squares.

Added together, it seemed a certainty that Christmas at Pemberley would be a raging success.

The emotions flowing through Darcy and Lizzy regarding the season varied, but one emotion absolutely shared was the priority in protecting Alexander. Darcy refused to allow his still recovering wife and fragile child to overextend, the very thought of them becoming ill sending frigid chills deep into the marrow of his bones. With typical Darcy dominance and severity, he bluntly reminded Lizzy that he would be in charge and would expect her to obey his orders in all matters. Lizzy flared in irritation briefly, but then laughed, Darcy frowning and preparing to puff intimidatingly, only to deflate and calm when she assured him she agreed and would bow to his will.

As it turned colder, Lizzy fretted constantly over Alexander, but the baby grew stronger, and his little body seemed to generate heat just as his father's did. Nonetheless, Lizzy kept him close to her chest as much as possible, dressed in warm clothing, and wrapped with thick blankets. Every fireplace in the inhabited areas of the mansion blazed from sunrise to well after sunset, dispelling the bulk of the cold and keeping the residents comfortable.

Colonel Fitzwilliam arrived two days after the Bennets, galloping in amid a swirl of snowflakes. Another snowstorm, this one fairly mild, had struck that morning, making for an uncomfortable ride from his parents' estate, but the battle-hardened soldier was impervious to the weather.

"Richard! Welcome, Cousin. You are just in time for luncheon." Darcy approached with a warm smile.

"Hello, Darcy. Good to see you, although yours is not the Darcy face I most wanted to greet first. Thank you, Mr. Taylor." He handed the last layer of jackets to the pile of over-clothing held by the butler, turning with a grin to clap his cousin on the back.

"We can readily divert to the nursery, as I assume this is your reference. Be warned, however: Alexander is asleep, so formal introductions must wait. Come, and while we walk you can tell me when your parents will be visiting."

"We arrived at Rivallain last evening. Mother was more than prepared to arise with the sun and travel on, but father wanted to settle for a day or two. I rather believe that, as in most matters, mother's will shall prevail and expect they will rattle into the courtyard tomorrow morning at the latest! She is anxious to meet your son and visit with Elizabeth, having brought the subject to the fore of all conversation at the breakfast table no less than a dozen times. I decided I needed to ride on if I wanted to see him myself, the women liable to monopolize all his waking moments discussing the joys of childbirth and motherhood!"

"You have no idea how accurate your jest, my friend. I have barely laid eyes on him since Elizabeth's family arrived and he is mine. Quite annoying actually, so I am forced to rise with the late night feedings just to steal precious time alone."

Darcy was speaking lightly, but Richard, who knew him so well, detected the undertone of irritation. In an attempt to soothe the easily somber Darcy, he said, "Surely you cannot be missing too much. After all, babies, so I am to understand, lie there as lumps and sleep all the time!"

Darcy bristled, the idea of his son a "lump" not appreciated, but one look at his cousin's face brought laughter to the surface. "Very well, Colonel, we shall see. I have it on good authority that he is the most adorable child in the universe, and thus far, all who lay eyes on him have fallen hopelessly in love. Be cautious, my friend, as your heart will be wrested away!"

They reached the nursery, Darcy entering cautiously although the well-oiled door was unlikely to squeak. Mrs. Hanford glanced up from the dresser where she was folding a pile of clothes, smiling at her Master and nodding toward the cradle.

"Mrs. Hanford, this is my cousin Colonel Fitzwilliam. Richard, our wonderful nanny, Mrs. Hanford."

"Madam," Richard bowed gallantly, turning into the room to follow Darcy, who had crossed swiftly to the cradle. Alexander lay curled on his right side, pink hands folded beside his parted lips as if in sleepy supplication to the Almighty. Auburn curls lay heavy over his now perfectly round head, longer wisps brushing his brows; skin porcelain with ruddy cheeks marred only by a faint pinpoint rash across his chin. Both the nanny and excellent in-house doctor assured the Darcys that these scattered rashes were normal as his delicate flesh adjusted to the outside world of fabrics and soaps. Despite the trivial imperfections, Alexander was beautiful, his father's assertions only a slim exaggeration, as everyone in the manor was adoring.

A softly smiling, prideful father competently bent with seeking hands to lift his son, Richard grabbing at his wrist. "Darcy, wait! Do not wake him!"

"He just finished eating and I know how to lift him without disturbing. Sit in the chair and you can hold him."

Richard blanched, arms instinctively clasping behind his back as he shook his head emphatically. "I do not think that a wise plan at all! If I drop him, I am quite certain you will be perturbed!"

"Heavens, Richard. The mighty man of His Majesty's Armed Forces who handles sword and musket in battle is afraid of a tiny baby?"

"Precisely. If I fail with any of those things, it is my own health and life that is forfeit."

"Sit and quit complaining. Besides, you have held Annabella's children, so stop pretending. Alexander is sturdy and I trust you completely."

Colonel Fitzwilliam sat as bid, his face yet pale. "Very well, but if something happens, I will tell Elizabeth it was your fault."

Darcy had lifted Alexander adeptly, the slumbering babe merely stretching slightly before nestling into the familiar warm shape of his father's embrace. As always, Darcy's heart swelled with a love indescribable and unique. Instantly, he was mesmerized by the breathing reality of his child, the living presence clutched close to his body, overwhelming his senses; his soul elevated by the tiny personality created with the woman he loved so profoundly.

Colonel Fitzwilliam observed his cousin, freshly amazed—even after the transitions of the past year—by how altered the serious, perpetually melancholic mien was that he had assumed was an integral trait in Darcy. Now it was entirely erased; Darcy, even in his intensity, displayed a tenderness and joy that was transparent. Richard privately challenged anyone who knew Darcy well to not be moved by the positive mutation of his character.

"Here he is, Richard. My son. Alexander William George Bennet Darcy. Did I not speak the truth in that he is amazing and adorable? Beautiful like his mother." Darcy secured him into Richard's arms, sitting on the chair beside and caressing one fingertip over the baby's cheek.

"Yes, he is a highly attractive lad. He definitely has Elizabeth's hair and nose, but he looks like you, Darcy. What about his eyes?"

"Blue, but shaped as his mother's. He actually seems to be a fair mixture of us both, although I am sure his features will evolve as he matures."

"Do not tell my sister I said this or I shall torture you, but he is far lovelier than any of her four children. Sadly, they inherited their father's physical characteristics."

Darcy smothered a laugh. "Shame, Richard. Lord Montgomery is a distinguished gentleman."

"Ha! He is grouchy, old, and sports an enormous nose! Makes yours look positively petite."

"Thanks," Darcy interrupted dryly.

"You are welcome, and thank you for not countering with an acerbic remark about my own nasal assets, as you surely could have. By the way, Annabella and the children accompanied us from London and are at Rivallain. Lord Montgomery may show up if his preferred pursuits bore him, but we are not holding our breath."

"Poor Annabella."

Richard shrugged faintly. "In truth, I believed she was relieved. Ah, you know my sister, Darcy. Money and place in society were always more important to her than affection. She has that as Lady Montgomery and is content."

"I suppose. It will be delightful to see her again, and I think I can now find it in me to endure her children."

Richard chuckled, glancing to his cousin with a sly smile. "Oh, I would not count on that! They are spoiled rotten and unruly. Your best bet is to hint they stay at Rivallain with their governess."

Darcy snorted. "Were we different as youths, Cousin? How many governesses labeled you incorrigible and me mischievous? I still have lash marks on my backside, I am sure."

"Let it be a lesson for you, father Darcy. 'Spare the rod, spoil the child,' as the Good Book says, or 'train a child in the way he should go and he will not depart from it.'"

Darcy shuddered, stroking his precious, innocent son's cheek. "Perhaps, although I cannot imagine taking a switch or belt to Alexander. I guess Elizabeth and I will need to be prepared. I know I shall not tolerate a disobedient child."

Lizzy discovered the two men a half hour later still fawning over the oblivious infant. She smiled at the tableau, like her husband never tiring of noting how everyone fell immediately in love with their child. Neither perceived her presence in the doorway until she cleared her throat. Darcy rose with a beaming grin, crossing to kiss her on the lips.

"Richard arrived, as you can see, and I could not resist introducing him to Alexander."

"So I gathered. We waited in the dining room wondering if you had gotten lost in your own house, Mr. Darcy. Mr. Taylor enlightened us to Colonel Fitzwilliam's arrival and I reckoned you had come here."

"I am so sorry, love! We completely lost track of the hour. Forgive me?"

"Naturally. However, you, Colonel Fitzwilliam, will be punished severely for your rudeness in not greeting Pemberley's Mistress, unless you pay penance by singing the praises of our incredible son."

"Thankfully, madam, I can accomplish this with ease. Honestly, Elizabeth, he is lovely. Of course, he has been sleeping the entire time and I have not been gifted with the vocal prowess I am certain he possesses."

Lizzy laughed. "Even his cries are rays of sunshine, Colonel. I think he has inherited his father's resonant tones, as his yells are not shrill, and only occur with appropriate incentive."

"He is demanding and with a wild temper, which could easily come from either of us," Darcy interjected.

"A melding most probably, which could mean it double in intensity. Woe to you both on that count. Remember the switch, Darcy."

"Very funny, Richard. Now, gentlemen, if I may be so bold as to insist we let the baby sleep in peace and eat lunch before it grows colder, and before he wakens to persistently request my presence. I have to schedule these things carefully."

The remaining days until Christmas counted down slowly, with the residents and guests of Pemberley contented in their seclusion behind sturdy stone walls and snow blanketed lawns.

The weather continued to be unpredictable. The sky was continually cloudy to one degree or another, but the snows fell randomly with little warning, even to the bizarrely astute Darcy. It was freezing cold, warming ever so slightly during the days when the sun was allowed to shine through. The small pond froze over, the last of the stubbornly clinging leaves fell, walkways slicked over with crunching ice, and evergreen trees and hedges transformed into wintry monuments. Rhododendrons, hellebore, jasmine, camellia, and cyclamen, as well as potted iris and daffodils sheltered on the terrace, fought to shine through the frosty quilt with varying degrees of colorful success.

Lizzy watched the changes to the surrounds from the thick windows of the manor, happy for one of the first times in her life to forego outdoor activities. Twice she bundled up with barely the tip of her nose visible and strolled along the balcony and private garden with her mother and sisters; however, she honestly did not wish to be far from Alexander. Her only excursions beyond the manor would be to visit the orphanage, bringing gifts to the children and for church on Christmas day. Their guests, on the other hand, delighted in the array of entertainments Pemberley had to offer both inside and out.

Georgiana shed the past year's maturity in the presence of Kitty, the two giggling and adolescent in their pursuits. Not surprisingly, it was Colonel Fitzwilliam who could generally be found in their company, as equal parts adult escort and fellow juvenile enthusiast. They skated, practiced dancing for the Masque, threw snowballs, and erected a well-accessorized snowman and snow-woman on the south lawn. Mary and Mr. Daniels tended to remain together most of the time in quieter activities, such as table games and conversation, although they did join the revelry surrounding the snow-couple's creation.

Dr. Darcy and Mr. Bennet renewed their acquaintance, the older gentlemen spending the bulk of their time in the library, although the chess set was put through its paces with neither claiming more victory than the other. Darcy joined them frequently, as did Mr. Daniels and Colonel Fitzwilliam when the ladies were engaged in female companionship. Every possible diversion offered was enjoyed by someone at sometime, and even Mr. Bennet was cajoled into a tennis tournament at one point, with the feminine cheering squad vocalizing their encouragement from the narrow spectator seats. It was George Darcy, of the long limber extremities and quick reflexes, who prevailed over them all. Naturally, he thoroughly delighted in the adulation from the rousing onlookers. Conversely, to the humorous delight of everyone in the Manor, the lanky physician was a disaster on ice skates! His loud declarations of donning slim blades to glide over frozen water being an unnatural and ridiculous activity only increased the laughter and teasing.

Mrs. Bennet flittered about, finding amusement wherever possible. She spent the majority of her time with Lizzy, in the nursery or her parlor with Alexander nearby. She did extend a vast amount of parenting advice, some of it filed in mental wastebaskets for disposal, but a quantity of it actually worthy. Lizzy and Darcy were delighted and a smidge dumbfounded to discover that the flighty, nervous woman actually possessed a rudimentary wisdom after raising five daughters.

Though Pemberley was a very large house, nonetheless, ten people roaming the corridors and haunting the public chambers was rather evident! Adding to the clamor was the arrival of Lord and Lady Matlock with Lady Annabella Montgomery the day after Colonel Fitzwilliam. Lizzy had been introduced to Richard's younger sister in London. Her husband's estate was in Hampshire, none of the family visiting with her often except during the season in London. Lizzy found her dull and haughty, resembling her eldest brother Jonathan in personality and none of the other Fitzwilliams. Annabella's reaction to her cousin's son and heir was vague, and after a brief pinch to a chubby cheek, she murmured, "How sweet," before moving away.

Lord Matlock smiled and declared him "handsome and strapping." Lady Matlock was composed and dignified as usual, but once Alexander was in her arms, it required a seriously vexed wail of extreme hunger to induce her to relinquish him.

In truth, although neither Lizzy nor Darcy would dream of verbalizing it, they were relieved when the three returned to Rivallain after a one day visit. However, the Gardiners arrived mere hours later, filling the brief respite with fresh exuberance. Further presentations of the newborn were performed, Alexander far more tolerant than was his father, who was becoming quite cross.

Despite their fears, Lizzy and Darcy admitted that Alexander was healthy, patient with all the handling, unperturbed, regular in his sleeping and eating patterns, and a certifiable smash with every last soul who laid eyes on him. He grew before their eyes, daily becoming increasingly alert with a rapidly blossoming personality uniquely his own. They were cautious, never allowing him to be taken far from the nursery or disturbed while napping. After his meals, he was held and rocked by his doting mother in solitude for long periods of time, Lizzy refusing to be influenced by family or Pemberley duties.

Unfortunately, Darcy was not so blessed. He was pulled in a dozen directions. Once dressed and separated from wife and son for the day, he rarely saw them again except in passing until late at night. As master and host, it was a responsibility keenly felt to ensure all guests were adequately entertained, nourished, comfortable, and content. As husband and father, it was his duty to guarantee his immediate family was not overwhelmed or unduly disturbed. Add to that the occasional Pemberley estate–related issue and he was busy from sunup to well after sundown. Lizzy fell asleep early, still recuperating from the birth and exhausted from the demands on her body. Darcy arrived later, snuggling close to her warmth in their temporary bedchamber close to the nursery. He made a point to rise with the predawn feeding, assuming the burping and rocking so Lizzy could return to sleep. It was the only time he managed to be alone with his son since the arrival of the Bennets, and after a week he was ready to burst.

Thankfully a day of fair weather dawned and a breakfast decision was made to travel to Matlock for last minute Christmas shopping. Everyone went except for Mr. Bennet and Mr. Gardiner, who opted to grasp onto the silence for placid perusal of the library shelves yet unexamined. Darcy begged liberation from the expedition, claiming business when the truth was he wanted to be alone with his wife and baby. The instant glitter to Lizzy's eyes as she snapped her gaze to his face clearly spoke of her own need and hope that he was dissembling regarding business. Darcy smiled, his blue eyes softening in a familiar way that Lizzy understood.

After waving farewell to the laughing occupants of three carriages, Darcy practically sprinted up the stairs. Lizzy sat on the bed with Alexander at her breast, raising adoring eyes and one hand to her spouse, who hastily discarded jacket and boots before joining her with a heady sigh.

He buried his face into her neck, kissing as he murmured, "I can only assume the good Lord has taken pity on me this day, as I absolutely would have exploded. I cannot survive another day without your kisses and touch, and our son's soft body against my heart. I love you so tremendously, my Lizzy."

"Has it been so awful for you having my family about?"

He lifted to look into her eyes. "It is not your family, my heart. It is anyone who takes me from you and Alexander. Honestly, I am having a delightful time with our guests. Did you know Miss Kitty is an excellent shuffleboard player?" Lizzy shook her head with a raised brow. "Well, she is. I spent roughly ten minutes showing her the basic moves and explaining the rules, and she nearly beat me the first game! Twice I have turned a corner to discover Miss Mary and Mr. Daniels indulging in the mistletoe custom. I think they both nearly suffered apoplexy and I have never laughed so hard—after I departed the scene that is. Your father and I have shared many a game and brandy, and even your mother has surprised me. No, dearest, I merely need to be alone with you and intend to do so all day today."

"I think this a wonderful plan. I do believe I can bear to be cooped up with you all day." She smiled brightly, reaching to palm his jaw and draw his mouth to hers for a lingering kiss, lasting until Alexander decided he was replete.

"Come to your father, sweet boy. Behave, as I do not have a cloth handy. Samuel likes you well enough, but not if you soil another garment. That's my good little man, what a strong burp you have! Yes you do, my precious. Give your papa a kiss. Hmm… delicious milk, so sweet. No wonder you like it so much. Perhaps soon your father can taste your mother's milk…"

"William!" Lizzy laughed nervously and sharply slapped his knee. "Do not corrupt his innocent ears."

"He has no idea what I am saying, but I do apologize and will attempt to refrain from verbalizing my desires in his presence. Look, he is falling asleep already, not at all perturbed or shocked. I could even express how urgently I wish to make love to you and he would not flinch. See?"

"Please, William, stop. You are embarrassing me."

Darcy peered closely at his wife's rosy cheeks and frowned faintly. "Forgive me, love. I was only jesting. Well, not entirely you understand, but I did not mean to make you uncomfortable."

Lizzy shook her head, dropping to rest on Darcy's shoulder, her face hidden from view. Silence fell, Darcy snuggling Alexander while his mind raced. That Darcy desired his wife was a given, and he had assumed she felt the same way, both patiently waiting until her body was restored. Now he was not so certain how she felt and the doubt rocked him. Naturally they had avoided undue intimate contact; Darcy out of respect for her health and Lizzy, he thought, out of respect for his unremitting amorousness. Despite his yearning, he was quite content to wait. He wanted to wait for her, dreamt of it incessantly, imagining how blissful it would be when they finally renewed their intimate marital relationship. Did she not dream of the same? Or was it merely speaking of it in front of the baby?

"I will lay him down," he said softly, kissing the top of her head. "Stay here, beloved."

When he returned Lizzy was lying partially propped on several pillows, smiling warmly, and opening her arms to him. Instantly he experienced a rush of relief, nestling close and drawing her against his strongly beating heart.

She squeezed him tightly, voice choking and tremulous. "I am sorry if I distressed you. I guess I am still a bit out of sorts. So many changes these past weeks, with adjustments to my body so suddenly and profoundly. And then all the visitors. I am so happy to have them all here, but it is tiring." She paused, resuming with a soft sob. "Mostly I want to be with you, truly and completely be with you, and I cannot. I am sorry."

"Elizabeth, hush. You do not need to explain, as I already understand. Just kiss me and tell me you love me." He cupped her dear face, pulling her upward so they could drink the other in.

"I love you, Fitzwilliam, with all my soul."

He smiled, whispering just before claiming her mouth thoroughly in a kiss that would leave them both breathless and desperately wanting more, "That is all I ever need to know. I love you, Mrs. Darcy."

Lizzy spent the next three days in the frustration of believing she would never manage to corner George alone. When it happened it was quite by accident. She entered the conservatory to pick flowers for Darcy's dressing room and discovered the usually sociable man alone, stretched on a lounge chair under a ripening orange tree with a book in his hands.

Biting her lip, suddenly shy after seeking his undivided attention, she hesitated before slowly approaching.

"Dr. Darcy."

Brows rising instantly, he replied, "Yes, Mrs. Darcy?"

Lizzy cleared her throat, glancing away from his unsettling and penetrating eyes. "I wished for your advice... medical advice, that is, on a matter of... some delicacy... and... well, a personal question if you take my meaning?" She was flushed nearly scarlet, with her eyes downcast.

"Have a seat, Elizabeth. I honestly have no idea to what you refer, but I rather think after the events of the past weeks we should be beyond such embarrassments. Speak as plainly as you can, child, and I will do what I can to help. Are you experiencing some residual pain or other discomfort?"

She shook her head vigorously, glancing up briefly. "No, in fact quite the opposite. I feel fine... in all ways. None of the symptoms you or Mrs. Henderson instructed me to watch for. I feel good as new, I suppose I could say."

"I see." He studied her face, beginning to suspect the train of her thoughts. "So, I am to understand the cramping is all gone? Good. And no further drainage or tenderness from... very good. I detect no lingering fatigue, other than what is normal with a baby, and your overall appearance is consistent with a state of health and vigor. Do you agree?"

She nodded, hoping he would put the pieces together and spare her further humiliation, but he remained silent. "It is just... You know we rely a great deal on the book for information, and well..." Another glance to his inscrutable face after which she bolted up and began pacing, continuing in a rush. "The book recommends waiting for... for... relations"—swallow—"for six weeks or so, but also states 'until the woman's body is fully healed.'"

She stopped abruptly, spinning around to face him with hands on her hips and voice strong. "Well, which is it? I feel healed, but it is not six weeks, so... this is my question." The gush of vim evaporated, voice falling into a whisper.

George's lips twitched, but he managed to avoid laughing, holding out his hand instead. "Relax, Elizabeth. Sit down and I will give the advice I give all my maternity patients, although it is doubtful most of them listen to me. The truth is we do not know what is happening internally after birth. Physicians can only guess what course a couple should take as far as marital relations. There is no accurate answer that is the same for all, as each birth is varied and the effects equally so. However, the standard recommendation is to let your heart and body guide you. When you feel capable and desirous of such activity both physically and emotionally, then that is your answer. I can tell you this with absolute certainty: Many resume within a couple of weeks and I have never known there to be a problem unless an issue already existed which was aggravated by the action. Does this answer your query adequately?"

Lizzy could only nod.

CHAPTER TWO

Christmas Eve Surprises

CHRISTMAS EVE DAY DAWNED with a brightly shining sun valiantly struggling to bestow heat onto the frozen lands, but sadly thwarted by persistent banks of gray clouds dotting the azure sky. It never did rain or snow, but the immobile clouds cast shadows all day. The mild weather would provide an excellent cap to what was universally agreed to be a fabulously successful week.

The tenant's feast and ball was a triumph. From a raised dais in the formal dining hall, the Darcys welcomed their guests, Mr. Darcy giving a short speech of gratitude and well wishes for a merry holiday and prosperous coming year. Alexander, awake and awed by the glittering chandeliers, was presented formally to the families whose diligent work made his life possible, many of whom would someday call him Master. The applause was deafening, hurrahs rising to the eaves with Lizzy barely managing a dignified retreat before the startled babe burst into wails!

Calming the upset infant was accomplished easily enough, but the revelry from the first floor chambers would continue late into the night—another tradition successfully reestablished by the new Mistress of Pemberley and savored by all.

The tenant packages were delivered by Miss Darcy, Miss Kitty, and Miss Mary. Kitty came along for the ride, offering cheery chatter in between the scattered cottages. Georgiana kept the detailed list tight in her hand, fretting over making a mistake or stuttering over the practiced speeches. Mary was the steadying influence, this sort of task not at all unusual for her, as charity work through the Meryton Church was a duty she had delighted in for many years. Everyone understood why Mrs. Darcy could not appear in person this year, and since they had already met the infant heir at the feast, no one felt slighted.

A letter from the Bingleys heralded the arrival of Miss Bingley and the Hursts. Greetings were conveyed to the Bennets, the decision being to wait until Christmas day to visit. Jane was not feeling too well, although she hastened to add it only within the expected range of symptoms, and both she and Charles desired to spend their first Christmas at Hasberry. This was comprehended by all, and as no one was exactly thrilled by the concept of extended time with Caroline and her snobbish sister and boorish brother-in-law, tears were definitely not shed.

Elizabeth and Darcy joined the older members for a stroll along the south terrace. Lizzy tightly clutched her husband's arm, not due to any unsteadiness but out of a pure desire to keep him close. Her conversation with George the previous morning had lightened her mood considerably, notable to all including Darcy, who had no idea the cause of her sudden ebullience, although it was he who would reap the greatest benefit! She avoided looking directly at the faintly smirking George, the doctor highly amused at her transparency.

"Mr. Darcy, do you imagine the fine trout will be biting this year as they did last?"

Darcy glanced to Mr. Gardiner with a smile. "I am quite certain they will. I am personally not fond of trout, so they are left greatly unmolested for the majority of the year. Help yourself, Mr. Gardiner."

"Lizzy loves trout," Mrs. Bennet declared. "She fished when young, always insisting on dining on her private catch. Do you remember, Edward?"

"Yes, I do. I taught her the rudimentary skills, although I seem to recall her having a penchant for falling into the lake rather than taking fish out of it."

Lizzy laughed gaily with cheeks flushing prettily, but Darcy was peering at her with a faint scowl. "You never told me you liked trout. Why have you not had the kitchen prepare it for dinner?"

She shrugged, beaming up into her husband's face. "It is not a favorite dish, William, and I know you dislike it. I guess a treat now and then would be nice, however."

"Mrs. Langton will prepare more than one entrée if you order it so, dearest."

"And the aroma of fresh trout will not send you screaming from the table as mutton surely would?" Her eyes twinkled as she teased, Darcy smiling wider and reaching to caress the hand resting on his arm.

"It is a large room. I can always sit at the opposite end."

Mr. Bennet observed the unconsciously affectionate interplay with an inner fount of peace, never tiring of seeing his children's happiness. *How maudlin I am in my old age*, he thought with a silent chuckle.

Mrs. Bennet was more oblivious to the romance. "Well, it is fortunate, Mr. Darcy, that Lizzy does not like mutton either! At least in that you will be spared any distress."

They had reached the eastern end of the lengthy terrace, pausing to absorb the sparkling landscape of white with glistening fountain and waterfall, the Greek Temple rising in a glory of marbled stone on the hill. The jolly squeals of skaters were audible, floating from the distant, small pond that was hidden from view by snow-topped trees and hedges.

"How about it, Thomas?" Mr. Gardiner turned to his brother-in-law. "In for a spell of fishing? I tell you, the trout practically jump onto the hooks. It is divine."

Mr. Bennet chuckled. "As long as you promise to maintain some awareness of the time. I have no desire to turn into an icicle."

"Dr. Darcy? Care to try your luck yet again?"

"Do you suppose there is any way to build a fire near the edge of the pond?" The shivering man, bundled in two wool coats, turned to his nephew with a pleading expression.

Darcy laughed, shaking his head negatively. "Sorry. Mr. Clark would strangle you if you marred his landscaping or damaged the dormant lawns. Afraid you just need to be tough."

"We can share a flask of brandy while we fish. That should help."

George shuddered, sighing in resignation. "Thank you, Mr. Bennet, but I think I shall bring my own flask, just to be on the safe side."

"You men enjoy yourselves. I, for one, am beginning to freeze already. Lizzy, Rose, care for a few hands of cards? You can bring Alexander for us to gush over and take turns holding."

Lizzy smiled at her aunt, eyes glowing happily. "Sounds wonderful. William, do you yet intend to go for a ride with Colonel Fitzwilliam?"

Darcy nodded. "As soon as he is done cavorting as a juvenile."

"I seem to remember a certain mature gentleman engaging in a fair amount of juvenile cavorting at the pond last year at this time, or so I was told," Mrs. Gardiner remarked with a grin to Mr. Darcy, who flushed slightly and coughed.

"Well, yes, but it was all the doings of my devious wife who claimed to be a novice skater in dire need of assistance and rescue."

"Lizzy a novice?" Mrs. Bennet exclaimed. "Why she has been on skates since she was three, although the winters are not as harsh as here and the skating opportunities fewer. Shame, Lizzy, deceiving your husband! What must you think of her, Mr. Darcy?"

"I assure you, madam, I have only the highest regard for your daughter. Her ruse was only in jest and thinly veiled. I knew she could skate all along, plying my own arts of deception. It was a friendly game with a pleasurably outcome." He smirked at his blushing bride, knowing full well she was recalling their interlude in her bathtub afterwards.

The afternoon waned into evening. The gentlemen, including Mr. Daniels and George, were invigorated by their brisk jaunt on horseback. Varied entertainments prevailed both before the excellent Christmas Eve dinner and after. Georgiana and Mary delighted with duets on the pianoforte, Kitty lifting her voice a time or two, as did Lizzy and Violet Gardiner. The guests differed from the prior year, but the revelry was in the same vein. Alexander joined the group for a time, alternating between wakefulness and slumber, but in good humor throughout and horribly spoilt by all.

Past Christmas reminiscences were shared as they sat in the cozy parlor with fire crackling. The rowdy Bennet celebrations differed hugely from the sedate festivities at Pemberley, but everyone delighted in the story telling. With his customary flair, George related the long ago holiday memories, clear from his dramatizing that the Darcy children of his generation possessed few of the strict manners of later generations.

"It was the only night of the year that we did not argue about retiring in our anxiousness to greet the dawn and open presents. And the only night we did not sneak into Estella's room after we were supposed to be asleep." George chuckled. "Our parents were ignorant of how late we often extended our ordered curfew, romping and mischief making until nearly midnight upon occasion."

"I doubt if they were as ignorant as you surmise," Darcy interjected with a smile, continuing at his uncle's questioning look. "Grandfather once said to me, when I was seven or so and upon the occasion of a visit from my cousin Anne with Richard and Jonathan here as well, that now I could, 'disobey as children ought, by pretending to be abed before traipsing the darkened halls to cavort with your siblings.'"

Richard was laughing. "Oh yes, I remember that! And I also remember how surprised you were, William, and Anne as well. Poor souls with no conspirators about on a regular basis! You two were scandalized at the idea of disobeying a parent."

"And you managed to break me sufficiently of that ridiculous notion. Bursting into my room with Anne being pulled along by Jonathan. I nearly screamed in fright. Dear Anne looked ready to collapse. This one"—he indicated Richard while glancing about at the grinning faces of his audience—"had gone so far as to steal food from the kitchen!"

"Ah yes. Fun times," Richard said, his face radiating puckishness.

George, however, was mournful. "I can't believe they knew! Rather spoils the whole purpose of being naughty and breaking the rules if the authority figure is aware of it. I am crushed."

"Do not be dismayed, Dr. Darcy," Mrs. Gardiner offered placatingly. "I imagine there was a wealth of roguish misbehavior they never knew of." George brightened considerably.

"How does one celebrate Christmas in India, Doctor?" Mary asked.

"It varied depending on where I was at the time. The English compounds held lavish parties, upholding the traditions for the children. But quite often I was traveling about. I never heeded calendar dates, simply going where I was needed or as whimsy inspired me. Obviously, the indigenous peoples of India do not celebrate Christmas."

"Did you not receive any gifts?" Kitty asked in shock, her young mind stunned at the idea.

George laughed. "I had little need of additional trinkets or possessions, Miss Kitty. I traveled with the barest necessities and my quarters in Bombay were modest. James always sent me something special, although I rarely received it before Christmas. I had a few close friends, both Christian and not, who expressed their affection with a token. In later years I had a dear friend who set the day aside, furnished me with a gift, and insisted I honor the birth of my Savior, even while gently teasing me about it." His smile was soft, eyes dreamy for several seconds before he shrugged, the lopsided grin again in place as he met Kitty's eyes. "Of course, shaking the gift was always an imperative! Have you shaken and guessed your gifts yet, Georgie?"

His gaze slid to Georgiana, the young woman startling and reddening instantly as her guilty eyes snapped briefly to Darcy even as she exclaimed, "Of course not!"

Laughter rang out. Darcy pretended a stern scowl, his smile evident nonetheless. "Shaking presents is forbidden in the Darcy household. Is that not so, Georgiana?"

"Yes, Brother."

But she glanced at George from under her lashes, meeting his wink with twinkling eyes.

It was early yet when Lizzy cornered her husband where he stood for a moment's solitary contemplation by a far window. She laid one hand gently on his arm, Darcy turning with a ready smile.

"Penny for your thoughts, Mr. Darcy."

"My thoughts are all of you and our family, my heart, and therefore price-less treasures."

"So romantic you are my darling. Impressive."

Unconsciously, he reached to stroke her cheek with a fingertip. "Must be the brandy, reminiscences, and excessive body heat pervading the room causing my mind to become all foggy and nonsensical."

"Whatever the stimulus, do not cease as I am deeply affected by the senti-ments." She ran one hand lightly down the lapels of his jacket, holding his tenderly piercing gaze. "It is time for Alexander's last meal. May I ask a favor? Can you form a polite reason to excuse yourself early and join us? I crave your undivided company and cuddling before the fire on our second Christmas Eve together."

He smiled, that singular smile that lit his entire being and was only for her, touching even his vocal cords as evidenced by the huskiness in his voice. "Nothing could be simpler, beloved. I will be right behind you."

And he was. Lizzy never knew the excuse he gave, although she would have been surprised to learn it was nothing more than the truth. Darcy declared that he wished to spend the evening alone with his wife and son, bowed gracefully if abruptly, and hastily exited the room. Having washed and divested himself of all clothing but his shirt and breeches, he entered the nursery as Lizzy was finishing the exhilarating task of nursing their son. He happily assumed the chore of final burping and rocking to sleep while Lizzy retreated to her dressing room.

Lizzy returned, pausing on the threshold and smiling at the scene. Darcy held Alexander as he rocked, whispering silly phrases of love and singing in his off-key resonant tones, bringing to life the vision of her dream from so long ago. That prescient image of Darcy calling their baby by name had cemented in her heart that they were to have a son. Brought to life innumerable times already, watching their son being adored by his father never ceased to move her.

"Is he asleep?" She whispered.

Darcy nodded, kissing the top of Alexander's curly head. "Out for the duration I believe. Yet I do have a difficult time parting from him, even knowing he is likely more comfortable on his cushiony mattress."

"I rather doubt he prefers the cradle to his papa's warmth, but tonight I want you for myself." Darcy looked at her with a raised brow and lilt to his full lips. "Yes, my selfishness unmasked. Put him down, love, and I will tell Mrs. Hanford we are retiring."

That accomplished, Lizzy laced her fingers between Darcy's, bending for a final kiss to the baby's forehead before steering him out the door. To his surprise she bypassed their temporary bedchamber, leading unerringly through the sitting room to the Master suite. Darcy had barely stepped foot in this room for nearly a month, almost forgetting how cozy and spacious it was, not to mention how much larger the bed. He crossed the threshold, Lizzy's hand warm in his, and halted thunderstruck.

A fire blazed, casting glows of red and amber across the bearskin rug and pillows before the hearth. A scattering of candles and oil lamps were lit, but the room was muted in soft rays of gold, warm and incredibly inviting. A bottle of champagne sat by the turned down bed, fluted glasses alongside a tray of fruits and sweets.

Lizzy had moved a few paces away, still clutching his hand, watching the dawning enlightenment spread over his features as his glittering blue eyes swept the scene and returned to her face. She smiled at the expression of mingled childish enthusiasm and raging ardor, his grin both breathtakingly seductive and frivolously exuberant. He truly was speechless.

She stepped closer, eyes shining as passion rose, raising the free hand to feather fingertips over his chest. "Merry Christmas, Fitzwilliam."

For a span of several harsh breaths they stared at each other, ignoring everything beyond their acutely alive bodies. Darcy pressed Lizzy's hand flat against his rapidly rising chest, her palm instantly burning as his skin transmit flares of heat through the linen of his shirt. Lizzy ached for his touch, yet she held still waiting for him to move. His eyes penetrated her soul, searing through her mind and body as he studied her intently as only he could.

The moments stretched, Darcy finally bending in increments that were agonizing in their sluggishness until he was inches from her upturned lips. His blue eyes were openly gazing into her brown depths, voice a bare hoarse whisper with breath brushing her sensitized mouth when he spoke.

"Are you absolutely certain, Elizabeth? Positive you are fully healed and ready for me? No reservations whatsoever? I must know because I do not think myself capable of stopping once we start. My desire for you, my hunger, burns as a consuming fire. God, how I need you, my Lizzy!"

She was already nodding as he teased the tip of his tongue over her lips. Involuntarily, a faint moaning sigh escaped her throat, Darcy shuddering as he fought for control. The urge to sweep her into his arms, carry her to their bed, and love her thirstily nearly overwhelmed him. Instead, he moved away from her deliciously devastating mouth, planting tender kisses down the sloping expanse of her neck.

Still gripping one of her hands by his side and tightly pressing the other over his wildly palpating heart, he kissed and huskily resumed his inquiry, "No lingering pain? No discomfort? I could not bear it if I hurt you even while bringing you great pleasure. We need not rush, my lover, as I will wait as long as you require…"

Lizzy halted his words by the straightforward method of clamping her mouth over his in a forceful kiss, lips parting demandingly and tongue seeking. Darcy groaned, releasing her hands to encircle her body, drawing her soft curves onto the hard planes of his entire torso… Some small section of his brain screamed to take it slowly, but Darcy was beyond reason. Even through the thick layers of his old robe that she now wore belted securely over her gown he could feel the mass of her breasts, the warmth of her flesh radiating through the fabric, her scent intoxicating and taste enthralling, as her lush figure yielded to his probing hands.

"Oh, sweet Lord, I love you, Elizabeth!" His voice was covetous, the fingers of one hand franticly fumbling with the knot at her waist, firmly compressing her upper body against his chest with the other, and simultaneously inching toward the bed.

"William, wait!" Lizzy grasped the hand at her waist, breathing so heavily she saw stars before her eyes. Darcy had halted at her cry although the effort was clearly a torture for him. "I just… need you to know that… I am not… that is, my shape is not exactly... what it was yet. I may never be... as thin again, and there are a few... marks. Just faint ones, but nonetheless they are visible and... I just thought you should be warned."

Darcy was staring at her in genuine shock and surging amusement. The combination worked to cool the craziness of his passion, a lazy smile spreading over his face while he calmly resumed untying the robe sash, peeling it unhurriedly off her delicate shoulders. "My beautiful, sensuous, absurdly silly, adored wife. I shall not waste words of praise in an attempt to convince you how absolutely stunning you are, how desirable, how perfect, how intoxicating, how adulated. Instead, I shall show you."

The robe fell to the ground. Lizzy stood before her besotted spouse in his silk shirt unbuttoned to below her abundant breasts, creamy skin glowing and chest rising thrillingly with each breath. Darcy's smoldering eyes raked possessively head to toe then back to her face, grinning purely lascivious as he huskily said, "Yes, indeed, I will show you."

And then he did sweep her into his arms, carrying her the remaining steps to their favorite bed. Laying her gently down, he kissed teasingly, running one hand the length of her body. "You shall have no doubt whatsoever how I feel about you and what you do to me," he murmured before pulling away. Stripping his shirt off and tossing it randomly, he then opened the top drawer to retrieve the nearly empty jar of massaging cream forgotten since the last application the day before Alexander's birth.

Lizzy giggled. "What are you doing with that? I think the stretching is done for the time being."

"Ah, but the effects of the ointment are not exhausted. Besides, a woman who has been through such travails and who works so hard deserves a lengthy massage from her appreciative husband, do you not agree?"

Lizzy nodded, smiling and sighing as happiness freshly washed over her. Her handsome husband settled onto his knees at the end of the bed, rubbing a glob of aromatic balm between his palms before grasping her feet. She giggled and wiggled slightly at the ticklish sensation, Darcy grinning and applying strong fingers to the task. He took his time, the visual enticements of his luscious wife more than a little bit arousing, but the need to allay her insecurity calmed his lust... somewhat. Besides, the pleasure derived from smoothing over her skin was heady, experience having proven that a checked passion once released was rapture heightened beyond comprehension.

Transferring gradually to silky legs and knees, the oil soaked as he massaged firmly into each muscle. Lizzy watched him closely, mouth parted, and panting as ardor rose rapidly from the combined stimulus of his amazing touch and the sight of his flexing muscles. She pressed wiggling toes up his inner thigh, Darcy playfully pushing her foot away.

"Behave, Mrs. Darcy, or the massage will not extend beyond your thighs."

"What a tragedy that would be."

"Perhaps not a tragedy, but assuredly not as pleasurable."

Her mumbled disagreement about the levels of pleasure was lost in a gasping moan as he pressed lips to her lower abdomen, hands stroking over her hips. The sensations raged, Lizzy completely forgetting to be embarrassed over the thin, silvery marks low on her belly or the residual mound of flesh by her navel. Darcy, as he had told her so long ago, adored all of her, especially these remnants of their child's first dwelling place. She was beautiful, her sacrifice in bringing their son safely to the world was beautiful, and her giving soul was beautiful. Nothing would change how he felt about her or quash his desire for her.

After a thoroughly enticing time, Darcy lifted, one by one unbuttoning the shirt to expose all of her. "So gorgeous," he whispered, eyes revealing devotion and candor. "Elizabeth, I love you."

She held out her arms, reaching, but he shook his head slightly, smiling as he scooped a second dose of ointment. "I have only traveled half way up your body, my lover. Some of my favorite parts yet require my meticulous attention."

"Fitzwilliam, I may well die if you do not kiss me!"

He did not respond other than to smile wider and resume his labors. Straddling her hips he navigated every inch—from her waist, around to buttocks and back, up her sides to arms which were freed from the shirt, across trembling shoulders, and finally to her breasts. Darcy had dreamt of this moment nearly as often as he had dreamt of making love to her. Always he loved her bosom, delighted in the softness, this utterly feminine aspect of her physique by far his favored and most arousing.

Now, after a month of observing Alexander nursing at a vastly increased fullness, the mingled faint jealousy and suppressed passion bubbled forth as an uncontainable yearning. Still, he played teasingly, employing all the usual tricks of fingers and tongue validated time and again to arouse them both profoundly. The added euphoria attained when he eventually gave in to the familiar pleasure of suckling at her breast, with that arousing activity heightened by the sweet taste of her milk, was shockingly intense. Her response with throaty groans of delight, arching body, and grasping hands spiraled his craving out of control.

Darcy lost all regulation. Not ceasing the inciting activity for a second, he tore at his breeches, Lizzy writhing and deliriously aiding the procedure.

Simultaneous exclamations of inexpressible bliss burst forth as they merged. Darcy only then released her breast to claim her mouth, entire body bearing hers down into the mattress as he clutched her. He could feel all of her! No bulge, as precious as it was, inhibiting. Her bountiful breasts pressed against his chest, thrilling him immeasurably, agile limbs clasping and pulling him even closer, bellies caressing as they swayed in harmonious rhythm.

As he had promised, they loved hard. Passion pent up and held for weeks built further. The life-altering events of the past month and awareness of the cherished infant sleeping two rooms away added a dimension to their lovemaking that was indescribable. Any doubts either may have harbored deep in their subconscious that parenthood would negatively affect their intimate rapport were shattered.

Darcy had told her once that their lovemaking would grow more powerful as their relationship matured, and now they completely acknowledged the reality.

Darcy shouted, shuddering, and collapsing onto his wife in gratification, Lizzy shivering uncontrollably, but clinging so inflexibly that he could not have moved had he wished to or been capable. It was a considerable period of time before she relaxed her crushing grip, Darcy lifting ponderously to brush tousled hair off her brow and kiss her tenderly.

He sighed deeply, laying his forehead onto hers, voice a grating rumble. "Have I told you lately how utterly amazing you are? It honestly staggers my mind the bliss I experience when loving you, Elizabeth. I cannot believe it possible for a body to feel such sensations and not splinter into a thousand pieces."

Lizzy chuckled, kissing his nose, her voice nearly as rough as his. "I understand completely, my love. I too am rocked to my very core and in awe. I love you, Fitzwilliam, forever."

Their eyes met briefly, closing again as they kissed. Lizzy ran a palm down his chest, pulling her lips away with a tiny squeal.

"Oh! I have leaked all over us! William, I am so sorry!"

He chuckled hoarsely, grasping her hand and licking the moist tips of her fingers. "I am not complaining."

"But I have made a mess."

He halted her with a kiss, hand reaching to one wet breast and squeezing gently. "Do not apologize, please. I confess to rather liking your milk. We Darcy men have that in common as well."

Rolling to his back he embraced her trembling body, a smile of sheer exhilaration lighting his visage. She sagged against his chest, her deep breathing leading to satisfied slumber. Lifting to retrieve the folded blankets, he nestled her snuggly and kissed her forehead. Champagne and treats were forgotten in lieu of blissful cuddling.

"Sleep well, precious wife. I will wake you when Mrs. Hanford rings."

The Darcys were not roused on this Christmas Day well after the dawn by a light knock on the door. Rather, it was a good two hours before the dawn to the sound of a ringing bell hanging by the bedside. Darcy was in a customary deep sleep augmented tremendously by sexual gratification. Lizzy, on the other hand, was already beginning to rise through the deepest stages of sleep due to the increasingly painful pressure in her breasts. Therefore, when the unfamiliar tone of a chiming bell invaded her consciousness she was instantly fully awake and alert.

She untangled her limbs from Darcy's with alacrity, out of the bed and retrieving her fallen robe before a breath was taken. The abrupt movement and sudden blast of chill air over his uncovered skin, Lizzy forgetting to re-tuck the blankets in her haste, roused Darcy.

"Elizabeth? What?"

"Alexander is awake. Go back to sleep, dearest."

"Bring him here," he mumbled, rising laboriously to stoke the fire as Lizzy dashed from the room. Angry howls greeted her from the middle of the sitting room, their son's lungs in no way fragile. Mrs. Hanford was completing the annoying task, in Alexander's opinion, of changing his diaper, the infant only calming when his crooning mother picked him up.

"Come, sweetheart, be patient. Let's go see your father. Not too far away, little love. No, no, do not cry!" But it was to no avail, Alexander's stomach especially empty after the nighttime stretch of sleep. If Darcy had managed to drift into a doze, it was shattered at the entry of his wife and hollering son. He merely chuckled though, withdrawing the blankets so Lizzy could nestle against his warmth, lying on her side and finally quieting the distressed babe at her breast.

Darcy leaned on an elbow, encircling his family with the other arm and stroking Alexander's back. "Yes, quite the temper, my lad, but it is good to know your appetite is a healthy one." He kissed Lizzy's neck, settling in the soft bend to observe the baby nursing.

"I love how he kneads against your breast while he sucks. Rather like a kitten." The smile could be heard in his voice, Darcy rubbing one finger over the tiny rhythmically opening and closing hand atop the breast he suckled on. The baby's eyes were closed in deep concentration, by all appearances unaware and unconcerned with the people around him. Of course, this was not true; Alexander was merely innocently confident and content in the love of his parents. "Merry Christmas, my little kitten. And to you as well, beloved wife."

The words were accented with a warm caress down her side, over hips to abdomen, pulling closer against his pelvis. He bestowed another kiss to her neck and sighed happily before settling to watch their son.

It was a wonderfully lazy way to begin their second Christmas together. Darcy had returned to sleep by the time Alexander finished. Mother and son drifted away within the heat of Darcy's embrace, the comfortable bed a haven on a wintry day. Lizzy woke over two hours later feeling cramped between two immobile bodies of raging internal temperatures. Alexander's brow was actually sweaty! She cautiously vacated the bed, carrying the baby to his cradle and then freshening up before returning to her husband.

Darcy lay much as she had left him, having shifted only slightly and still soundly asleep. It was unusual for him to sleep so late, the sun well over the hazy horizon and casting bright beams of light around the gaps in the curtains. Lizzy smiled as she paused to observe him.

Did our activities last night wear you out, my lover? she thought with a sensuous grin. *Well, I do hope your energy is restored!*

And with that libidinous thought, she shed her robe and crawled under the covers. He gathered her instinctively, but was not fully awake until her lips had completed their leisurely travels from the hollow of his throat to his navel. Darcy woke a happy and satisfied man. The vision of his wife, the touch of his wife, and the love of his wife combined to nearly be more than one man, even as virile and lusty as Darcy, could handle.

Yet he handled it well.

"Merry Christmas, Fitzwilliam," were the only words she uttered as she straddled his hips, unifying beautifully and proceeding to show him how he thrilled her, how she adored him, how perfect he was, and how profound her love.

CHAPTER THREE

The Second Noël

THE RELATIVELY FAIR WEATHER from the prior day lasted, allowing for ease in travel both to the quaint chapel in the Village and for their evening's guests. Traditions prevailed in both breakfast foods as well as Christmas activities, meaning that in many ways this Christmas was indistinguishable from last year and all the ones that would follow. Mrs. Langton and her staff had prepared a stupendous breakfast heartily enjoyed by everyone in the elaborately bedecked dining room. Everyone wore his or her finest garments, Mr. Bennet dashing in the new suit purchased for his trip to visit Lizzy in London the previous spring. Marguerite and Samuel's consulting was now an expected arrangement, Lizzy and Darcy therefore dressing in nearly identical shades of blue with silver threads and trim.

Reverend Bertram preached a flawlessly constructed if unsurprising sermon on the birth of Christ. Lizzy had learned over the past year that the children of the parish performed at least three times a year: at Easter, for All Saint's Day, and during Christmas. It varied from celebration to celebration, either with a play or singing or, in the case of Easter, a puppet show. This year the youngsters gathered in the chancel dressed in choir robes, accompanied by the organist as they lifted their childish voices in a number of seasonal hymns. The finale was the older children singing "The Twelve Days of Christmas" while the tiniest held up corresponding signs with painted pictures of the vocalized gifts. Naturally there were mishaps, especially as the singers inevitably sped up the rhythm as the lengthy song progressed, but the resulting mistakes added to the fun. Once again, the worshippers exited the chapel with laughter and smiles.

As delightful as it was, Lizzy had a hard time relaxing and was anxious to return to the manor. She worried that Alexander may need her, although it was unlikely as he had eaten well and it was less than two hours since departing. To her faint dismay the pleasant weather meant that folks lingered in the modest courtyard, all desirous to congratulate their Master and Mistress on their son. Darcy, unlike years past, was reveling in the praise. His smile was barely contained behind the usual mask of reserved supremacy, lending him an approachable air perceived by all and, to Lizzy's veiled chagrin, acted upon by every last one of them! Yet despite her worries, they made it safely back to Pemberley before the baby woke.

Opening of the presents necessarily had to wait until Alexander was fed. Then it would take the greater bulk of the afternoon to complete due to the massive quantity of gifts and frequent interruptions. Lord and Lady Matlock arrived shortly after noon with enough wrapped packages to fill the space created by those already opened. Then, approximately an hour and a half later, it was the Bingley carriages.

The cacophony of voices and laughter was overwhelming at times. The ample parlor filled to standing room only, even with additional settees and chairs hastily provided. Any attempt at order was ludicrous. Lord Matlock trapped Mr. Bennet, Mr. Gardiner, and Dr. Darcy, the older gentlemen retreating to a far corner for relatively sedate conversation. Mr. Hurst made a beeline to the liquor cabinet and rarely wandered more than a few feet from it throughout the entire afternoon. Caroline Bingley and Louisa Hurst sat apart, gazing down their noses at the rowdy Bennets and Gardiners, feeling superior and unaware that Lady Annabella Montgomery was wrinkling her nose at them.

Lizzy had handed the baby to Darcy when Mr. Taylor announced the arrival of the Bingleys, Darcy now happily encumbered in a chair away from the fray. Alexander was awake in Darcy's lap, his chubby body erupting with newborn wiggles at the silly faces created by his father and the tickles delivered.

"My goodness he has grown!" It was Charles talking, eyes wide in astonishment.

"Welcome to Pemberley, Charles," Darcy spoke with a laugh. "I would rise and bow properly, but I am otherwise engaged. Pull up a chair and say hello to my son."

This he did, Colonel Fitzwilliam standing beside Darcy with a broad grin. Alexander's gaze moved from face to face, intently studying. "He looks so like you, Darcy. It is uncanny! Even your penetrating gaze. Rather disconcerting actually, to have an infant piercing me with your blue eyes."

Darcy smiled with pride. "I will consider that a compliment, Bingley. He is intelligent and it shows. Is that not the way of it my precious, wise little boy?" The picture of infantile acumen abruptly lost as Darcy attacked his son's soft neck with nibbling kisses, fistfuls of his hair seized painfully.

"Ouch! Help please!" Darcy pleaded from the depths of Alexander's neck. Richard laughingly untangled the amazingly tough fingers from Darcy's locks.

"You need a haircut, Cousin."

"So I have been informed." He nestled Alexander against his chest, soft head tucked under his chin, and rocked gently. Alexander instinctively found two fingers to suck on as he relaxed contentedly into the warmth of his father's body. "How was Christmas at Hasberry, Bingley?"

"Delightful. Jane decorated so beautifully and our cook prepared an amazing breakfast feast. We attended church in Buxton and we, that is Jane and I, thought it perfect."

Richard hid his smile, Darcy glancing toward Bingley's sisters who sat rigid on the sofa. Caroline looked up, briefly meeting Darcy's eyes and raking over the tiny body secured by his broad hands before glancing away with disinterest. "I gather Miss Bingley and the Hursts were not as enthused?"

"Well, you know how it is. Nothing compares to London or, surprisingly, Essex."

"Essex?" Richard asked in surprise. "What does Essex have to offer?"

"Hanged if I know. She spent several weeks there with a society friend of hers, Miss Beatrice Dandridge, and now suddenly its Essex this and Essex that. She slips it in somewhere every other sentence. Frankly, it is driving me mad."

"Essex has its charms, especially the coastal areas. Remember Mr. Hardin, Richard? He has a lovely estate near Southend-on-Sea. I spent a few weeks there one summer while at Cambridge."

"Perhaps so Darcy, but Miss Dandridge lives near Chelmsford. It is not that far from Hertford, and we all know how enthusiastic she was about the country surrounding Netherfield." The sarcasm was evident in Charles's voice. He shook his head, "It makes no sense whatsoever."

"Who can understand a woman, eh, Darcy?" Richard said with a nudge to his cousin's booted foot. "Unfathomable creatures all, but we love them nonetheless. Here's to the fairer sex!" He lifted his glass toward Bingley and Darcy, who both laughed, Darcy shaking his head.

"Pathetic. I do pity the woman who ensnares you, dear cousin. Now, if you both will excuse me a moment, I think my son needs to be put to bed." Darcy rose, Alexander a limp weight although he continued to suck sleepily on his first two fingers. Lizzy was approaching Caroline and Louisa as Darcy drew near.

"Miss Bingley, Mrs. Hurst, forgive me for not properly greeting you sooner. It has been rather chaotic. Welcome to Pemberley and merry Christmas. Mr. Darcy and I are delighted to have you celebrate with us." She turned to her husband with a smile, laying one hand lightly on his arm.

"Welcome, Miss Bingley, Mrs. Hurst. How long has it been, Mrs. Hurst? At least two years?"

"Approximately, Mr. Darcy. Many things have altered. I do not believe I have ever seen Pemberley so elaborately adorned. It is lovely."

Darcy smiled and bowed slightly, Alexander clutched securely. "Thank you. Many things have changed here at Pemberley, Mrs. Hurst, aside from the decorations."

"So it seems. Congratulations on the birth of your son. He appears to be a healthy infant."

"Quite healthy, and asleep and heavy." He turned to his wife. "Elizabeth, I will put him to bed. Pardon me ladies, I will return momentarily." And with another short bow, he left.

Lizzy watched him depart with a happy smile, unconsciously releasing a sigh before turning her attention to her guests.

"Mr. Darcy certainly is an attentive father," Caroline said. "Who would have thought him the type? Playing foolishly in plain sight of all and now attending to the task of carrying to the nursery! Do you not have a nanny for such things, Mrs. Darcy?"

"We do, but as I recall stating many months ago within your hearing, Miss Bingley, we intend to provide for our child's needs as much as possible. It is a joy to do so, a joy we both treasure." She chose not to comment on the fact that Mr.

Darcy was precisely the "type" to cater ridiculously to his loved ones, a fact Miss Bingley should be aware of given his long standing devotion to Mr. Bingley.

"How was your sojourn in Essex? Jane said you spent over a month there at the Dandridge estate. I recall meeting Miss Dandridge at the soiree at Lord Calvin's. I was not aware she was a close friend of yours. I have a cousin who lives near Braintree and know how beautiful the countryside is thereabouts. Not particularly exotic or glamorous, but certainly refreshing and good for a horseback ride if nothing else."

Caroline smiled. "Indeed. Thankfully, I do adore riding so was not too terribly bored. There were enough diversions to entertain." She finished softly with a faint flush spreading over her cheeks. Lizzy cocked her head in puzzlement, her musings interrupted by an exclamation from Kitty.

"Can we finish opening presents now, please? Papa, this is from Mary and me."

The revealing commenced. Lizzy sat beside a mildly paler Jane, squeezing her hand. The gentlemen assumed the roles of couriers, delivering labeled packages to the ladies. Every attempt was made to open neatly, one at a time, but enthusiasm occasionally overcame caution with ribbons and paper flying. Darcy rejoined a group in a state of moderate, lively chaos. Laughter was rampant with frequent jumping up to hug someone across the room, gifts being passed about for inspection, and exclamations of appreciation.

Darcy stood beside his wife, hand warm on her shoulder. She glanced upward, eyes sparkling as she clasped his fingers, lifting for a kiss to his knuckles. He smiled, brushing across her cheek before turning to Richard. "Colonel Fitzwilliam, the gold wrapped box to your right is addressed to Mrs. Darcy. Yes, that one. Bring it here please."

"For you, my lady," Richard bowed gallantly, placing the flat box onto her lap.

"Thank you, Richard. William, I thought we were done. You already gifted me three new gowns, the sardonyx cameo brooch of a mother and child that I absolutely adore, the leather bound edition of Wordsworth's *Lyrical Ballads*, two new pairs of gloves, handkerchiefs, and what else… oh yes, the wooden table with drawers to sit beside my chair!"

"Trifles, my dear. The latter essentially because I was weary of seeing your sewing scattered all over the ground." He grinned and squeezed her shoulder. "This, in addition to the larger box in yonder corner"—he pointed to a now visible package previously buried under the mound of presents—"is your main gift from me."

"William, really…"

"You may as well just open it, Lizzy," Jane interjected, smiling at her brother-in-law. "It is purchased and wrapped. I doubt if there is any chance it will be returned."

"Absolutely none. Thank you, Mrs. Bingley, for your support. My wife has yet to comprehend the realities of being spoiled by her husband. I pray you do not torment Bingley with useless arguments and quibbling."

"I fear she does," Charles said with a laugh. "However, I do believe we should be thankful, Darcy. After all it was the modesty, virtue, and economy of spirit which partially drew us to the Bennet sisters, along with other stellar attributes I hasten to add."

"Lord have mercy! We will be here until next Christmas at this rate! Open it, Elizabeth, before these two begin reciting poetry and destroy all our appetites!" George declared, Mr. Bennet laughing and nodding in agreement.

Jane blushed, Lizzy laughing as she began untying the ribbons.

"Honestly, Lizzy, and you too, Jane, be thankful you have husbands able to present such treasures! How fortunate you both are!"

"Thank you for the reminder, Mama," Lizzy said with sarcasm.

Of course Lizzy was quite familiar with her husband's need to shower her with gifts. It was a habit borne of his deep love for all those dearest to him; an expression established long before she entered his life. The logical conclusion was simply to accept it, but her nature would not allow her to ever be mercenary or greedy and, therefore, it was mildly uncomfortable. She glanced upon his glowing visage, much like a child with a secret, and could only say a silent prayer of thankfulness.

The box contained a book bound with fine calf leather dyed a deep blue with gold leaf etching along the spine. The pages inside were blank, the intent of which was unmistakably indicated by the gold emblazoned Alexander William George Bennet Darcy scrolled across the front cover.

Before Lizzy could find her voice, Darcy was kneeling with hands caressing over the exquisite binding. "It is a memory book. I saw something similar in Derby. I had this made by a bookbinding establishment in London that has restored numerous antique volumes I have purchased over the years. You can write your thoughts, facts as he grows, ink prints of his feet, memories of first words, when he walks, and anything else that comes to mind. Is it not a fabulous idea?"

"Darcy, this is marvelous!" It was Charles, face suffused with enthusiasm. "Where did you get it?" The new father and father-to-be launched into a discussion, Jane and Lizzy exchanging amused glances.

"William, thank you so much! It is a marvelous concept, keeping an itemized log, so to speak, of his transitions and growth. Will you write in it as well?"

"If you wish. My mother kept a similar journal for Georgie and me. I ran across them in the attic, having not thought on it for years." His voice grew quiet, eyes far away for a spell as he stroked the embossed name of their son. "Such memories are priceless." He cleared his throat gruffly with a slight shrug, voice firmer as he resumed. "The other gift accompanies and is the last, I promise. Merry Christmas, my love."

It was a trunk of cedar, approximately three feet cubed with short legs, sturdily if plainly constructed with no embellishment other than "Alexander" carved in rough block letters across the lid. The sweet aroma of cedar pervaded the air, every eye lifting from individual unwrapping to observe the scene.

"Mother kept particular artifacts in a series of boxes, some that I discovered damaged. I did not want that to happen to Alexander's favorite toy, first shoes, blanket, or anything else we deem worthy of keeping. So I built this..."

"You built it?" Caroline interrupted in astonishment, Darcy glancing to her face with a smile.

"I am quite skillful with my hands, Miss Bingley. Unfortunately, I do not have the talent for whittling or engraving as did my grandfather, so it is unadorned, but it will withstand the test of time and any pounding by a rowdy son! I thought it would fit nicely below the window in the nursery."

"Absolutely! It is fantastic." Lizzy raised one hand to lightly brush his cheek. "Thank you, William, again."

"I do hope you kept the pattern, William, so you can create more. I think you will need an entire collection in due course." George declared with a wink, Lizzy blushing but Darcy meeting his eyes boldly.

"Not a problem, Uncle. I have a very good memory."

"I pray you are an adequate instructor as well, Darcy, as I want you to teach me how to construct a cedar box for our child. I have never worked with wood, so it shall be a challenge for you." Charles looked at his friend with a grin.

"Really, Charles! Carpentry? Is not sheep farming and walnut harvesting enough manual labor for you? It is so, so… common!" Caroline was truly aghast.

Darcy's mumbled and sarcastic thank you was lost behind Bingley's reply, "Honestly, Caroline! It is not as if I pick the nuts myself or shovel manure. I manage an estate, and none of this has any bearing on desiring to construct a memory box for my firstborn."

"Attaboy, Mr. Bingley!" George declared with a stunning clap to the younger man's shoulder. "Artistic creativity is food for the brain! Keeps the nerve's firing, eh, Mr. Bennet?"

"I cannot claim any particular skills with my hands, Dr. Darcy, but I do agree with the philosophy. Although, I have assisted in the mending of the fence a time or two and did apply saw and hammer to create a finely wrought birdhouse and feeder which yet graces the east garden."

"Oh, I remember that!" Mary spoke up with a rare burst of enthusiasm. "I was but seven or so, Papa, and I recall you let each of us hammer a bit and Lizzy sawed. Jane, you carved the perches, is that not so?"

Jane was blushing, Charles gazing at her with pride. "It was a small thing really. I merely smoothed several branches. We all worked on it together. Even Lydia, who was barely four or five, was placed in charge of handing each nail."

Lizzy and Kitty were smiling in memory. Caroline sniffed, "Well, I suppose such an endeavor could be amusing, in certain circumstances. Seems a trifle rustic to me. Artistry is one thing, but pounding wood strikes me as a menial chore destined for the working man."

Darcy was stiff with indignation, hand tight on Lizzy's shoulder. She caressed his white knuckles tenderly, opening her mouth to flash a retort, but was halted by her mother's voice, "Of course, Miss Bingley, you have a point! I am certain the venture will not be a frequent activity for either Mr. Darcy or Mr. Bingley. Men of their fine stature and finances have no need to lower themselves to such base levels, naturally. Do not fret!"

"I am of the opinion that talent of all kind, whether it be musical or architectural or scientific or any of a million other realms are all gifts inspired of God and, therefore, to be acknowledged and pursued extensively, otherwise it is an insult to the Giver. As the Declaration penned by the founders of the Americas states, 'all men are created equal, that they are endowed, by their Creator.' No tasks are too menial or unnecessary, Miss Bingley."

All in the room were staring with amazement at Mary, who had delivered this quietly voiced speech. The attitudes may have varied as to the veracity of her words, but all were momentarily speechless. Not surprisingly, it was Dr. Darcy who shattered the silence first with a raised cup of tea and ringing endorsement, "Here, here, Miss Bennet! Well said indeed. I'll drink to that!"

The mood thus lightened, Lizzy turned to Richard, "Colonel, now that my husband has finally exhausted the gift giving, it would be an appropriate time to retrieve the package you assured me was in your safekeeping. If you please?"

Richard bowed formally. "As you wish, Mrs. Darcy. Pardon me a moment." And with a brisk clap of his military boot heels, he pivoted and exited the room.

"Secrets, Mrs. Darcy?" Darcy asked with a raised brow.

"It is Christmas, my dear."

"While we are waiting, Lizzy, this is from all of us Bennets. We pooled our resources." Kitty placed a smallish, but heavy gift on her lap, stooping to kiss her cheek. "Merry Christmas."

The wrapping hid a roughly cigar box–sized, highly glossed, cherry wood musical box! The glass panel in the ornately carved lid displayed the copper cylinder and shiny mechanical devices required to turn the cylinder and elicit the sounds. Lizzy gasped, hand instantly over her heart in awe and delighted expressions of thanks pouring forth. It was a stunning piece of workmanship, instantly drawing the attention of most in the room, especially the ever invention-fascinated Darcy.

"Incredible! Where did you acquire one so large and sporting a cylinder rather than disk, Mr. Bennet?" He was already lightly touching the internal springs and motor.

"One of the advantages to having a brother in trade," he answered with a smile and nod toward Mr. Gardiner.

"I have an associate who deals with various Swiss manufacturers of timepieces. He occasionally acquires musical boxes as well. These are new, Mr. Darcy, created by Recordon and Jundon. This one plays a compilation of Mozart's sonatas."

"I have two musical snuff boxes purchased in Paris and London, one of which I gave to Elizabeth to listen while at her desk. I dismantled a third in an attempt to figure how it worked, failing miserably as I was unable to completely fathom the mechanics nor reassemble properly." His voice dropped to a tone of inner musing as he intently investigated the visible parts, Lizzy playfully batting his hands away with a laugh.

"Get your own musical box to dissect, Mr. Darcy! This one is mine."

He straightened with a faint blush. "Of course, dearest. I was merely looking."

Several snickers erupted, Colonel Fitzwilliam returning to a room of polite twitters and flushed cousin. "What have you done now, Darcy?"

Darcy, however, had no response forthcoming. Rather, his gaze was riveted to the wooden case Richard held in both arms. It was well over five feet in length yet only a foot wide, which would have strongly hinted to Darcy what it contained even if it was not branded with the label Knopf Bros. of Shenandoah Valley, Virginia. His mouth fell open and immobility gripped all four extremities.

"How did you...?" He stopped, speechless.

Lizzy was grinning broadly, face rosy with delight as she jumped up to stand beside her paralyzed spouse. Placing one hand tenderly on his arm, she explained, "I know you have coveted one for your collection. Richard was able to acquire an original, dated 1786. I have yet to see it myself, not that I would know what I was inspecting, so I pray it meets your expectations. Open it!"

Richard laid the case onto the table, stepping back as Darcy approached with reverence. "This is unbelievable. I cannot thank you both enough."

"I should have thought of it myself and claimed all the glory," Richard said. "After all, years of immersing yourself in the journals of William Bartram and Jonathan Carver, as well as other American frontiersmen, and the undoubtedly embellished tales of Daniel Boone, should have enlightened me."

Darcy had opened the case, nearly the entire room's occupants now clustered about to watch, revealing a pristine condition rifle. But not just any rifle. A uniquely American invention of the 18th century frontiersman: a long rifle. This one sported a stock of beautifully grained wood, lacquered and decorated with silver and brass inlays fancily scrolled, the stamped and dated emblem of its makers, and a barrel easily four feet in length. Every surface, both wooden and metal, gleamed. It was exquisite.

Collectively, the men in the room, even Mr. Hurst who had left his vigil by the liquor cabinet, whistled in appreciative awe. The women, unschooled in the artistry of firearms, nonetheless could readily grasp the fine quality and sheer beauty of the displayed specimen.

Darcy grasped the weapon, lifting with steady and competent hands, as Richard continued his narrative. "This one reputedly has a range of nearly four hundred yards in the hands of an experienced marksman. You should be able to achieve that, Cousin, with practice."

"Four hundred yards!" Mr. Bennet gasped. "I would love to see that!"

Colonel Fitzwilliam turned to the skeptical Mr. Bennet. "A general I know has a long rifle and has reached four hundred seventy yards. Of course, he is our regiment's finest marksman, actually trained as a sharpshooter, but Darcy here is quite an excellent shot. An English Baker rifle can nearly attain that distance, but not as reliably. Nor are they as imposing in appearance or as beautifully designed. I daresay these American rifles are the most elaborate I have ever seen, as painful as that is to admit."

Darcy's eyes were glittering as he sighted down the barrel, stock end nestled flawlessly against his shoulder. "I do not know about four hundred yards, but I certainly will attempt it. The balance is excellent, weight perfect, and you are correct Richard, no English or German firearm compares. Damned Americans!"

"Do you like it then?" Lizzy asked teasingly. "I am sure Richard could get my money back."

He lowered the weapon to his side, encircled his surprised wife's waist, and drew her in for a firm kiss. "I love it almost as much as I love you. You keep your paws off my rifle and I shall leave your musical box unmolested. Agreed?" Lizzy nodded, several eruptions of laughter ensuing around the massed observers.

An hour later, all the gifts were finally unwrapped and organized in individual piles. The strewn papers and ribbons were discarded, and the satisfied Pemberley inhabitants relaxed as they awaited the call to dinner. Select items were inspected and shared with others while the men loitered in a knot around the corner table where the rifle case now sat. The rifle itself was passed from hand to hand, all delighting in the temporary joy of imagining firing the stupendous weapon at unsuspecting game. Darcy was already arranging a target session for the morrow, graciously offering to allow each man the opportunity to test his skill.

Jane sat next to Lizzy, admiring the locket lying on a pillowy cushion of velvet. "This truly is exquisite, Miss Darcy. You must whisper in Mr. Darcy's ear to casually mention to my husband where it was purchased. I would dearly love one myself."

Georgiana smiled. "I shall tell Mr. Bingley myself! It would make a perfect Christmas gift next year or perhaps for your birthday. The jeweler in Matlock,

Mr. Ingalls, is quite excellent and reasonably priced compared to most found in Town. He has quite an extensive selection of lockets, in fact. I thought Lizzy would like this one," she finished shyly.

"And you are absolutely correct, Georgie. I adore it! In fact, if it is not a bother, can you clasp it on for me? Fortunately, I did not take the time this morning to don a necklace. A fortuitous oversight on my part."

The locket in question, a gift from Georgiana to her new sister, was of silver. In size it was only a half-inch diameter with a raised and exceptionally detailed picture on the lid of a sleeping infant in profile with tiny hands folded by his cheek. Georgiana had presented it with the humble suggestion of placing a lock of Alexander's hair inside. Lizzy was still choked up and Darcy quite smug in that he knew of the gift before her, although hastening to clarify that it was entirely Georgiana's idea and chosen without any input from him.

Not a soul was left wanting or dissatisfied. Lizzy played hostess, engaging and gregarious so that even Lady Annabella was drawn into frequent conversation and stilted laughter. Dinner was marvelous, a dozen courses served over nearly two hours as humor and conversation raged. The Master and Mistress sat at opposite ends of the long, elegantly adorned table sharing frequent warm gazes. The weather held fair if bitterly cold, permitting after dinner walks in the waning light. Early evening entertainment lapsed in the music room with a splendid array of instruments played and vocal ranges lifted to the delight of all. Alexander joined the group for a spell, awake and happily passed from embrace to embrace until eventually falling asleep in his grandfather's arms.

It was late in the evening, music and singing issuing forth gaily, when Mr. Taylor circumspectly approached his Master and leaned for a whispered conference. Darcy's face instantly tightened, lips a thin line as he nodded brusquely and rose, leaving the room without a word.

"How extraordinary!" Mrs. Bennet exclaimed. "I thought Mr. Darcy's former rudeness was extinguished with marital felicity."

"Mother, please," Lizzy said. "Remember that my husband manages a vast estate which occasionally requires problem solving of a serious nature. Papa, do you mind holding Alexander for a bit longer? Good. Excuse me please." And with a nod toward the group in general, she followed her husband.

As suspected, he had removed to his study with Mr. Taylor and Mr. Keith and was standing before the desk where he sat scribbling on a piece of parchment, another lying by his left hand.

"Mr. Keith, I should be no more than a few days. These envelopes here"—
he tapped a stack with the end of his pen—"are ready to post. These papers
here are signed." He tapped another pile. "Issue payment draughts as necessary,
address and post. I will be staying at the Georgian as usual."

"Very good, sir." Mr. Keith replied.

"Mr. Taylor, alert Samuel to pack a small travel bag for me, then inform
the stables to prepare Parsifal. I will depart within the hour."

"Depart! Where?" Darcy glanced up in surprise, not aware Lizzy had
entered the room.

"Derby," he answered shortly, eyes returning to the parchment.

"William, it is already dark outside…"

"I am well aware of the time, Mrs. Darcy!" He snapped, eyes troubled and
blazing as he glanced at her briefly. "Thank you, Mr. Taylor, Mr. Keith. Follow
my orders. You are dismissed."

"Yes, sir." And with a bow both men left.

Lizzy stood in silence, embarrassed, angry, and worried. Darcy seemed to
be ignoring her. She bit her lip, slowly stepping toward the desk. "William,
what has happened?"

He sighed and melted at her tender tone, falling into his chair and running
one hand through his hair. He closed his eyes and gesticulated to the left hand
paper. "There was a fire today at my mill in Derby. Much has been destroyed,
two men badly wounded, and three dead. Thankfully, as it was Christmas, most
were home with their families," he finished flatly.

Lizzy's breath caught, eyes glazing with tears. "Oh, love! I am so sorry!" She
crossed quickly, placing a hand onto his shoulder. The gesture woke Darcy from
his stasis, and he stood up briskly and stepped past Lizzy impatiently.

"Thank you. I am afraid I must attend to the aftermath personally. I am
sorry, Elizabeth, but there is no choice."

"I understand, dearest, I truly do and would think less of you if you
did not go. However, must you leave tonight? Traveling in the dark is not
safe and I would worry so. Nothing can be accomplished until tomorrow
in any case."

"I have traveled in the dark many times before. I can be there in a few
hours, attain information, and be on site at first light. Time is precious in
situations such as these, Elizabeth."

"William, please be reasonable…"

"There is nothing to discuss! It is my decision and I am in no mood to argue the matter."

"At best you would arrive by eleven, far too late to do anything of consequence. I am merely asking you to stay safe with us tonight and leave at first light tomorrow. What difference can a few hours make? The damage has already been done, dearest."

"I cannot stay here, laughing and amusing myself when people in my employ are suffering. It is unconscionable!"

"What is unconscionable is the possibility of injury while galloping full bore, as you would, on a dark and muddy road for two hours! What is unconscionable is that you would not rationally consider your safekeeping and the anxiety of your family!"

"I am an excellent rider, madam, as you know. Nothing will happen to me."

"You can assure this, sir? You have the gift of foresight? How delightful it is to know this! Or is it that you are immortal and I was unaware? Whatever the case, thank you for explaining. By all means then, ride on! I shall return to our guests with a cheery heart knowing that I have no fear of surviving without you and raising our son fatherless!"

And with that ringing impeachment, she stormed from the room, slamming the door behind. Darcy stood rooted to the floor, furious, but also stricken by her horrifying allegation. Lizzy, meanwhile, was pulled up short five steps past the still reverberating door when she realized she did not know where to go. Lost in confusion with rage and terror warring, she did not readily note her father lurking in the hall several paces away.

"Lizzy?"

She started, glancing upward and instantly losing control at the sight of her concerned father and sleeping baby. With a choking sob, she spun about and dashed down the corridor to her parlor. Naturally, Mr. Bennet followed, laying Alexander down onto a settee and walking to where Lizzy leaned against the windowsill weeping. He stood silently, concerned, but he was not one who easily dealt with women's hysterics despite, or probably because of, long years in a household with six women. Reverting to the simple comfort of patting her shoulder and uttering a sympathetic *there, there*, he waited.

Eventually, Lizzy calmed enough to relate the dilemma. Mr. Bennet offered no answers or advice, being of the mind that marital difficulties were of an intimate nature beyond parental purview. He had only one statement, convincingly presented.

"As painful as Mr. Darcy's decision, Lizzy, it will be compounded if you do not talk to him prior to his departure. The affection you two have for each other is too great to easily endure days apart under misspoken words and emotional estrangement."

In time, they left the parlor, Alexander beginning to stir in Lizzy's arms, just as Darcy neared the music room. The lovers' eyes met in the dim expanse between, Lizzy's swollen, red, and filled with pain and Darcy's dull and inscrutable. He bowed slightly, turning without a word into the music room. Lizzy and Mr. Bennet trailed, Darcy already addressing the assembly when they entered and halted by the doorway.

"Forgive my abrupt exodus a while ago. I regret I have received ill news from Derby necessitating an early retirement, as I must depart at first light tomorrow. Please, enjoy yourselves fully. All that Pemberley has to offer is at your immediate disposal. Your most excellent hostess will ensure your comfort. Good night." Another bow, this one formally proffered, was followed by a stiff pivot and swift exit, not glancing at Lizzy or her father.

Alexander, to Lizzy's relief, chose that moment to release a loud yell, providing a logical excuse to leave. She nursed him alone, Darcy not joining her as he had nearly every night since Alexander's birth. When she later entered their bedchamber, dressed in a gauzy gown of blue, he stood by the far window gazing outward at the visible stars and pale moonlight.

Lizzy had had plenty of time to think. She knew he was likely still angry and riddled with grief and misplaced guilt over the mill disaster, yet she could not deny her own overwhelming relief at his decision to stay. Correct she may have been, but there was no sense of victory in the idea. Only one thing was certain: she loved him far too much to part on negative terms. Her father was accurate on that count.

Darcy did not hear her steps on the thick carpet, lost in reverie and contemplation of the stars. She said nothing, merely standing behind his left shoulder and absorbing his beloved profile until the drifting scent of lavender reached his nostrils. He turned, countenance composed as he leaned into the wall and stared at her mutely.

The moment stretched, Lizzy finally reaching one hand and laying it on his chest. "Thank you for staying." She spoke in a bare whisper, breathing deeply before continuing in the face of his silence. "I know you are angry with me, perhaps rightfully so, but I am not sorry for anything I said if it induced you to stay. I too feel grief for the families afflicted, William, but I am not ashamed to confess my selfishness. I cannot bear the thought of anything happening to you. We need you; it is as simple as that," she finished firmly.

She lifted her chin bravely, holding his indecipherable gaze. It had been over a year since she had last been the recipient of the unreadable Darcy stare and she did not like it. The urgent desire to wrap her arms around him was unbearably painful to resist.

When Darcy moved, it startled her. He cupped her face with sturdy hands, bending until he was inches away, voice hoarse as emotion abruptly surged over his features. "I absolutely hate it when you are right and I am wrong, Mrs. Darcy. Please try not to make a habit out of the tendency." His mouth curled faintly in a soft smile, eyes tender as they engaged hers.

And then he kissed her hard, absolving sobs caught in both throats as bodies melted together. It continued for a long time, spirits meshing as breath was shared. Lizzy was crushed against every plane of his body, but she did not care. When they pulled apart it was out of necessity for deep respirations, neither letting go. Darcy drew her head under his chin, holding her as physically close as possible. She rubbed her cheek against the mildly rough hairs on his chest, warmth flooding even in the midst of the cool window embrasure.

"I love you so much, Fitzwilliam! I am so, so sorry!"

He released an enormous sigh. "So am I."

Taking her by the hand, he led her to the bearskin rug, fur burnished amber in the firelight. Wordlessly, he removed his robe, bare skin reflecting the flames, and reached dexterous fingers to untie each ribbon of her robe and discard it unhurriedly. The sadness in his eyes tore at her soul. Always naked before her as he was to no one else, she had often seen the pain of grief both past and present in his eyes. It ripped her heart, but she understood now that it was who he was. Tomorrow, in Derby, he would be the man of strength and serene control; everyone looking to him for the answers that he would give without hesitation. Tonight, in the privacy of their bedchamber with his soul mate, he could relax.

He ran heated palms down her arms, goose pimples rising in the wake of his touch, clasping each hand and pulling her onto the rug. He sat propped on the mass of cushions, Lizzy in his arms with back nestled to his chest. He said nothing, staring into the flickering flames with cheek pressed against her temple. He made no move other than to tenderly caress slightly calloused fingertips over her shoulders and arms. When he did speak, his tone was low and anguished.

"Is it wrong to be so content when people I am responsible for are suffering?"

"There are always people suffering, everywhere and at all times. Do not all individuals, even in the midst of travails, deserve happiness as it comes to them?"

Silence. Then, "Do you think less of me if I confess there are times I want to run from it all, forget about being 'Master of Pemberley' and just live simply somewhere with you and Alexander? No responsibilities except to love you eternally and play with our children as a child myself?"

She turned in his arms, pushing unruly locks away from his troubled eyes and feathering over each feature. "How could I think less of you for being human?"

They made love then. Slowly, long into the night, comfort and peace attained in the rapturous expression of bonding and love.

Lizzy woke as the first rays of dim sunlight peeked through the curtains. Darcy, fully clothed in traveling attire, entered their chambers with a squalling son in his arms. He smiled sunnily at his wife as she sat up in the bed, breasts full and ready.

"He has no interest in silly faces or words of devotion. Your breasts take precedence each time, not that I cannot relate to the sentiment."

He sat beside her as Alexander ravenously attacked the nipple, Lizzy wincing slightly. Infant placated, she peered into her husband's face, reaching her free hand to cup his jaw. He kissed her palm, smiling with only a hint of lingering pain evident.

"I will miss you, Mrs. Darcy."

"I know. And I you. Be careful, my heart, and return to us quickly. I love you."

"I know," he grinned. "Thank you, my Lizzy, for being my comfort. You are my life and I will return quickly." He kissed her temple then bent to nibble Alexander's toes and bestow tiny kisses to chubby feet and hands. Returning to Lizzy's mouth, they kissed lingeringly. With a final brush over her lips with his thumb and repeated *I love you*, he rose.

She watched him walk to the door, back straight with figure flawlessly masculine and controlled. He turned and, after a blown kiss and airy wave, was gone.

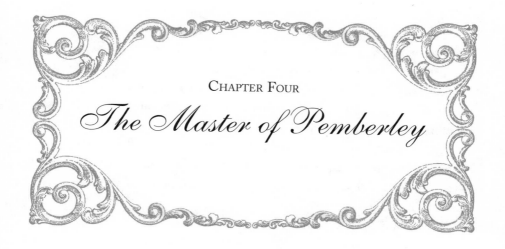

CHAPTER FOUR

The Master of Pemberley

DARCY WAS FOUR MILES south of Pemberley, clopping along at a swift gallop when the echoing thud of horse's hooves not belonging to his mount penetrated his awareness. Glancing over his shoulder, he grunted once and lightly pulled on the reins, Parsifal slowing to a sedate walk. He had given no details as to why he was departing so early in the morning, had not asked for company, and assuredly did not need a bodyguard, yet found he was not the slightest bit surprised. Annoyed, yes, but not surprised.

The other horse pulled alongside, Darcy slowing to a halt and gracing its sunnily smiling rider with a decidedly unfriendly scowl. He leaned forward and growled, "Why are you here? I did not ask for company."

"Can a fellow not take a morning ride in the bracing air? Are you the boss of the road, Mr. Darcy?"

"Yes, as a matter of fact I am. This is my land and I did not give you permission to be here."

The intruder looked around at the endless plains of frosted pasture and smoke-emitting chimneys rising from the numerous brick cottages nestled in between the empty fields. All was silent in the misty dawn gloom, only the faint scattered barks of dogs and lowing of cows needing to be milked a subtle reminder of life beyond the two horsemen. He shrugged unperturbed. "Very well, I will give you that, but as a sworn defender of the Crown, I think I outrank you even here and can, therefore, travel wherever I see fit."

"Hogwash. And you are not even in uniform. Seriously, Richard, did Elizabeth send you to watch over me?"

"Unruffle your proud tail feathers, Cousin. I came of my own volition. Your wife is under the impression you can tread water and calm raging seas; therefore, she is unlikely to request me to play protector."

"I can assure you that my wife is fully aware of every flaw I possess and reminds me of them frequently, but that's beside the point. I have no humor today, am quite foul as a matter of fact, and in no mood for your acerbic wit and lame jokes."

Richard nodded, face suddenly devoid of any trace of jocularity. "I gathered as much. Ride on then and enlighten me as to the problem. I am at your disposal in any way you see fit."

Darcy stared at his serious cousin for a moment more, grunted again, but argued no further. Instead, he tightened his leather-clad grip on the reins, and with a short command to Parsifal, they set off at a brisk canter while Darcy imparted the facts as he knew them.

The ride was uneventful and thankfully free of rain or snow, although the wind was biting. The roads were frozen solid, with scattered slick patches of ice and a fair amount of slushy mud ofttimes covering their mounts to the fetlocks. Few words were spoken after the brief discourse on the mill fire, the fast pace and stiff breeze not conducive to conversation even if Darcy had been in the mood. Despite the pleasant evening spent with his wife, the idyllic hours spent loving each other so deliriously, her ceaseless empathy which calmed his turbulent soul, and the brief interlude of family felicity that morning, Darcy was still deeply disturbed.

His years as Master of an enormous estate had been relatively disaster free. Only nine deaths had occurred as a result of accidents and three men who were maimed to the point of requiring retirement from their duties. It was not a bad record compared to most men in his position. He knew this, was proud of the fact, and strove to find ways to ensure safety among his tenants and employees, but the simple reality was that many of the jobs necessary to keep the Pemberley estate functioning were of a dangerous nature. The number of injuries and near misses was substantially higher, and Darcy looked upon each incidence as a personal affront and failing.

Darcy was a rational man by nature. Rationally, he knew the blaze at the mill, however it had occurred, was completely beyond his control. Rationally, he knew that it was in no way his blunder. Rationally, he knew that these events were called accidents for a reason. Rationally, he knew that no one would place blame on him. Rationally, he knew that he and his partners would financially survive the disaster and deal with the trauma, as they were each wise businessmen and astute managers.

However, Darcy was also a man who cared deeply. Logic would triumph over emotion, but the emotion would not merely disappear. He would fight it every step of the way, with every breath, and not a single person he encountered would have the vaguest clue as to his struggle. Such was the disposition of the man who, after roughly two hours of hard riding with Richard keeping pace, drew into the wide gravelly area before the main entrance of the mill in Derby.

It was not yet eight-thirty in the morning, the sun well risen in the eastern sky and casting a strong light if little warmth. The cotton mill co-owned by Darcy was located on the western bank of the River Derwent, near the northern borders of the town proper. Several mills of various types had, for centuries, utilized the power of the briskly flowing river to process the wool and flax that was abundantly grown on the fertile fields of Derbyshire, as well as imported silk and cotton. Derby, like many other towns situated fortuitously on rapid rivers throughout England, had evolved in the past fifty years from a sleepy fishing and farming village to a center of industry. As inventions designed to speed up the laborious and costly processes of rendering textiles useful had emerged, an industrial revolution had waved across the county. Derby had benefited significantly and prospered as a result, as had forward-thinking men such as Darcy. Uncounted persons of modest means had grown rich through wise investments while men of wealth had grown even wealthier. Darcy invested financially in Derby's Silk Mill, the oldest such factory in all of England, as well as one of the three wool mills located nearby. However, the cotton mill was the only one he was an actual owner of; therefore, he was actively involved in the management policies.

From a distance, the four-storied red brick building's jutting towers and visible eaves appeared undamaged. This did not particularly surprise Darcy, as he figured the bulk of the damage would be internal. The note had been written hastily by the surviving foreman, giving no specific details other than the loss of life and that the blaze was quenched. Nonetheless, it takes a massive amount of heat to mar brick.

Darcy and Colonel Fitzwilliam were greeted by a group of several men knotted by the front entrance to the mill. Two of the gentlemen were his partners, Mr. Kinnison and Mr. Shultz, while the others were a mixture of workers, foremen, and, undoubtedly, city officials sent to investigate the incident.

"Ah! Darcy!" Mr. Kinnison boomed. "We figured you would be here soon. I wish I could say it was good to see you but…" He spread his hands and shrugged.

Darcy dismounted, Richard doing the same but hanging back while his cousin shook hands brusquely with his partners.

"Kinnison. Shultz." He nodded to the stocky German who had stepped forward. "I came as quickly as I could manage. It was quite late when I received the message. How did you make it here so speedily, Kinnison?"

Mr. Kinnison shrugged again. "I was in Spondon for Christmas. My wife's family dwells there. Shultz and I had lunch three days ago, so he knew I was in the area; otherwise, the messenger would probably still be riding from Claycross. We just arrived here, having spent the past hour with the injured men."

Kinnison was the youngest of the three men, only four and twenty. It was actually his father who had partnered with Darcy and Mr. Shultz eight years ago to buy the decrepit old mill. Always a man fascinated by technology and gadgets, Darcy was also an evolving, wise businessman. He immediately saw the advantage to embracing the wave of manufacturing sweeping through England and was especially proud of the acquisition, as it was the first independent venture he had entered into after assuming the mantle of Master of Pemberley. Twice he had discussed the prospect with his father, the first when he was twenty-one and home for the summer.

Not in his wildest dreams did he imagine at the time that in just over a year he would be Master of Pemberley. His father was in excellent health by all appearances, the ravages of his unrelenting grief visible in the haggard lines around his eyes and hollowed cheeks, but otherwise, James Darcy was robust. Father and son had developed an easy relationship, one that was of mutual respect and affection if a trifle distant due to James's tendency toward moroseness and Darcy's reticence. Their times together were invariably centered on discussing Pemberley affairs rather than personal issues, although as Darcy matured, he found it was as if the gap in their ages dwindled. In later years, on those rare occasions when he allowed himself to reminisce and muse on could-have-beens, he firmly believed that in time, he and his father would have become great friends. But at twenty-one those tragic events were future and unthinkable. Rather, both Darcy men imagined and openly planned for a future similar to what James had developed with his father: co-management of Pemberley. Only in this instance, James desired to relinquish the horse breeding and training aspects to his vastly competent son while he continued to manage the farming and livestock ventures. It was an arrangement that appealed to both of them. Darcy's obsession for all matters horse related was legendary, the only other niggle in his brain that of modern inventions. Hence, he approached his father about milling cotton.

James sat at the desk that Darcy would inherit, smiling in true pleasure and pride as he watched his tall son pace before him with caged energy, talking vociferously and gesturing wildly.

"It is truly a marvel, Father. Just think! We could double, probably triple, our income by entering into the cotton trade and milling it. Of course, depending on the initial layout, it may take a few years to recoup, but eventually. And what is to stop us from delving further and milling our own wool as well? The process is a bit more expensive, but you see the figures?" He stopped abruptly, tapping one long index finger on the parchment page lying on the desktop.

James opened his mouth to speak, but Darcy resumed pacing and speaking, "I confess I need to do a bit more research to be absolutely sure, but I am fairly confident we could handle it. In fact, I spoke with Mr. Castledon of London Textile just last month. His company owns several mills of all varieties and he gave me excellent advice. My thought had been to build our own mill here, starting from scratch. He suggested looking into buying an existing mill, preferably one a bit rundown or mismanaged that could be attained at a lowered price. I took the liberty of asking Mr. Daniels to nose around a bit, drop a few hints discreetly. He says there are a couple of possibilities near Stavely on the Rother or Buxton on the Wye and in Derby. Any location would do nicely. Perhaps I could have him send you the specifications, Father, and you could look into it?"

"Perhaps—"

"Of course with steam engines," Darcy interrupted, hardly aware his father had spoken, "we do not have to look along rivers. They make the need for a water source unnecessary! Although it is still wise, I am convinced, for shipping and safety reasons. We could, possibly, build one from the ground up near Pemberley, or expand the existing facilities where we sheer and scour our wool. Although I do believe that might still be more expensive than obtaining an already existing structure designed for the task. I need to obtain further figures on that, but you can see that we have numerous options."

"I do not think I would want a loud manufacturing monstrosity so near the manor, Son."

"Yes, yes, you are correct, Father! That would not be wise, I agree." He paused momentarily, fingers fidgeting by his sides as he stared into space sightlessly. James observed him silently, the turning wheels of his son's brain practically visible to the naked eye. "With a steam engine we could fully prepare the cotton. Clean it, card it, comb it, everything. Then spin it and weave it as well. Maybe in time expand further and develop rooms for dyeing and finishing the cloth. Yes, Derby would be best, as the population is higher and it is on the main thoroughfare to London and beyond. Think of all the people we could employ! Profits and community benefit!"

James was laughing and shaking his head slowly. "Hold on a minute, my boy! You know I appreciate your enthusiasm, but are you not supposed to be carousing with your friends, engaging in endless fox hunts and billiard tournaments and other frivolous pursuits of youth? You are on vacation and have one more year of leisurely studies at University, not that you ever study leisurely, but you get the idea. Enjoy yourself for a change and we can deal with this in a year."

"I do not carouse, Father, but trust me, I partake in plenty of extracurricular activities. Did I tell you I won the fencing tournament for my House? Plaque on the wall next to Grandfather's!"

James laughed at Darcy's sudden youthful boasting. "Yes, you told me, lad. I am quite proud of you and delighted to know your nose is not always pressed between the pages of a book. So do me a favor: Relax, gather information if you wish, but complete your education and enjoy life for a while before you immerse yourself in work."

"But…"

"No buts, William! You know I personally have no interest in the endeavor. That is not to say I disagree with your research and concept, so do not frown at me! I merely insist it wait for now. Take your time, enjoy the summer, and finish your education. Next summer, we can discuss it at length and I will trust you to pursue to your heart's content."

So Darcy had grudgingly agreed, not really having much choice in the matter. A year later, he was home and barely unpacked ere broaching the topic with his father yet again. He had not relented in his desire, had only increased his enthusiasm with further study and discussion with professors, businessmen, and even the average working man during his haunts at the mills near Cambridge. James was agreeable if not newly inspired, permitting his son to look seriously into the matter at the mills to be found locally and promising to allow him to proceed once the particulars were known. It was a short conversation, Darcy wasting no time in riding to Alfreton where a potential mill had been unearthed by Mr. Wickham. It ended up not being the best candidate, but before Darcy could pursue other options, his father suffered a massive heart attack and, a week later, died.

It was over six months before Darcy could begin even to think about starting an entirely new project, yet despite the overwhelming chaos, tremendous grief, and burdens suddenly thrust upon his shoulders, the tiny flame of desire had kept burning deep inside. Nonetheless, it was a coincidence that brought the cotton mill in Derby to his attention. Mr. Kinnison the elder was good friends with Mr. Henry Vernor and rather casually mentioned to him that the old mill was for sale and he was contemplating buying. Mr. Vernor knew of Darcy's interest via his son, Gerald. One thing led to another, as the old saying goes, and within a month, Darcy, Kinnison, and Mr. Shultz, an associate of Kinnison's, formed a partnership and bought the dilapidated mill. DKS Midlands, Inc., was born.

Mr. Shultz was a German immigrant of some fifty years, a self-made man who had begun his employment history as a youth working at every job in a cotton mill in Yorkshire before rising to the rank of foreman. Thrifty by nature, he saved and eventually invested in the very mill he had worked in since the tender age of nine. A few more years went by, a total of ten mills invested in at the pinnacle of his career, and Mr. Shultz was counted among the comfortably rich. He liquefied it all, moved to Derby, and started over where no one would know he had once been a lowly mill drudge. Darcy would know none of this history until five years into their partnership, trusting to the man's obvious knowledge of the business and to Mr. Kinnison's recommendation and personal reputation.

The project was a success from the beginning. The partnership allowed for the financial resources to purchase a number of machines that Darcy had not imagined in his early figuring. In the end, revenue was made in two years time. It was a small profit for the first three years and the money was reinvested, which substantially benefited the company. For two years now, the proceeds were significant. The elder Mr. Kinnison had died not quite two years prior, his son proving to be as excellent a businessman, and trustworthy partner, as had his father. All three men were abundantly content with the project.

The milling process utilized by DKS Midlands was typical of all cotton mills of that day. Raw cotton fibers were imported in vast quantities, primarily via British East India Trading vessels that acquired the product from India and other Far East nations, as well as the former American colonies. Certain areas of England, Yorkshire, and Manchester, for instance, became synonymous with the cotton trade. Other towns followed suit to varying degrees, cashing in on the wealth to be found. English inventors by the dozens devoted their lives to improving the machinery necessary to enhance the process. American inventor Eli Whitney's cotton gin was one of the prime revolutionary devices ever invented. Every worker of cotton in England owned a cotton gin by the early 1800s, speeding the initial process unbelievably. Raw, baled cotton was transported to the large and complete mill in Derby, just one of hundreds throughout the country.

The massive four-story building was laid out with each floor devoted to the sequential procedures necessary to take the raw product and render it into useable cloth, from opening the five-hundred-pound bales of crude cotton to begin the ginning and cleaning process, to the finer tasks of separating the fibers, spinning the slivered threads into yarns, weaving the yarns into cloth, and finishing the fabric with various chemicals, from bleaching to dyeing. All of this was accomplished through complicated and innovative machinery operated by human hands. It was a lengthy practice requiring hundreds of employees even in such a relatively modest mill.

Mr. Shultz lived in Derby and personally handled difficulties as they arose, Darcy and Kinnison rarely needing to get involved with the day-to-day functioning. Rather, they dealt with the business side of affairs. Mr. Kinnison managed the storage warehouses, distribution, and transport to local markets and London. Darcy arranged the exchange with markets beyond London and abroad as well as the political issues, dealing extensively with the East India Company and, to a lesser degree, his own ships. These contacts contributed to their rapid success.

Thus far, the mishaps had been nominal; a few minor injuries and broken down machines all that had upset the flow. This positive record was highly irregular in the danger fraught machinations of a mill and all the persons involved recognized their good fortune. "Darcy." Mr. Shultz shook his hand, jerking his head toward the smoldering mill. "We were just discussing the details of what occurred. Kinnison and I were here until late last night, but it was not safe to inspect and far too disordered. And we were busily dealing with the injuries and fatalities, and assuring the fire was out." He shrugged, pausing briefly before continuing. "We lost the foreman Hendle and two workers, Spreckle and Trillis. Good workers."

Darcy nodded solemnly. His personal knowledge of most of the personnel was nonexistent. However, this did not mean he did not care. "Any family? Widows?"

"The men chosen for the Christmas holiday were unmarried per protocol. Hendle was the foreman who drew lots this year and he has… had a family. It will be dealt with according to our policy, Darcy." Shultz answered wearily but matter-of-factly. "She works in the weaving room and knows her position will be held for two weeks with compensation for Hendle until she decides what to do. They have four children, two who work as spinners, so I do not know what to expect."

Kinnison spoke up then, "The two men injured are Haggar and Merran. They suffered minor burns and breathing difficulties from the smoke. The surgeon says they will be fine."

They began walking toward the large front doors, Richard joining the other men to follow behind while Shultz resumed his narrative. "We were not able to speak with either man until an hour ago, so it was unclear what had occurred. The other watchmen were not at the scene until after the fire was well ablaze, making their rounds and checking equipment as expected, so they were little help. One fellow, Stevenson, let it slip that alcohol was present." He paused for an angry glower. Shultz was a staunch Methodist and abstainer from all alcoholic beverages, even to the point of actively participating in a thus far unpopular temperance society in Derby.

Kinnison shared a sideways grin with Darcy, who nodded and smiled faintly. Darcy was not a heavy drinker by any means, a few youthful overindulgences having taught him severe lessons in moderation; but he did not fully ascribe to the near satanic, sinful qualities attributed to alcohol by some. Nonetheless, having been witness to the tragic results of drunkenness in terms of domestic violence and financial ruin—especially amongst the lower classes, although on occasion in his own peer group—he did sympathize with the temperance movement. Frankly, as a man of superior self-control, Darcy had little patience for men who chronically over imbibed and considered it a hideous character flaw.

As a company policy, alcohol of any kind was prohibited on the mill grounds. Its possession was grounds for immediate dismissal. The idea that employees would jeopardize their livelihood and lives for a drink filled him with a simmering rage. "Do we know the finer details?"

Kinnison spoke up, Shultz still glowering and muttering under his breath. "It took a bit of time. A few threats, intimidation, and cajoling, but they finally gave us enough."

They were inside now, the aroma of smoke and burnt cotton heavy in the air in spite of the widely open windows. Unconsciously, each man retrieved a handkerchief to place over his nose. They walked down the seemingly endless rows of liquid-filled vats and gigantic tables where the bleaching, scouring, dyeing, and other finishing procedures were carried out. Darcy was relieved to note that they were heading away from the separated rooms where the two steam engines were located, those machines being by far the most expensive, not to mention necessary for all other operations to take place. They walked up a curved stairway to the second floor where they traversed long aisles between the weaving looms. Now standing idle with the threads in various stages of completion, the powerful machines were undamaged. They mounted the sooty stairs leading to the third floor spinning room while Kinnison continued, voice muffled behind cloth.

"Not too original, Darcy. A bit of holiday cheer, as it were, to accompany a lively faro game. They holed up by the stacks of rovings where it is warmer. It was early afternoon, but yesterday was cloudy, so apparently they brought in extra oil lamps; the better to see the cards, you understand?" He finished with heavy sarcasm and a shake of his head. "Plain stupidity!"

"The lamps are to be kept mounted and well away from the cotton; they all know that." Shultz mumbled, faint German accent notable as it always was when distressed or angry.

"Apparently, Hendle happened upon their entertainment, demanded they clear out, but the four were well into their cups and a fight ensued. Somehow a lamp was overturned." He paused to rub his eyes, continuing in a thick voice, "Hendle ran to the water pumps they tell me, but it gets confused from there on out. The others joined the scene and quenched the fire eventually, but not before Hendle and the others had died. What a waste!"

They halted before a bank of spinning mules, blackened with ash and soot but otherwise intact. Beyond was a scorched, smoking, wet mess of destroyed machinery and piles of burned fiber bundles extending thirty feet to the southern brick wall. Jagged, blackened gaps were visible in the floor and the ceiling, the fire having obviously risen to encompass the fourth level. The ceiling was essentially gone, with thick crossbeams in varying degrees of charred thickness the only support for the ruined carding machines above. The massive contraptions were scorched and twisted with melted metal pieces jutting, the entire row of mangled devices perched precariously.

Shultz gestured above. "The spinners and rovings acted as wicks, funneling the flames to the fourth floor. It looks like the damage is worst up there. Thanks to you, Darcy, we had those water pumps installed, otherwise the fire would have raged unchecked."

"Our first order of business is to remove those carders before they break the beams and plummet through to the bottom floors and cause more damage." Darcy said with a curt signal to several of the loitering men, who nodded and hastened to organize a group of workers for the task. "Any idea how much cleaned cotton was sitting here?"

Shultz scratched at his chin and sighed. "Well, the stacks line the walls here, piled to just below the windows. Freshly prepared bundles are replenished via the far lifts as quickly as they are set to the spinners. I have detailed invoices in my office. Looks like those on the extreme edges may be salvageable."

While he spoke he indicated the area of destruction before them, Darcy's mind performing rapid calculations as he considered the quantities. The walls between floors rose roughly fifteen feet with wide windows all around. The southern wall spanned at least fifty feet, the middle bulk of which was a black, faintly smoldering, and soggy mess.

Shultz was continuing, "Some of these spinners may be repairable. I have three new mules in the warehouse and dozens of spare parts from others that have worn out. Guess we should head upstairs. At least this end of the top floor is just machinery. The raw bales are at the northern end where they are hoisted up."

The group made their way to the stairs, Shultz relating the warehouse inventory as they walked. The inspection was thorough, Darcy calling for parchment and quill to take detailed notes. Eventually, Richard left per Darcy's request to secure rooms for them at the Georgian and to dispatch a note to Pemberley assuring of their safe arrival. It was a long day with Darcy and

Kinnison spending the bulk of it in Shultz's office on the ground level, bent over the desk and long table with jackets removed and shirt sleeves rolled up as they pored over invoices and inventory lists. Pages of parchment were written in Darcy's firm hand, itemizing the damage.

Most of the men were put to work on the cleaning and removing. Others returned to the unscathed portions of the factory where the women waited; the steam engines powered up as the sequence of milling cotton from its raw, ginned state to completed weave resumed. Cotton needed processing and orders needed filling, no one wanting to waste any more time or revenue than necessary.

It was well after sundown when Darcy finally eased his aching, exhausted body into a hot tub. With a groan of relief, he sank into the water, eyes closing. For the first time since leaving home, he allowed his thoughts to stray toward wife and son. With clarity, he conjured the image of his family lounging in the parlor, son complacently being passed from devoted relative to relative with serious countenance breaking into sunny smiles at each face encountered. Darcy could hear the adult laughter and infant giggles as he was tickled and nuzzled, always the beloved center of attention.

As an abrupt epiphany, it dawned on him that he would miss his baby's one-month birthday! His eyes flew open and chest constricted in true sorrow. The ironic part was that he and Elizabeth had not talked about celebrating the date, nor had it consciously occurred to Darcy to mark it in any significant way, yet he knew without any doubt that they would have done so. In disgust, he sat up in the bathtub, irritatingly grabbing the soap and attacking his grimy skin with force.

In London, upon the incident of their first lengthy separation, Darcy had foolishly believed that separating from his wife would grow easier with time. He now accepted that the distress merely multiplied. Now he had to add to the agony of missing Elizabeth the pain of missing Alexander. It came as a bit of a surprise to recognize how thoroughly Alexander had wrapped around his father's heart as an individual.

He joined Richard for a delicious and much needed full course dinner feeling depressed and subdued. Richard seemed uncommonly downcast as well, conversation was minimal, and both men retired to their rooms immediately after dinner. Darcy spent what remaining energy he possessed writing to Lizzy, telling about the day's events and assuring her that he would be home well before the christening.

The second day broke with Darcy renewed in his vigor to deal with all the complex issues as rapidly as possible so he could return to his family. He was surly and he knew it, but under the circumstances, no one questioned the cause. Mr. Shultz handled the manual labor aspects, Darcy and Kinnison thrilled to note that every remaining machine was up and running with six of the damaged ones revamped before the day was done. All of the debris was cleaned away and fresh timber was ordered to begin the structural repairs. Areas were rearranged to compensate for the lost space, every employee responding to the orders of Shultz and his foremen with competence. Richard donned casual attire and assisted Mr. Shultz, the military man being quite adept at both receiving and giving orders.

Kinnison concentrated on the reordering of supplies and notification of both buyers and sellers as to the delays incurred due to the fire. Darcy focused on the finances. That there would be a substantial impact fiscally was a given, but the reality was that the combination of careful planning, diligent saving, and significant personal wealth well diversified by all three meant that the impact would readily be absorbed and overcome.

When it came to managing the business aspects, Darcy was in his element and supremely proficient. The years of governing a vast estate had taught him how to deal with the varied array of complications that inevitably arose. Therefore, despite never facing the aftermath of a fire, praise God, Darcy instinctively and through experience dealing with other traumas knew precisely what to do.

It was the human element that was distressing to him. As distasteful as it was in one respect, there was no option but to dismiss Haggar and Merran for imbibing alcohol while on duty. There were a number of other mills in the area where they could seek employment, but Derby was a small community and word would spread. Few employers were as strict regarding the no alcohol rule as Mr. Shultz, but a fire was universally looked upon with horror. Whether the men would be able to attain adequately paying work locally was questionable. Shultz was far more pragmatic than his partners, and he simply shrugged his shoulders, completely unmoved. Kinnison and Darcy wavered a bit, but in the end the decision was clear.

On the third day, Darcy rode with Richard and a foreman named Rhodes to the tiny house in the middle of town where the widow Hendle resided. Mrs. Hendle greeted them with subdued politeness, eyes swollen and red.

The Hendle children clustered around her, the youngest of four and five years clutching her skirts and staring with wide-eyed fright at the tall, well-dressed, formal man. The eldest, a skinny boy of thirteen, halted his chore of chopping wood and stood with sharpened axe in hand as he glowered at the men.

Darcy bowed. "Mrs. Hendle, I am Mr. Darcy. Please accept my deepest sympathies for your loss." She nodded, wiping at teary eyes and murmuring her thanks. Darcy continued, "I confess I did not personally know your husband, but Mr. Shultz assures me he was an excellent foreman." He handed her a parchment wrapped bundle. "Per DKS Midlands policy, Mrs. Hendle, you will find the equivalent of one month's salary. Your position will be held for two weeks, as you have been informed, to allow for grieving. Please let us know as soon as you possibly can what your plans are."

Mrs. Hendle sniffled. "This is our home, sir. We got no place to go. The mill's been good to us so we'll be back, me and the young 'uns." Her hand swept the yard to encompass her son as well as the twelve-year-old girl standing behind her. "DKS has the best pay and all, we won't go nowheres else, milord."

Darcy nodded, opening his mouth to speak, but the eldest son had stepped closer and interrupted with a grumble, "If it's so great how come my da is dead?"

"Jerome!" His mother gasped. "I am so sorry, sir! You watch your tongue young man and apologize to Mr. Darcy this instant!"

"I will not! His stupid mill killed my da!"

Mrs. Hendle was crying in earnest, attempting to choke out something, anything, to placate the tall, stern man with the reputation for kindness and fairness, but also stringency and nobility. Darcy cut her spluttering short with nothing more than one raised finger her direction, piercing gaze riveted on the teenager.

Jerome flushed under Darcy's forceful but sympathetic stare, but he bravely stared back, lifting his chin slightly as if to challenge. When Darcy spoke it was softly, but with an unmistakable edge of authority and faint contempt. "Mr. Hendle, is it your opinion that your father was a fool?"

"No! How could you—"

"A man makes his own decisions in life, Mr. Hendle. Your father made his. He was a miller, a foreman in my company, and trusted with tremendous responsibility. He worked hard for his place and knew precisely what it entailed. Do you mean to slander his name by insinuating he was ignorant of the risks?" He paused, allowing the grieving boy to assimilate his words. "He took great pride in his work, was brave and strong. His sacrifice will not be forgotten. Do not allow your sorrow to cloud your judgment, Mr. Hendle. I do not claim to be an expert on theological matters, but I believe that our loved ones watch us from the Heavens. Do you wish for your father to witness your disrespect?"

Jerome shook his head shortly, eyes now downcast and axe fallen to rest on the ground, but he held his back straight and shoulders firm. Darcy smiled faintly, glancing to Mrs. Hendle and nodding slightly. The poor woman was speechless, tears falling in huge glistening drops down her cheeks.

"You are the man of the house now, Mr. Hendle. Make your father proud. Mrs. Hendle, you have my sympathies. If there is anything you require, Mr. Shultz will assist you."

She curtseyed shakily, Darcy bowing again before he turned and mounted Parsifal. Rhodes leaned close and said, "I will keep a close eye on that boy, Mr. Darcy. He may give us trouble."

"There is no need. Take him out of the spinning room, away from his mother. Give him more responsibility. The carding machine, I think. Work him hard for a while, exhaust him, and he will give you no trouble." Rhodes looked dubious, Darcy smiling grimly and finishing with confidence as they rode away, "Trust me, I know how best to deal with grief."

"Today is Alexander's birthday and I am missing it."

Colonel Fitzwilliam, out of uniform and comfortable in a black suit of wool, peered over the rim of his wine glass at the morose cousin sitting across their secluded table in the Georgian's opulent dining hall. Darcy was staring at his plate, mien serious as he played with the remains of dinner, fork absently scoring trenches through a small pile of mashed yams. Richard frowned, completely at a loss as to what Darcy meant.

"Ah, Cousin, unless I have slept through all of 1818, a year has not passed."

Darcy chuckled, putting down his fork and picking up his own wine glass. "No, I meant his one-month birthday."

Richard raised his brows. "Do people actually celebrate such a thing? I certainly pray you did not expect me to provide a present. This could become costly after a time."

"No gifts or parties. I just wanted to be there is all." He sighed, sitting back in the chair. "I miss my family, Richard." He took a sip, glancing to his cousin's humorous face. "Go ahead, laugh. Make a joke. I need to be cheered."

Richard shrugged. "I was just thinking that there was a time when all you needed in life was my sparkling personality and delightful company. How things change!"

Darcy laughed in earnest. "Never have I thought you were all I needed, my friend, but you do in a pinch."

Richard lifted his glass in salute. "We shall be back at Pemberley in a day or two. You seem to have things well in hand, and there really are no reasons to stay around for the reconstruction, are there?"

"I do not want to desert my partners, but I suppose I can complete the rest from home. It is primarily paperwork from here on. Mr. Keith and I will work on it, and I will likely send him to London next month. I refuse to leave again, barring another catastrophe. It is too difficult."

Richard was smiling at his once again morose cousin now fiddling with his wedding ring, a gleam of something indiscernible in his eyes. "I know I have said it before, but it still shocks me how profoundly matrimony has affected you."

"And I have said it before, wait until it is your turn. It is marvelous, beautiful, the very best feeling in the world. Love and now fatherhood. Ach! I need to go home! Tomorrow afternoon, Richard. We will be home by dinner. What? Why are you looking at me like that?"

"Do you remember Lord Fotherby?"

Darcy blinked in surprise. "Naturally. One of our greatest members of Parliament. How could I not? Terrible loss to our country when he passed. Why do you ask?"

Richard looked embarrassed, ruddy face flushing further. "Well, he has been a friend to our family for decades, as you know, he and our grandfather contemporaries. Considering his age, I guess none of us were too surprised at his death, but then again there are some people who seem immortal. He was so spry."

"He assuredly was spry. We saw him in London and I never would have imagined him dying a few months later. He was dancing with his wife at Lord Ivers's ball more often than Elizabeth and me. Yes, a shock and loss to be sure." He noted Richard's grimace, chuckling and leaning forward. "So are you going to tell me the thought behind this line of questioning?"

"It is entirely your fault you know. Walking about with that ridiculous grin all the time, peace and tranquility oozing from every pore, and pardon my crudeness, but the obvious sexual satisfaction radiating continually is enough to make the most confirmed bachelor vacillate!"

Darcy grinned, flushing slightly and ducking his head in embarrassment, but not in the least offended. "Whom are we talking about? The lucky lady to turn my wayward cousin's heart and bring me such utter joy as I now can tease him mercilessly in return? Pray tell!"

"Go easy on me, Darcy. I think I am in love, yes, but I am caught up in my own Shakespearean tragedy."

"Does this have to do with Miss Ulster? I would have imagined the Admiral presenting her on a silver platter if you asked. No, wait!" Suddenly the pieces fell into place and he gazed at his cousin with amazement. "You are speaking of Lady Fotherby."

"Now you see my dilemma?"

"When did this take place? How could you…? I mean, she has only been widowed for a few months and sequestered at the estate in Buckinghamshire I understand."

"Very well, you want the sordid details? I have known Lady Fotherby nearly all my life if you recollect. Her mother and mine have been friends since their society days, although I paid her scant attention, I confess, until University. I would encounter the then Lady Simone Halifax at various soirees and balls. You were there upon occasion, Darcy. She had matured into a true beauty and so utterly perfect."

He paused, shaking his head and taking a drink of wine. "Timing is everything, I have come to believe," his voice low as he swirled the red liquid and lost himself in musings. "Certainly this is true in military matters, but also in life and love. I knew I loved her and that she returned the affection. What could I do about the feelings I had? I was young and naïve with dreams of glory in battle and killing Napoleon personally, far too foolish to recognize true love. Not that I could have done a thing about it as a second son with a small inheritance." He shrugged. "By the time I could possibly give matrimony any serious consideration, she was long since married to Lord Fotherby."

"I remember you fancied her a bit but had no idea the emotions were deep. Forgive me, my friend, I never knew."

"Oh, be still, William. I cannot proclaim to any great passion. Again, I was young and not sparing undue contemplation on a hopeless situation. It is more the wisdom of age that enables me to relive the feelings and see them for what they were. That and you all dreamy and radiating disgusting happiness every waking hour of the day."

Darcy smiled and Richard laughed, both men silent for a while. "I had not seen her in years. The rumors would reach my ears from time to time. Her marriage to the far older Lord Fotherby, the birth of their two children, the elaborate galas at their homes in Town and High Wycombe. I wondered, as I am sure so many others did, whether the marriage was based on affection or merely an old man wanting a young wife." He shook his head and grimaced. "Whatever the case, I pushed it all aside until two seasons ago when I saw her at the symphony. It was all back in a rush. Quite took my breath away, actually."

"That is how it was to see Elizabeth at Rosings and later at Pemberley, and every day when I wake next to her, matter of fact. Must have been horrible for you. I am so sorry and wish you had shared with me."

"Shared that I am in love with another man's wife? Yes, I can only imagine how you would have accepted that news! Your sense of morality would have been highly offended and the prudish expressions and lecturing would not have been welcome, I can assure you."

"You did not act on your inclinations, and when it comes to losing the woman you love, I can fully comprehend the agony. No, I would not have lectured, Cousin. In fact, I am not now offended and actually a bit confused. Why do you see it as a tragedy, Richard? As sad as the passing of Lord Fotherby, it does free her, given appropriate mourning period of course. And now you are in a better position to offer yourself as suitor."

"I suppose, although it seems rather distasteful to consider it at this juncture. The man is barely cold in his grave. Besides..." He stopped, lips pressed together and face filled with a rare bitterness.

"What? Do you judge there no chance she may return your interest?"

"Difficult to ascertain, under the circumstances. We spoke a few times at various functions in Town. Lord and Lady Fotherby were everywhere, to my dismay. She was polite and proper, our conversations always restrained and in the presence of others. It was probably just my romantic fancy overwhelming me, but I sensed a current between us. Fills me with guilt even to contemplate the subject! Lord, Darcy, I am not capable of judging! I am a soldier. How can I compare to a man of Lord Fotherby's caliber?"

"Oh, nonsense! You are a nobleman's son, an officer of His Majesty's army, young and dashingly handsome, rich, charming. Need I go on? You have far more to offer than even the famous Lord Fotherby, no matter how virile he may have been in his seniority." He sat back and picked up his glass. "I really cannot tell you precisely how to proceed. I believe in fate, but also think one needs to encourage it along."

Silence descended yet again, plates cleared by servants, and the dessert course served before either man spoke. Darcy was shaken by the atypical expression of sadness on Colonel Fitzwilliam's face, having come to rely on his irrepressible affability. When he broke the quiet, his voice was husky with emotion.

"I saw her a couple of weeks ago. Mother insisted on diverting northwest to pay her respects as friend to her mother. We only stayed the afternoon, had teas and cakes. Father related fond memories of Lord Fotherby in action during sessions of the House of Lords. Lady Fotherby smiled kindly, but did not seem comfortable with the topic. Even in the black of mourning she was beautiful." He sighed deeply. "How can you judge a woman's face, William? Especially when so controlled?"

Darcy shrugged and shook his head. "I am not the one to ask, I am afraid. I can read Elizabeth perfectly now, but assuredly misconstrued horribly early in our acquaintance. Even when love was apparent on her face, I refused to embrace it out of fear. Did you sense anything from Lady Fotherby? Any hope?"

"Perhaps. She looked at me quite a bit, but maybe that is because I kept staring at her! When we said our good-byes and I kissed her fingers, I swear she pressed against my lips and she definitely squeezed my hand. I was shocked at the boldness—too flummoxed to make sense of it and do more than stammer something stupid." He laughed faintly and shook his head. "Go ahead and laugh, Cousin, I deserve it!"

Darcy was grinning, an amused twinkle in his eyes. "I have not seen you so flustered since Miss Susanne Carmichael kissed you under the mistletoe when you were fifteen! What a joy! The particularly amusing part of it all is that you are far more worldly than I, yet here you sit, as affected by a woman as all the rest of us mortals. Refreshing, actually."

"You are enjoying this, aren't you?"

"Immensely!"

"No further sympathy for the man of constant sorrows? The broken-hearted romantic fool doomed to traverse the earth in pitiful loneliness? The woeful puppy with hanging tail and ears?"

"Pah!" Darcy interrupted. "I am as pathetically inept as they come when pertaining to divining romantic clues. However, even I can determine there is hope. Give it time, Richard. I am convinced I shall be raising a glass at your wedding ere the year is out. Worse come to worst, you can enlist Aunt Madeline's aid. She would do anything to see you married and bringing more grandchildren her way."

Richard cringed, and Darcy laughed as he bit into his apple pie.

The conversation turned to unrelated business and political topics as they finished their brandies. Finally, Darcy said, "Well, I think I shall retire, my friend. Sooner I am asleep, the sooner tomorrow will arrive."

"You sound like a child awaiting Christmas."

"Ah, but this is far superior. My wife's arms and son's grasping hands transcend any gift delivered. Remember this, Cousin. It will keep you motivated in your pursuit."

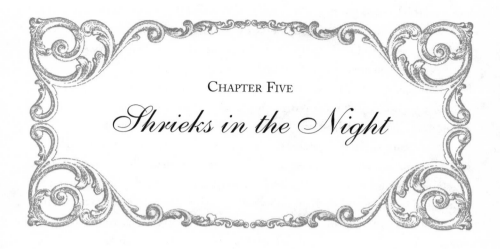

CHAPTER FIVE

Shrieks in the Night

Honestly, Darcy, we can manage matters from here on. I was going to be tarrying hereabouts with my wife's family for a couple of weeks anyway. Frankly, this will give me something to occupy my time besides pretending to enjoy their chatter." Kinnison grinned. "Go home to your new wife and child. We will send regular dispatches, I promise."

"You and Mr. Keith are far more proficient at the paperwork and financial issues," Shultz grumbled from where he reclined and fanned his perspiring face. He was covered with soot and grime, having spent the past three hours revamping several of the damaged spinning mules. It was actually very cold outside, clouds gathering rapidly and darkening threateningly by the moment. "You better get a move on if you want to beat the storm. I think it bodes to be a bad one."

He was right. Flurries were already falling by the time Colonel Fitzwilliam and Darcy mounted their stallions and headed out of town. Richard was questioning the wisdom in riding through what promised to become a blizzard before it was over. Darcy, however, refused to discuss waiting. His prescient prediction of Derbyshire weather was not failing him; he simply ignored it in the urgent need to be home. It would prove to be a horrible mistake, one that he was rapidly recognizing before they were three miles north of town.

It was miserable. Snow fell in thick sheets, wind hitching furiously and driving the increasingly solidified ice into their faces, cold seeping through the layers of thick woolens they wore, and visibility falling to near zero. The horses plodded along slowly, riders bent double over their backs. It was when they passed the barely seen sign for "Belper, 2 miles" that Richard grabbed Darcy's arm.

"William, we have traveled eight miles in nearly an hour, with twenty more to go! We cannot do this. I say we stop in Belper for the night."

Darcy nodded, heart sinking; with the storm raging, he would have no method of alerting Elizabeth. Being comfortably settled at the small but hospitable carriage inn in Belper, dry and warm in front of the blazing fire with steaming mugs of coffee and a platter of roasted lamb with sautéed vegetables did little to ease the ache in his heart. Richard prattled on in his typical humorous fashion, the room was lively with other waylaid travelers and a country fiddler in the corner, but Darcy volunteered little. Eventually he would relax, make the best of a troublesome situation, and even join in a game of darts that Richard won, naturally.

The bed was comfortable and clean, welcomed by a weary Darcy even if it was the fourth night of sleeping alone. He tossed a bit, always finding it difficult to settle now that he was so dependent on his wife's warm and soft body molded into his, but finally drifted asleep. He dreamt happily, confident that he would see their beloved faces, kiss their beloved lips, and hold their beloved bodies close on the morrow.

He had no way of knowing that he was wrong.

The blizzard raged all through the dark hours of the night. Wind screeched wildly in tones reminiscent of fighting tomcats or a woman in pain. It was one of those rare storms that old men would talk about in decades to come: "Remember the blizzard of 1817? Ushered in the new year with a vengeance, that one!" Temperatures dropped to alarming levels, with negative consequences to some livestock and vegetation that would be felt in a variety of ways. Snow fell in record amounts, the landscape as white as an untouched canvas. It was the singular object that marred the otherwise pristine surrounds; vague flashes of brown tree trunks, the multihued bricks and stones of buildings, and partially frozen blues of waterways and lakes the only spots of color between the lopsided blown drifts of powdery snow.

Darcy woke hours before the dawn, shivering under the pile of blankets. It required an exceptional cold to cause his internal furnace to dampen, evidenced further by visible mist with each shuddering exhale. He rose, struggling into trousers and a thick robe to aid the apparently useless nightshirt in warding off the chill. With a sleep numbed mind, he jerked to the dead fireplace, shaking as he set about the familiar task of building a fire and sending a thankful prayer heavenward for the competent Pemberley staff that he knew would not allow his family and friends to suffer unduly from the extreme weather. Without the slightest doubt, he knew that fires would be raging in all the occupied bedchambers, especially those of his wife and son.

In minutes he had a steady blaze going, chafed hands practically touching the flames in order to absorb the heat. He sat on the hearth, momentarily too cold to think of rising and checking the outside. It was yet too dark anyway, but he could tell that the violent wind had died down somewhat and the furious tinkling of icy flakes hitting glass was no more. Darcy's lifetime of dwelling in Derbyshire told him what he already needed to know without the necessity of gazing upon the countryside: the snow would be deep. Whether his faithful and vigorous mount could trudge through the banked flakes was not the question; it was whether the storm had abated enough to allow for travel. He sighed deeply, closing weary eyes for a moment and leaning his head onto the warming stones. The worst of the winds and thrashing snow may have dissipated, but he knew the storm continued.

Anger rose in his chest, aiding in warming his flesh but causing fists to clench and fresh shaking to erupt. *I must get home!* Darcy had never been the type of man to suffer from bouts of impatience, being generally reasonably long-suffering, but at the present, his impetuosity consumed him. With forced effort he inhaled deeply numerous times, struggling with eventual success to calm the turbulence. Oddly, he discovered that meditating on Elizabeth's face, envisioning her sitting placidly with Alexander at her breast, aided his serenity.

The hours passed as the obscured sun slowly rose. Darcy eventually lit several lamps, passing the time in relative peace with book in hand as he sat near the fire. He must have dozed off without realizing it because the sudden earsplitting scream which rent the silence jolted him from his chair. He grasped the chair arm to steady himself, moving toward the door seconds later.

The hallway was rapidly becoming a mass of surging bodies and rising noise as doors opened all along the passageway. Servants and inn guests appeared by the dozens it seemed, confusion abounding as all eyes swiveled to the hysterically shrieking maid embraced by a middle-aged man wearing a robe where they stood blocking a widely open door near the end of the long hallway. From Darcy's room some forty feet away, nothing in the room could be seen, but from the antics of the maid and pallor of the gentleman, it must be bad.

He stood under the jamb observing the mayhem in silent bafflement and started slightly when Richard spoke into his ear. "What is going on?"

"No idea. Fix your hair."

Richard ran fingers through his unruly russet locks absently, glancing at Darcy who was attending to the chaos at the end of the hallway. "Tighten your robe." Darcy did so, flushing faintly at the realization that his entire upper chest was exposed, but no one was looking their direction, and all the abruptly roused guests were in varying states of undress.

At that moment, the innkeeper, Mr. Allenton, appeared on the landing, voice raised loudly as he inquired as to the upset. The maid had calmed somewhat, no longer yelling, but now sobbing uncontrollably in the obviously dazed man's arms.

"What is all the fuss?" Mr. Allenton asked, waving and nodding apologetically to the agitated guests. "So sorry, ladies and gentlemen. Please accept my apologies for the disturbance. So excitable these young girls are. Please excuse me. Pardon me, sir. Now, Alice, what is the meaning of this unseemly display? Quite horrid of you! Really should be more control…"

At which point he glanced into the room and halted with a gasp and hand raised to his mouth. Instantly, all the blood drained from his face. "Merciful God! Spare us!" He whispered.

This supplication was followed by a fresh screech from a woman who had eased herself through the crowd to peek over Mr. Allenton's shoulder. "She is dead! Saint's preserve us! A girl, dead!"

At that proclamation, pandemonium broke loose. Yells and cries, bodies backing into each other in a frantic effort to escape, frightened eyes suspiciously gazing at their neighbor, and families grasping onto loved ones to ensure their existence. Nothing remotely resembling order prevailed; even the innkeeper was paralyzed in the doorway.

A shrill whistle pierced the uproar. All voices fell, the silence abrupt and complete. Darcy swiveled to his cousin who seemed to have grown taller and added years in a matter of seconds. A uniform was not necessary for all instantly to sense that here was a man of authority.

"Listen here!" he commanded forcefully. "You all must return to your rooms and stay inside until the matter can be appropriately dealt with. Now!" Only a heartbeat's hesitation before every last soul responded to the directive, shuffling hastily and quietly. In seconds, the corridor was empty of all but Colonel Fitzwilliam, Darcy, Mr. Allenton, a handful of servants, and the befuddled gentleman comforting the weeping maid.

Richard approached the innkeeper, Darcy trailing behind. "Mr. Allenton, I am Colonel Fitzwilliam if you recall. This is Mr. Darcy of Pemberley. Perhaps we may be of assistance." He looked into the room, expression unchanged as he returned his attention to the innkeeper.

Mr. Allenton peered into Richard's face blankly for a moment, the man clearly stunned. "I do not... What?"

"Get a grip on yourself, man! You, sir, whom might you be?" Richard said, the latter addressed to the older man holding the maid.

"I am Carlyle, Colonel. Room nine, here, across the hall. I heard the girl and responded first. She, well, she is obviously distraught."

Richard nodded crisply. "You there!" He gestured to a servant, a boy of approximately fifteen. "Take Miss Alice to the common room. Give her some warm tea and a shot of brandy. No one is to leave this establishment, do you understand?" The boy nodded, eyes round and frightened. Richard turned to Mr. Allenton. "Who of your staff is the most trustworthy? We need to send for the Sheriff."

Mr. Allenton had managed to collect himself. He remained pale but was focused and responded in a firm voice. "Milton," he said to the boy, "take Alice as the Colonel commands. Bolton," he signaled to another lurking servant, this one an enormous black man, as Milton and Alice moved away. "Send Mackenzie for the Sheriff. The remainder of the staff is to wait in the common room. No one is to leave! You guard the door."

This accomplished, Richard again addressed the innkeeper. "Do you recognize the young lady, Mr. Allenton?"

He swallowed, eyes closing in silent prayer before bravely looking into the room and taking a hesitant step over the threshold. Richard followed, Darcy pausing in the doorway.

The girl was no more than sixteen. There was no doubt that, in life, she would have been a pretty thing, shapely figure with full breasts and narrow waist, all of which were tragically on display. She lay exposed on the bed, chemise ripped open and body splayed in a bizarre angle with smudges of blood on her thighs and the bed sheets by her legs. Her once lovely, innocent face now bluish tinged and frozen in an expression of horror. Darcy had witnessed death in all its ugliness on more occasions then he wished to recall, but nothing that compared with the raw brutality before him. It required every ounce of discipline at his disposal to remain standing calmly, but his stomach churned.

Mr. Allenton released a moan, fist clenched before his mouth with voice faint. "It is Mr. Hazeldon's daughter. Oh sweet Jesus! How could this happen? In my inn!" He broke down in sobs, rushing from the room and leaning into the hallway wall where Mr. Carlyle still stood.

"Richard, how should we handle this?" Darcy asked in a quiet, sick tone.

Richard was staring at the girl with a frown on his face. "I remember her. In the dining room with her parents, I assume, and a younger sister. I only noticed because I thought the gentleman looked vaguely familiar. I could not place from where, and as I do not know a Mr. Hazeldon, it must just be that he resembles another. Be that as it may, I was startled at one point because this young lady was staring at me with a flirtatious expression. I have been on the receiving end of enough such coquettishness to recognize it. This startled me, however, as she is so young and I am not in uniform, which is generally the stimulus."

"I do not recall her at all."

"Of course not. You were brooding far too much and rarely noticed a pretty face even when you were unattached. What an absolute pity! Come. We should leave her be and let the Sheriff deal with this."

"Someone needs to find the parents. They obviously do not know she is missing." He stopped, throat tight and eyes misty. "Can we not at least cover her?"

Richard nodded tersely, lips compressed as he stepped to the bed and drew the counterpane over her pale and lifeless body. "Go with God, little one," he murmured.

The following hours were tense ones to be sure. Richard and Darcy retired to their respective rooms to shave and dress. Mr. Allenton coped with the situation as well as possible, placing a guard in front of the ill-fated girl's door and appeasing the upset staff. He prayed that the Hazeldon family, who were situated in two rooms on the third floor, would remain asleep until the Sheriff arrived. In this, at least, he was fortunate.

Those guests and servants who knew of the tragedy trembled in their chambers behind stoutly locked doors. It would be the Sheriff who first uttered the word, but they were all thinking it: Murder.

Richard joined Darcy in his room once dressed. The two sat in silence, waiting.

Now that the sun was well over the horizon, the outer world beyond the cold glass and benumbed atmosphere within the walls could be seen. Darcy's prediction was accurate. Snow sat in deep drifts with fresh flakes falling airily. The sky was grayish-black with thick clouds offering nominal breaks to visualize sunny blue sky. The winds had died, thankfully, but the snowfall itself volunteered no hint of abating anytime soon.

He experienced pangs of guilt over the thought, but the honest truth was that Darcy merely wanted to be home. He did not know the girl, but that did not preclude him from sympathizing with the family. In fact, it was the image of his beloved sister, who was not much older that the stricken girl, in such a horrific pose that increased his urgency to be with his family. The additional responsibilities now lying upon his shoulders as a husband and father were keenly felt and taken very seriously. He trusted the Pemberley staff, knew with fair certainty that the house and its occupants were well protected, but this incident proved that the criminal element stalked and would strike indeterminately. In a reaction typical of most men, he illogically believed that his mere presence would shield his family from any tragedy.

"As soon as feasible, I wish to depart. Are you prepared to brave the cold?"

"Under the circumstances, yes. Suddenly Pemberley has never appealed to me more, or Rivallain for that matter. Depending on whether we ever have breakfast, I may desert you at Matlock."

Darcy sighed. "I would be delighted just to have coffee. What will be the procedure, Richard? You know more of the law than I do."

Richard shrugged. "I know military law, which is different. I imagine the Sheriff will need to question everyone, try to piece together what happened. My God, William! A crime such as this not eight doors down! Did you hear anything?"

"A number of doors opening and closing as you and I retired earlier, but nothing untoward. Just the wind howling incessantly. I slept well, but woke at four-thirty absolutely freezing. The wind had died down to a moderate whine, and it was fairly quiet aside from the usual crashing of over-burdened tree branches. Whatever transpired was likely long since concluded."

"She was strangled." Richard said softly from where he stood by the window. "That was evident. I have seen death from strangulation a number of times, although not as often as…" He paused, turning to Darcy. "She was violated, William, before. I am sure of it. Someone who is here, a guest or servant perhaps."

Darcy stared at his cousin, neither man speaking for a time. Colonel Fitzwilliam, commander of soldiers in numerous battles, warrior and dealer of death in times of war, was no stranger to the evil that haunted this world. There were things he had seen, things he himself had done in the name of Country and Honor that no one knew, not even Darcy. He was far from innocent, by any stretch of the imagination. Serving the Crown was frequently the polar opposite of glorious. It was more often ugly, dirty, brutal, messy, repugnant, and hellish. The contemptible reality of the baser elements had hardened his heart to a great degree. Nothing truly shocked him.

Darcy, on the other hand, for all his education and awareness of the broader world, was an innocent. His knowledge of evil in its myriad manifestations was primarily read about in books and newspapers. The death and subsequent grief that was a part of his life was of a normal nature, the result of accidents or fate. Other than a couple of incidents of thievery among his workers and once with a Pemberley servant, the typical scheming machinations of businessmen, and cheating with cards or dice, Darcy had no personal experience of truly heinous sinfulness.

The sound of footsteps in the corridor and lifted voices reached their ears. Individual words could not be distinguished, Richard returning to his contemplation of the snow while Darcy closed his eyes.

When the agonizing wails of a man and woman reached their ears, they barely flinched. Unconsciously, they had been expecting it and were strangely relieved to have the tormenting anticipation over. The muffled murmur of placating voices filtered through the cries, the sporadic bark of a dictate uttered by a voice of authority, and the tread of multiple feet.

It was Richard who answered the knock when it came. A deputy stood without, bowing briskly. "Mr. Darcy?"

"I am afraid not. I am Colonel Fitzwilliam."

"Excellent! Sheriff Weeden wishes to speak with you Colonel as well as Mr. Darcy. If you please?"

Bypassing the brawny attendant guarding the scene of the crime, they followed the deputy down the stairs and eventually to a cluttered office located beyond the kitchen. The clink of pans and pottery mingled with pleasing aromas caused both men's hungry stomachs to growl. Sheriff Weeden sat behind the desk, several pieces of parchment laid before him as he scribbled. Without glancing up at the Deputy's introduction, he waved both men to the seats situated before the desk.

"Cross, bring us fresh coffee and a tray of something to eat. I do not know about you gents, but I am famished. Roused from my warm bed with news of a murder does not allot the liberty of a leisurely breakfast." As he spoke, the Sheriff continued to write, not yet formally acknowledging either gentleman nor even meeting their eyes.

Darcy frowned, not at all used to such rudeness, glancing toward Richard whose brows were raised with a similar expression of surprise. The room was small and windowless, disorderly with stacks of papers and boxes stuffed to overflowing with an assortment of items. A pair of mounted, smoky oil sconces and one lamp on the messy desk provided the only illumination. The fastidious Darcy found the whole environment depressing. His desk may be a bit cluttered, but it was an organized clutter and always clean.

The Sheriff of Belper was a middle-aged man, short and portly, with graying black hair and a face tired and lined. Thick, bushy eyebrows framed small, sunken eyes aside the bulbous nose of a chronic drinker.

"Colonel Fitzwilliam," the Sheriff spoke abruptly, looking at Richard with an intimidating stare. "I am to understand that you were the first to look closely at the deceased?"

"I suppose that is true."

"Why?"

"I beg your pardon? I do not understand—"

"Why did you feel it your place to exert your authority and examine a crime scene? Are you a professional investigator?"

Richard bristled. "I believe you are mistaken, Sheriff Weeden. I did not 'examine' anything. We entered with Mr. Allenton to identify the girl. That is all."

"You covered her, yes?"

"Only to preserve decency. I disturbed nothing, I can assure you."

"Hmmm. Perhaps. Why did you feel the need to get involved at all?"

"It was utter chaos and Mr. Allenton was unable to cope with the situation. I was merely trying to help."

"Did you know the girl, Colonel?"

Richard inhaled several times in an attempt to calm his irritation before replying. "Sheriff Weeden, I am not appreciative of your tone. I comprehend that you have questions but do not approve of the rudely accusatory inflections."

"A crime of the most heinous variety took place in this establishment last night, Colonel, and I intend to find out who did it. Forgive me for not extending the customary pleasantries, but under the circumstances, it is a waste of my time. I repeat: did you know the girl?" His voice had risen slightly, fleshy chin thrust forward pugnaciously.

"No, I did not. I recall seeing her with her family while dining and later in the common room briefly. I did not speak to her, exchanged the merest glances, do not know her family, nor did I see when she left the room."

"You were present as well, Mr. Darcy?" Darcy nodded, face a mask of regulated disapproval. "Did you know the girl or speak to her at any time?"

"I did not notice her at all."

"What brings you two to Belper?"

Darcy answered, "We were caught in the storm and could go no further. I am sure it is a similar tale for most of the guests."

"Traveling north or south?"

"North from Derby."

"Why, pray tell, were you in Derby so soon after Christmas? Why would you not be at Pemberley with your new wife, Mr. Darcy?" Darcy's eyes were flinty, lips a tight line as he pierced the Sheriff with his most menacing stare. He did not reply. The Sheriff steepled his fingers and sat back into the chair, meeting Darcy's gaze unflinchingly. "Refusing to answer me is not wise, Mr. Darcy."

"I will answer any question you place before me that is of relevance to the matter at hand. My personal affairs have no bearing."

"Oh, but they do. A young girl was raped and killed. And I have before me two men without female companionship who leapt at the opportunity to place themselves on the scene, a devious method of displacing suspicion, one of whom it was reported to me had a light shining from his room at the wee hours of the night! Can you explain that, Mr. Darcy?"

Darcy was absolutely livid. He stood stiffly, back straight and tense fury emanating from him in waves. Nonetheless, his voice was soft and calm, "I regret that I can shed no light on this tragedy, Sheriff Weeden. I heard nothing and saw nothing until the tumult this morning. I awoke at 4:30 and started a fire as my room was cold. I rang no one, instead sitting and reading. That is all I have to offer on the subject I am afraid. If you have further need of me, I will be at Pemberley."

He turned to exit the room, the Sheriff's smug voice staying his steps. "You will be going nowhere, Mr. Darcy. Until the guilty party is discovered, all here are suspects, including yourself. I am the authority now, sir. Remember this. Colonel, you may go back to your room as well. I will call if I have further questions." And he recommenced his writing without another word.

Noon approached with the atmosphere unchanged. The staff resumed some of their duties, primarily the preparation of food, always watched over by the deputy guarding the rear door. Rooms were not cleaned or beds made, baths were not drawn, and most of the guests preferred to dress themselves rather than interact with anyone. Meals of plain fare were served in the dining room, people sitting alone and eating quickly. Conversation was minimal and suspicious glances abounded. Word had spread despite the subdued environment, the full fate of the girl known by all.

A pall of death had fallen over the entire building. The weather remained cloudy, with steadily falling snow fostering the sensation of exclusion from the rest of the world. The exception to the rule was the coroner and undertaker, who reported by mid-morning, and later left with the shrouded body accompanied by a grieving father. Mrs. Hazeldon remained in their chambers, well sedated thanks to the laudanum graciously supplied by a fellow guest.

It seemed to bode well for the investigation that the inn was not filled to capacity. Overall, the establishment was of modest size, a small country coaching public house frequently bypassed for the fancier places in Derby or Matlock. Being the holiday season as well as a particularly cruel winter, travelers were few, and thus, nearly half the available rooms were vacant. Aside from the Hazeldons, the only other entire family was the Westmorelands. Both groups were returning home after spending Christmas with relatives, tarrying only due to the inclement weather. The remaining guests were mostly single men journeying for a variety of business or pleasure purposes, such as were Richard and Darcy, and two couples. Sheriff Weeden suspected everyone, granting no quarter arbitrarily.

One by one, each male resident was filed into the dank office where Sheriff Weeden presided. Every man was treated to his tactics with abrupt questions and harshly glaring beady eyes. It would continue at a snail's pace for many hours.

Darcy exited the interrogation absolutely fuming. With back stiff and tread a hairbreadth away from stomping, he ascended the stairs with Colonel Fitzwilliam trailing silently behind him. Richard was offended by the Sheriff's tone and disgusting insinuations, but could tolerate the intimations with equanimity, as he understood to a degree why they had been rendered and he was not as easily affronted as his morally staunch cousin. They entered Darcy's chamber, the incensed man heading directly to the armoire and removing his saddle bag. Without a word, he yanked the fastidiously hung shirts and jackets, shoving them into the large pockets with angry vigor.

"Ah, Darcy? What, pray tell, are you doing?"

"I am packing and I am leaving. You can accompany me or not, I do not care which, but I am going home."

Richard drew close, voice soft but firm. "William, listen to me. I sympathize with your feelings, I truly do, but you cannot leave."

"Watch me."

"What I will watch is one, or probably all three, of those burly deputies tackle you to the ground, clap you in irons, and lock you in one of the basement storage rooms. Furthermore, such an action will only cast greater doubt on your innocence. Aside from the distress this will cause your wife, imagine the confusion it will cause. You must think beyond your own selfish desires!"

Darcy had continued to thrust items haphazardly into the pouches, apparently ignoring Richard, until the final words, at which point he rounded on him with a visage of icy fury. "Speak cautiously, Cousin."

"I will speak sense and it would behoove you to calm down and listen! A girl has been murdered, William! This horrendous occurrence takes precedence over your wishes. I am sorry for the brutality of that truth, but there it is. Sheriff Weeden may be a bit rough around the edges, but he has a job to do. Our responsibility as citizens of Derbyshire is to assist him in any way possible, and certainly do nothing that will distract him."

"It is ludicrous, Richard. We have nothing to do with this and he knows that. The man merely wants to exert his authority and is taking advantage of a woeful calamity to do so. It is disgusting."

"All that is true, but you are forgetting one incontrovertible fact, Cousin."

"What?"

"He is the Sheriff and even you, Master of Pemberley, cannot overcome that. Do you think I like this any better? Being ordered about by a subordinate? I am a colonel for God's sake!" He shrugged and spread his hands, mouth lifted in a faint smile.

Darcy was assuredly not in the mood for humor, but Richard's words did have the effect of dousing his anger. He sat onto the edge of the bed, hands falling between his knees as he leaned forward with a deep sigh. "How long do you think this will take? I do not have much faith in the murderer stepping forward and confessing his crimes, do you?"

"Not especially. I suppose it depends on the situation." Darcy looked at him questioningly. Richard shrugged again and sat next to his cousin on the bed. "I do not claim to be an expert in these sorts of crimes, but I do have some experience with the lower dregs of society and criminal element. Either this man is a calculated killer and has likely done such a thing before, or it was an accident. If it the former, then it may be impossible to discover the culprit, unless Sheriff Weeden is an excellent interrogator. If the latter—which is what I tend to believe—the perpetrator will be easier to crack."

Darcy smiled and lifted a brow. "You have a theory, Inspector Fitzwilliam?"

He shook his head and laughed faintly. "Not really. Perhaps I simply prefer to think we do not have a soulless, homicidal maniac lurking about." He slapped his palms onto his knees and stood up abruptly, "Enough speculating! I am famished, and I know food will improve your disposition. Let us see what the cooks have managed to throw together. Cheer up, Cousin! You still have me for company!"

Darcy met Richard's grin with a sardonic shake of his head. "Marvelous."

Darcy's attitude was not much improved by coffee and a full stomach, but physically he felt better. He and Richard reposed in friendly companionship at the small table nestled near the fire. Darcy had purposefully crossed to the table farthest away from the window, having no wish to stare at the gloomy surroundings. The dining room was empty except for two other tables, one with an elderly couple and the other with a distinguished gentleman of some sixty years. They ignored each other completely. The girl who nervously served related that the other guests had all eaten and quickly returned to their rooms.

The food was plain but satisfying. Aside from the undercurrent of persistent tension, it was a relaxing interval in a cozily warm room. The cousins conversed softly about a variety of subjects, none of which involved the current crisis. Mr. Allenton entered at one point, speaking timidly with Darcy and Richard before moving on to the other guests.

"Poor man," Richard said. "I doubt anything remotely like this has ever happened to him."

"I do pray his business does not suffer due to this event."

At that instant, a handsome young man of approximately twenty years appeared on the threshold. He was well dressed, comportment clearly revealing him to be a gentleman of means, but there was an air of distress about him that was equally evident. An accompanying servant pointed to Mr. Allenton and the young man hastily approached. Richard and Darcy curiously observed the interaction as Mr. Allenton frowned, then paled and glanced about the room. With readily apparent relief, he settled on Richard and Darcy, striding swiftly toward their table with the young man trailing him.

"Mr. Darcy, Colonel Fitzwilliam, this is Mr. Hugh Stafford. He and his brother are guests here, have been for a week now. Anyway, he is concerned as his brother, Mr. Jared Stafford, is not answering the knock at his door and Mr. Stafford here says he heard odd noises coming from inside."

"What sort of odd noises?"

Mr. Stafford swallowed, clearing his throat nervously before answering. "It makes no sense at all, Mr. Darcy. We retired to our rooms late having, well, imbibed fiercely." His face was beet red, head hanging as if expecting the older men to scold him. Richard smiled faintly, recalling his first youthful indiscretions and feeling for the lad. However, the events of late did not lend well to humor. Mr. Stafford resumed, "I was worse off than Jared, but we were both well in our cups. He is younger then I, but generally better able to recuperate from these overindulgences. Not that we do this often, you understand!"

"Of course not, Mr. Stafford." Darcy said placatingly. "Continue."

"I just rose an hour ago and was surprised Jared had not woken me earlier. I went to his room, but the door is locked and he does not answer. I hear banging about and"—he hesitated in embarrassment, face flushing—"I think… crying."

The three older men exchanged significant glances. "Mr. Stafford, are you aware of what has transpired at the inn today?"

"No, Mr. Darcy."

"A girl was murdered last night, Mr. Stafford. Miss Hazeldon. Do you know her?"

But the question was redundant, as all the blood had drained from Mr. Stafford's face, his knees giving out as he sank into a nearby chair. "Sweet Jesus! Miss Felicity? Do you mean Miss Felicity? Murdered? No! It cannot be! Oh dear God! Who could do such a thing? How..." His voice broke in a sob, "How did she...? Oh God!"

"How well did you know the young lady, Mr. Stafford?" Richard asked sharply.

"I... That is, I knew her a little. They have... the Hazeldons have been here for, what four days now, Mr. Allenton? She is a lovely young lady, so sweet and kind. Jared will be crushed! He fancied her a bit, you see. Her poor, poor parents! This is horrible! Too horrible!" He released a moan, head cradled in shaking hands. "Have they caught the villain who did this?"

Mr. Allenton had watched and listened with a dawning fear that he attempted with all his might to submerge. He honestly liked both young men, judged them of the finest caliber, so the thought of either of them being involved had not entered his mind despite the friendly association between the two families. Mr. and Mrs. Hazeldon were also fond of the fellows, knew them to be reputedly of an excellent family, so had not inhibited the acquaintance between their eldest daughter and Mr. Jared Stafford. The innkeeper had placed their names last on the guest list given to Sheriff Weeden and obviously Mr. Hazeldon had not mentioned their names with any sort of suspicion. Given the rather flirtatious and forwardly improper personality of the deceased girl, Mr. Allenton had reckoned it could be any of the dozen men currently residing at his establishment.

Darcy and Richard were grim. "Mr. Allenton, has Sheriff Weeden spoken with Mr. Jared Stafford? Does he know about the girl?"

"I have not seen him yet this morning, sir. The Staffords are last on the list and I know the Sheriff has not seen everyone yet." He paused, spreading his hands. "I do not know for certain, sir, but think it unlikely. They were quite intoxicated last night."

Richard looked at Darcy. "Locked in his room and sobbing? Seems an odd crapulent reaction, no matter how intense the headache. Sounds like guilt to me."

"Or fear."

"Wait, what are you talking about?" Mr. Stafford was glancing from one troubled face to the other in confusion. "Are you suggesting... Wait!" He jumped up angrily, "Are you suggesting my brother had something to do with Miss Felicity? That is absurd! How dare you—"

"Calm down, Mr. Stafford." Richard rose and placed his hand lightly onto the upset young man's shoulder. "Lead us to your brother's room and let's see what we can discover."

The chamber of Mr. Jared Stafford was at the end of the hallway, just beyond Richard and Darcy's chambers. The three older men stepped in the wake of a fuming Mr. Hugh Stafford, who paused before the closed door and angrily glanced at the others before pressing his lips together and rapping on the solid wood.

"Jared? It's Hugh. Open up and let me in." Silence. "Come on, Jared! It is well past the lunch hour and I am famished. We need food, Brother." Nothing. "Jared, you are worrying me. Open the door, please."

"Go away, Hugh," a muffled, slurry voice issued from behind the stout door. "Run back to mother and father. Tell them I am dead. Gone, gone… into the abyss… no hope… no bloody hope…" The words trailed off into hushed gibberish accented by the crash of something glass shattering against the wall.

No longer angry but merely frightened, Hugh looked to the older men. The face barely on the edge of manhood was now reverted to the pleading desolation of a confused youth. Darcy nodded to Mr. Allenton who retrieved a bundle of keys from his pocket. The muted scrape of a heavy object dragging across the wooden floor reached their ears as Mr. Allenton finally found the correct key and inserted it into the lock. He turned the knob, throwing the door open and nimbly stepping aside, clearly not wishing to be the first to view what they all feared to behold.

It was far worse than any of them had imagined.

The small chamber was freezing cold from the yawning windows and in utter ruin. Broken shards of glass and pottery lay everywhere; the linens had been violently flung off the bed with numerous ripped strips of fabric littering the floor; the curtains had been slashed with a knife and then wrenched from the wall, rod and all, to lie in a heap by the window; the tall mirror was smashed in four places by the heavy crystal tumblers whose remains could be seen in a pile at the mirror's base; pictures were jerked from their wall hooks and tossed randomly; deep gashes marred one of the thick bedposts as if a sword fight had ensued with the unoffending column; and through it all were splatters of blood and bloody footprints.

As appalling as the room itself, even more gruesome was the sight of the eighteen-year-old boy slumped in the chair positioned before the unlit fireplace. He stared with lifeless eyes into the ashes, holding a sharp knife in his right hand and a nearly empty bottle of whiskey in the other. Whether he was a handsome lad could not be discerned, so ravaged was his visage. His entire being was depraved: shoulder-length blond hair loose and snarled; eyes red rimmed and bloodshot; four deep, bloody fingernail scratches down his left cheek; torn, gaping, and blood smeared linen shirt displaying a bruised upper chest; stocking clad feet lacerated and bleeding from a dozen shard-inflicted wounds; and tremoring hands with swollen, bruised knuckles lifting the bottle to pale, dry lips. He muttered indecipherable words under his breath, momentarily unaware of the four shocked men standing in the doorway.

"Jared!" Hugh whispered. "My God, what happened to you?"

Jared glanced up blearily, blinking several times to focus, eyes alighting on his elder brother with bare recognition. "Brother. I told you to leave. Let me die as I deserve. Tell Mother… tell her I love her. Now, go away." His voice was flat and low, and he turned away dismissively for further contemplation of the ashes.

Richard and Darcy shared glances. Richard cleared his throat and stepped forward, while Darcy whispered to Mr. Allenton to fetch the Sheriff. Hugh was shocked beyond words or coherent thought and stood pale and silent.

"Mr. Stafford, my name is Colonel Fitzwilliam. This is Mr. Darcy of Pemberley. We are here at your brother's behest to offer assistance." He stepped closer, carefully avoiding the glass. "Perhaps you can share with us what has you so distraught?"

Jared shook his head, tears springing to his eyes. "No point. There is no point. It is over… my life is over." He choked out a sob, drinking the last drops of whiskey and then staring into the container as if baffled why it was empty. "Over… over and done." He laughed hysterically then frowned, his face darkening as rage abruptly swept through each feature. With a harsh yell he heaved the drained decanter at the opposite wall where it shattered.

"All over!" Jared screamed, lurching unsteadily to his feet and fixing Richard with a baleful glare. "Because she lied to me! Lied and screamed and screamed and screamed!"

"Calm yourself, Mr. Stafford. Are you talking about Miss Hazeldon?"

"Yes! Her! The lying strumpet! Said she loved me, wanted me!" He was raging and pacing imperviously through the rubble, dangerously brandishing the long knife, and words barely decipherable. "Said, 'Meet me, Jared. Once we are truly lovers we can be together forever. No one can stop us.' Then she says no. No! Can you believe it? First she wants it, wants me, then she doesn't! Tease! Whore! A woman cannot do that! Then she starts screaming and would not stop! I told her to stop, begged her to stop, but she wouldn't. Told me I was hurting her. Why would I hurt her? I was making love to her! I loved her!"

He halted suddenly, swaying as he glowered defiantly toward Richard. Darcy had moved cautiously into the room, circling to the left. Hugh was crying unabashedly from his weak slouch near the door, hands covering his face. None of them noticed the return of Mr. Allenton with Sheriff Weeden and two deputies by his side.

"Mr. Stafford, please, put down the knife and…"

"No! Go away I tell you! All of you!" Twirling about toward Darcy with knife raised in a surprisingly firm grip given his obvious level of intoxication, Jared stepped backward toward the open balcony doors. "Stay away! Leave me be so I can die in peace. Die like she… like… Oh God!" Releasing wracking sobs with head hanging dejectedly and knife dangling loose at his side, Jared succumbed momentarily to grief and remorse.

Darcy, who was now nearer, leapt forward and grasped onto the weapon-wielding arm of the deranged youth. His control was fleeting, however, as Jared reared precipitously, bodily knocking into the far larger man. Surprise was on his side, as Darcy was unbalanced and lost his grip. The knife was jerked out of Jared's hand and flew through the air, nearly impaling Richard, who again called upon his excellent reflexes and ducked just in time.

An animalistic growl erupted from the young man's throat, eyes scanning the room and noting the additional men. With a final shove square on Darcy's chest, sending him staggering backward into the splintered bedpost, Jared pivoted and dashed toward the balcony.

"Jared, no!" Hugh yelled, brought out of his stasis and launching after his brother, but they were too late. Jared catapulted himself off the balcony.

Darcy and Hugh reached the railing simultaneously, just in time to see a miraculously unhurt Jared struggling to free himself from an enormous snowdrift mere inches from the rearward side of the solid woodshed. Covered with powdery snow, he managed to right himself enough to commence plowing through the knee-high drifts, heading in a zigzag pattern toward the woods.

"Jared!" Hugh yelled.

"He is heading for the woods." Darcy proclaimed, twirling and hastening toward the door with long strides. "Damned fool will die out there dressed like that."

"Thankfully his trail will be easy to follow," Richard added, joining his cousin in his rapid exodus from the devastated chamber, Sheriff Weeden and the deputies marching along behind.

What ensued was a wild trek through the wet, frigid surrounds. The snow was thick in places; the terrain obscured so that frequent submersions into pits or painful collisions with bushes occurred. The continued snowfall and winds created flurries and fogs that distorted vision. Nonetheless, a weakened, inebriated youth was no match for six healthy men on his trail.

Jared Stafford was finally cornered against the trunk of a broad oak, huddled and shivering on a bare patch of frozen ground. The shock of all that had transpired in the past twelve or so hours caught up to him, and from there it was an easy matter, the tragic youth no longer offering any fight.

Richard and Darcy gladly returned to the warmth of the inn, leaving the issue in the capable, legal hands of the Sheriff. Word of the murderer's capture spread hastily through the halls; the mixture of horror and relief generated an atmosphere of bizarre giddiness that would reign until late in the night. Neither Darcy nor Colonel Fitzwilliam were in the mood to share their part in the tale, retreating to their respective rooms early in the evening, thankful that the drama was behind them and abundantly prepared to return to the seclusion of Pemberley.

I T WAS TWO DAMP, cold, and exhausted men who finally rode into the stable courtyard the following afternoon. The ride from Derby was miserable, despite the abated storm and rays of sunlight that now succeeded in piercing the scattering clouds. Stomping muddy boots and shaking snow-drenched cloaks in the north entrance foyer, servants dashing to assist, the men breathed deep sighs of relief.

Richard made a beeline for his room while Darcy inquired as to the whereabouts of Mrs. Darcy, informed that she and everyone else were in the court room cheering a tennis tournament. This was certainly the truth as far as it went. Georgiana and Kitty were currently engaged in a fierce competition, George playing referee from the net line, and the remainder of Pemberley's guests applauding, whistling, and shouting encouragement. However, a rapid sweep of the room revealed that Lizzy and Jane were absent.

Darcy's heart fell, but he had no time to deal with the disappointment before George spotted him. "William! It is about time! We thought you had gotten buried in a snow bank." The lanky physician crossed the room in long strides, enfolding his nephew in a bone-cracking embrace and bestowing a stunning blow to his shoulder. "It is good to have you back, son. We have all missed your serious face, but none more so than your lovely wife and precious son."

"Thank you, Uncle. Where might I find them?"

"In the conservatory. Your son decided it was mealtime and disrupted the entire game. Quite threw Georgie off and she completely missed the ball, match point to Miss Kitty." He grinned.

Darcy grinned in return. "Extend my apologies to my sister. I am sure she will overcome. Now, if you will excuse me?" George nodded and Darcy waved a general greeting toward the crowd, hastily retreating before anyone else felt the urgent need to accost him.

The conservatory was an enormous room, easy to become lost in, but there were only three alcoves sheltering enough for Mrs. Darcy's purpose. The nearest to the entrance was the wisteria arbor, so there Darcy headed. His choice was correct, the murmur of voices reaching his ears as he approached. Lizzy's tinkling laugh at some quip of Jane's sent his heart soaring.

A gentle rap on the trellis edge to alert to his presence was followed with a declaration, "Pardon me, ladies, but may I interrupt your pleasant interlude?" He peeked around the frame just as Lizzy released a gasp, meeting her instantly shining eyes with his own radiant smile. The sisters sat and gently rocked on the wide swing, Alexander nuzzled against Lizzy's shoulder, apparently finished with his meal and currently staring raptly at the brilliant purple blooms draped behind his mother.

Jane stood, approaching her brother-in-law with a dimpled smile. "William, how delightful to have you home. We have missed you and Colonel Fitzwilliam most profoundly. Far too many females languishing about without male attitude to sustain a balance."

Darcy took her hand, kissing fingers with a courtly bow. "Dear Jane. You look beautiful and in excellent health. I pray all is well?"

"Excellent, sir. I have little to complain about. Thank you for asking, but I am quite certain you do not wish for a protracted conversation about my health. If you will excuse me, I do believe I shall see how the tennis match is proceeding." And with a smile toward Lizzy, she departed.

Lizzy already had one arm extended toward her husband, fingers beckoning and instantly entangling into his damp hair when he sat. She drew him close, Darcy offering no resistance as he met her lips for a hungry kiss. He encircled her with one arm, palm cool on her face as fingers stroked, the other hand joining hers on Alexander's back.

The kiss lasted for a long time. Only the burning need to taste her flesh moved him away from her intoxicating mouth to trail moist kisses over jaw and neck.

"Oh, William, I missed you so! I know it has only been five days, but it feels like an eternity. And then this horrid blizzard! I so feared you would be stranded in Derby for longer. I could not bear it!"

He had reached her ear, scattering kisses and nibbles amid gentle flicks of his tongue and hot breath. "I promised I would be home for the christening, my heart. Nothing would keep me from you and our son." He returned to her mouth vehemently for another extensive kiss, both panting heavily when he finally withdrew to rest his forehead onto hers.

"You must tell me everything."

He pulled away with a smile, needing to gaze into her stunning eyes. "I will, naturally, but not yet. I simply require your voice and touch to comfort me. Your beauty soothes me. Are you well, my dearest wife? All has passed quietly in my absence? You weathered the storm safely?"

Lizzy laughed, kissing him tenderly. "Listen to you! You are the one off having adventures and you ask what we have been doing? I can assure you, it was much as you have already seen. Constant entertaining larks. The men were devastated to have their target practice cancelled. Be prepared for an urgent need to brave the ice and cold for a chance to fire your new rifle."

Darcy laughed as she continued, fingers ruffling through his hair as she spoke, "George regaled us with stories of past Derbyshire storms, although he recalls none as violent as this one. The lightning was an entertaining treat if frightening. Noses were pressed to available windows facing west as the bolts were spectacular. Mr. Keith was relieved to report no damage done. A billiard tournament was attempted, and although George was thrilled to win for a change, they all agreed it was a dismal failure without you."

"I am touched."

"So, as you can see, it was uneventful. Lazy, endless hours of lying about with the only interruptions of import being your son's appetite, which shows no imminent signs of waning."

Alexander had finally recognized his father's voice, head bobbing in a determined attempt to turn away from the wisteria but not having great success. Darcy laughed, removing his arm from about Lizzy's shoulders and pulling the babe into his lap with broad hands supporting.

"Let me look at you, little one. Have you been a good boy? Taking care of your mother? Yes? That is papa's bright boy. Give me a kiss, sweet love." And he proceeded to shower tiny kisses all over Alexander's face and chubby neck, the infant fidgeting irritably at the cold skin and fabric. Darcy hugged him close to his chest and reached a hand to cup Lizzy's face. "I am happy to be home."

❧

"There you are!" Lizzy laid her embroidery hoop aside and smiled up at her weary but handsome husband, who had entered their sitting room with a contented sigh.

"Yes, finally. Forgive me for ignoring you. I wanted to settle a few matters with Mr. Keith before they escaped my tired brain." He crossed to his wife, sitting on the ottoman before her chair and leaning for a kiss, hands warm and soothing on her knees. "Thank you for waiting so patiently."

"I cannot claim any great patience, as I was near to storming into your study and evicting you forcefully." She smiled but reached up to stroke his cheek with concern evident in her eyes. "You have had a grueling few days, my heart. I can see it in your eyes without knowing the specifics. I should scold you for insisting we retire early only to spend the past hour with your steward, but I shall not. I am just happy you are here. Shall I call for tea?"

Darcy shook negative, hands clasping hers and stroking gently. "No thank you. I had some tea in my study. All I wish for now is to disrobe and relax with you." He kissed her cheek, nuzzling against her soft skin and inhaling deeply. "Alexander is asleep?" He inquired, following with a gentle suck to her earlobe.

"Hmmm. For the present. He will require a snack in two hours or so before satiated enough for a long sleep." She withdrew to gaze into his beautiful eyes. "We have time to enjoy each other before the other man in my life demands my attention."

Darcy chuckled, initiating a long and lazy kiss while Lizzy began working the various buttons and knots necessary to accomplish her spouse's desire to be unclothed.

The afternoon and early evening after the two snow-encrusted, frozen men finally arrived home had been filled with greetings and conversation, neither man elucidating their adventures. They barely managed to bath and change clothing before being accosted joyously and distracted with refreshing cuisine and glittering entertainment. Richard, generally the hardy soul square in the thick of any revelry offered until late in the night, had pleaded weariness, retiring immediately after dinner. Darcy politely requested the same, only to then retreat to his study for a "brief" interview with Mr. Keith.

Now that he was here, Lizzy's heart and soul were complete, yet she was worried. That he was physically exhausted was clear; but it was also glaringly evident, at least to her, that the trip had taken an emotional toll that transcended the physical. Never in their time together thus far had she sensed this degree of disquietude in his soul. That he would share all the recent events was not an issue for contemplation, as she knew absolutely that he would. Her uncertainty was in how best to comfort him.

However, within seconds of entering, his wishes were abundantly clarified. Lizzy smiled as she pulled the choking cravat free and tossed it aside. Her William may have been a complex person, but in the end he was simply a man, and she estimated, even in her ignorance on the subject, that the male species were all the same. Sexual pleasure would always be preferable, offering a release unique and cleansing under any circumstance. Knowing her husband's rampant amorousness and considerable virility, she rather doubted any amount of weariness or distress could staunch his desire for her. If making love was the foremost urging of his heart, then she would happily acquiesce.

She slithered from his tight grip, kneeling between his knees to remove boots and stockings. Darcy took advantage of the position to unclasp the jeweled combs from her hair and thrilled in the vibrancy of her fragrant tresses flowing through his fingers.

"I missed you, my beautiful wife. More than I have the words to convey. My bed was lonely and cold, my sleep troubled with the want of your body in my arms. I even missed our son waking me at ungodly hours of the night."

Lizzy rose, clasping arms about his waist while Darcy dexterously attacked the row of buttons down her back. "I missed you as well, love, although I had the advantage of nestling Alexander against my chest. It is not nearly as glorious as your nakedness surrounding me, but it soothed me to a degree."

"He slept with you?"

Lizzy nodded. "I could not bear to sleep alone. I hate it so! Besides, it was terribly cold and I worried for him. At least that was the excuse I used." She smiled, leaning into his body to bestow sucking kisses to his exposed neck. Darcy shivered and moaned, hands tightening on her waist as he succumbed to the exhilarating sensations.

"Oh, Lizzy! How desperately I need you." He whispered faintly, vocal cords overwhelmed, and fingers trembling against the thin chemise covering her exposed back. His eyes were closed, ardor rising rapidly as she unbuttoned his shirt, with lips as warm and soft as finest velvet trailing down the midline of his chest. Delicate hands moved gracefully over his torso, grazing puckered nipples before stripping the linen off broad shoulders and reaching to trace the strong bones of his back.

Halting and pulling away after an electrifying dip of her tongue into his navel, Darcy jerking and gasping in delight, she stood and peeled the gown off her shoulders. The corset joined the puddle of fabric at her feet. Darcy groaned, reaching instantly to encircle her hips and draw her toward his aching mouth, but she chuckled softly and clasped his hands. Tugging gently, she stepped backward and drew him to his feet, Darcy swaying slightly.

"Come, lover. Follow me and hold tight to my hands. I would not wish you to faint from the sudden lack of proper blood circulation to other muscles of your body!" The last uttered with a playfully arch glance to his groin and wide grin.

"You minx! Seducing me to achieve such a state and then teasing mercilessly! Do not fear, my beloved vixen, I am quite capable of standing, walking, and doing a great deal more. Lead on and I shall follow happily, but hasten, my sweet, or I will be convincing you of my capabilities on this chair!"

Lizzy laughed, turning and steering the few feet to their bedchamber with her enchanted and extremely aroused spouse inches behind. His breath brushed over her bare shoulder, lips grazing, the rising heat of his body felt deep into her bones, and his free hand roamed insistently over hip and thigh as she walked. The second they entered their favored sanctuary, he flattened his palm over her lower abdomen, hauling her backward onto the hard surfaces of his chest.

With intimately probing fingers rendering her breathless and incoherent, she listened as whispering lips brushed her ear, "I do pray you have slept well over the past days, Elizabeth, as I intend to keep you awake most of the night. Loving you once will not satiate me, I can assure you. I require the glorious sounds of your ecstasy and erotic writhing of your body numerous times to quench my thirst even partially. The hunger to feel your warmth encasing me as we love cannot be satisfied until a banquet course has been served. I need to feast on every inch of you to be truly satisfied. Lord, my precious wife, how beautiful you are and how deeply I love you!" The latter breathless exclamation was uttered as he tenderly rotated her now naked form to face him, eyes afire as he inspected head to toe while fingertips breezily traced her curves.

Lizzy groaned, moving decisively and clasping his face in her palms, lifting on tiptoes to passionately claim his mouth. His poetic words, always so spontaneously expressed from the heart, never failed to stir her tremendously.

Over the course of their marriage, they had learned the blissful happiness achieved in intuitively seeking to discover the innermost yearnings of their partner. A mere glance, fleeting touch, whispered word, or barest kiss was enough to sense the internal necessity. In the main, they discovered that their individual cravings at any given interlude were inevitably hungry for the same level of intensity, be it slow and languorous or fast and furious.

Yet there were those occasions of altered synchronicity. One would wish for a crazy, scorching assignation with rapture attained in a swift, blinding crescendo, while the other preferred gradually building to a prolonged, soothing climatic wave. One would wish for the comfort and intimate familiarity of their bed with bodies pressed together naturally, while the other longed for an exotic locale or position. It was at those times when the full nature of their love for each other was called forth, as the ability to sense the emotional reasoning behind their lover's wishes and then cheerfully granting that wish brought the highest pleasure and joy.

Such was the case now. Lizzy was in a sudden fever of desire, yet she knew that this was one of those times when Darcy's deepest needs transcended her own. Instinctively, she recognized that her husband ached to be tenderly loved. His arousal was swift and marked, but his softly spoken words and gentle caresses as well as something indefinable alerted her to his unspoken plea.

With a coarse groan, she softened her kiss, hands loosening their crushing grip to his face and traveling to tangle in his hair. The sensation of firm muscles and the rigid length of him brought shudders to her flesh, but she forced each sinew to relax, pliantly melting into his embrace. Eventually their eyes met. Darcy smiled gently as he stroked over her back, the knowledge of her sacrifice and his gratefulness clear in the glittering blue of his gaze.

"Elizabeth Darcy," he murmured reverently. "My wife."

While nibbling kisses to swollen, ruddy lips, he clutched her upper thighs and hoisted her up. She instinctively wrapped legs about his waist while he walked sedately toward their bed. Within minutes, Lizzy would forget her prior salacious insanity. They nestled under a blanket, bodies entwined as they commenced a languid exploration with Darcy fulfilling each spoken phrase as he feasted. Hands and mouths were everywhere; Darcy leading and Lizzy responding as sensations blazed and ebbed only to blaze anew at some fresh sensory assault.

It was cathartic. All the moans and sighs of his beloved purging; each stroke within her purifying; every successive level of passion attained supplanting the sorrow until there was no room for anything but happiness. It was then and only then that he fully surrendered to the pure, absolving pleasure to be found only with his wife.

Mutual cries reverberated. Darcy's guttural shouts rose to the rafters; Lizzy's release paling under the intensity of her husband's unleashed climax. "I love you, Fitzwilliam," she gasped hoarsely, Darcy far too caught up to be more than peripherally aware of her declaration.

But he felt the sentiment emanating, and embraced her even tighter if that was possible. They lay on their sides with limbs tangled and flesh connected on multiple planes, clasping and caressing as hearts gradually returned to a normal pace. The tenderness and vulnerability of being so rawly exposed aided their ever increasing melding as one soul and, in this particular situation, assisted the final dissipation of Darcy's dolor.

He pulled her head gently onto his shoulder, kissed the top of her head, and sighed. "I do not think I have ever needed to love you more, my heart. Thank you. I am unsure if I can express how urgently I required your love, but I will try. Be patient with me."

"You have all the time in the world. I am not going anywhere."

"Hmmm... Yes, I know this to be true and it fills me with bliss. My good fortune staggers me, but I accept it nonetheless."

"And so you should. How deficient of you to not accept the Almighty's wondrous blessing... me!" And she leaned her head back to meet his sparkling eyes with her own, both chuckling.

He stroked her cheek, happiness radiating. "Guess who else is in love?"
"Who?"

"The confirmed bachelor himself. Our wayward cousin Richard."
"You jest!"

"God's truth. Behind that flippant exterior beats a heart as sappy as my own. He confessed over dinner one night to harboring a years-long affection that I had no clue about whatsoever." He paused, running the back of his hand along her clavicle and neck. "You remember our attending Lord Ivers's ball in London?"

Lizzy blinked, eyebrows rising in a surprised expression much as Darcy had worn when Richard seemed to abruptly change the subject. "I... do, yes."

"You recall Lord and Lady Fotherby? I believe you conversed with Lady Fotherby, did you not?"

She nodded, still puzzled. "I spoke with them both briefly and Lady Fotherby sat near me for a spell at one point. They are lovely people, or rather I suppose I should say Lord Fotherby was. He rather intimidated me I confess. I do not know if I will ever accustom myself to actually speaking with people who are so noteworthy, the legendary famous who are names read about in newspapers. I think I stammered a bit, but his wife was unassuming, and we shared a time of stimulating conversation."

"You never stammered, beloved. Were always charming and witty, my perfect Mistress of Pemberley, exceeding all my expectations and swelling my ego outrageously."

"Pride, Mr. Darcy. Tsk, tsk."

"Indubitably. But also merely the truth."

He bestowed several kisses, Lizzy finally murmuring against his lips, "We were discussing Richard's love life."

"Hmmm... Were we?" He captured her lower lip, sucking gently.

Lizzy giggled, pulling away, but he only followed, her giggles increasing and voice mumbling without the ability to articulate properly. "William, finish your tale. Curiosity is killing me!"

He let go of her lip with a laugh. "A rumormonger you are, Mrs. Darcy."

"You started it! And quit changing the subject. One minute Richard in love, the next a ball attended months ago. Focus, my dear, and tell me... Wait!" Her eyes opened wide as comprehension dawned, Darcy observing her with a broad grin. "You mean Lady Fotherby?" Nod. "Richard is in love with Lady Fotherby?" Nod. "How? When? I do not see..."

"Allow me to enlighten you, and rest assured, I was as flabbergasted and I have known the man all my life." He proceeded to tell her the entire woeful tale as recounted to him, leaving nothing out, and adding his own commentaries from recollected incidents of ages past. "I remember the two flirting a bit, but it is standard practice amongst most of the society seekers, as you witnessed yourself. A time or two he mentioned Lady Simone's beauty or grace, repeated a handful of witty ripostes or clever stories with a gleam in his eye. The gents teased him a bit, but that too was standard practice so I thought little of it."

He chuckled, closing his eyes in humored remembrance. "It was dangerous, Elizabeth. Merely glancing at a lady was fodder for merciless teasing, let alone speaking of one. Luckily, it was an equal opportunity mocking torment so no one took it seriously."

"How about you? I know how you despise being teased."

He smiled. "I avoided looking at or talking to any women as much as possible, which was not too difficult since they all frightened me half to death."

Lizzy burst out laughing, Darcy rolling to his back with her in his arms and laughing as well. "There! You now know all of my secrets. You were not the first woman to leave me hopelessly tongue-tied, although the reasons were quite different. Social skills were never my forte, especially when in my teens. Thankfully, I was ridiculous and boring so the young ladies ignored me as well, saving me from the worst of my friends' innuendos and taunting."

"I rather doubt they ignored you, after all I have seen your portrait from the year you left for Cambridge and you were entirely too dashing to be ignored. So what is Richard to do?"

Darcy shrugged, eyes on the breasts so gloriously displayed resting on his chest as Lizzy was propped on her elbows above him. Reaching to trace an index finger over the softness, dipping into the welcoming cleavage, he answered absently, "Not much he can do at this juncture. Lady Fotherby is in mourning and will be for a few more months. Eventually, however, she will return to society functions. Richard should have no trouble encountering her from time to time, especially if he is proactive as I suggested he be. His greatest obstacle will be the other men placing themselves in her path. A wealthy widow of her beauty will be sought after. I encouraged him to press his suit forthwith. If she holds any affection for him, which seems at least possible, given the clues extended, he should have no trouble."

"Who would have thought you would ever be giving another advice on romance?"

He glanced up at her teasing face with a grin. "My arts worked on you, did they not? Found me irresistible, charming, dashing? Had to have me as yours immediately? Wanted me desperately?" He accented the huskily uttered words with firm strokes down her sides and a tight squeeze into his pelvis.

Lizzy squirmed and laughed. "Live with your delusions if you must, Mr. Darcy, although rewriting history is considered a sin in some quarters."

He merely grinned and returned to the delightful contemplation of her bosom. "You no longer leak milk and feel softer, not so... lumpy."

"Lumpy? Yes, I suppose they did at times." She shook her head in amusement. "My body seems to have adjusted." She smiled at Darcy's rapt attention, running fingers through his thick, messy hair while she observed the play of expressions crossing his elegant features. His thoughts were transparent, thus she was not even slightly surprised when he gently rolled her onto her back and buried his face into her chest with a happy sigh.

His playful delight did not last long, however, as the bell above the right side of the bed rang. With a final kiss to each pert nipple, Darcy rose, kissing her lips before exiting the bed.

They had come to refer to this final nursing as Alexander's bedtime snack, as he inevitably ate voraciously prior and needed merely to fill the tiny void before succumbing to a deep Darcy-style sleep that lasted for six to sometimes eight hours. Naturally, he was not always so predictable, often waking in the darkest hours of the night for nourishment or comforting. Mrs. Hanford assured them this was typical and to be expected for months to come. Generally, the nanny attempted to calm the baby herself, not wishing to disturb her Mistress unless essential; however, she was under orders to alert the Darcys the moment Alexander was inconsolable. Neither regarded it as a burden to attend to their son's needs.

They were fortunate in that Alexander was a temperate infant. He had only suffered two episodes of severe infantile colic, probably as a result of something Lizzy had eaten, Mrs. Hanford informed. Those two nights of pacing and rocking with a disconsolate, screaming baby were hideously memorable. The three had taken turns attempting to placate the suffering and irritated babe, only Lizzy managing limited success at her breast. The frantic parents were distraught, doubly so by the increasing hoarseness of their son's voice and purple cast to his face. The first night, Darcy was so worried that he woke George, insisting he examine Alexander, which the good doctor was more than happy to do. He and Mrs. Hanford exchanged understanding glances, George assuring the new parents that it was normal albeit distressful. He personally brewed a concoction of herbals, including fennel, chamomile, anise, and dill that did seem to help, or maybe Alexander just wore himself out. Whatever the case, they kept a bottle of the extract in the nursery just in case.

Darcy particularly enjoyed this late night snack, as Alexander was not so ravenous and more apt to willingly play with his father. He walked slowly into the bedchamber, Alexander placated for the moment with his father's little finger. "Have you been a good boy while I was gone, my sweet? I believe you have gained another half a pound, you gorger. You nearly have two chins!" He laughed, Alexander pausing his steady sucking to gaze into Darcy's eyes. He had a firm grip to the index finger, chubby fist curled tight, and his legs kept a regular rhythm of strong kicks. He was always moving, Darcy had discovered. Unless asleep or completely satiated with mother's milk, his body was in action. The day before Christmas he had kicked so hard that he flipped from his side to back, limbs flailing wildly and eyes wide in amazement at the abrupt change.

Darcy sat on the bed beside a reclining Lizzy, not ready to relinquish the lively bundle cuddled in his arms. With eyes locked onto his son's face, he asked of his wife, "Has he had any bouts of colic while I was away?"

"No. He was a bit fussy two nights ago and slow to suckle contentedly. I gave him a few drops of tonic and we rocked. I discovered that gazing into the flames soothes him. Finally he nursed and slept well. I was relieved it did not ripen into a serious episode, as you were not here to sing to him." She chuckled at Darcy's wry smile. "I would not count on him being musically inclined, as he seems to prefer your singing voice to mine."

"Have no fear, love. Georgie adored my singing and she is incredibly talented. Maybe you will be the Darcy male to break the mold, my darling." He brought the baby to his lips for a number of tender kisses, Alexander patiently enduring. Darcy ran a hand all over his son's round body, marveling anew at the combination of vulnerable softness and solid strength. Developing rolls of fat could be felt on his arms and legs, his entire body dominated by an enormous abdomen, and his head hard was still covered with a mass of brown curls. Darcy removed one thick knitted bootie to nibble kisses to a plump, pink foot.

"Praise be to God for keeping you so healthy and perfect," Darcy whispered, kissing the baby's brow. "I love you, my son, my precious, precious son."

"We received a few more gifts before the storm struck. I piled them with the others in the parlor." She reached up to tickle over Alexander's exposed toes, dropping her hand to caress lightly over Darcy's bare knee emerged from an open robe. "We received a package from Lady Catherine and Anne, including an envelope addressed to us which I assume is a wedding invitation."

"You did not open it?"

"I wished to wait for you. I heard from Charlotte as well, a brief note as they likely all will be for a time to come. She says that the girls are in excellent health; the youngest, Rachel if you recall, has nearly caught up to her sister Leah. What a relief it must be for them."

"Rachel and Leah. Lovely names, although I find myself thankful they were not male children or they may have been christened Cain and Abel."

Lizzy laughed. "Or Jacob and Esau, neither option boding well for future sibling tranquility. Anyway, Charlotte says the wedding plans are consuming life at Rosings. I gather it is to be an extravaganza. Apparently, Mr. Collins was disappointed that the ceremony would be taking place in the Ashford Cathedral with the Bishop presiding."

"Foolish man! What did he think?"

"You know the answer to that question! The date is officially set as February twenty-seven, a week after Mary and Mr. Daniels. That is fortunate if we decide to travel."

Darcy patted the hand lying on his knee, smiling sympathetically. "Do not worry over it, love. I will do all in my power to ensure you are present at your sister's wedding and that Alexander is safe. The carriage is solid and we possess a plethora of thick quilts and down comforters. Alexander is healthy and a temperate infant who will travel well, I judge, especially cuddled by us. We can journey in short stages over several days. Of course, all this depends on you, my wee love," he paused for fresh kisses, Alexander wiggling. "Stay strong and grow stout so we can proudly show you to the rest of your relatives."

Lizzy smiled joyously at her husband's antics, nodding in agreement. "Let me see, what else happened while you were gone? Reverend Bertram visited to say he cleared and cleaned the balcony and opened the side rooms to allot more space."

Darcy laughed. "I have told him at least three times not to fret over it. He seems to imagine half of Derbyshire showing up for the affair, which I deem unlikely. We may esteem our son's christening as a premiere event, but I assured him that a baby's naming in general is not a cause of major enthusiasm."

"It has been many years since a Darcy heir was christened, so to the good Reverend, it is an event of momentous importance. Allow him his moment of glory. By the way, I took the liberty of planning a luncheon party of sorts for that afternoon. Mrs. Langton was instructed to keep it simple and not lavish too much attention on the meal or christening cake, orders that I am sure she will ignore. I trust this meets with your approval?"

He looked at her with a humorous smile and twinkling eyes. "Yes, it meets with my approval, Mistress Darcy. Another occasion to swell with pride at the

SHARON LATHAN

blessings gifted me in you and our son is always welcomed. Although you, my little ball of energy, will not be attending I am afraid. We have been fortunate thus far to avoid any illness and I will not press our luck." Alexander erupted in fresh squirms at his father's tickling fingers under his chunky arms.

"Care to hazard a guess as to who else is in love or a reasonable facsimile thereof?" Darcy lifted the left brow inquiringly. "You will never guess."

"If you say my baby sister I may have to cry."

"No, silly. I am speaking of Miss Bingley."

"You are not serious? Who is the unfortunate gentleman?"

"Fitzwilliam Darcy! Shame." But she was laughing and he was unrepentant. Lizzy shook her head, slapping him playfully on the knee. "His name is Sir Wallace Dandridge of Chelmsford, Essex."

"Ah, that mystery is solved."

"Pardon?"

He shrugged, telling her of Bingley's frustration regarding endless references to Essex. "I do not believe she has thus far confided in her brother. How did you discover this piece of stunning news?"

"Girl talk, my love." She replied sweetly with a flutter of her lashes.

Darcy grunted. "Female blathering is the germane phrase, but I am thankful you were not bored in my absence."

She raised her chin at his lopsided grin, pouting adorably. "I see. And you and Colonel Fitzwilliam swapping romantic advice qualify as professional consultation?"

"Precisely! So when shall Miss Bingley become Lady Dandridge?"

"We gather that it is not official as yet. She hints strongly to an 'understanding' of some nature, reveling in the secrecy of it all. Perhaps Sir Wallace is waiting on an opportune moment to speak with Charles."

"Do you judge her truly in love?" His inflection clearly indicating his dubiousness.

"Difficult to say. Charles is right. Every other sentence is 'Sir Wallace this' or 'Sir Wallace that' and once she even called him 'Wally,' then blushed crimson. It was hysterical. Still, I speculate that she is as enamored by the gentleman's title as the gentleman himself. Perhaps I am being uncivil, but she does seem particularly smug over the fact that he bears a title and none of our husbands do."

"I am positive I could buy myself a title if it would please you." Lizzy snorted and pinched his knee. "Ouch!"

"You deserved that, ridiculous man."

"All flippancy aside, I do pray she has found true emotion and happiness. I am acquainted with Sir Wallace and he strikes me as a kind man. If they are blessed with a fourth our joy, they will be content. Of course, no child could possibly surpass my Alexander for sheer cuteness and sweetness, is that not correct, my pudgy lamb?" He clutched the baby under his arms, bringing the round abdomen to his mouth for blowing tickles.

Alexander released a short squeal, fingers instantly grasping fistfuls of Darcy's hair with legs kicking crazily.

Shortly, Alexander's tolerance gave out, and his tiny face lost all serenity. "My turn," Lizzy said with a laugh, pulling the blanket away as Darcy positioned a now seriously hungry baby at his mother's breast. After adding three more logs to the fire, Darcy stripped off his robe and joined his family on the comfortable bed.

There was something incredibly intimate and peaceful about these interludes with their son nestled between their bodies. Watching him suckle from Elizabeth, the most basic of maternal acts, was joyous. Darcy could not quite explain it, but it brought a level of tranquility and pride to his soul that was immeasurable.

He snuggled close, nose pressed to Alexander's curls and fingertips caressing lightly. "I missed his birthday."

Lizzy frowned in puzzlement. "I beg your pardon? William, you were only gone five days."

He smiled into Alexander's hair. "His one-month birthday, and do not pretend you did not note the day, my heart."

"I bestowed an extra dose of kisses, told him he was a month old, and confirmed the all consuming love his parents hold for him. Otherwise it was just another day. Do not fret so." She stroked over his cheek. "You were merely melancholy about the mill catastrophe and being away."

"I suppose." He sighed, rolling away slightly and meeting her eyes. "I missed you both terribly, but I confess having Richard as companion eased the pain. I am afraid I was not initially too pleased, quite rude to him actually. I thought you had sent him, which irritated me, but now that I think on it I would have appreciated the gesture."

"Thank you, but I had nothing to do with it. We were informed of his departure by a hastily penned note found on his breakfast setting. I wished I had thought of it, in fact, and was grateful that he chose to insinuate himself. It eased my mind to know you would have him there to cheer your gloominess."

"That he did, to a degree, as well as rolling up his sleeves and working alongside the others." He paused, collecting his thoughts, and launched into the details of the fire and its repercussion.

Lizzy had turned to the other side to nurse Alexander on the opposite breast, Darcy spooning wholly head to toe and continuing his account with chin resting into the bend of her neck.

"The poor boy," she said, speaking of the Hendle youth, "so tragic to lose your father so young. I am sure your words encouraged him to dwell on his father in a positive light."

He ran a finger down Alexander's downy cheek, voice thick and low, "I thought of Alexander and remembered your chastisement before I departed..."

"William, don't..."

"No, it is all right, beloved. You were correct, completely. Life is uncertain, naturally, and I do not plan on leaving this earth anytime near soon, but I would like to hope that my death, when it comes, will be later rather than sooner." He paused yet again, Lizzy waiting. She did not need to see his face to know that he was struggling with how to express a painful sentiment. "I never imagined that I would be able to consider my father's death as it occurred a... positive, so to speak, from a certain point of view. I have such full memories of him, joyous times, years of mentorship and friendship. The years we shared taught me how to be a man, a husband, a father, a Master, and so many other qualities that I cannot fathom them all. Now I have been gifted the opportunity to pass on this knowledge to Alexander and any other children we are blessed with. God, what a fortunate man I am!"

He reflexively clutched her tighter into his body, face pressed into the tender flesh of her neck with eyes on their sleeping son. "Forgive me, Elizabeth, for momentarily forgetting to prioritize my responsibilities. If this time away has taught me anything, it is how important family is above all. And how fragile life is," he finished quietly.

Lizzy rubbed the thigh lying on top of hers then removed the slack mouthed infant from her breast, nestling him away before turning in Darcy's arms to gaze into his face. She embraced him, palms soothing over his back, and kissed tenderly. "You are the best man in the entire world, Fitzwilliam, and need never apologize to me for being human and vulnerable. But I do appreciate it." She smiled with that humorous lilt to her lips that he so adored. "I never thought I would be saying this to that stoic, reserved man I met in Meryton, but you need to learn to suppress your reckless impetuousness to a degree. And listen to the superior wisdom of your wife."

She grinned sunnily, Darcy grinning and laughing in return. "Agreed."

"Do you truly predict no financial deficits from the fire?"

He was stretched above her, propped on one elbow with head resting in his hand, the other breezily running over her body. He shook his head negative. "We spent hours over the figures. I am confident that our capital is abundantly sufficient to cover the cost of repairs and buying new machines. I trust Mr. Shultz to handle those aspects efficiently."

"So what still worries you?" She asked, fingering the tiny creases between his brows.

"Until we have everything restored, there is no way we can fulfill our current contracts. Fortunately, it is the slow time of year, but there are nonetheless stacks of waiting cotton that needs to be processed and more constantly arriving from warehouses. That is one of the issues I discussed with Mr. Keith. I will be writing several letters over the following days to placate our clients."

"Surely they will understand and sympathize with your plight."

"Undoubtedly they will. But business is business. Their livelihood depends on us processing the raw cotton and providing cloth. Our livelihood depends on a finished product, with orders needing to be filled on the other end to keep contacts happy; and so if necessary, our buyers will go elsewhere. I do not blame them, as I would do the same. Financially, it is not the here and now that concerns me, but the future five, six, eight months down the line. It is imperative that we not lose clients for the future profits and function of our company."

"So... will you give incentives? Offer discounts if they stay with you? Process some bales for free or half cost, that sort of thing?"

Darcy smiled and cupped her cheek. "Very wise, Mrs. Darcy. You have learned from my rambling orations after all."

"I always listen and attempt to understand."

"We have considered all options. The mill will be running for longer hours than usual, although we are limited there as well, since I refuse to allow the women and children to work for more than ten hours a day. Mr. Shultz plans to hire additional workers on a temporary basis to keep the mill operating as long as possible."

He bent for a kiss and then resumed his pose with a serious cast to his face. "I warn you now, Elizabeth, I will be busy for a time and will need to travel over the next several weeks. Day trips, for the most part, to those clients in the vicinity, and I will avoid traveling if possible. Mr. Keith will make the trip to London in my stead."

"Will you need to return to Derby anytime soon?"

A shadow flickered over his features and he averted his eyes. His jaw clenched briefly and lips pressed together for only a moment, but Lizzy frowned. "I will, yes, but on another matter."

"What other matter? William?"

He looked into her eyes, shaking his head slightly and forcing a smile. "Later, my love, later. Do you trust me?"

Her eyebrows rose. "Absolutely! Do not be ridiculous!"

He smiled again, a true smile from the heart. "Then put it aside for now and just let me love you." And without further ado, he rolled his body onto hers, fitting naturally within clasping limbs as flawlessly as lock and key. He pressed firmly and insistently but with the utmost tenderness, and captured her mouth for a prolonged kiss. He ran both palms gradually up her sides, under her arms, pressing with firm fingers the entire length of each round arm, stretching over her head until reaching her flattened palms, and holding tight with fingers laced between hers.

He left her mouth finally, traversing the expanse of her neck to an ear for teasing licks and nibbles. Lizzy was breathless with desire but managed to choke out a few words, "William, we should... the baby is... Oh God! I... that is, we should put him in his cradle."

"I want him to stay with us tonight," he murmured huskily, hot breath waving over her ear and sending shivers cascading through her body.

"But, we should not do..." Gasp! "...this with him..." Moan. "...here."

"He is soundly asleep and likes to be rocked anyway." He lifted slightly to meet her eyes, both of them smoldering with dark passion, but his additionally sparkled with humor. He clasped both wrists in one strong hand, keeping her arms extended, and leisurely rubbed back down her side, firm strokes and squeezes to a round buttock, then drawing the knee up and over his waist. "He will be unaffected, my lover. You will not be."

And with that grating declaration, he dove in, hard and all at once. He groaned deeply in his throat, eyes closing in exalting pleasure. "Oh my Lizzy! I love you!"

He was correct; Alexander never flinched. The antics of his loving, impassioned parents registered not at all unless it was to be soothed into an even deeper sleep by the rhythmic swaying and cadenced gasps. Lizzy was granted her earlier wish in experiencing a lovemaking session of highly intense enthusiasm. There was little in the way of gentleness in their uninhibited passion, but much in the way of furious innervations. Before the need was comfort and cleansing, now the need was a celebration of life and vitality. The emotion was ferocious, the energy spent exorbitant, the excitement fervent, and the release euphoric.

Darcy rolled away, shuddering and inhaling vigorous lungfuls of air. Rarely did they break intimate contact immediately, but the basic need for oxygen called for it. He clasped Lizzy's hand tightly, silence descending except for their rasping respirations.

Lizzy recovered her faculties first, reaching to brush her knuckles over Alexander's rosy cheek, and then turning to her husband's side. She kissed his shoulder, sighing in utter contentment. He kissed the crown of her head, rubbing against the soft tresses, his voice rough and low, "I fear I may need to rescind my earlier promise."

"Which promise is that?"

"That I keep you awake all night with constant loving. I believe you have unhinged me and depleted me wholly. Not that I am complaining, mind you."

She could feel the smile and giggled, kissing the sweaty muscular shoulder again. "I can live with the disappointment. Until some time tomorrow, that is." She lifted, running a hand down the damp hairs on his chest while peering into sparkling blue eyes. "I love you, Fitzwilliam Darcy, with all my being."

Darcy cupped her chin, feathering fingertips along her skin. He stared, simply stared, for several minutes, only then pulling in for a soft kiss. Lizzy brushed the hair away from his noble brow, bestowing a tiny nibble to his upper lip. She tried to withdraw, but he held her close, airily skimming pecks and nuzzles about her face.

"Elizabeth," he whispered. "My beautiful Elizabeth. You heal me with your devotion. You infuse me with your life and verve and goodness. I now have the strength to share the remainder of my trip with you."

She shook her head. "You are tired, my love. I can see the circles under your eyes and hear the weariness in your voice. Your adventures can wait until you have slept."

Darcy, however, was shaking his head negative. "I appreciate your concern, dearest, and I do need to sleep. First, though, I want to tell you all. It is important to me."

"You are frightening me, William. Are you sure you are well?"

"Forgive me! I do not mean to imply anything ill with my health. Have I not proven my vigor?" He grinned and Lizzy chuckled despite her unease.

"You are incorrigible! And you should not jest with my worries. I have sensed from the moment I saw you in the arbor that something serious was amiss, but convinced myself it was merely weariness or thought it related to the fire. Now I am truly alarmed."

He pulled her closer and kissed tenderly. "I accept your chastisement, love, and beg your pardon. I have a story to tell, it is true, but I desire to keep it from you completely. I abhor the very idea of causing you pain."

"William, sharing your life means sharing everyth—"

He halted her with another kiss. "Do not say it, Elizabeth. Trust me, I have learned the lesson of hiding anything from you or making an attempt to shield. I cannot say it is easy, as I always endeavor to bring you only joy and contentment, but I promised to be forthright at all times and I will. This is why I want to reveal all, so I can sleep with you in my arms knowing there are no lingering secrets to disturb my blissful dreams."

She was staring intently into his eyes, frowning. "Thank you. I could not bear it if there was turmoil in your soul or some actual circumstance transpiring that I was not aware of and given the opportunity to alleviate. I love you, William, far too much to allow you to suffer if there is anything I can do to help."

He smiled and nodded, bringing her hands to lie against his chest, and with a sigh, began.

"Richard and I left Derby the day before yesterday."

"Two days ago? During the blizzard?" She blurted, biting her lip instantly. "Sorry."

He chuckled faintly. "Yes, it was appallingly foolish. I allowed my impetuosity to rule, as you recently scolded me. We barely made it unfrozen to Belper, finding shelter at the inn. I was in a foul mood, Elizabeth, I admit with shame. I wanted to be home so dreadfully, missed you and Alexander, and wholly ignored my normal wisdom and temperance."

He closed his eyes and, in a muted tone, told her the entire tale, leaving only the most gruesome details out. Lizzy gasped a time or two but remained silent until he reached the part where he almost left against the Sheriff's command.

"I am ashamed to admit that I nearly slugged Richard. Thankfully, he spoke sensible words that penetrated my thick skull, or I probably would have acted rashly and still be clapped in irons as he predicted."

Surprisingly, Lizzy was giggling, her smothered chuckling breaking Darcy from his narrative. "You find this amusing, Mrs. Darcy?" He cocked an eyebrow.

"I suddenly had a mental picture of you and Richard grappling about on the floor, pummeling each other as unruly boys."

She continued to giggle, Darcy chuckling as well. "Nearly, but I finally called upon the restraint and forbearance generally a chief character trait. I saw reason, or more aptly accepted the futility of my situation."

"So, did they catch the villain? He is not still running loose, is he?" Her voice unconsciously raised an octave, eyes wide with fright.

Darcy draped her with one arm and a leg, drawing her closer and kissing her forehead before tucking under his chin. "We caught him. A young man just eighteen on a pleasure tour with his brother. Fancied himself in love with Miss Hazeldon and thought she returned his affection, and…"

He fell silent, trembles and pounding heart felt by Lizzy. He did not speak for several minutes, and when he did, his voice was agonized. "I thought of Georgiana, Elizabeth. I have never seen anything quite this horrible, but I know what unscrupulous men are capable of, what they believe is their right, what is somehow owed them as the natural conclusion to a flirtation and roused desire. How some regard women as property and worthy of only what pleasure can be taken from them, forcefully or willingly it matters naught. Wickham was such a person, as I knew so well. When I arrived at Ramsgate, unexpectedly discovering his plot, my greatest fear was that he had violated Georgie. I knew it to be a real possibility. Praise God, I was in time, as I am absolutely convinced he would have taken her virtue either to secure her or wound me without the slightest consideration to her fragility or sensibilities. Yet never did it occur to me that she could have died. Some say rape is a fate worse then death. As a man I cannot judge whether this is true or not, but I believe I am sensitive enough to fathom the horror of it. However, nothing could be worse then what happened in Belper," he finished in a bare whisper.

"You were correct to scold me for being foolhardy," he continued, "for forgetting my responsibilities to you and my family. I will not forget it again.

My place is here, protecting you and our son, and all the others dependent on me. I cannot allow myself to brainlessly or selfishly bring harm to my person because I must be diligent in my duties! I will not fail you, Elizabeth."

"I know—"

"I promise to safeguard you, my wife, and you must promise to be wise, wary, sensible, and aware. Elizabeth, I cannot survive without you. I know this to be true as a mere five days drives me insane!"

Darcy trailed his fingers and lips airily over her face. Exhaustion washed over him in waves as the final vestiges of the tragedies were illuminated and scattered. He ached deep into his bones with sleep clawing at the edges of his consciousness, yet he could not halt hands and mouth which urgently required the final cathartic sensation of touching his wife's vibrant flesh.

Lizzy, by the same token, experienced a similar abrupt weariness of heart and body. Her husband's troubles had shaken her, and she felt his sorrow. Yet, with each unifying act of lovemaking, with each cleansing conversation, and with each current kiss and caress, she knew he was healed. Although weary, her heart nonetheless leapt for joy in the knowledge that their unique bond had worked another miracle.

Considering the expended energy and emotions of the evening thus far, it was a marvel that either would respond sensually. Then again, never could Darcy touch his wife without desiring to arouse her. He was well down the luscious curves of her body before fully comprehending her rising ardor, the lush swell of her breasts his personal undoing.

"I love you immeasurably, Elizabeth," he whispered between tender licks and kisses, fingering through the tousled curls cascading wildly over their pillows. "Always and for all eternity you are mine. Only mine."

Darcy was quite certain he could fall asleep in seconds and not budge for hours, but the titillation of his wife was irresistible. While his increasingly foggy brain fought succumbing to the oblivion of sleep, his potent manliness responded to her enchantment and touch.

Lizzy took charge. Rolling him onto his back, she rapidly straddled his hips. Darcy groaned weakly, hands slack on her thighs, misty eyes shining with profound contentment at the electrifying feel of her surrounding him and the captivating vision of her feminine figure with luxuriant tresses tumbling rising above him.

"I love you eternally, Fitzwilliam. Only for you, my life and breath. Always and forever, you are mine."

It did not take long. A few minutes of tender motions and he yielded to the comforting surge of pleasure procured only with her. His satiated, stuporous brain was only vaguely aware of her moving away afterwards to add a log to the fire. He opened his eyes briefly, ponderously scooting closer to Alexander and laying one broad hand onto the baby's back before falling into a daze. A brief rush of air over his back was quickly supplanted by the radiant warmth of Elizabeth nuzzling between his shoulder blades. Her arm snaked over his waist and her breath soothingly wafted across the nape of his neck.

"Good night, my darling. Sleep well." A tender kiss planted at the top of his spine was his last memory. His final thought was a reciprocated wish for refreshing sleep, but the sentiment would remain unspoken as consuming, blissful, therapeutic, and revitalizing sleep overwhelmed.

CHAPTER SEVEN

Thanksgiving for the Gift of a Child

ALEXANDER HAD NOT RECEIVED any Christmas gifts per se. All the gifts addressed to the young master which began arriving some three weeks after his birth were set aside to be opened nearer to his christening. Lizzy was stunned by the barrage of packages delivered by Royal Mail or servants or the hands of the gifter. Once again she was struck by the prestige and eminence of her husband as Master of Pemberley; the full scope of what that title portended was signified by the wealth of accolades and blessings pouring in.

The red velvet drape once encumbered with wrapped holiday presents was now equally laden with gilded and sparkling packages of all sizes from all over England. A number had arrived with the Bennets from the relatives and friends of Lizzy. A package containing three wrapped gifts was sent from Darcy's family in Devon. There were parcels from Lady Catherine, Anne and Raul, and the Collinses, all delivered together while Darcy was away. They had received an abundance of written congratulations with a smattering of small gifts from friends and associates in London and elsewhere. No word yet from Austria, but the birth announcement had likely barely been conveyed. Other more modestly wrapped presents mysteriously appeared at all hours of the day and were clearly from the staff. The biggest surprise was a complete layette of quality Irish linen dyed a brilliant sky blue from Darcy's Uncle Phillip and his family.

Opening the surfeit of gifts became part of the evening's entertainment for the three nights following Darcy's return from Derby. The bulk of offerings consisted of knitted blankets and quilts; cotton, wool, and linen baby dresses in every color of the rainbow with matching bonnets; an adorable collection of toddler boy outfits with small trousers, ruffled shirts, and tiny jackets; several rattles and teething rings; a profusion of bibs in all sizes; and a dozen satin pillows.

"I will need to change his clothing three times a day for the next six months to wear all these dresses," Lizzy exclaimed. She held up a lovely gown of faded pink with white ribbons crisscrossed down the front and along the hemline, a gift from Jonathan and Priscilla Fitzwilliam.

"I am surprised you are not weeping at all the time wasted sewing gowns yourself, considering how you detest such activity." It was Jane, teasing from where she sat beside her sister, refolding and repacking the individual presents to be put away later.

Darcy hid a smile in the rim of his teacup. He stood across the room, ostensibly watching the unwrapping, although in truth the procedure was becoming a bit boring. Not that he would confess this to his wife or any of the other women in the room, who seemed to be inexhaustible in their enchantment over each item, many of which looked identical as far as he was concerned. All the other men had pretended attentiveness for thirty minutes maximum before meandering to far corners. Darcy maintained his vigil from a purposefully selected locale near enough to partake in the festivities when necessary, but also converse covertly with Bingley and Colonel Fitzwilliam. For two nights he had diligently observed the unmasking with a mixture of the extreme pleasure experienced with anything regarding his son and an ennui that he vaguely felt guilty about, but could not control. Tonight, thankfully, they had finally worked methodically through the gifts from business associates, friends, staff, and distant relatives to the ones presented by close family and friends.

"I cannot argue with the truth of that statement, Jane." Lizzy responded to her jest while looking to her husband's glittering eyes with a faint shake of her head. Darcy merely raised one brow.

"Mrs. Darcy, this is from me. You saw the beginning pattern and have been gifted an array of quilts, but I do hope you will like it."

"Thank you, Miss Bingley! I am sure we will love it. And have no fear, as cold as it is here in Derbyshire, I am sure we will have great need of blankets and quilts aplenty. Jane has already informed me of the beauty of your creation, and I see she was not exaggerating. Look William! Oh, Miss Bingley, it is truly incredible."

Darcy drew near in honest awe. The quilt in question was magnificent: a collage of poplin pieces in varying degrees of brightness exceptionally woven into a Crown of Thorns pattern. The entire quilt was a bit larger than a true infant-sized blanket, which was a bonus.

"Caroline, this is a marvel!" Darcy exclaimed, losing his usual formality in surprise. "How wise of you to create it larger, as it will fit well over his toddler bed. The colors are remarkable! Thank you, Caroline. We will treasure it always."

Caroline was beaming, all the typical arrogance erased in the light of the Darcys' praise. For one of the first times in all his years of acquaintance with her, it suddenly struck him how truly beautiful she was when her features were allowed to relax and light with an honest smile. Abruptly, the epiphany bolted through him that this is what his wife and friends saw in his countenance now as compared to the severe façade presented for most of his life. With a surge of emotion bordering on affection, he grasped one of Caroline's hands and brought the fingers to his lips for a thankful kiss.

"Thank you, Caroline, from the bottom of my heart." He spoke softly, the words reaching only the immediate bystanders. "Elizabeth and I will cherish this gift created from your heart. Our greatest wish is that someday we may be honored to return the gesture when you are blessed with the exalted joy of motherhood."

Caroline's mouth had fallen open, eyes misty as she gazed into Darcy's shining visage, swallowing the lump formed with difficulty before murmuring, "You are welcome, Mr. Darcy."

Kitty stepped into the slightly awkward tableau, handing her gift to Lizzy. "It is no big thing," she stated apologetically, "but I did do all the work myself!"

Lizzy laughed. Of all the Bennet sisters, Jane and Mary were the only two who excelled and actually enjoyed working with needles in all the various methods. Lydia hated it the most, probably never finishing a project in all her life, but Kitty came second. Lizzy delighted in embroidery, as long as it was not too complicated a pattern, and found a relaxation in knitting, but that was it. Crocheting was out of the question and sewing she abhorred. Lizzy had noticed a calming of Kitty since Lydia's departure and, upon rare occasion, observed her head bent over a hoop. If she had created a gift of any sort with her own hands, it would be a prize to be sure, no matter the caliber of craftsmanship.

As anticipated, the gown sewn and detailed by Kitty was not a masterpiece. But its beauty was in the simplicity of design, especially as compared to many of the fancy infant dresses thus far given. Constructed of plain white cotton with eyelet lace along the collar and sleeve edges, the gown itself was pure in its minimalism. Clearly, Kitty had devoted her skill and time to the embroidered border of the skirt. In painstakingly perfect stitches and every color imaginable, she had fabricated a flowing pattern of inch-high stick figure children at play: skipping rope, swinging, bouncing a ball, running, jumping, rolling a hoop, swatting a shuttlecock, tumbling, and blowing soap bubbles. It was playful, colorful, and utterly delightful.

"Oh, Kitty! I love it! The pattern is wonderful! I can imagine Alexander doing all these fun pastimes. Thank you so much!" Darcy thanked a blushing Kitty with a regal bow and courtly kiss to the fingers.

Hugs and kisses became rampant and enthusiastic as the family gifts were gradually unveiled. The men began to drift closer to the fray with sincere smiles of delight. The presents varied widely and reflected the personalities of the individuals involved. Silver implements abounded per tradition, with Alexander provided a wealth of eating utensils, porridge bowls, and cups. The Gardiners, Bennets, and Lady Catherine, as the eldest family members, especially adhered to the tradition of silver, each implement beautifully carved and shiny. Lord and Lady Matlock gifted a gorgeous silver and lapis lazuli inlaid brush and comb.

Anne and Raul sent the complete series of S. & J. Fuller paper doll books. These were instantly popular among the guests, and the precious books were passed from hand to hand with each adult reverting to childhood as the dolls were dressed and the story verses read aloud. Darcy finally confiscated the expensive books before "they are smudged and creased beyond Alexander being able to read them."

Samuel and Marguerite kept to the theme of literature with both volumes of Ann and Jane Taylor's *Poems for Infant Minds*, *Rhymes for the Nursery*, and *Hymns for Infant Minds*, signed to Alexander Darcy by the loyal personal servants. Not surprisingly, Mary and Mr. Daniels gifted a small white-dyed leather Bible and accompanied publication of inspirational quotations from spiritual writers.

Numerous gifts came from the servants, most of a simple nature such as the crocheted blanket with embroidered clusters of Sweet William from Phillips and his wife, but two stood out from the rest. Mr. Clark and the entire grounds-keeping staff presented Lizzy and Darcy formally with a three-year-old oak sapling, carefully cultivated in the orangery from an acorn harvested off the enormous oak marking the eastern boundary of the private garden.

Standing with grubby hat in hand, his staff crowded behind, Mr. Clark had nervously delivered his speech to the touched Darcys that afternoon in the Conservatory. "Reckoning how much you enjoy gardening, Mrs. Darcy, and as Pemberley for generations now has gained renown for her landscaping, we"—he swept the hat toward the shuffling gardeners—"figured a tree to mark the young Master's birth was appropriate. It will grow with him, strong and enduring, so it had to be an oak. There is a perfect plot in the garden for it, with a few re-plantings come spring, but of course you can decide to plant it wherever you wish it to be." The Darcys assured him that the private garden would be preferred, trusting to his expertise. Lizzy was so choked up she could barely speak, Darcy maintaining his equilibrium adequately enough to thank the groundskeeper and his excellent staff with the essential pomp and formality.

Mrs. Reynolds provided the final habiliments to the christening outfit with a superbly crafted bonnet of lace and satin, and tiny slippers of pliant kid leather sewn by her hand. She had produced both with Darcy's christening gown in mind, keeping to the old-fashioned style and sparing no expense in purchasing fine Alençon lace similar to the original. The entire project was taken on faith, hoping that her Master and Mistress would choose her gift over the ones worn by Darcy. The finishing touch came from the Bingleys. As godparents, they added an elaborately carved stout silver cross pendant on an ebony and ruby beaded chain. The necklace was stunning, the fiery red and bold black a masculine contrast to the ruffles and lace. Darcy was elated.

Richard, typical man, went farther afield from the standard infant paraphernalia. His box was far and away the largest, too big to set into a lap. Rather, he deposited the hefty, and obviously heavy, unwrapped parcel onto the low table before Elizabeth. Grinning widely, he addressed Darcy and Lizzy, "I am well aware that this is not a customary christening gift, but then neither is the gift you bestowed upon your son, Darcy."

Darcy raised a brow. "What are you referring to?"

Richard grinned further, glancing to Lizzy's baffled face. "Surely you have informed your wife of the generous bequest awarded to your infant son?"

Lizzy started laughing. "Shame on you, Colonel, trying to cause your cousin trouble. Of course he told me about Wolfram. Asked my permission, if you must know, although I judge he would have finagled the transaction somehow whether I deemed it suitable or not. My only stipulation was that he forbids Alexander to ride a fully grown stallion until he can competently manage a pony."

"Which will be by the time he is six or seven," Darcy stated firmly, prideful assurance evident on his face. Lizzy merely shook her head, but Darcy was lost momentarily in dreamy visions of squiring his son about the corral. Horses never far from his thoughts upon any given day, it had occurred to him soon after Alexander's birth that the year old colt Wolfram would be in the full bloom of his maturity when Alexander was ready to make the transition from pony to horse. Lizzy may not be thrilled with the idea of her son atop a feisty horse, but marriage to Darcy made it inevitable, so she had happily agreed to his desire to deed Wolfram to Alexander.

"In all honesty, Elizabeth, horses are as important to me as Darcy." Lizzy smiled at that understatement, Richard continuing without pause, "I think Wolfram an excellent choice, but in the meantime, until he is strong enough to ride a full grown horse he will need to ride a pony. If I know my cousin he already has one of the Connemaras picked out for him." He glanced at Darcy with a questioning grin, but Darcy merely pressed his lips together, his expression speaking volumes nonetheless. "So, with that in mind, I had this fashioned for my newest cousin by a leather maker named Anderson in London."

Darcy was already whistling, familiar with the prestigious Anderson and his equestrian products, and standing with unveiled excitement to lay eyes on what he now suspected was in the box. He was correct. It was a pony-sized saddle crafted for dressage in the fashion of Gueriniere and included all necessary tack. Fine cowhide tanned and dyed a deep brown then polished and oiled until gleaming and supple. "Alexander" was stamped into each saddle flap in a stylized script with a shooting star bursting off the R's final curve. The entire ensemble was exquisitely constructed.

"Along with this saddle ensemble, I vow to lend my superb horsemanship skills to teaching Alexander to be a superior rider. I am better than Darcy, so it only fitting I extend my expertise."

Darcy merely grunted his disdain toward that statement, otherwise ignoring the grinning Richard for meticulous examination of the saddle. Collectively the men assembled for inspection, offering vastly superior interest over this one item to all the others combined.

Georgiana and George applied their artistic talents to their offerings. In the case of Georgiana this was to be expected, but George's was a complete surprise. Georgiana had begun creating a wealth of baby items upon first hearing the news, even when it was not a certainty. Therefore, Lizzy and Darcy had already been the grateful recipients of numerous garments, decorative furnishings for the nursery such as floral adorned silk lampshades, a painted tile table sitting next to Lizzy's rocking chair, and two enamel decorated porcelain flower vases. Her gift for the christening was equally stunning and exhibitive of her talent.

Painted on miniature ovals of silk were striking likenesses of Lizzy and Darcy from the shoulders up, the portraits sewn above each other onto a twelve inch square quilted wall hanging with the following poem masterfully stitched alongside:

This little tiny baby
Was sent from God above
To fill our hearts with happiness
And touch our lives with love
He must have known
We'd give our all
And always do our best
To give our precious baby love
And be grateful and so blessed

"Georgie! Oh! It is so beautiful!" Lizzy jumped up, handing the picture to a dazzled Darcy, and embraced her sister tightly.

"This is incredible, Georgiana. Precisely as we look now, when Alexander was born. How absolutely marvelous!" Darcy smiled incandescently. "You truly astound me, baby sister. Now I only wonder why I pay anyone else to paint portraits when I have a remarkable artist within my household." He cupped her head, leaning for a kiss to her forehead.

"I love you with all my soul, Georgie. This will hang above Alexander's cradle, the faces of his adoring parents watching over him eternally and the poetic phrases conveying our everlasting sentiments." He enfolded her against his chest, murmuring into her hair, "How fortunate our boy is to have such a fabulous auntie. Thank you my dearest, thank you."

"Enough mushiness! Break it up so Elizabeth can open my presents. Two! For you, my darling niece." George breezed in, bowing with a flourish and handing the largest of the last two presents to Elizabeth while linking arms with Georgiana. "I would say the best has been saved for last, but I doubt my meager offering can transcend Georgie's. I shall boast, nonetheless, as I too created these masterpieces with mine own hands." He lifted his long fingered appendages, digits waving. "Skilled surgeon's instruments employed in the creative process for my grand nephew and partial namesake."

Lizzy laughed, shaking her head. "Are you ever serious, Uncle?"

"Rarely, my dear. Only when delivering babies. Now open."

The formless, cushiony bundle was wrapped in one of his Indian scarves—a particularly flamboyant one of chartreuse and orange, all tied with blue string. Lizzy was smiling even before revealing the contents, upon which she burst into huge gales of laughter. Darcy merely shook his head in resignation. Nestled between sheets of tissue paper was a wardrobe of baby and toddler sized Indian outfits! Casual dhotis, salwar, kurti, salwar kameez, all in bright colors and exotic prints, and one formal khalat robe of thick wool lined satin in turquoise with woven peacocks and Bengal tigers.

Gasps and exclamations of awe rose from the gathering crowd as every hand reached to inspect the kaleidoscopic miniature garments. "Elizabeth dear, I fashioned these from the cloths I brought with me or new ones purchased in Town. My nephew deserves to be breezy and as handsome as his Grand Uncle, do you not agree? On a practical note, youngsters should wear clothing that is unencumbering to developing extremities and allows the genitalia to freely grow."

"Uncle!" Darcy chastised with a pointed glance to Georgiana's reddening cheeks.

George merely shrugged unperturbed. "It is the truth of it, William. That *khalat,*" he nodded toward the robe Darcy held in his hands, "is of the same fabric as mine. Very elegant, I daresay, and Alexander will be exceedingly comfortable while reclining with his favored companion: me!" His grin was broad, Darcy laughing and rolling his eyes.

"Do Indian children really dress like this, Dr. Darcy?"

"Actually, Miss Kitty, Indian children rarely wear more than a loincloth. It is far hotter in India, if you recall. But on occasion they do, yes, although I confess the colors are traditionally beige hues. For some unfathomable reason neutral tones do not appeal to me," he concluded with false confusion.

"I adore your attire, Dr. Darcy, and so admire your bravery in wearing brilliant colors. Goodness knows I would never have the nerve." Mrs. Gardiner offered, George bowing gallantly in her direction.

Mrs. Bennet was closely examining one of the kurtis. "I am extremely impressed, sir, at your sewing abilities. These stitches are remarkable!"

"Thank you, Mrs. Bennet. I do have vast experience with needle and thread, although not often utilized with fabrics you understand." He grinned, Mrs. Bennet staring incomprehensively for several seconds, then paling and eyes widening humorously as understanding dawned. Muted snickers rippled through the assembly.

George continued, "Of course, as a bachelor I am not blessed with the joy of a loving, devoted wife to darn my socks and mend ripped hems, therefore I must attend to such tasks myself. Tragic really." He hung his head, tone mournful as the women collectively *Aaahed*.

Mr. Bennet snorted and Mr. Gardiner coughed a laugh, George winking sidelong. Darcy was inspecting the exquisite two-year-old-sized robe, speaking with skepticism, "You intend to maintain you sewed this yourself? Forgive me, Uncle, as I have no experience with needlework, but my wife informs me that working with such a delicate fabric is incredibly difficult."

"I would not be too swift in gauging sewing skills in general against anything Lizzy has told you, Mr. Darcy." Mary interjected with a teasing glance to her sister, who retaliated by sticking out her tongue.

Darcy's lips twitched, but he held his laughter in check. "Be that as it may, Miss Mary, I persist in believe my uncle dissembling."

"Oh very well! If you must know I had assistance from a seamstress in Lambton. The patterns, however, were all mine and I picked the materials specifically so Alexander will be most adorably adorned."

"Well, I love them!" Lizzy declared and lifted on tiptoes to kiss her uncle's cheek. "Alexander will be adorable. I can already see him dashing up and down Pemberley's halls in a flash of color. Thank you, George."

He smiled, kissing Elizabeth's forehead. "You are welcome, my dear. Well, William?" He turned to his nephew with a raised brow.

"I concede that six months ago I would have been horrified at the prospect, but I suppose I have grown accustomed to the attire." He smiled dreamily. "Yes, Alexander will look adorable. Very well then, I like them as well, as long as you realize they are for private only. We have our public reputations to maintain."

"What an old fogy you are!" Richard asserted with a laugh.

"I do not see you dashing out to garb yourself in flamboyant Indian wear, Colonel," Darcy said primly, fresh laughter erupting.

"Now I have the opportunity to redeem myself after being revealed as a sewing incompetent." George handed a small package to Darcy. "This I did create with my own hands, honest to God." He smiled sweetly and sincerely, speaking with emotion, "It is important to me that Alexander have something from me that he can carry with him always. An everlasting remembrance of his beloved uncle and godfather."

"Oh! George! It is exquisite!"

Lying in the palm of Darcy's hand and taking up the entire area was a finely detailed, three-dimensional carving of an Asian elephant in pristine ivory. With white trunk raised in the air, mouth agape, curved tusks proudly lifted, small ears erect, legs spread in a run, and tail swishing, the inanimate pachyderm projected a realism so astounding that one held their breath waiting for the trumpet sound to burst forth. Each crease of the rubbery skin and coarse hair was etched in meticulous technicality, the artisanship clearly a gift of expert proportions.

"When did you learn to whittle? I had no idea." Darcy paused, choked up from the breathtaking beauty of the object in his hand coupled with the rushing memories of his grandfather creating such miniature works of art. Of all the various visions burned upon his memory, the sight of his beloved grandfather with hands masterfully wielding a whittling knife as a flawless creation of wood or other raw, shapeless material gradually evolved into a work of art was foremost.

"My father taught us all. You remember how much he loved to carve. My twin and I were the only ones who inherited the propensity, although after Alex died I refused to touch a sculpting knife for years. Now I find it calms me and the aptitude remains within my hands."

"Have you seen many elephants?" Kitty asked in awe.

"Hundreds, Miss Kitty. They roam freely in certain regions and the locals do ride them as the stories proclaim."

"Have you ridden one?"

"Dozens of times." He chuckled at the wondrous expression on her face. "They look as if they would be slow and plodding, but the contrary is true." He launched into a lengthy dissertation of Indian mammals and lifestyle that filled the bulk of the evening. The sculptured elephant would eventually be encased in glass and placed next to Darcy's christening bonnet and shoes in the nursery. Alexander would treasure the figurine for all his life, adding many others sculpted by Uncle Goj to his collection, the marvels always gracing a place of prominence in whatever room he dwelt in.

∼✠∼

Per tradition and the precepts of the Anglican Church of England, the christening ceremony served two vitally important objectives. One was the official naming and declaration of the child before the congregation, family, and God. The second was to receive the baptism into the Body of Christ, ensuring that the child begins his or her life on the proper pathway toward a mature affirmation of faith leading to complete salvation.

In order to correctly fulfill the first objective, the christening was to take place on Sunday during the normal worship service when the local congregants were assembled as witnesses. These witnesses accepted the partial responsibility of overseeing the spiritual upbringing of the child, who was henceforth a part of the flock. With this idea in mind, it was also critical to perform the rite at the parish church where the parents were members and by the pastor who ministered to them.

Due to the irrefutable fact of infant illness and subsequent death being a frequent harsh reality, the christening of Alexander William George Bennet Darcy was scheduled for the Sunday that fell three days after Christmas. The hasty departure of his father to Derby had necessitated a postponement until the following Sunday, arranged by Mr. Keith as one of the tasks assigned at the last minute by his Master.

The dawn of January fourth, 1818, with Alexander now a full five weeks old and stout, should have brought nothing but high enthusiasm to both his parents.

In the case of his father, this was true. The past days had been hectic ones between duties to his guests, endless hours opening presents, and extended hours with Mr. Keith, and three days on horseback to visit local clients, but the robust man in the prime of his life suffered no depreciation. Being home within the bosom of his family amid the comforting rooms, entertained and well fed, was all he needed to restore his equilibrium. The final crown to his joy was the formal presentation of his son and heir and the necessity of ensuring the new life's dedication to Christ. With these pleasant thoughts premiere, Darcy woke as the first rays of sunlight bathed the snow drenched landscape and drew his sleeping wife closer with a dreamy smile, then drifted back into a doze.

In contrast, Lizzy roused roughly an hour later and vaulted from the bed. She dashed to the nearest window and ripped the curtain aside. Darcy jerked upright in sheer panic, shock rendering him speechless.

"The sun is shining!" She exclaimed ecstatically, glancing to her befuddled spouse then turning back to contemplate the outside. "No wind or rain or clouds! Oh thank you, Lord! Do you think it warmer?"

She whirled back to Darcy, who was now faintly smiling in amusement. His answer was to gaze pointedly at her rock hard nipples and spreading goose bumps as the frigid cold of the chamber waved over her bare flesh. He quite enjoyed the view of her alabaster nakedness and wildly disheveled hair as illuminated by the filtered beams of light, but she was beginning to shiver so he held out his arm beckoningly.

"I think you know the answer to that question, my darling. Come back to bed and let me warm you." She hesitated, her face falling slightly as she glanced outside again before sighing and turning toward the welcoming bed and spouse. Darcy enfolded her, pulling down into the cushions, and covering with thick comforter and radiant body. He kissed her forehead, "Do not fret so. He will be bundled securely up to his eyeballs. No harm will come, I promise. He must travel beyond Pemberley sooner or later, and this is the appropriate occasion."

"I know," she mumbled petulantly. "I just... worry."

Darcy smoothed the hair from her brow, kissing tenderly. "Focus instead on how precious he will look in his gown, fat rosy cheeks surrounded by lace, while we stand together at the altar with his godparents. This is a magnificent day! Be filled with only cheer, I beg you. I know for me it is a day I have longed for, for many years, one of the best days of my life after the day you married me."

"Of course you are correct. Thank you, love." She smiled. "He will be absolutely adorable, to be sure. Oh, I just love him so much! And you too, my dear husband." And she hugged him tightly, the lovers losing themselves in soft kisses and caresses until Alexander's hunger overruled.

⁓❦⁓

"There, there, my darling. Hush now and do not be so vexed with your mama. You look absolutely adorable."

"I thought he had grown so big until now. That gown swallows him! No wonder you are irritated, my lamb." Darcy bent to kiss the flushed cheek of his fussing son, securing waving hands. "Only for a short time must you endure.

It is important, even if you do resemble a blob of meringue confection. Be strong, my son, as life is full of these travails and clothing is rarely comfortable." Alexander had calmed somewhat at the resonant murmurings of his father, but additional wails were clearly bubbling under the surface.

"Hold the skirts up so I can find his feet. Thank you. I should have placed the stockings and slippers on first. Oh, there he goes! Ticklish feet. Talk to him before he loses all control and wrinkles the material beyond repair."

Darcy bent again to croon placatingly into a tiny ear while Lizzy finished the difficult task of placing small garments on a flailing limb. Mrs. Hanford stood nearby with the bonnet and silver cross in hand, smiling at the scene. Alexander was well fed and wishing to fall asleep as was typical, but instead was being subjected to the horrors of dressing in a lace encrusted gown with dozens of buttons that had required him to lie on his abdomen for far too long. At least now he was on his back, so all the surroundings, including the two beloved adults who cared for him so devotedly, could be visualized in the appropriate perspective.

"It is understandable, my sweet, cry if you must. I cannot say that I blame you, as you do look rather ridiculous…"

"William! He does not! He is adorable."

"He looks like a girl or a doll all smothered in satin and lace. I cannot believe I ever had to wear this frippery, but traditions must be adhered to. Yes, that is the way of life, my son, lesson number two after the revelation is that clothing is generally uncomfortable." He nibbled on Alexander's neck, whose slow crying was replaced with baby giggles.

"I am sure you were equally adorable in this gown, although you would have filled it out better, since you weighed nearly two pounds heavier than Alexander at birth. Your poor mother."

The christening gown currently disturbing Alexander had been sewn by Anne Darcy during her first pregnancy, expressly to be worn by the Heir to Pemberley. When that first child had ended up being a girl, Alexandria, she had instead been christened in the gown worn by her mother, the far more elaborate gown packed away until Fitzwilliam was christened.

Initially, Lizzy had imagined sewing a gown as well, but the plain reality was that she was not very skilled with a needle, especially when dealing with fragile fabrics. While in London she had examined several readymade garments, considered purchasing one that she liked, but was too embarrassed to do so. Darcy would laugh at her later when she finally confessed that she was ashamed to admit her deficiency to him. As sentimental as Darcy tended to be in many respects, he honestly could care less what his child wore during the baptism ceremony. It was only upon one of his excursions through the stacks of boxes stored in the attic that the resolution presented itself: the gown worn by him and sewn by his mother, discovered among the stacked boxes of memorabilia.

"Finished!" Lizzy gently patted the silver cross lying square on Alexander's chest. "He is perfect."

"Yes, he is."

Alexander was finally succumbing to the draw of infant slumber, allowing the donning of bonnet and pendant to proceed with minimal pique. He was resplendent. Wispy chestnut curls escaped the lacy edges of the bonnet, framing his round face and accenting the alabaster fairness of his skin. Pudgy body encased in flowing white lace and satin with the train extending well beyond his leather slippered feet and cascading over the side of the dresser. Darcy had jokily added a daub of his cologne, declaring that Alexander needed a dose of manliness to augment the bold pendant in counteracting the frilly gown.

"Are we ready then?" Mrs. Hanford asked. She held the blanket, a thick one of bleached spun wool trimmed with lace and ribbon.

Lizzy nodded. Darcy lifted his sleeping son carefully so as not to startle, while Lizzy assisted with arranging the gown. The trio of adults, all dressed in fine garments for the momentous event, gingerly made their way to the main parlor where their friends and family awaited. Everyone was there dressed in his or her Sunday best: Lord and Lady Matlock with Lady Montgomery and the Fitzwilliams, all four of the Vernors, the Hugheses, the entire Bennet clan and Mr. Daniels, the Gardiners, Colonel Fitzwilliam and Dr. Darcy, the three Bingleys and two Hursts, the senior staff members, and Georgiana.

Quiet conversation drifted as all eagerly waited. A hush descended as the Darcys appeared on the threshold. Darcy wore a broad grin, happiness ebullient as he crossed to the three godparents.

"This is it. Are you ready?" His answer was a trio of radiant smiles and affirmative nods in concert.

CHAPTER EIGHT

Christening

A S LIZZY HAD NOTED upon rising that morning, the sun was blazing in a brilliant cobalt, cloudless sky, bathing the earth in eye piercing sparkles reflecting off the banks of snow. Yet, despite the reality of a fierce sun, the air was only a few degrees above freezing. The faint rays of warmth able to radiate through the chill succeeded in melting the layered frozen flakes enough to edge the chapel's eaves with glistening spikes of twisted icicles and provide background sounds of muffled drips from snow-laden trees.

Bundled to his eyeballs, as promised by a protective father, Alexander was rosy-cheeked and red-nosed, but otherwise unfazed by his first excursion abroad. He slept through the entire short jaunt to the church, nestled in Darcy's arms with Lizzy incessantly retucking the tightly wrapped blankets, only blinking and stretching briefly upon alighting from the carriage. Reverend Bertram assured that the wide drive and stone pathways leading to Pemberley's quaint house of worship were scoured clean of every speck of ice. This allowed not only for safe passage, but also for an accumulated crowd of local citizens craning for a second glimpse of the young Master.

Darcy undertook this event with the utmost seriousness. If there was one aspect of his existence he understood deep into the core of his being, it was the significance of this moment and the obligatory protocol associated. He was not about to allow several dozen people to touch or breath on his newborn son, nor subject him to the atmospheric elements for longer than absolutely necessary. So he turned to offer a hand to his wife, lent an arm to her dainty gloved hand, and imperiously walked into the brightly candlelit interior with nary a glance to either side. It was left to Mrs. Darcy to extend kind smiles to the onlookers.

The front pews were reserved for the Darcy family and friends, some of whom were already seated. Reverend Bertram greeted from the inner narthex, bowing properly at the Darcys and exchanging a short whispered conversation. His estimation that the modest chapel would be bursting at the seams with attendees proved to be inaccurate, but the seats were filled to a capacity not seen in many a year. Darcy submerged his emotions behind a composed façade, but he was profoundly moved by the devotion expressed in their participation.

A hush fell over the previously talkative assembly as Mr. and Mrs. Darcy carried their son to the designated bench in the front row. The sanctuary was pleasantly warm due to the combined effects of thick stonewalls, a mass of bodies, and the four braziers burning coal in each corner. Lizzy gently worked to remove the woolen blankets, revealing Alexander in all his lacy satin glory. A ripple of whispered awe ran through the congregants. Lizzy and Darcy shared a private smile and loving glance, hearts swelling with immeasurable pride and happiness.

Resplendent in his formal vestments, black cassock covered by a delicate white surplice and accented with a stunning cross of gold and green satin stole, Reverend Bertram stood in regal command behind the pulpit. The kindly face of the grey haired elderly gentleman shone upon each person equally, caring eyes touching every face. He signaled his wife, who sat at the five-year-old pianoforte which was a gift from their patron when the prior one grew impossible to tune adequately, and she applied competent fingertips to the ivory keys for the initial bars of "Come, and Let Us Sweetly Join" by Charles Wesley as the white robed choir entered to stand in their designated location.

Alexander's eyes opened as the first voices rose in song. With the serious expression typical of the weeks old infant, he gazed up at his father, who was concentrating on the choir, and quietly settled in to listen to the disembodied singing and cadenced music as it lifted, harmonized, and swirled about the chamber.

The good reverend had long ago learned the necessity of keeping the introductory worship as short as feasible in hopes that infantile fortitude would persevere throughout the ritual itself. Even at that, there had been many a child whose wails nearly drowned out the verbalized blessings well before the assault with tepid water to a delicate forehead. Thus it was that as soon as the final strains of echoing music died, he lifted his hands and requested the congregation join him in prayer.

With bowed head, Darcy listened to the invocation while smiling at the blue-eyed stare fixed on his face. One chubby hand was wrapped around his thumb, and it was no surprise when Lizzy's soft hand crept over, fingers lacing and simultaneously caressing both husband and son.

"Gentlemen and ladies of Pemberley Parish, welcome to this first Sunday of the year of our Lord eighteen hundred eighteen. Every day and every year granted to us by the gracious Hand of our merciful God is to be treasured and accepted as a gift. Nonetheless, there are certain days, certain years, and certain events that are marked as momentous. Supreme over all human celebrations are those that exalt our awesome Father, sacrificial Savior, and renewing Spirit. Yet, in the process of uplifting our hearts and minds in honoring and commemorating human occurrences, we are also reminded of the grace and mercy of the Creator of all. Today is such a day."

Reverend Bertram paused, eyes sweeping the assembly and resting lastly on the Darcys. He smiled, continuing in his ringing voice, "Of all the miracles we daily witness, second to the reawakening of a lost soul finding Christ is the miracle of a new life created in the union between two who love and are joined in the Holy State of Matrimony. Today, this Fourth day of January, we gather here in God's sanctified House to welcome a new life. Further, it is our joy and honor to perform the sacred ritual that will set this innocent babe, born into sin and darkness, upon the true path of Light and forgiveness.

"The Christening Sacrament, baptizing a soul in need of redemption, serves numerous functions. It is a welcoming of the child into the family, community, church, and the world. It is a formal blessing of the child, just as Jesus blessed the children in Mark chapter ten, verses thirteen to sixteen. It is a celebration of the life given, a life that is treasured and loved, a way to publicly thank God for this transcendent joy. It is to dedicate the child to God, vowing to raise him in the tenets of Christian faith. It is to purify by the washing of water, symbolically cleansing of the stain of Original Sin and imparting rebirth through Christ and the power of the Holy Spirit. It is a time of formal naming and presentation of the reborn Child of Christ to God and the parish community.

"All of these functions are willingly and wholeheartedly entered into today by Mr. and Mrs. Fitzwilliam Darcy. With unification of purpose and free submission to God, they bring their first-born child, a son, before us now to receive the Sacrament. Mr. and Mrs. Darcy, if you will join me here with the godparents as well?"

Darcy rose, heart surging with joy. Glancing to his misty-eyed wife, he fleetingly envied the societal custom that said it was acceptable for women to shed tears but not men! The five of them, with Alexander quietly awake from the comfortable position nestled against his papa's solid chest, gathered next to Reverend Bertram on the elevated chancel where he now stood beside the baptismal font.

Darcy stared into the beaming faces of each godparent, one by one meeting their eyes to convey an unspoken message of thankfulness and abiding affection. Jane Bingley, serene and beautiful in a pale yellow gown, golden locks shimmering in innumerable curls upon her head, cerulean blue eyes shining and brimming with steady love. Charles Bingley, stately in a tailored suit of brown, red hair gleaming in the sunrays through the high windows, eyes wide with lingering traces of amazement, but tender with eternal friendship. And lastly, George Darcy, resplendent in a modern suit of vivid blue with long fitted trousers and waistcoat of cream velvet, brown curls lying impishly over a high noble brow, dimpled and toothy grin extending to identical Darcy blue eyes with fathomless depths of compassion, twinkles of humor, and profound familial devotion.

Darcy and Lizzy turned their attention to Reverend Bertram, confident in the certain knowledge that Alexander was to be perpetually surrounded by the best of souls.

Reverend Bertram's elderly but trained speaking voice rang out, easily reaching to the farthest ear and readily commanding the attention of the vigilant flock. "Loving parents, family, and friends, you have come to witness the dedication of this blessed child to God. Realizing that this baby is special because by his birthright he is a Child of God."

He turned to Darcy and Lizzy. "Mr. and Mrs. Darcy, your gift of love for each other made this child possible, and your guidance, wisdom, and love assures the happiness of this new life. May you remember to listen with your heart to the indwelling Christ as you nurture, love, and watch this loving Child of God grow into his divinely inspired potential. Do you receive this child as a gift from God?"

In a clear voice they both responded, "Yes, we do."

"Do you wish to give thanks to God and receive His blessing?"

"Yes, we do."

"Then let us pray. God our Creator, we thank you for the wonder and miracle of new life and for the mystery of human love. We thank you that we are known to you by name and loved by you from eternity past. We thank you for Jesus Christ who has shown us the way of love. Bless these parents that they may cherish their child. Make them wise, patient, and understanding to help him grow as he ought. Surround this family with the light of your truth and the warmth of your love. We praise you Father, Son, and Holy Ghost. Amen."

"Blessed be God forever," the entire assembly intoned.

"What name have you given to this child?"

"Alexander William George Bennet Darcy," carefully articulated in ringing tones by a proud father.

"Who stands with you as persons of testified faith to offer their willing services as support in bringing Alexander to a conscious knowledge of Christ at the earliest possible age?"

Each godparent answered by stating their names, Reverend Bertram then asking, "Do you vow to withhold the tenets of your faith, set an example of Christian life and behavior, do all within your power to maintain a lasting relationship with Alexander and the Darcys, and be a support to them in the fulfillment of their vows until such time as God releases you when called home to Him?"

"I do."

"I do."

"I do."

Lizzy was furtively dabbing at her teary eyes. She was afraid to look at Darcy, who she felt standing stiffly beside her; one glance at what she knew for certain was his patented rigid expression when overcome would surely send her over the emotional edge. She was correct, of course, as Darcy's jaws were beginning to hurt from the tight grip he forced upon each muscle and bone. Alexander, in contrast, had accidentally wrapped his fingers around the ties to his bonnet and was happily ignoring all the drama about him in the delightful contemplation of flapping lace.

In fact, he was noticeably more disturbed by the sudden interruption to his play when passed from the familiar location next to the strongly beating heart of his father into the strange arms of another man than by anything that had transpired thus far. The surprising motion caused his arms to flail and partially lose their clasp on the entertaining ribbons, and then to make matters worse, his mother leaned over and removed the bonnet entirely! The indignity and annoyance of it all was almost too much to bear and his face screwed up in preparation to vocalize his opinion on the subject.

Fortunately, Darcy could read his son's thoughts quite well and placed a firm hand onto his chest, leaning slightly to hush placatingly and capture Alexander's gaze before it was too late. His timing was impeccable, Alexander calmed and distracted by the beloved face and voice.

Reverend Bertram chuckled, beaming upon the assembly. "Father to the rescue! Thank you Mr. Darcy for saving me from the arduous task of raising my age-crusted voice above the din!"

Darcy bowed slightly with a soft smile as the crowd rippled with quiet laughter. Reverend Bertram stepped behind the venerable baptismal font, a thick pedestal of white marble with curved inlaid strips of black marble and beaten copper between the four sides richly carved with images of Jesus blessing the little children. On top sat a bowl of intricately scrolled sterling silver, very old with aged tarnish spots impervious to the diligent efforts of numerous Pemberley servants on down through the centuries. This bowl served one purpose only: to hold the blessed water for christening Darcy children. Last used for Georgiana, the bowl had nonetheless been polished regularly and stored safely awaiting this very day.

Now Alexander's head of massed brown curls dangled over the water-filled bowl as Reverend Bertram plunged his hand into the tepid liquid and said, "Alexander William George Bennet Darcy, I baptize thee in the Name of the Father and the Son and the Holy Spirit."

Alexander blinked and flinched in surprise at the sensation of water poured onto his head, but remained peacefully gazing into the rector's face. Lizzy squeezed Darcy's arm, impulsively laying her head onto his shoulder while he blinked so furiously as to be unaware of anything but his own struggles to retain control.

Dipping into the small chalice of oil, Reverend Bertram anointed the babe's forehead with the shape of a cross, speaking clearly, "I sign thee, Alexander, with the cross; the sign of Christ and His Church."

Mrs. Bertram approached, handing a lighted candle to Darcy, Lizzy, and each godparent, while the Reverend completed the sacrament, "Shine as a light in the world to fight against sin and the devil." Rotating and lifting Alexander so all could easily see his face, he finished in a booming voice, "Congregants, I present to you Alexander Darcy!"

A cheer went up, claps resounded, and shouts of *Alleluia* burst forth, as Mrs. Bertram and the choir added to the clamor with a rousing hymn. The noise was the final straw for Alexander who broke into serious cries just as Darcy hastily handed his candle to Lizzy and reached to rescue the upset infant from the Reverend's arms.

After the service, a relieved and ebullient Darcy gladly welcomed the congratulations of the citizens, his jovial smile a sharp contrast to the somber man who had entered the chapel. For some reason that he could not properly identify, he felt as if a weight was lifted. In a perhaps illogical rationale, it was as if Alexander was more real now, permanent and protected in a way he had not quite been before. The final crescendo was the formal entry into the parish registry of Alexander's full name, birth date, parents' names, and father's listed occupation as Master of Pemberley. A gathering of family and friends observed the procedure, Darcy applying quill to parchment page with studious intensity and writing each letter in his firm hand with precise penmanship. Legibility for centuries to come would not be an issue.

He turned with a broad grin, the last vestiges of proper reserve erased momentarily at the sea of shining faces. George clapped him on the shoulder, glancing at the register and nodding.

"Excellently done, William! All spelled correctly too. Amazing." Darcy merely grinned wider.

The intended quiet, intimate luncheon was anything but. True to Lizzy's speculation, Mrs. Langton and the entire staff had ignored any urgings of the Mistress and thus presented a meal of stupendous proportions. The already elaborate holiday decorations were enhanced, the table dazzling with candles and ribbons in abundance, and the christening cake a masterpiece of exquisite artwork. The "cake" was actually three cakes stacked, each one less in diameter to the one below and of a variant flavor and custard filling, but equally thick. It was covered in creamy white frosting, pearls, and cascading flowers in multiple colors. The enormous concoction stood nearly three-feet high and required a table all by itself.

George presented the Bingleys with a gift identical to what he proudly displayed on his lapel: a triangular shaped pin of gold with the etched relief of a cherub in one corner and the words, "Alexander's Godparent" scrolled below. This one item would be a topic of amused conversation for the bulk of the evening.

The humble gathering visualized evolved into a full-scale fête. Lizzy received numerous praises for the lavish affair and was too embarrassed to confess that she had little to do with it. The guest of honor made a brief appearance, dressed in a lovely but practical gown and staring with wide-eyed intensity from the security of his mother's arms.

Georgiana and Mary played a duet on the pianoforte, voices raised in harmony with Kitty in a lyric paean to Alexander. The lyrics were a compilation of poems and nursery rhymes placed to music written by Georgiana. It was an excellent cap to the afternoon.

The guests said their adieus as the sun sat low on the horizon, darkness and icy roads not conducive to staying any later. By nightfall the Vernors, Sitwells, Hugheses, and Lord and Lady Matlock were safely ensconced in their own Manors, leaving the Darcys, Bennets, Gardiners, and Mr. Daniels to lazy and sedate companionship until bedtime.

Darcy joined his wife in the nursery, relieved to have removed his formal attire and anxious to devote attention to wife and son. Although they had carefully shielded Alexander from the festivities, he seemed unusually weary; not even nursing as well as typical and falling asleep at Lizzy's breast rather than on Darcy's shoulder as was his norm.

Darcy noted the concern on Lizzy's face. "He has had a busy day, that's all. There is no fever and his color is unchanged." He kissed the tiny forehead nestled under his chin. "Tomorrow he will wake frequently demanding your attention to make up."

Lizzy chuckled, smoothing the blanket tight over his body. "Most likely that is true. I know I am exhausted by the day's events so can commiserate." She leaned onto her husband's arm, yawning hugely. "I can hardly keep my eyes open! One of these days I am going to fall asleep while rocking him and he will tumble to the floor, I just know it! Perhaps this comfortable chair was not such a wise idea."

Darcy laughed, rising and extending a hand. "I have no fear that you will ever drop our son. Come, dearest, there is one last ritual we must attend before I can tuck you both into bed. Grab that candelabrum."

Lizzy raised a quizzical brow, but he merely smiled and wiggled his fingers, so she took the proffered hand and lit candelabrum without a word. Darcy led out of the warm chambers into the chill of the hall. As always, spaced lamps were lit so safe navigation was not an issue. Unerringly, he led them down the staircase, along the silent second floor hallways to the Grand Staircase, and down again to the massive foyer.

Slippered and bare feet made no sound on the marble expanse as they crossed to the blue tapestry. Darcy pointed, voice hushed but throbbing with emotion, "Look there."

"Oh!" Lizzy covered her mouth as tears sprung.

Darcy cautiously readjusted the inert body of his son until he was facing the woolen veiled wall and stepped closer. "Alexander Darcy, our son. There you are, my wee love, forever a part of a noble heritage," he whispered, fingertip tracing the embroidered rendering of Alexander's name and birth date. Lizzy's fingertip followed, tears freely spilling down her cheeks but chin lifted with immeasurable pride.

They stood for several minutes, Alexander sleeping on and unaware of the importance. Darcy, like his uncle and every Darcy child before, had spent hours examining these tapestries, often considering them the bane of his existence. Only with maturity did the true significance of family and ancestry dawn. He chuckled now in remembrance, Lizzy glancing into his amused visage.

"What is so funny?"

"Currently, Alexander is innocently indifferent to the history unfolding here, and in years to come, he will grow to hate the convoluted connections and bizarre names. I can assure you from personal experience that it will probably not be until he stands here with his wife and child years hence that he will fully appreciate what is revealed on these walls."

"Perhaps. Nonetheless, it is a wonderful accomplishment and we can be proud for him."

Darcy nodded. Lizzy sat the candelabrum on the floor and encircled her spouse's waist, snuggling securely into his warmth and sturdiness as his free arm drew her tight. For a long while they remained gazing in silence until the cold of winter seeped into even Darcy's bones, only then retiring to their warm bedchamber.

CHAPTER NINE

Encourage Affection

Hold still, crazy little man, or soap will fly into your eyes! He is nearly outgrowing this tub. I believe more water ends up sloshed onto the floor than left in the basin." Darcy said as he handed his wife a soft bristled brush, returning to his seat well away from the splash zone.

Lizzy attacked Alexander's hair with a chuckle. "Indeed. I have come to consider the wisdom of simply taking him into the tub with me, since I end up practically soaked as it is. Be still, my sweet, or you will get soap in your eyes as Papa predicted. Ah, thank you, Mrs. Hanford."

Bathing the rambunctious infant was rapidly becoming a three-person job. Alexander loved the water, limbs thrashing in delight throughout, but more than once, Lizzy had lost her slippery grip only to have Alexander slide under the surface. Alexander did not seem to mind these mishaps and the fine castile soap was mild so he was unfazed.

The towel-covered stone tiles immediately before the nursery's Franklin style wood stove were nearly saturated by the time Darcy stepped in with warm, dry towels.

"Was that not tremendous fun, my lamb? How clean you are! You smell sweet enough to eat even without the coconut oil slathered onto your skin."

Afternoon playtime continued, Darcy thrilled to be a part of it. Too often he was tied up with work or entertaining, not able to leave and assist Lizzy with the bathing procedure. As with all afternoon bath times, this one ended with the babe at his mother's breast. Darcy sat beside Lizzy, gently caressing wife and son while joyously observing a healthy appetite illustrated.

"I thought we could bring him downstairs tomorrow since it shall just be the six of us. Your father has had scant time alone with his grandson," he said in a hushed voice.

"How thoughtful of you! He will be thrilled. I know he is saddened at the reality of their visit soon coming to an end. Of course it eases the separation, knowing that we will be traveling south next month." She sighed, leaning her head onto Darcy's shoulder. "I confess I am looking forward to the respite. Peace and quiet sounds blissful right about now. Even tomorrow evening is an anticipatory caesura from the hectic environment of late."

"You are not the least bit grieved to miss the Masque?"

"No. Oh, I would adore dancing with the handsomest man at the assembly, naturally. You, you understand?" She glanced up at his face with a playful lilt to her lips, Darcy merely smiling. "Yet all matters considered, I would much rather have you all to myself here, with Alexander. Besides, all the dancing over the past several days has quite exhausted me! I judge I can happily eschew the activity until the spring."

"What a pity," he whispered into her hair. "I was planning to ask for your favor once Alexander completed his meal. Hopes dashed once again!"

"Do not be so hasty, sir! A properly extended dance request from a worthy gentleman is rarely refused by an interested lady, no matter how weary she may be of the pursuit."

"So the challenge is for me to couch my appeal in flowery prose? Hmmm… Not quite sure I am up to the test."

"My soul weeps at the discovery of your pessimism, Mr. Darcy. I thought you brave and wholly stalwart, willing and able to face a contest head on. How disappointing."

He chuckled and then fell silent, kissing the crown of her head. Eventually Alexander was satiated, mouth slack with sticky drool inevitably staining his father's shoulder. From that point on, it was a simple matter of nestling him onto his round abdomen and tucking the blanket.

"Here, let me take care of that so Samuel will not scold you yet again." Lizzy approached with a wet cloth, attacking the milk spot with vigor while shaking her head. "Why do you not place the cloth over your shirt?"

"I cannot feel him as well then. It is a small price to pay for the sensation of his pliant warmth and breathing. Actually, I should just remove the shirt as I prefer his skin touching mine, but do not think it wise to appear so with Mrs. Hanford nearby." He chuckled, as did Lizzy still busily blotting the sullied linen. "Besides, Samuel has given up scolding, merely glaring and frowning with pursed lips."

"There. The wet spot is larger, but at least the milk is gone."

She turned toward her dressing room, intent on returning the wet cloth, but Darcy stayed her with a firm grasp. He tossed the cloth onto the floor, hands claiming both her dainty ones and placing them securely against his chest. His mien was utterly serious, blue eyes rapt and capturing her surprised gaze. Standing a proper distance but with a slight bow nearer her mesmerized face, he spoke in resonant oratory tones.

> "Come live with me and be my love,
> And we will all the pleasures prove,
> That valleys, groves, hills and fields,
> Woods or steepy mountains yields.
>
> "And we will sit upon the rocks,
> Seeing the shepherds feed their flocks
> By shallow rivers, to whose falls
> Melodious birds sing madrigals.
>
> "And I will make thee beds of roses,
> And a thousand fragrant posies,
> A cap of flowers and a kirtle
> Embroidered all with leaves of myrtle;
>
> "A gown made of the finest wool,
> Which from our pretty lambs we pull;
> Fair-lined slippers for the cold,
> With buckles of the purest gold;
>
> "A belt of straw and ivy buds,
> With coral clasps and amber studs;

And if these pleasures may thee move,
Come live with me and be my love.

"The shepherd swains shall dance and sing
For thy delight each May morning;
If these delights thy mind may move,
Then live with me and be my love.

"Dance with me, my lovely Elizabeth?" he finished in a bare whisper.

She rose on tiptoes, kissing sweetly and murmuring against his full, moist lips, "Quoting Marlowe will never lead to a refusal. Yes, I will dance with you, my love."

In their typical modified waltz pose, they began. Over time their amusement of private dancing had evolved, incorporating steps from numerous established dances with those created spontaneously as they swayed and glided about the room. The choreography changed from time to time, Darcy leading and Lizzy responding with flawless grace, adding her own twists and bodily gyrations as the emotions moved her. Neither pretended even for a second that the activity was anything other than an erotic precursor to astounding lovemaking. Yet, it was enjoyable in its own right, both of them being fond of dancing.

Boundaries of social decorum found in a ballroom setting were thrown aside. Caresses were intimate, bodies entwined, and kisses interspersed all while spinning, undulating, circling, weaving, and floating. They became increasingly daring, experimenting with sensual motions purely designed to arouse each other.

Today Darcy rose to her challenge, huskily whispering snippets of poetry as they danced. Usually it was Darcy who lost all restraint long before Lizzy, but today he seemed determined to drive her mad with desire. Never losing the faint humorous lilt upon his lush lips, voice especially sonorous, eyes lusty and trenchant, rhythm elegant and nimble, figure powerful and masculine, in all ways spiraling her sensibilities insanely.

Thus it was she who harshly pulled him into her where she leaned breathlessly against the bedpost. Frantic fingers attacked buttons while he loomed placidly before her. She feverishly removed impeding clothing while he feathered steady fingertips over her neck and exposed skin, mouth exhaling hotly breathed poetry onto a tingling scalp and sensitive ear.

"Your smile stops the minutes
 And as moments they dance in candlelight.
While your eyes whisper secrets,
My heart with wings takes flight.
In search for more of you to know,
Of why and what make you so,
Then mystery pleads her case
And once again I found your face.
There to know beauty true
And gentle winds of peace and love,
With eyes like jewels shining,
Looking to the One above.
And the moments which find life there
Become the brightest stars above,
Which live forever beautiful
In the sky of my heart's love."

Lizzy paused, having managed to bare the majority of their bodies, hands now stilled at his waist as she listened to the romantic words.

"I recognized Marlowe, Shakespeare, Lord Byron, and Keats. Who wrote the last one?" She withdrew, gazing upward into his glowing visage.

"Did you like it?"

"Very much. It was beautiful."

He smiled, bending closer and grazing along her cheek with his lips. "I wrote it for you, my heart's love."

"You wrote it?"

He chuckled, tickling her ear. "You sound shocked. I was once forcefully informed that only a fine, stout love is nourished by poetry. I do believe ours qualifies. Besides, Jane should not be the only Bennet daughter to have pretty verse written for her." He nibbled tiny bites across fragile collarbones, hands airily removing her thin chemise. "Has my ideal method of encouraging affection borne fruit?"

She nodded, moaning in response to stimulating fingers. "Indeed. As has my recommendation of dancing. You appear highly affectionate."

"Indeed," he rasped, claiming her mouth in an impassioned kiss while pressing harshly against her, his wide palms flattened on her bottom.

Unhurriedly they kissed, Darcy voracious, but in no rush to halt the pleasure found in her mouth. Until, that is, the rising appetite to taste the other delectable parts of her body overrode. Steadily moving lower, he assaulted her flesh, hands and mouth utilized effectively.

Lizzy truly thought she would faint. "Fitzwilliam!" she pleaded, not certain if she was begging for him to pause for a moment's respite or to hurry ere she perished from the aching need for him.

"Hold on," he commanded gruffly. Lizzy was momentarily too befuddled to understand what he meant, but clarity was provided seconds later. Lizzy gasped and reached to cling to the mahogany carved post above her head, abundantly thankful that her husband had a firm grip.

"William, please!"

Darcy rose, holding securely to her shivering body. Lizzy clutched onto his rigid muscles, hands weaving through his hair.

"Dancing and poetry," he said, his impassioned, rough voice casting jolts along sensitized nerves. "A lethal combination. I love you so desperately, my Lizzy!"

One short step to the left and they fell together onto the blanket chest at the end of their enormous bed, Darcy never relinquishing the hold on his wife. Subsequent words either of poetry or anything remotely coherent were forgotten. The only dancing hereon was the timeless dance of passionate lovemaking.

"Please hold still, Miss Bennet. I do not wish to prick you with the needle."

"Yes, be cautious, Kitty, or you will end up with a blood spot on your gown. Georgiana could hide such a flaw, but you may have difficulty!"

Lizzy laughed at Mary's quip, Kitty ignoring all of them as she continued to attempt craning for a glimpse of the trailing yards of organza bustled over her bottom. Madame du Loire knelt behind Kitty, needle and thread busily cinching the gathers along the waistline.

The modiste and her assistants were attending to the final alterations to Kitty and Georgiana's gowns, the annual Twelfth Night Masquerade Ball held by Sir Cole scheduled for that evening. Kitty had chosen an organza in pale turquoise, delicate lace edging the entire creation. Madame du Loire worked her magic, crafting a ball dress exquisite and stylish. It was far and away the most elegant gown Kitty had ever owned and her delight was uncontainable.

Fortunately, the couturier was experienced in dealing with fidgety young girls, managing the minute alterations without mishap.

Georgiana, in sharp contrast, stood nearby on a chair in a pose of serene passiveness. Far more accustomed to the ofttimes time-consuming task of painstaking tailoring, Georgiana gazed composedly into the tall mirror while the seamstress adjusted the hemline. Her gown was velvet in a vibrant maroon. The sleeves to both dresses were elbow length, modest in style generally speaking, except for daring necklines that displayed maturing décolletages.

Lizzy sat on the sofa beside Mary, Alexander asleep against her chest within a swaddle of purple and yellow Indian linen, eyeballing the figure of her newest sister with tremendous amusement. Her humor arose from the visualized expression she knew would cross her husband's face upon seeing his "baby" sister so attired. While Darcy plotted Georgiana's official introduction into Society come spring with businesslike precision, he nonetheless persisted in thinking of her as yet a child. Lizzy teased him for this paradoxical attitude, but he always looked at her with utter incomprehension. He had not quite figured out how to deal with the contradiction that a Georgiana of marriageable eighteen and a debutante was no longer the grubby faced youngster in his mind's eye.

"Mary dear, it is not yet too late to fashion a gown for you," Georgiana spoke softly at the reflected Mary sitting beside Lizzy. "Please reconsider!"

Mary lifted her chin stubbornly but did smile faintly at her dear friend. "Have we not exhausted this discussion, Georgiana? Balls hold no interest to me, which is fortuitous. A solicitor and his wife will likely receive few invitations to fancy dances, a fact that is abundantly pleasing to both Mr. Daniels and me."

Lizzy hid a smile into the top of Alexander's curly haired head. As news regarding the upcoming Masque became a prime topic of conversation, the inevitable subject of Mary and her betrothed attending was advanced. Lizzy vividly recollected the expression of utter horror that flew over Mr. Daniels's instantly pale face. He had snapped his eyes to Mary with such mute pleading that everyone in the room had collectively coughed to avoid laughter.

Gradually over the past weeks, the young man had relaxed his glaring discomfiture at being a guest in Mr. Darcy's home, the extended hours with his fiancée greatly easing the embarrassment. He had even loosened enough to join the family in several entertainments, including the manly pursuits partaken of each evening. Nevertheless, the concept of dressing the part of high society and attending a formal function was beyond endurance, and privately, he prayed for the days to pass speedily, fearful that at any moment his normally sober, rational fiancée would succumb to the female twittering and change her mind.

It did not help that hours were passed in the ballroom as Darcy, Richard, Charles, and George led the ladies in waltz lessons and dancing practice. Georgiana was fairly proficient, but neither Kitty nor Jane had ever attempted the waltz. In two short years, the scandalous dance of Vienna had spread like wildfire through England, even making an appearance at Almack's. Although generally frowned upon and denounced harshly by some commentators, it increasingly showed up at even remote village assembly halls. Per typical human nature, this antagonism only served to advance the popularity of the intimate dance. Also typical was the blind eye turned to all historical evidence regarding the acceptance and fame of far more sensational dances, such as the volta, by royalty past.

Mr. Daniels need not have worried, as Mary viewed the waltz as further indication of the steady slide into debauchery and sinfulness! She could not deny that the couples were graceful in how they glided about the room, but her cheeks flamed and lips pursed nonetheless. Georgiana and Kitty were oblivious, far too enamored with the entertainment. Jane's natural poise ensured her ability to adapt, but Kitty was unfamiliar with the stilted formality of a grand ball. Meryton Assembly country dancing was of a different character altogether, so studious attention was paid to teaching her the propriety demanded.

It was tremendous fun and was added to the entertainments utilized to wile away the hours between Christmas and Twelfth Night. The Matlocks and Bennets even joined the lessons upon occasion. In the comfortable environment of his own ballroom and surrounded by familiars, Darcy displayed his feline grace and dancing expertise. It was an eye-opener to most in the household, even those closest to him, as such fluency was a rare spectacle. Caroline was stupefied, her past dances with Mr. Darcy leaving her with the opinion that, for all his stellar qualities, the man had no balletic facility whatsoever! Lizzy delighted in the activity. Not since their impromptu dancing on the pier at Caister-on-Sea had the lovers embraced in rhythmic twirls and steps outside of their bedchamber. All the frivolity mollified Lizzy and Darcy in their mild sadness over not being able to attend this year's Masque.

The final session during the early afternoon of the fifth of January, the day of the Masque, was purely for enjoyment. The Matlocks, Gardiners, and

Bingleys had returned to their respective homes, the remaining Pemberley inhabitants eventually breaking from the light-hearted amusement to seek rest in preparation for a late night.

Georgiana gently grasped Richard's elbow as they exited the ballroom. "Cousin," she whispered, cheeks flushed as she eyed the retreating bodies nervously, exhaling in relief when none noted them hanging back. "I request a moment of your time."

Richard smiled. "Why so formal, Georgie?" He lifted her chin until meeting her gaze. "What disturbs you, little mouse?"

"Will you ever cease calling me that?"

"Probably not. What is it?"

"I… want to ask a favor of you… for tonight." Richard nodded encouragingly. "Will you stay close to me? Ensure I do not err in any way or make a fool of myself or do anything untoward?"

Richard frowned. "Why in the world would you think this possible, my dear? You are a proper lady, graceful and beautiful, decorous, a perfect Darcy in every way."

"That is precisely the point!" She flared, pacing away a couple of steps then turning to him with teary eyes. "I am a Darcy and as such the expectations are so high! People will be looking at me, judging, waiting for me to misstep. And if I do… I do not want to disappoint William or any of you."

He crossed the short distance, placing tender hands onto her shoulders. "Listen to me, dearest. Firstly, I am your guardian, a position I take quite seriously, as well as your cousin and friend. Of course I will be there for you, my sweet mouse. As will your uncles, Aunt Madeline, and the Bingleys. You will be amongst friends of Derbyshire. This is an excellent introduction for you and you will perform brilliantly, I know it! Do not fret so."

"But I do not know anyone else! I never made friends with other girls, except for Bertha Vernor and Amy Hughes. I wish I could be as frivolous as Kitty," she finished in a rueful tone.

Richard laughed. "As much as I admire Miss Kitty, you are not so blithe and should not wish to be other than who you are. Did you not relax and enjoy yourself at the dances in Wales? Father and mother said you loved it and were fabulous. They were proud of you and I know their recommendation is what swayed your overbearing brother's protectiveness into allowing your attendance at the Masque. You requested to attend with enthusiasm, or so I was informed."

"It seemed like a good idea at the time."

"It is a good idea. Georgiana, let me assure you that Derbyshire events, for all the outward pomp and circumstance, are not all that formalized. I have attended thousands of balls, cotillions, soirees, military receptions, and the rest. Trust me, Sir Cole's Masquerade is a relatively carefree extravaganza. You will have a marvelous time, I promise." He offered an arm, steering toward the door. "Besides, you will have that ridiculous mask to hide behind. Pretend you are an exotic lady of the orient, a world-traveling Princess deigning to mix with the mere mortals of this quaint Shire, imperiously granting your expert dancing capabilities to the country bumpkins with two left feet, bestowing precious smiles and prized witticisms uttered in dulcet tones to the fortunate, flirting outrageously with fluttering fan and batting eyelashes as they swoon at your feet..."

And on it went down the corridor, with Georgiana's nervousness mostly evaporating in the face of her cousin's nonsense.

⁓❦⁓

"Are we still waiting on the ladies?" George boomed, breezing through the open parlor doors, scanning the room, and quickly noting the absence of Kitty and Georgiana.

"Did you seriously expect them to be prepared prior to you?" Darcy inquired with a laugh. "You truly are innocent of a woman's ways."

"Humorous, Mr. Darcy." Lizzy sniffed. "George, you are supremely handsome in that outfit. I believe you and Richard will be competing for who is the most sought after bachelor."

George wore a formal sherwani in emerald green with elaborate gold embroidery covering the front—far more sedate than the majority of his outfits but impeccably tailored and exotic nonetheless. Richard, of course, was in full dress uniform, resplendent in red and white. Both men cut striking, if very different, figures. The gallant bows directed Lizzy's way in response to her compliment were identically flamboyant however, except for the crisp military heel click that Richard added compared to George's tip of an invisible hat. Darcy groaned dramatically, shaking his head.

"I must disagree with you slightly Lizzy," Mr. Bennet spoke with a grin from his casual stance near the fireplace. "As debonair as I am certain Dr. Darcy would be considered in most quarters, I do have it on good authority that nothing quite sets a female's heart to racing as a man in uniform. Watch your p's and q's, Colonel, or you may end the evening inadvertently engaged to a plethora of ladies."

"Thank you for the warning, Mr. Bennet. I shall be cautious."

"Perhaps I should advance the rumor that my garment is the official uniform of the Indian army. A man my age must resort to devious means and grasp onto any advantage possible."

"Do the Indians have an official army, Dr. Darcy?" Mr. Daniels asked in confusion.

"Only in Punjab, but do you imagine that most of the naive girls of Derbyshire know this?" He grinned lecherously.

"My uncle. Godfather to my son. I am so proud." Darcy declared dryly, the room erupting in laughter.

Voices and giggling interrupted further banter, a sudden flurry of colorful fabrics appearing at the wide double doorway. Mrs. Bennet led the pack, breathlessly fluttering in with voice raised over the din, "Oh how I wish I were young again! So marvelous, a Masque! Mr. Bennet! Look at our little Kitty. Is she not a vision of perfection? Wealthy suitors will be falling at her feet, I am sure of it!"

Katherine Bennet, nineteen years of age, rosy dimpled cheeks and sunny smile, was indeed a vision. The chosen turquoise gown was superbly fitted to accentuate her generous bosom and each voluptuous curve. Her hair was styled with a mass of curls held in check by a thin, jewel-encrusted tiara. Of all the Bennet girls Kitty most resembled her mother in both figure and character. Not overly intelligent, but with a sunny disposition and infectious smile that easily captivated men and women alike. Kitty would never lack for friends or suitors, although the acceptability of such acquaintances may be suspect, as Kitty did not possess a discerning nature. Like her mother, she had a tendency to blurt without thinking, to avoid any activity requiring extensive reasoning, to speak and laugh boisterously, and to ignore many of the finer nuances of etiquette and propriety. With maturity and positive outside influences some of the worst of these characteristics were tempering, but it seemed unlikely that Kitty would ever attain the level of grace and elegance that high society demanded. However, unlike her mother, she was rarely somber or distressed. All was gay and delightful to her. Georgiana Darcy, eighteen years of age, tall and slender, was equally a vision. Apropos for her stature and natural regality, the gown of thick maroon velvet lent an air of heightened prestige and maturity. The alterations of the past year were glaringly obvious to all who knew her, but never as forcefully as at this moment. Georgiana stood at five foot eight inches tall, figure svelte but with a curvaceousness that Lizzy only now in her maternal state had acquired. She was well proportioned with an ample bust line, delicate waist, long limbs, and sloping neck. Eyes slightly deeper blue than her brother's, hair golden blonde, features dainty, and skin fair combined for a vision of loveliness.

Lizzy kept her gaze directed toward her husband, transfixed by the play of emotions that crossed his face. Initially it was shock; eyes bulging mildly and mouth dropping at the notable womanly figure. This was followed by a deep flush with lips pressed tightly, eyebrow creases formed instantly, and the flash of irritation with clenched fists as she had expected. What surprised and moved her was the gradual transition from protective anger to what could only be described as mournful remembrance; vivid mental portraits of his beloved mother now manifested before his eyes in the body of his sister. Lastly was the abrupt lifted chin and proud cast to his face, as with a beaming smile he strode toward her.

Georgiana too had swung her gaze to her brother upon entering the room. As well as she knew him, the rigid control he maintained at all times outside the privacy of his innermost sanctuaries meant that even she could not always correctly interpret his thoughts. Tonight, however, the naked displays were evident and she silently responded to each expression. Embarrassment at his shocked perusal of her body; shame and fear at his anger; tears and trembling at his mute grief, knowing that she resembled her mother; and finally a feeling of relief.

He reached for her outstretched hands, enfolding warmly. Voice husky, he murmured, "Georgiana Darcy. How beautiful you are. When did you become a woman? If only Father and Mother could see you now. How proud they would be!"

"You are not displeased, Brother?"

"No, my dearest. Merely woeful that my innocent, pubescent sister has apparently disappeared. I have a terrible need to be relied upon and now it fully strikes me that this role is rapidly dissipating. My selfish heart may well suffer with the blow of losing you, baby sister."

Georgiana giggled, a decidedly unsophisticated sound. "I am only going to a ball, William. Tomorrow I shall be back for you to boss around and brood over."

"Where does this sharp tongue come from?" he asked with a laugh.

"Try to blame me if you must," George interjected, "or perhaps even your wife who has a sharp intellect and independent streak a mile wide, but actually she inherits the tendency from your mother. Anne was blessed with a piquant wit and James encouraged it. Neither ascribed to the idea of women as weak-minded vessels, thank God. Georgiana, you are radiant! Red is assuredly the color for you."

Both girls were swarmed under a barrage of gushing accolades; the men appropriately complimenting their beauty and the ladies fawning over each button and ribbon. In a scene reminiscent of last Twelfth Night, it was Darcy who assumed control and ushered the group toward the waiting carriage, well aware that the flattering could go on forever.

Darcy personally assisted Georgiana into the carriage with a farewell kiss to her fingers and proud smile. Then he turned to George and Richard waiting on the gravel drive. All humor was erased, eyes piercing as he flatly stated, "I am trusting you two to keep a diligent guard over my sisters. Do not let me down."

Richard nodded soberly. George squeezed his nephew's shoulder, his eyes equally serious but voice soft, "Have no fears, William. We will vigilantly protect with our lives if need be. The girls will only have joyful stories to tell, I promise."

Darcy searched their faces for a moment more, nodding once in satisfaction before rejoining Lizzy on the steps.

Kitty had badgered Georgiana into accenting with a mask, informed by Madame du Loire that the affectation was highly in style amongst the youthful singles this year for some unknown reason. Strangely, Georgiana had embraced the idea, displaying an unusual playful side at odds with her natural shyness. Obviously, Kitty's silliness was influencing Georgiana as much as her steadiness was influencing Kitty! No one was surprised when George whipped out a peacock mask, with authentic feathers. It was quite spectacular and worn with a panache truly breathtaking to behold.

Later that evening, the Darcys lounged in their darkened sitting room. Darcy sat furthest from the blazing fireplace with feet bare and robe gaping open to reveal unclothed legs and exposed chest, yet he actually felt sweaty. Darcy read the book propped on a small pillow while caressing Alexander, the sleeping baby's tiny body generating heat in droves. Darcy was bestowing occasional kisses to the curly head while absorbing the printed words of Goethe, the inconvenience in personal comfort well worth the joy.

Lizzy sat in an identical chair beside her husband with only a small table separating and less than three feet away from the fireplace. She wore Darcy's old robe belted securely and drawn taut, and burrowed her stocking clad feet between his warm soles on the ottoman.

Normally, Lizzy relaxed into these moments of domestic felicity as thoroughly as did her spouse, but not tonight. She glanced at his intently placid mien, simultaneously amazed and annoyed at his apparent lack of distraction. She too held a book in her hands, but could not focus on the words.

"What do you think the girls are doing now?" She asked suddenly, rupturing the tranquility.

Darcy looked to his wife with a raised brow, eyes glancing to the softly ticking longcase clock in the corner. "Well, let me see. It is nearly eleven, which means that dinner is completed, yet it is not time to crown the King and Queen, therefore dancing is the primary diversion. Consequently, they are most likely standing in an unobtrusive corner talking with a well selected collective of unsociable individuals, praying that the night will end as rapidly and painlessly as possible."

He turned with a shrug, Lizzy snorting and rolling her eyes. "Somehow I rather doubt that!"

"Then why did you ask me? I can only venture a guess based on personal experience, hence my answer. You would have a far better grasp on the possible activities, which, God help me, undoubtedly include flirting and dancing with lustful adolescent boys." He shuddered, Alexander startling faintly and releasing a gurgling sigh.

"More personal experience, Mr. Darcy?" She laughed at his flush, then also released a sigh and tossed the unread book onto the floor. "I wish I could observe them dazzling, and I am dying to hear all the details!" She slyly glanced at her smiling spouse. "And do not pretend you are not wishing you could be there as well, to intimidate those lustful boys if nothing else."

He shrugged again. "I trust Richard and Uncle George. They know I would skin them alive if any harm came to the girls. As for the details, there is no question we will hear all about it, especially you, who will surely be sequestered most of the day in your parlor reliving each second. Thankfully, I have a hunt planned so will only suffer the synopsis." He too put the book aside, neatly onto the table, holding Lizzy's gaze with a tender smile. "Perhaps I should relinquish our son to his cradle and engage you in an activity that will divert your attention away from useless pondering."

Lizzy grinned salaciously, eyes brightening, and ran one foot seductively along his bare leg to inner thigh. "Hmmm… What sort of activity, Mr. Darcy?"

Darcy burst out laughing, again startling Alexander who jerked and fluttered his eyelids, wiggled and rubbed his tiny face into his father's scratchy, hair-covered skin before capturing the first two fingers of his right hand and returning to slumber happily sucking. Darcy patted the infant's back placatingly, attempting to croon amid the escaping chuckles.

"You, my insatiable love, have a wicked mind! I was referring to a competition over the backgammon board, as your fangs always come out with that game. However, I suppose my direction could be altered if you so desire. I intend to stay awake until Watson informs me the celebrants have returned anyway."

Now he was grinning salaciously while Lizzy reddened slightly, but returned his smile. "Well, since we have until then I imagine we can do both. I have not properly trounced you in backgammon for weeks, so a humbling is in order." She jumped up, leaning over husband and baby and bestowing a chaste kiss to inviting lips. "I will put him to bed while you set up the board. Say your prayers, Mr. Darcy, as I fully intend to spank you until you beg for mercy."

Darcy grasped behind her neck, halting her mere inches away from his mouth. "Are we still talking about backgammon?"

But she did not answer, smirking instead with a lifted brow and tiny shrug.

The first three games were serious affairs. Darcy had discovered far back in his youth the horrid ill luck he possessed with dice and cards. It was a running jest for as long as he could remember and legendary amongst his peers. That is not to say he never prevailed in the rare game of chance or refused to partake altogether. Rory Sitwell, especially, was fond of gambling card games and Darcy had learned that even though he would likely eventually lose every last pence, the competition and male camaraderie could be moderately amusing. The main problem, aside from inherently being a man of financial sensibility, was that Darcy hated defeat.

Backgammon was a game that required a melding of both skill and luck at dice. Lizzy was blessed with an eerily magical talent for rolling doubles or the precise combination needed to either hit Darcy's checker and send it to the bar or keep her checkers together. Darcy seldom rolled doubles and was forever forced to separate his checkers into lone blots on a pip just waiting for his ruthless wife to knock them back. Lizzy was a fierce competitor, which Darcy loved, as he was also. His saving grace was a patience and tactical strategy that Lizzy lacked. Her swift, impulsive moves often proved her undoing. Although in the long run Darcy lost more often than he won, the victories were enough to sustain his interest and retard utter humiliation. Plus, he simply adored any entertainment undertaken with his wife.

Darcy surprisingly won the first game, barely. Lizzy won the second by a fair margin and the third was a slaughter with Darcy passing three rolls of his dice unable to release the two checkers captured on the middle bar. Lizzy gloated while setting up the board yet again, Darcy suddenly distracted by the fact that during the intensity of the past rounds, the old, voluminous robe had loosened and was now gaping open to reveal tantalizing glimpses of a succulent bosom. He opted not to point out the fact, praying fervently that she would remain ignorant as the game commenced.

For the first time in a long while, Darcy paid not the slightest attention to plotting and maneuvering. In fact, he barely noticed the fall of the dice, absently relocating from pip to pip before returning his rapt gaze to the ever increasing view of flesh before him. Lizzy's frown deepened as she studied the board with undisguised chagrin. Her husband was thwarting her every move, rolling the perfect combinations, and clearly on the road to annihilating her! With more than half her checkers still scattered about, Darcy rolled a shocking double six, taking his blood-deprived brain completely by surprise upon realizing that he had just won the game! He blinked several times, Lizzy releasing a snort of disgust as she fell back into her chair.

The abrupt movement and contact with the hard chair back caused her breasts to bounce delightfully above their stays, Lizzy flushing as she realized her entire front torso and one shoulder were exposed.

Darcy's gaze was instantly riveted, the final checker falling randomly onto the board. "Stop," he commanded when she reached to close the robe. In seconds he was beside her, Lizzy standing without thought, separating the robe completely and running warm hands around her waist toward the short corset's ties in back. He pulled her tightly into his body and bent to administer lazy licks to her breasts; his pleased wife encircled his broad shoulders and moaning faintly. Darcy skillfully released the undergarment, never halting the delicious and highly arousing oral attention given to each breast.

"Are we finished with backgammon then?" Lizzy whispered in a voice caught between breathless excitement and teasing sauciness, fingers tightly enmeshed in his thick brown hair.

Darcy's husky voice rose from the depths of her cleavage, words spaced as lips continued their assault, "I am now more than ready to cry for mercy while you spank or in any way choose to exert your superiority over me, Mrs. Darcy. I am utterly at your disposal and in your power."

"Careful what you wish for, my lover. I am very clever, remember?"

She tugged his head away, meeting darkly glittering orbs of blue before pulling in for a searing kiss, running forceful hands down his robe covered back until encountering a firm derriere.

Darcy's knees buckled slightly at her rough clench to his bottom, gasping for air as he withdrew an inch or so from her devastating lips while simultaneously crushing her lower body into his with a grinding writhe. "Lizzy! Unbelievable minx and temptress. Anything... anything you want of me and it is yours!"

She answered with a tender bite to his lower lip. "I only want you, Fitzwilliam. Take me to bed."

Darcy was no longer stupefied by the apparently bottomless depths of amorous arousal they both elicited in the other. He never took it for granted, but had gradually come to accept it as what was obviously a natural offshoot of their tremendous love. Perhaps in some small part of his psyche he sheltered an egotistical sliver of pride at his raging virility, but he gave the credit to her. The undeniable fact was that, although virtuous upon his marriage, Darcy was a functional man and never had he attained the levels of arousal, even when in the first blooms of manhood, that he did with Elizabeth.

Lizzy suffered no shock at her wantonness and was abundantly clear about how smug she was in the power to raise her husband's passion. She wasted no mental effort in analyzing their desire for each other, simply employing every tactic that occurred to her at any given moment to please him, which always worked and in turn massively pleased her.

Their lovemaking had assumed a life of its own, and tonight they entered a place caught blissfully between wild, animalistic fervor and playful teasing. They reached heavenly completion in unity, their bodies not once more than inches apart and hands constantly moving.

Still gasping, sight and clarity slowly restored as Lizzy stroked the rigid thigh lying alongside hers while his sweaty and shaking body adhered to her backside and crushed her into the soft mattress. Lizzy murmured into the pillow, "This is far better than dancing at a ball."

Darcy chuckled, breath tickling her ear and hoarse voice reverberating through her back. "No regrets, my lover?"

"Lord no! Only in that I must request you move as I cannot breathe."

He chuckled again, kissing softly to the luscious bend of her neck before complying. He rolled away from her back, but brought her with him, wide palms supporting full breasts and fingers teasing sensitive nipples. She allowed this erotic after-play for a moment and then turned in his arms.

"I love you, William."

"I love you, Elizabeth." He kissed her nose.

"Do you still intend to stay awake until they return? After expending this much energy, I find it difficult to believe you will manage it." She accentuated her tease with a well placed fondle, Darcy retrieving her gentle fingers with a heavenly sigh.

"You know me well, dearest. It will not be easy at all to hold you in my arms and not surrender to gratified slumber, but I want to make sure they arrive safely. The roads are slick in places." He embraced her tighter, nestling into the bed as they naturally assumed their customary positions with her head lying perfectly on his inner shoulder with body loosely draped over and molding to his.

She idly played with the damp hairs on his chest, sleep rapidly consuming her malleable flesh, contentment and sheer sexual gratification overflowing. "You are a good man." She yawned, snuggling even closer. "I fear you have expertly leeched every ounce of energy from my bones so I make no promise to wait with you."

"Do not try, love." He kissed her head. "Alexander will have you up soon enough. Sleep, my Lizzy."

CHAPTER TEN

Masquerade

T HE COLE FAMILY WAS a Derbyshire staple for nearly as long as the Darcys. Only slightly less wealthy and with acreage roughly three-fourths the size of Pemberley, the Coles were the second largest landowners of the region. As one of the foremost landed gentry for centuries, the Coles—even without Sir Walter Cole's honorary title gained as a reward for bravery during the Anglo-Dutch War of 1780—were a prestigious family and their home reflected their prominence. Not quite as grand as Pemberley, Melcourt Hall was nonetheless an imposing structure and currently extravagantly festooned and ablaze with light.

Caroline Bingley did not approach tonight's ball with the thinly veiled contempt felt at the Meryton assemblies. She had never resided at Pemberley during the winter season so had not attended one of Sir Cole's masquerades, but she knew the family's reputation as a distinguished one. Moreover, the opportunity to dazzle and further advance her fame was always grasped onto with vigor. One never knew what possibilities could arise at such an affair.

Kitty was innocently exuberant. The thought of dancing and being amid a festival atmosphere was enough to enthuse, and despite the caution impressed upon her over the past week as to proper society behavior, she was musing on little besides the potential fun to be had. Georgiana felt residuals of nervousness, but excitement had overtaken the jitters. Warm, encouraging smiles from Richard greatly calmed her fears. Jane Bingley, much like Lizzy the year before, felt the need to present herself in the most positive light feasible. Charles Bingley's residence was recent, but with the hope of constructing the foundation for a future in the community, this Derbyshire societal fête was step one in establishing those roots.

The annual masque truly was an event with a capital E. Peers of the realm and elite gentry from all over Derbyshire as well as a handful from nearby Cheshire, Nottinghamshire, and South Yorkshire attended. Hazardous weather often influenced the resultant luminaries, but never was the ball a failure. Thankfully, the climate over the past several days had mellowed somewhat, with no fresh snow falling and the skies fairly clear. It remained bitterly cold, but this fact inhibited no one from traveling nor affected the abundant display of female flesh in stylish gowns. Rather, it provided the excuse to don fine furs as an additional example of one's wealth and prestige.

Fashions alter during a year, both men's and women's. Hairstyles change, trendy accessories vary, topics of gossip fluctuate, dance techniques and music transform, entertainments differ, and even the privileged bon ton suffer vacillating membership. Certain traditions do persevere, however, and one was the apparent necessity for the youthful single ladies to collect strategically, so as to chatter about the latest happenings while unobtrusively observing the arrivals. Strict, unwritten codes of etiquette meant that the now married ladies who had contributed to the rumor mongering last year now stood with their peers. This in no way diminished the group, as there were always new additions to take their place. Thus a knot of glitteringly dressed and adorned debutantes on the prowl stood in several loose clusters about the foyer edges.

"Oh! Here comes Miss Vernor!" Miss Hattie Kennan declared. All eyes turned to the doorway with enthusiasm as the Vernors, older and younger, completed their greetings with the Coles. Miss Bertha broke away from her parents, smile brilliant and left hand extended as she dashed to meet her friends. Finally putting aside her acute disappointment and anguish over losing Mr. Darcy, Bertha had discovered a wealth of suitors clamoring for her attention. The past year had been quite a delightful one for the stunned young lady, and her maneuvering mother, as the prospective choices multiplied. Sadly for Mr. Bates and Mr. Sitwell, Bertha was not inclined toward either. Rather, she had immersed herself in the exhilarating amusement to be found with a myriad of beaus, waiting patiently for the right one. That place was eventually inhabited by the eminently worthy and deliciously handsome Baronet Niles Ramsey from Nottinghamshire, the engagement having been announced just last month.

"Dear Bertha!" Miss Astin Fairholm cried. "I have been dying to talk to you and see the ring! Look! Oh, how beautiful."

Congratulations and swooning persisted for quite some time, other friends meandering by to gush over the ring and her conquest. Miss Vernor was not the only newly affianced, Miss Ewell and Miss Irvine also receiving and accepting proposals in recent months. Of course, as exciting as secured engagements, and they most assuredly were since every last maiden there dreamed of little else, the discussions involved a glut of intriguing material with voices frequently colliding.

"My brother tells me that Lord Blaisdale is coming to the Masque," Miss Amy Hughes offered into the clamor, to the united gasp of each girl.

"Are you certain?"

"Here in Derbyshire?"

"You tease!"

"I think I shall faint!"

"Have you seen him?"

"Is he not yet in mourning?"

"Is he alone?"

The questions and exclamations surged forth, Miss Hughes flushing at the barrage of attention. This was truly momentous news, as she had known prior to breaking it, but the response quite took her breath away. It was several minutes before anyone gave her the chance to answer.

"He is reportedly a guest of Lord Mather for the Christmas holiday, thus invited to the Masque. No, I have not seen him. I do believe his sister is accompanying him, and their mourning is not officially over, but I am sure they will adhere to the proper customs."

John Clay-Powell, the Earl of Blaisdale, was one of hundreds of titled peers of the Realm known by name and reputation. No one could possibly list all of them. Certainly those ladies currently gathered at Melcourt Hall had no interest in the vast number of royalty, or non-royalty for that matter, who ran the country. It was a perhaps sad reality that immature females of society were abundantly fascinated by the trappings that wealth and prestige provided, but bored by how that wealth was acquired. Therefore, it was only those noble gentlemen of available status who piqued their interest. Lord Blaisdale was one such man.

New to his title and seat in the House of Lords as of eight months ago, Lord Blaisdale was a childless widower in his late thirties with an enormous estate in Staffordshire; a country home in Fife, Scotland; a townhouse in London; tremendous affluence and prominence; and considerable magnetism and attractiveness. If the murmurings of his womanizing, gambling, and borderline roguish behavior had reached their innocent ears, each young lady chose to ignore it. It was an accepted fact that a man in Lord Blaisdale's position needed only one thing: a wife. And nearly every girl there judged herself up to fulfilling that post.

Georgiana and Kitty alighted from the Darcy carriage with sparkling eyes darting everywhere at once in a vain attempt to absorb it all. Two years ago the fashionable ball gown choice had been white. Not so this year. Color abounded in every hue imaginable with elaborate masks prominently veiling many faces. No real attempt at disguise was intended, the embellishments an amusement. Strains of music filtered through the raised voices and laughter. Crowds of bodies occupied nearly every available space with the line of carriages without visible end. Not a single fireplace burned, a supplementary heat source unnecessary even on this chill night in early January.

Lord and Lady Matlock were found in the parlor, George and Richard gradually drifting to join them with numerous halts along the path to engage in conversation. It had been three years since Colonel Fitzwilliam had been able to attend the Masque, many of the Derbyshire residents having not seen him in years. Dr. Darcy was remembered by dozens of old friends and anxiously accosted by strangers who merely desired meeting the legendary, world traveling, eccentric Darcy.

Richard suffered a momentary panic when Georgiana, with Kitty in tow, was waylaid immediately after passing through the formal reception line by Miss Vernor and Miss Hughes. Cognizant of the promise he had made to his cousin, he fully intended to be a chaperone, of sorts; but it quickly became clear that she was managing fine. George kept one eye centered on his niece no matter where she and Kitty migrated.

The young ladies sincerely welcomed Miss Darcy into the fold, thrilled to have a new member and confident in the indisputable reality that she was of the highest class. Miss Bennet was welcomed equally without question, few even remembering in the sprightliness of the moment that she was of a lower class. As Darcy had predicted to Lizzy, these inconsequentials disintegrated in time.

This was especially true in what was, for all its glamour, nonetheless a country gathering far removed from the inherent snobbishness of a London society event.

The Bingleys arrived shortly thereafter. After long years of association with Darcy, Bingley was passably acquainted with several of the male citizens of Derbyshire. The short months of his and Jane's residence had not afforded them the opportunity to socialize too often except for a handful of dinner invitations with prominent families near Hasberry Hall and the village of Winster. Jane's exposure to the women of the region was limited to the aforementioned local couples and the friends of Lizzy, who had embraced her readily as Mrs. Darcy's sister, but also on her own merits. Gerald and Harriet Vernor greeted them effusively, including Caroline in the welcome, and each took a Bingley under their wing for the evening.

While the single ladies giggled and gossiped, the bachelors surveyed their prospective dance partners with glee. Naturally there were the older gentlemen who had mastered the giddy emotions of youth; they appraised from a respectable distance with outward indifference and generally tended to favor the slightly older unattached females who had also regulated their flightiness. Nonetheless, the groups of excitable single men grew with each passing year and were more than adequately numbered to squire the energized girls.

A barely discernable ripple passed through the company, a signal from who knew where, that the dancing was about to begin. Brothers sought sisters and vice versa, as a way to be properly introduced and initiate conversation with those of the opposite sex.

Georgiana, to her shocked delight, found herself amid a thick cluster of admirers. Her innocence and sheltered existence did not prepare her for the full impact of being a Darcy. As her brother had for years been the prime bull of Derbyshire, Georgiana was the prized heifer. This would have been the case regardless of her semblance, but, again like her brother, Georgiana's physical beauty heightened the attraction. There was not a man in the place unaffected by her presence.

"Brother," began Miss Hughes, "allow me to introduce Miss Darcy and Miss Bennet. This is my brother, Mr. Avery Hughes, and my cousin Mr. Tyndale." Bows and curtseys all around, Kitty dimpling flirtatiously and Georgiana shyly flushing.

"Mr. Hughes, it is a pleasure to see you again," Georgiana said. "How are you enjoying Cambridge?"

"Very much, Miss Darcy. Of course, I am rather obligated to respond positively or my father will chastise me for not embracing my studies."

Georgiana laughed. "Well, I do hope the sentiment is largely true. My brother speaks fondly of his time at University. Quite makes me jealous at times, in fact."

Mr. Tyndale interjected with a smile. "It is a pity females cannot attend, I believe. Certainly would liven up the occasional stuffiness of the atmosphere."

"Be careful what you say aloud, Mr. Tyndale," Miss Vera Stolesk declared with a flick of her folded fan. "Such scandalous talk has no place at a ball."

Mr. Tyndale bowed her direction. "Forgive me, madam. Permit me to beg your forgiveness by complimenting you on your ensemble. Lovely mask. I hardly recognized you until hearing your voice."

"Oh, posh Rydell! Quit flirting so outrageously. You have known Miss Stolesk since you were a baby!" It was his sister, Miss Hilary Tyndale teasing, the group laughing as Mr. Tyndale again bowed with a flourish.

"Miss Bennet, how are you enjoying Derbyshire?"

"It has been delightful, Mr. Blake, thank you. Primarily I have been visiting my sister and snowed in at Pemberley, but that has allotted me time to play with my nephew."

"You have unfortunately arrived at the worst time of the year for sightseeing."

"But at the perfect time to attend a Masque!" Kitty retorted with a giggle.

"Indeed, and most fortunate for us." This minor flattery was uttered quietly by a young man yet introduced: a tall, dark haired gentleman of twenty years standing silently at the edge of the group. He smiled, deep dimples flashing and several female knees instantly grew weak.

"Mr. Falke, you have an annoying habit of sneaking!" Miss Trent declared with a dramatic hand over her heart.

"I beg your pardon, Miss Trent. I did not wish to intrude unwarranted, but did wish to make the acquaintance of these two lovely ladies if at all possible." Georgiana blushed prettily, Kitty boldly flashing her own devastating dimples in his direction.

"Subtle, Mr. Falke," Miss Vernor laughed. "This is my dear friend Miss Georgiana Darcy and her sister-in-law Miss Katherine Bennet. Ladies, Mr. Anthony Falke of Haddison Manor in Chapel-en-le-Frith."

"That is in the High Peak District, Miss Bennet, which I am grieved to overhear you have not been so fortunate as to see."

"As am I, Mr. Falke. Luckily my sister, Mrs. Darcy, will be residing in Derbyshire for many years to come, so perhaps someday I will be fortunate enough to travel."

"Let us pray this is so." He smiled again, turning to Georgiana. "Miss Darcy, the pleasure to make your acquaintance is profound. My father speaks highly of Mr. Darcy. I have had the pleasure of meeting your esteemed brother on two occasions. My congratulations on the new addition to your family."

"Thank you, sir."

He turned again to Kitty. "Miss Bennet, may I have the honor of the first dance?"

"I do believe Miss Bennet has promised the first dance to me." A surprised Kitty glanced upward into the face of Colonel Fitzwilliam, her gloved hand automatically clasping the larger one offered. "She has promised me only one, however, so perhaps the second set will be gifted to you, Mr. Falke, if you ask so appropriately once again. Miss Bennet?"

She hesitated for another second, Richard gravely observing with only the hint of a smile.

"I will happily wait upon Miss Bennet's pleasure. As long as my name appears upon her dance card at least once I shall be satisfied."

Kitty gazed into Mr. Falke's undeterred eyes, her coquettish nature rising to the fore. "The second set is yours, Mr. Falke, if you wish it." He bowed gallantly, dimples making another brief appearance before moving away.

"Well, well! These evenings always start with a dazzle." George stood behind Georgiana, grinning as he extended one hand. "Miss Darcy, you promised to dance with your decrepit uncle first so as not to shame me later in the evening when my ancient brain can no longer recall the steps. Gentlemen, I regret I must steal my niece away. Shall give you all time to reconnoiter and plan further attacks. Draw straws amongst yourselves for the hand of the assembled ladies. Miss Vernor, Miss Hughes, quite charming. I am breathless in the sight of all this beauty." He bowed politely. "Miss Darcy, shall we?"

"Uncle," Georgiana whispered as they maneuvered toward the dance floor, "I have quite a good memory and am sure that neither Kitty nor I promised our dances! Is this a plot of my oppressive brother's to keep me from enjoying the company of other gentlemen?"

George laughed. "Not at all my dear! This is a scheme devised by the good Colonel and me with the opposite effect, which would likely aggravate your oppressive brother." She looked at him suspiciously. "You see, every eye will be on you and Miss Kitty. You are two of the surprises of the night. The mystery girls who have sparked the interest of every eligible male in the room. We are two of them, so understand how these emotions work. You are a Darcy, which instantly excites them, plus you are beautiful. Miss Kitty is an enigma, also beautiful, and the sister of Mrs. Darcy, who created such a wave last year. Now they will observe you with increased engrossment as you both glide so elegantly about the floor. By the time you reach the edges after this set, you will have every man engaging you. You, my sweet, and Miss Kitty will not sit down for the rest of the evening, I can assure you."

They took their places in line, Georgiana blushing adorably. George bowed, Richard doing the same toward Kitty from their location three couples away. The notes of the allemande began, the partners stepping to meet each other, as George continued, "Of course, this likely would have been the case without our interference, and so it was most probably a ploy concocted out of selfishness so that the Colonel and I could dance with two of the prettiest ladies in the house."

Georgiana laughed, a musical sound reaching the ears of many a spellbound lad standing nearby as George had presumed. "You, Uncle, are a tease and a fibber. I think this ploy was to heighten your own intrigue amongst the eligible women! You snared partners who could not refuse so that the scrutinizing ladies will see how debonair and graceful you two are. No one will refuse either of you from here on out!"

George grinned, laying one bony finger alongside his nose. "Entirely too clever for your own good, Miss Darcy. Since we now understand each other, let us show these people how it is done!"

Whether the tactic had any bearing whatsoever, who knows? Dancing partners were in abundance for all folks involved. George and Richard did sit out for a set or two as the night progressed. Kitty and Georgiana did not.

The arrival of Lord Blaisdale occurred while the girls were dancing the second set: Georgiana with Mr. Avery Hughes and Kitty with Mr. Falke. Therefore, they missed the spectacle.

The aristocratic trio consisting of Lord Mather; his betrothed, the Lady Sybil Clay-Powell; and her brother, Lord Blaisdale; entered the glittering foyer of Melcourt Hall without overt fanfare, but the clustered guests paused as surely as if a trumpet had sounded. Although Lord Mather as a near neighbor was the invited guest, there was no doubt in anyone's mind that the presence of the higher ranked and well-known Earl of Blaisdale was the star attraction.

Dressed in the sober black of mourning, the man was an imposing figure. Standing at an even six feet, burly built with a slight tendency toward heaviness, Lord Blaisdale had wholly inherited the traits of a Nordic ancestry. Thick hair so blonde as to be nearly white was worn long and tied with a ribbon in the back, narrow eyes a striking pale green spaced closely aside a broad nose, pale skin, high cheekbones, prominent eyebrow ridges, and full lips perpetually lifted with an expression of amusement or perhaps constant derision completed the picture of an icy northern origin. Yet the features combined beautifully, and to claim that he was merely handsome would be an understatement.

His sister was equally arresting. Not much shorter than her brother and every inch as Nordic in coloring and physical features, she was a beauty long sought after by dozens of suitors. Darcy knew her and had briefly considered her, but aside from the fact that she would likely not have returned the interest as his income was not up to the standards she desired, he found her to be cold and superior. Even then, always in fact, Darcy had sought a woman of passion and liveliness. Lady Sybil Clay-Powell did not possess those traits. It was Lord Mather who had finally won her hand, undoubtedly due to his supreme income and title. Unfortunately, the planned summer wedding had been postponed as a result of her father's death.

The three of them entered in a stately fashion, all dressed in colors of mourning. Rules of mourning were vague other than the requirement for sober colors and minimal decoration to garments, only nominal entertaining for a period of at least six months and up to two years in the case of widows, and public appearances only if vitally important. Conventions of grief were often put aside out of necessity, such as the widow or widower who needed to remarry due to income essentials or for the care of parentless children. Hasty remarriages and renewal of social engagements may have been frowned upon and gossiped about, but were generally overlooked if the cause was legitimate and decorum maintained.

Therefore, the appearance of the Clay-Powells, whose father had now been deceased for eight months, was not fodder even for a minor rumble except for those inevitable old-fashioned folks who relish finding fault with just about anything. The excitement in mingling with persons of such luminosity outweighed any vague feelings of improper behavior and the aloof trio quickly found themselves surrounded by dozens.

Caroline Bingley sat on a settee in a parlor located away from direct view of the foyer amid a group of women conversing quietly. She affected a pose of detached indifference, but sitting serenely with a cluster of married women was not precisely to her taste. Caroline may have had snobbery perfected as an art form, but she did enjoy dancing, friendly gossip, and witty repartee with handsome gentlemen.

Providentially, just as she was about to yawn from boredom, she noticed a trio of ladies known to her from London society crossing a far hallway heading toward the ballroom. With a murmured excuse to Jane, she stood and gracefully steered toward the direction taken by her friends.

It was a ghostly impression of being watched that caused her steps to pause and she glanced over her shoulder toward the foyer.

Her breath caught at the pair of vivid green eyes fixed upon her. Suddenly as if in a dream where the press of bodies disappeared into thin air, Caroline's only awareness was of the regal presence bearing down upon her.

"Miss Bingley, what an absolutely exquisite delight it is to see you here. I had no idea I would be blessed by the miracle of your presence, but I am thrilled beyond comprehension."

"Lord Blaisdale. Surely the pleasure is all mine."

He smiled, the gesture the merest lift to the corners of his mouth, and bowed slightly as he raised her fingers to his cool lips. "I assure you, that is not the truth."

His pale eyes boldly swept over her face, moving on brazenly to inventory the rest of her body. Caroline felt an unaccountable flare of heat rising, her mind both numb with shock and acutely aware.

She opened her mouth to speak, although words seemed to fail her. Fortunately for Caroline, the awkward encounter was interrupted.

"Caroline! What a wonder. We were hoping you were planning to attend!"

Lord Blaisdale released Caroline's hand, the flicker of anger that crossed his features gone as rapidly as it came. Caroline jerked, turning to the speaker, one of her friends, Miss Fay Cross, who not surprisingly was gazing intently and with hope at Lord Blaisdale, as were the other two young ladies in her wake.

Lord Blaisdale smoothly excused himself, leaving Caroline to deal with a fount of questions she was unwilling and unable to answer. Attempting to ignore the tingling sensation of being watched and the bizarre currents his gaze roused did not aid the restoration of her haughty tranquility.

The man unnerved her. He always had. It was a feeling that in and of itself was unsettling and actually made her angry. Caroline prided herself on being in control of her emotions and never ruffled.

She first met Lord Blaisdale, then the Viscount Monthorpe, at a dinner party in Town four seasons ago. He was married at the time, thus dismissed and invisible as far as Caroline was concerned. She had heard of the Clay-Powell family, naturally, their wealth and power too vast to be ignored, but with the only son wedded he simply was not a topic of interest to the socially grasping women of the ton. That he was handsome could not be denied, but her gaze was riveted on Mr. Darcy to the point of nearly excluding everyone else, especially an unavailable man. The only reason he entered her consciousness at all was due to the pointed stares directed her way all evening.

For the next two years, she would encounter him and his timid wife at various events. Always she felt his eyes upon her, examining as one would a fascinating piece of art with cryptic meanings discernible only to the artist. Whenever they happened to be at a function together, he inevitably incorporated into her group, welcomed wholeheartedly by everyone of course, and occupied her in direct conversation with his strange penetrating eyes. Caroline was not stupid and understood that he was intrigued by her. From anyone else, especially Mr. Darcy, she would have responded with perfected coquettishness. Instead, she was merely annoyed at his rudeness and impropriety in engaging her in unwanted conversations.

Only once did she chance upon him after his wife's death.

It was the middle of August in 1816, weeks before her hopes would come crashing down upon her head when Mr. Darcy proposed to Elizabeth Bennet. That horrid event was future, however, and Caroline was attending a symphony performance with her brother, sister and Mr. Hurst, and Mr. Darcy. The appearance of John Clay-Powell, the Viscount Monthorpe, less than three months after his wife's untimely demise was cause for a minor scandal. Talk rippled through the assembly, even the generally regulated and tight-lipped Mr. Darcy scowling and verbalizing his moral disgust. It was no great secret that the marriage between Lady Susanna Knowles and John Clay-Powell was one of social arrangement, but this was typical and no reason to ignore rules of decorum.

When Lord Monthorpe approached, Darcy's scorn was reserved but apparent nonetheless. Bingley was confused, having no idea why they were being addressed in the first place and not sure how to act under the strange circumstances; Mr. Hurst was partially inebriated as usual and Louisa embarrassed; but none of that truly mattered as Lord Monthorpe offered only brief greetings, focusing the longest on Caroline with a lingering kiss to her gloved knuckles and prolonged stare. Darcy's scowl deepened, not due to any affection for Miss Bingley, but some actions were simply not right no matter who was the recipient.

Caroline maintained her aloof demeanor, curtseying gracefully and ignoring the bewildering stirrings evoked by his bizarre intensity. Any attempt to understand the situation faded when Mr. Darcy urbanely stepped in with an offered arm, brusquely extending his condolences for Monthorpe's loss. It was a pointed reminder of impudent behavior that even a notorious rogue like the Viscount could not ignore. He bowed politely, departing the scene but clearly irritated by Darcy's interference. Caroline was left unsettled, as always when the Viscount gazed upon her so pointedly, but she rapidly disregarded the negative emotions in the rising hope over what she perceived as jealous interest from Mr. Darcy.

In the year since, Caroline had spared no thought for Lord Blaisdale. His name was uttered numerous times in gossipy circles, but no more than many other gentlemen of prestige and availability. Caroline's focus became firmly planted upon Sir Dandridge, the faint fluttering within her body elicited by his touch pleasant but governable. Now, within the space of a few minutes, after one brief touch and a searing look from a pair of green eyes, her insides were surging. Her world was again rocked, but rather than the previous displeasure, she discovered her mind spinning with possibility.

Kitty was having the time of her life. Always vivacious and naturally congenial, she readily made friends among those humble Derbyshire youth who accepted her regardless of her rumored low station. Naturally there were a number of haughty socialites who refused to acknowledge those beneath them, even if they did arrive with family connections of the highest caliber, but they in no way dampened the overall spirit of merriment. Besides, Kitty was blessed with a general naiveté and natural nescience to events beyond her immediate sphere.

Since dance partners clamored for her favor and pauses found her in the midst of lively clusters of young people, she had no reason to fret over murmurings from the imperious.

"What part of Hertfordshire do you dwell in, Miss Bennet?" Mr. Falke asked. His socially allotted two dance sets were passed, much to his annoyance, but that did not mean he could not converse with Kitty as much as possible.

"Our estate, Longbourn, is near Meryton, Mr. Falke."

"Oh! Meryton! We have passed through your quaint village many times on our way to my uncle's cottage!" Miss Vera Stolesk declared with enthusiasm. "You remember, Alicia, do you not?" She turned to her cousin, Lady Alicia Nash, laying a hand on her arm. "We paused there two summers ago to water the horses. When the bridle broke. Anyway, we visited this delightful confectionary to pass the time and enjoyed these gooseberry pastries that were simply to die for!"

"Yes, I do recall that. Oh, the pastries were divine."

"You must mean Mr. Janssen's shop. He is Dutch and creates true marvels. My mother is particularly fond of his treats, to Papa's dismay!" Kitty giggled at the understatement.

"Last summer we begged Father to stop, but he was anxious to reach our destination." Miss Stolesk continued. "I was quite cross about that and pouted as prettily as I could, but he would not be swayed!" Several laughs followed that statement, especially as Miss Stolesk demonstrated the adorable pout.

"I would surely never be able to deny you anything after such an expression, Miss Stolesk." Mr. Geoffrey Teddington offered with a florid bow, Miss Vera fluttering her lashes playfully.

"You must join us this summer, Miss Bennet." Lady Alicia stated firmly.

"Oh yes! You must!" Miss Stolesk emphatically agreed.

"Our family owns a country cottage north of Stevenage and we spend each summer there, after the season in London—days upon days of horseback riding, picnics by the river, strolls along the country lanes, and evening soirees. It is my favorite time of the year."

"Would it not be an inconvenience?" Kitty asked politely, vainly trying to keep the excitement from creeping into her voice.

Miss Stolesk waved her hand breezily with a shake of her head, Lady Alicia answering, "Gracious no! We have people in and out all summer long! Father goes for the shooting, declaring that the birds are far and away the best in

Hertfordshire." Her tone clearly indicating her disinterest in the subject while the young men all nodded sagely in agreement with Lord Nash's assessment. "Mother paints and grows orchids, an award winning member of the Orchid Society you see, while we frolic and amuse ourselves in any way possible. It is decided then!" She briskly declared with a clap of hands. "Miss Bennet will join us. If, that is, you believe your father will allow it?"

The truth was Kitty had no idea if Mr. Bennet would allow such an excursion, but she refused to face that horrid possibility. Smiles greeted her affirmative from numerous sources, several of the gentlemen already glowing with delight as the Earl of Stevenage's summer extravaganzas were famous and widely attended. The "cottage" humbly described by Lady Alicia was in point of fact an enormous manor rivaling Pemberley.

"Miss Darcy," Miss Vera Stolesk interjected, Georgiana startling and flushing instantly as a dozen set of eyes alit on her face. "You must join us as well. The more the merrier as they say!"

"Well, I..." she stammered, blush deepening, which the enchanted men thought endearing. "I cannot promise... my brother, well, he is... protective, to say the least."

Lady Alicia laughed, clicking her folded fan lightly onto Georgiana's hand. "Oh, yes! We all know the reputation of the formidable Mr. Darcy! I will talk to my father. He is quite persuasive and knows Mr. Darcy well. I am certain he can arrange it to my satisfaction." She sounded confident.

Mr. Falke chuckled. "Perhaps you should practice your pout, Lady Alicia, to ensure it has greater influence than Miss Stolesk's."

"I have no need to stoop to such devious tactics, Mr. Falke. I simply wait until he is enmeshed in a game of cards and he will absently grant me anything!"

They all laughed, Mr. Falke's dimples flashing as he bowed slightly. "Indeed, far more straightforward and honest."

The frivolous banter continued with plans laid for Derbyshire winter diversions and springtime London amusements until the orchestra signaled the beginning of the next set. Mr. Falke claimed Georgiana and Mr. Teddington escorted Kitty.

Colonel Fitzwilliam and Dr. Darcy honestly did strive to oversee the interactions of the flittering girls, but it was an assignment not always successful. Melcourt Hall was an enormous structure with a dozen of the main rooms open for the party. Crowds of bodies occupied every space and the flood of traffic was incessant with celebrants constantly on the move as they danced and socialized. Keeping track of two girls amid the ebb and flow of activity was extremely difficult. Add to those facts their own socializing and the truth was that the older gentlemen, for all their good intentions, lost track of their energetic relatives far more than they would ever confess to Darcy.

Fifty-four years is far from ancient, especially when one possesses a sparkling personality, limitless charm, extreme handsomeness, youthful vigor, and wealth. Dr. George Darcy was gifted with all these traits and many more so was thus a sought after guest from numerous quarters. Ladies were quite infatuated and flirty, which George shamelessly encouraged and relished. Unlike his nephew, George indulged in the joy of notoriety, jolly banter, and frivolous entertainment.

"Are there truly lions and tigers running wild in India, Dr. Darcy?"

"Indeed, Mrs. Longham. Majestic creatures. Exotic flora and fauna unseen here, although I am sure you have been so blessed to view wild animals from time to time in circuses?"

"Of course, but one imagines they are vastly differing in their natural habitats."

"This is true, madam. Unfortunately, the specimens displayed in such venues are generally weakened and domesticated to a degree. Certainly not allowed to interact and perform normally."

"I saw a lion tamer once with three ferocious beasts," Miss Carmichael breathlessly interjected. "It was terrifying! Their fangs and razor sharp claws!" She shuddered dramatically, fan fluttering. "Surely they could not be any more horrifying!"

"Quite the contrary, dear lady. Once, not but one year after arriving in Bombay while yet young and incredibly naïve, I traveled with another physician up the Ulhas River. We were on our way to a remote village in the jungles where a pestilence had erupted. It was my first extensive journey away from the immediate, more civilized regions around that great city, and you can imagine how enthusiastic I was. But also rather frightened, not that I would have confessed this to my wiser mentor and experienced native guides!"

His audience was spellbound, George's Darcy-inherited flair for the dramatic enhanced over the years by listening to the indigenous people's storytellers who had perfected the art form. His voice naturally assumed a slightly singsong rhythm with gestures and facial expressions adding emphasis and enlightenment. His choice of garment, handsome face mildly lined from years of harsh sun, and modulation of voice to a Hindu flavored accent augmented the effect. None of this was accidental on his part and he reveled in the attention.

"We sailed on a machwa. That is an open decked fishing vessel built by the natives, wide but offering no protection from the elements, you see, and sitting quite low in the water. The Indians use poles to propel the boat along with the currents, wind upon occasion aids movement, but this was in the hottest part of the year when breezes were rare. Ofttimes, we would creep along not much faster than a snail. I found it all so fascinating! Vegetation of a lushness and variety not seen here. Colors vivid, leaves appearing as if polished with fine lacquer. And the wildlife! Ah, teeming it is."

"Were there crocodiles?" Interrupted one wide-eyed woman.

"Indeed, madam! Enormous brutes, which thankfully prefer to hide along the shores under the shaded waters. There are other reptiles of stunning variety as well as birds vibrantly colored who mimic extraordinary sounds, insects of truly hideous sizes and shapes. It would be far too terrifying for me to elaborate further. Even I grow squeamish at the vision of the monstrous spiders and beetles." He shuddered, eyes closing momentarily as the women collectively shivered.

Resuming after a melodramatic pause, "I cannot fabricate nor embellish, so must truthfully confess that I did not espy the full complement of Indian creatures indigenous to the region upon this first trip. Over time, as I was there for some thirty years, I would become closely acquainted with the beasts both large and minute which inhabit the waters, jungles, and deserts. Ah, the stories I could tell! But we would be here all night listening to me drone on and that would not be entertaining in the least!"

Instantly several voices, both male and female, rushed to assure him that it was decidedly entertaining and none would wish to be elsewhere, *Oh absolutely not!* George humbly accepted the accolades, hesitantly resuming his tale upon the urging of an increasing fan club, twinkling eyes in sharp contrast to the meek tilt to his head. He described the verdant jungle, open grasslands, murky waters, insect-riddled air, and sultry atmosphere rife with alien odors so vividly that each listener was instantly transported to the foreign land.

"I sat on the edge of our machwa, bare feet dangling in the tepid waters, simply absorbing it all. Suddenly"—spoken with an abrupt tonal catch, causing everyone to jolt slightly—"my mentor, Dr. Ullas yelled, 'Dr. Darcy! Look quickly!' Naturally I obeyed, leaping up so rapidly that the boat swayed dangerously. Our driver scowled at me, but I ignored him because the sight before my eyes was riveting. There, roaming majestically over a mangrove-ringed valley covered with tall grasses was a group of leopards."

The *oohs* and *aahs* were intense. "What were they doing, Dr. Darcy?"

"That is the exciting part, Mrs. Allen. Leopards, like all the great cats, are shy creatures. They tend to hide in shady areas away from any traffic zones, stealthily lurking and gliding through the forests, nearly undetected in the thick underbrush or high within the tree branches. Of course, the river was not exactly a major thoroughfare, so we were invading their solitude. Unlike lions, who travel in large packs called prides, leopards prefer small clusters of three or four. Also, they generally are nocturnally active so what we witnessed, I came to realize in time, was extremely rare indeed."

Another infinitesimal caesura, the rapt audience holding their breath. "It was mating season, you see, and two males were in the throes of a serious dispute over an outstanding specimen of a feline female. All species on earth, so it appears, become incensed and foolishly aggressive when captured by an attractive lady." He flashed a dazzling smile and nod toward each captivated woman, blushes flaring prettily all around. "She paced imperiously, tail swishing while her suitors circled each other a time or two before engaging. It was brutal and noisy. Roars, fangs, and claws."

"Was there... blood?"

"Some, yes. All thoughts of medicinal treatments for the stricken villagers fled my mind, I daresay. Both leopards appeared evenly matched. Easily five feet long, not counting the tails, two hundred pounds with stocky bodies covered with gorgeous black spots on tannish brown fur. Incredible animals! Jaws squared and strong, teeth as needles, and a growling roar that sent shivers up my spine."

"Did they notice your boat? Were they angry?" Gasping with a hand to her mouth, Mrs. Longham whispered, "They did not... attack, did they?"

"Be still, dear lady. They were far too caught up in the moment to notice us. We glided silently and slowly past, for the first time truly grateful for the lack of breeze, as we were able to observe the entire spectacle. The fight itself was not lengthy, but intense with ferociousness and animalistic power. They did not seem to seriously be attempting to kill the other, but merely to display their prowess and superiority. They would stalk each other for a few moments, angry eyes locked with ears flattened on their massive heads. Then they would leap.

Several times they embraced in combat, the noises rising while the she-leopard observed her would-be mates. A particularly vicious swipe with half-foot-long claws across the nose of one effectively ended the battle. He slunk away while the victor wasted no time in approaching his harshly won mate."

"Was she impressed and amenable to the winner?" Mr. Longham asked.

"Apparently, she was quite impressed as they instantly attended to those activities I believe most species would consider a pleasurable reward for such valor and exhibited virility." He grinned widely, the ladies flushing and twittering as decorum demanded although it was clear that most were energized by his allusion.

While George Darcy charmed his way through every available and unavailable woman in the entire establishment, Colonel Fitzwilliam's heart was firmly planted in High Wycombe with Lady Simone Fotherby. George enchanted with a flamboyant cheekiness fully intended to sow the seeds for future socializing and romantic trysts if possible, whereas Richard congenially socialized for the sheer enjoyment factor. Bachelors of all ages were in abundance, but the son of Lord Matlock, a colonel in His Majesty's service, and a man of no mean attractiveness and wealth was a prime object of flirtatious advances in varying degrees. Simply put, the good Colonel was not in danger of boredom from lack of receptive dancing partners, but he might well have been in danger of bold female advances! Thus, he primarily visited with his oldest friends from childhood.

"After tonight's revelry I am not so certain a hunt scheduled for the morrow was a wise idea. Who thought of that anyway?" Gerald Vernor asked.

"Obviously the one man who is not here imbibing imprudently and is undoubtedly already sleeping!" Rory Sitwell answered with a laugh.

"Be cheered, Vernor. At least we are trekking through your lands, so you have that advantage over the rest of us."

"True, Colonel, but he has that fabulous long rifle. Gerald tells me he managed quite well with it, at targeting anyway." Mr. Henry Vernor gestured toward his son, who nodded affirmative.

"Yes, he did well, but you know Darcy. He can hit nearly anything. Almost as good as I am as annoying as that is to confess." Richard winced.

Lord Matlock spoke in his quiet tenor, "Did he reach four hundred yards?"

Richard shook his head. "Not quite. Probably 300, 325 would you say, Hughes?" Mr. Hughes nodded. "Fairly impressive for the first go around. Took a bit of sighting it in and compensating for the dimensions and weight, but

Darcy has a knack for firearms. Sitwell did quite well also," Richard concluded with a clap to his friend's shoulder.

Mr. Sitwell had a glow of heavenly rapture upon his face. "It was stupendous. Exquisite instrument! Well worth trudging through the snow from Reniswahl Hall. I may never have forgiven him if not invited. You really must shoot it, Lord Matlock."

"I shall be joining you tomorrow, if I can drag my old bones out of bed by noon. I will ask Darcy if I may try it out. Prove to you young bucks that the mature stag can aim true."

They all laughed, Mr. Gerald Vernor voicing their admiration, "We have no doubt of that, my Lord. My father can outshoot me any day of the week."

"And don't you forget it, my boy," Henry Vernor declared with an authoritative scowl leveled at his son, who flippantly saluted in return. Mr. Vernor the elder smiled and chuckled. "You may need to exert your familial clout, Lord Matlock, as I doubt Darcy will readily part with his weapon on this first hunt utilizing it. You know how serious he can be."

"Well there is the understatement of the century," Richard intoned under his breath, earning a humorous nudge from Albert Hughes and chuckle from Charles Bingley.

"Not a problem. One of the advantages of closely knit families is knowing things, you see. Blackmail, if all else fails, Mr. Vernor." Lord Matlock winked broadly, eliciting more laughter.

"When do you return to your regiment, Colonel Fitzwilliam?" Mr. George Fitzherbert asked.

"In two days. This is why the hunt was scheduled for tomorrow. So we can teasingly blame Darcy, but honestly it was due to me."

"At least it is for mid-afternoon, and if the weather remains fair, it should be tolerable. Worse come to worse we can always retire to Sanburl Hall sooner than expected where the fireplaces are ablaze and the brandy flows."

"Here! Here!" Several glasses lifted at that pleasant vision.

"How shocking. Thank goodness the womenfolk no longer solely rely on tough manly men to provide our sustenance or we would likely starve." They collectively turned at the words of Harriet Vernor who had arrived with the wives and a few hopeful singles as the strains of music recommenced for another set of dancing. "Afraid to be rained upon, my dear?" She smiled at her husband.

"Moisture is damaging to the mechanisms, Harriet," he answered dryly. "We would hate to see Darcy's fine weapon suffer. Think how upsetting that would be to Mrs. Darcy."

"Of course. Mr. Bingley, your lovely wife sent me to request your company on the terrace. She was in need of fresh air. Just through the music room there."

"Thank you, Mrs. Vernor. Excuse me."

"Is she well, Mrs. Vernor?"

"Merely with child, Colonel, as you would not quite comprehend... yet." Richard blushed and smiled before remembering to grimace as he normally would have.

Across the room a trio stood apart, one pair of vivid green eyes following the movements of a certain jewel-adorned, red-haired coiffure.

"John, you cannot be serious," Lady Sybil Clay-Powell uttered with disgust. "Her family's wealth is from trade, for heaven's sake!"

"All families make money from trade of some sort, Sybil, whether they acknowledge it or not. Besides, that was generations ago; her brother now is a landowner, and frankly I can do whatever I want. Who is going to shun me, for goodness sake?"

Lady Sybil released an indelicate sound, adequately voicing her contempt. "Be that as it may, I still do not comprehend the attraction you hold for her."

"Of course you do, my dear," Lord Mather interjected. "You simply choose to ignore it."

"What is it with you and red hair, John?" His sister asked with a sigh.

"Red haired women have fire, a passion hidden beneath waiting to be awoken. It is intoxicating!"

"So keep bedding your flaming-tressed harlots. Satisfy your lusts there. Why marry this one?"

"Because she fascinates me, Sybil. Always has. Besides, it is not just the hair, as you well know."

"So make her your mistress. You can conquer this fire you claim she has, have her whenever you want, and marry someone of your station."

Lord Blaisdale shook his head. "No, not now. Three years ago I considered it, although I do not think she would have agreed. Fire, Sybil, and a strong will. It is different now. Nothing hinders me. She is poised, beautiful, fashionable, highly accomplished, and socially acceptable. All traits for an excellent Lady Blaisdale. And, if I may remind you, I did marry as our parents and you judged worthy and look at what a disaster that was. Susanna was a timid mouse! Three months before I could consummate our marriage and it proceeded to be a struggle thereafter. Each time I felt as if I was assaulting her! Nine years to conceive and then she miscarried and died." He shook his head in remembered grief and repulsion.

"I will not argue the inadequacies of your late, lamented wife, John, but I do not think her failings had anything to do with hair color."

"Perhaps not, but I have yet to entertain a red-haired woman who was not passionate."

"The fact that they were mostly prostitutes may have something to do with that, Blaisdale," Lord Mather offered with a smirk.

Lord Blaisdale smiled at his friend, but shook his head. "Not all, as you well know, Mather. Nor do I only refer to bedroom activities. Passion extends into all areas of life."

"You men are disgusting."

"Save your false fastidiousness for mixed company, darling. I do not appreciate it otherwise." Lord Mather lifted Sybil's hand for a proper kiss, randy eyes engaging hers while the other hand stroked over her derriere.

"Good Lord I will be relieved to see you two married! I just pray you can keep up, Robert."

"Have no fear, Johnny. We are equals."

"Indeed, Sybil. This is precisely why you of all people should comprehend my desiring a union of equal passion. This may shock you, dear sister, but I am actually weary of brothels and chambermaids. And, be prepared for further amazement: I truly do want legitimate children. Little red-haired children who will try my patience, but keep my life lively."

"How can you be so certain she will provide an heir?"

"I cannot be certain unless I marry someone who has already procreated, and I refuse anyone else's seconds. Only a virgin will do, my own to awaken and possess."

"Surely you are not claiming to love her?"

"Do not be ridiculous! Love is for children and fools. I am talking about stability, perhaps even felicity, but with spice and entertainment."

"Then marry Lady Anne Hathers. She has red hair and an enormous dowry."

"As well as an enormous body and a face like a horse! Be serious, Sybil. Red hair alone is not enough to raise my desire."

"Perhaps Miss Evelyn Newton? She is quite lovely and from a distinguished family."

"And she is sixteen. A bit of maturity would be preferable and I do not find bedding a girl who could feasibly be my daughter appealing. And do not dare mention Miss Haskell or Lady Prudence Caraway." He shuddered. "Caroline Bingley is perfect and you know it. Stop arguing with me and just accept it. I will have her now that I am free and she is past her ridiculous infatuation with Darcy. That man is as cold as stone and never would have appreciated her anyway."

"You may have waited too long. I hear she is on quite friendly terms with Sir Wallace Dandridge. Practically engaged, so the tale goes."

Lord Blaisdale pivoted to his sister abruptly, face tight and eyes blazing. "Where did you hear this? Is there any truth to it?"

She shrugged, unmoved by his intensity and hint of anguished voice. "Just rumors at the moment. She spent weeks there this summer becoming acquainted. Perhaps he discovered and awoke this hidden passion you exult in."

"Sybil, I could strangle you right now. Luckily, I am familiar with Sir Dandridge and the man is a milksop, so I have no fear of him awakening anyone's passion as he likely possesses none of his own!"

"I believe that he is considered a gentleman by most definitions of the word," Lord Mather intoned with a grin.

"Well, good thing I do not hold to those restrictive definitions then."

"I pray you are right about her, Brother. She has never stuck me as particularly passionate. Rather cool and arrogant, far more than she has a right to be—disdainfully looking down that long nose at everyone, eyes calculating, and pose rigid. Cold fish, I fear."

Lord Mather laughed aloud. "You just described yourself, my love. I thought the same for years, until that day in the library, alone. Changed my opinion fast, did you not?" Lady Sybil smiled faintly, a coy glint from her green eyes as she glanced to her betrothed.

"You two are making me ill. You do give me an idea, however. Excuse me." Lord Blaisdale left his sister and best friend, walking purposefully toward the object of his interest.

Unlike Caroline, Lord Blaisdale had never forgotten the red-haired woman who fascinated him. His anger toward Darcy for interfering in what he had seen as a fortuitous opportunity to ingratiate himself with Miss Bingley was intense.

Additionally, it seemed quite clear to him at the time that Miss Bingley's overt stalking of the elusive Mr. Darcy had finally paid off. When the word reached his ears that Darcy was engaged to an unknown country girl, he was overwhelmed with personal trials, as his father was stricken with the wasting illness that would eventually claim his life. He did spare some occasional thought to the possibilities of seriously pursuing Miss Bingley, but fortune had not shined upon him. Until now.

His surprise at seeing Miss Bingley at the Cole's Masque was genuine. The Blaisdale estate lay far to the south in Staffordshire, near Cannock, whereas the Mather estate rested on the Derbyshire border east of Leek, hence why Lord Mather and his guests were invited. The life-altering developments of the past year had allotted scant time for the newly titled Lord Blaisdale to dwell on gossip. He had heard of Mr. Charles Bingley settling in Derbyshire, but had not consciously considered the whereabouts of Miss Bingley when urged by Lord Mather to accept the invitation to the ball. It was primarily Sybil who desired entertainment after months of mourning-restricted socializing. Even a country Twelfth Night Masque was preferable to another night of forced solitude with which her brother could not argue.

Whatever the impetus, be it divine fate or dumb luck, he intended to grasp onto it.

"Miss Bingley," he bowed low, standing directly in front of her and barely glancing at her companions, "I do believe the waltz is next on the dancing agenda. I would be deeply honored if you agreed to dance with me."

"It would be my pleasure as well, Lord Blaisdale," she responded with a regal incline of her head.

Caroline and Lord Blaisdale felt the currents running over and through them as they assumed a waltz pose. For Caroline the sensations were new and electrifying. Lord Blaisdale knew precisely what the sensations meant and what he desired. Yet despite the force of emotions, both were in clear control of their faculties. Similar calculating minds were judging, analyzing, and gauging the situation as they flawlessly glided about the room and shared the standard dialogue.

"Lord Blaisdale, I must first extend my condolences for your loss."

"Thank you, Miss Bingley. It has been a difficult adjustment. You have lost a father so surely relate to my grief."

"Indeed I do. I discovered that family surrounding me tremendously aided in the grieving process. Have you found the same to be true?"

"Absolutely."

"Your mother is well I trust?"

"Quite well. Managing admirably, in fact. She is a wonder of strength in crisis. We all look to her for guidance and example. It has been enlightening to me."

"How do you mean?"

"To observe the fortitude a woman can possess. To fully grasp what it is to be 'Lady Blaisdale' clarifies in my own mind how essential it is for me to select wisely, when the time comes again."

"I see your point. I do pray your decision adequate to your needs."

"I intend to ensure it is, Miss Bingley. I must compliment you on your gown if I may be so bold. Quite stunning. I admire ladies who are not afraid to embrace the latest fashions, who set trends. You have the grace and figure to do so and should never allow anyone to convince you otherwise."

"Thank you, my Lord. You are very kind."

"Merely speaking the truth, madam. How is Mr. Bingley finding Derbyshire?"

"He loves it. Wholly assuming the life of a gentleman farmer."

"And you, Miss Bingley? Do you appreciate the country?"

"Absolutely. For a time, that is. Society is less diverse than in Town and I confess that by the end of winter, I shall be screaming for the delights London has to offer. I think a balance is best, do you not agree?"

"Indeed I do. We appear to be quite similar in our thought processes, Miss Bingley. This pleases me. I tend to prefer London and will now be required to pass large portions of my time there, so it is fortunate that I own a comfortable townhouse and enjoy entertaining. Now I must attend diligently to the task of finding a woman to stand at my side. Someone accomplished, beautiful, and hospitable."

"I wish you luck in your search, Lord Blaisdale."

"It has reached my ears that congratulations on your engagement may soon be in order, Miss Bingley. Is there truth in the rumor?"

"Truth can be a relative term, my Lord. Official congratulations would be presumptuous at this juncture, but I am anticipating a positive development in that quarter soon."

The song ended at that point. He offered his arm, walking off the floor toward the terrace doors. "Your cheeks are a bit flushed, madam. I deem a breath of fresh air is requisite. And, if you wish to know the truth, I do not want to part from your glittering company."

"And do you always get what you want?"

"Generally, yes." He smiled down at her, steering to the railing and slowly detouring past the clustered guests to the shadows beyond. "You dance exquisitely, Miss Bingley. Another stellar quality to add to your growing list of attributes."

"You are quite full of compliments, sir. I hardly know how to express my continued thankfulness."

"Add it to all the other expressions of thanks you now owe me and we shall mutually devise a way for you to adequately communicate your gratitude that will be pleasurable for us both." They paused in a narrow alcove, only the dim echo of music and laughter and subdued glow of gaslight on the damp, snowy surrounds a reminder of others. Essentially they were utterly secluded and the gleam in Lord Blaisdale's eyes and suggestive huskiness of voice caused a shiver to run up Caroline's spine.

The friendly, borderline flirtatious banter while dancing had relaxed Caroline. It was familiar and comfortable, making her forget the past intensity of the man before her. Now her breath caught and the odd tingles rippled anew over her skin, vulnerability and faint anxiety causing her heart to palpitate as her eyes locked with his.

Lord Blaisdale read her expressions with glee. He leaned back slightly, smiling with confidence. "Miss Bingley, I am aware that you do not know me well, not at all really, so permit me a moment to share myself with you. I am a forthright man, for the most part. Confident, assured, cognizant of what I want in my life. And, as you aptly pointed out, I almost always get what I want. Any time I allowed others to lead me, it was a disaster. My marriage is a perfect example." He paused, watching her closely. Caroline was engrossed, her mind racing. "I never wished for my wife's death, but cannot pretend that it was an event of overwhelming grief to me. She was a disappointment on numerous levels, intimately and publicly. I vowed never to make such a horrendous mistake again. You are shivering, my lady. How thoughtless of me! Here, allow me."

He removed his jacket, stepping within inches of her body and pulling the fine woolen fabric over her slender shoulders, fingers purposefully brushing along the skin of her collarbones. "There. Is that better?" He whispered.

Caroline nodded, afraid to meet his eyes. "Much better. Thank you, sir."

"Caroline. May I call you Caroline?" She nodded. "Excellent. Now, look at me, Caroline." He spoke with a ring of authority, her eyes rising involuntarily but then flashing in irritation as she boldly stared back. He smiled suddenly, quite brilliantly, and leaned against the railing, putting a safe space between them. "Excellent again, Caroline. I knew you had fire."

"I beg your pardon?"

"Let me be blunt, my dear. You would have to be an idiot, which I do not think you are, not to know that I have been infatuated with you for years. Yes, even when my wife was still alive. You intrigue me, Caroline. I have watched you, learned about you, wondered, and wished. Does this flatter or frighten you?"

"A little of both, my Lord."

"Good. Obviously when I was married, my desire for you was unattainable, at least I did not reckon you would be amenable to anything other than marriage… Ah, I see that is correct. Good. My esteem for you would be diminished if that were so. However, I did seriously contemplate approaching you for an arrangement. Are you shocked by this, Caroline?"

"Not completely, sir. I am not a fool. I know gentlemen keep mistresses, although I would not have entered such a relationship. The question is why you are telling me all this."

"Do not play coy with me! Because I still desire you, Caroline. Only now you can be my wife. I can give you all that you have ever wanted, more than you would have with Dandridge. Does this idea appeal to you? Or do you harbor romantic notions of true love?"

"Not completely, no. I think it possible for some, but not necessary and certainly not common. However, I do not merely want a marriage of cold convenience. It is undeniably true that you can provide materialistically and grant a prestige that I would enjoy. I may not be a romantic fool, Lord Blaisdale; nonetheless, I have learned in recent months that a marriage can offer an abundance of pleasures beyond the mercenary."

He grinned wickedly. "Are you referring to sexual pleasures, Caroline? If you are, then you are correct."

Caroline reddened, glancing away for a moment. When her gaze returned to his face, it was calm and composed yet with a hint of rosiness. "I am referring to communication, respect, affection, joy, and even peace. Are these characteristics you would want in a marriage?"

"Considering my marriage possessed none of those, or sensual satisfaction for that matter, then I think I can answer in the affirmative." He stepped nearer.

"I do admire you, Caroline. I think we are much alike, you and I. This frank conversation proves that communication should not be a problem with the other named virtues falling naturally in the aftermath. What about intimacy? Do you suspect this essential aspect of a good marriage to be one you can also desire?"

"I have no experience in the matter, my Lord, so cannot answer with any reliability."

"I think you are flirting with me, Miss Bingley! Be cautious, my dear, as it is vital to me that my next marriage be one of passion and I do intend to ensure it will be before I commit myself in any way."

"How do you mean? Would you take advantage of me, sir? Ruin my reputation and be branded a scoundrel in the process?"

"Many already consider me a scoundrel, and if I was proved wrong in my judgment of you, then I would care not one whit for your shattered reputation. Are you virtuous, Caroline? Seductive teasing has its place and is welcomed, but I will not take a wife who has known another. I refuse used property. And I want to be the one who unleashes your potential, who teaches you the ways of love."

He quietly observed her flushing face. He detected the demure and innocent flashes in her eyes that a virginal woman, no matter how skilled at saucy flirting, cannot hide. He smiled in satisfaction.

"You do not need to answer. It is apparent. Ah! How greatly will I enjoy being your teacher, Caroline!"

He was very close to her now, reaching one finger and running softly over the bare flesh of her neck. His finger stroked lower, Caroline's breath now exhaling in short fits as a result of his mesmerizing touch. "I want a lively wife, Caroline. One who will embrace adventure, crave passion, and be witty and charming. But I also insist on propriety, faithfulness, and submission to my dominance. Only in our bed will I submit and only then if it brings mutual delight. I want Lady Blaisdale by day and wanton lover by night. I want a mother for my children, manager of my households, elegant hostess when entertaining, proud and beautiful wife on my arm, and savage temptress in my chambers. Can you accept this, Caroline?"

His lips were almost brushing hers. Caroline could hardly breathe, let alone think coherently. Never had she experienced such rushing and crashing sensations. The previous reactions to his presence were weak compared to the fire now racing through her body. Dimly, she heard his words and filtered through

SHARON LATHAN

them, nodding slowly as she realized she had never wanted anything in all her life more than him and all he promised.

Steeling herself, she withdrew a pace and forced the tremors of fear aside. Determined to risk potentially losing him, she lifted her chin and met his fierce stare. Her voice was firm when she spoke, "I can accept this, Lord Blaisdale, and will do my best to comply with your demands. However, I must be honest and confess that I do not know if I am capable of the more... private requirements you wish for."

"Do you truly doubt your potential or are you toying with me?"

"You have stressed your repugnance for such behavior, my Lord. Another attribute of a successful marriage that has been revealed to me is honesty. This has not necessarily been a natural trait of mine, but I have seen the positive affects of the quality in my brother's union. Additionally, you have been exceedingly forthright with me so it is only proper for me to extend the same. You are offering me an incredible opportunity and I would be a fool to pass it up. Perhaps I am a fool for risking your rejection, but I..." She swallowed, dropping her gaze from his penetrating stare.

"Yes, Caroline? Tell me."

She glanced away, noting afresh their solitude. With eyes averted, she haltingly resumed. "You intrigue me as well, Lord Blaisdale. I... feel... strange sensations... when near you. But I do not... I have not..."

He clasped her upper arms, gently pushing her against the stone wall. He began the kiss with light pressure before deepening to an unrestrained passion. Caroline was taken utterly by surprise, stiffening for a second before the surging waves washed all innocent hesitation away. His hands roamed unchecked, stirring and rousing skillfully, his hard body pressed into hers.

Never had any man handled her in such a way. Sir Dandridge's tentative touches and timid kisses had educed vague flutters but none of the shivers currently overwhelming her. Lord Blaisdale's assault overpowered her to the point where she mustered not the slightest embarrassment or offense at the breach in gentlemanly behavior.

Caroline came alive in places unknown to have perception. She soared to raging heights of pure passion as he skillfully caressed and surveyed her figure. All the while the fiery kiss continued and intensified.

She discovered her hands and arms wrapping around his body and boldly exploring in return. Lord Blaisdale trailed his lips down her neck toward her bosom, releasing a guttural growl and grinding so harshly against her that even the layers of clothing were irrelevant.

Caroline's legs grew weak, her muscles failing as a low moan escaped. She was clutching onto him for stability when he pulled away, panting heavily and grinning with supreme satisfaction. He stroked lightly over her cheek, lust-filled green eyes engaging her dazed ones.

"Delicious, Caroline. You are well, love? No further doubts?"

"Lord Blaisdale, please. I…"

"Do not fear. You have proven what I already knew. And I believe you can now address me as John."

CHAPTER ELEVEN

The Court of St. James

T HE HORSES TURNED THE corner onto Grosvenor Square, hoofs clomping loudly on the perfectly laid stones as Mr. Anders tugged slightly on the reins. The well-trained animals slowed in response, the vehicle's occupants noting the deceleration but not needing that clue to know they were nearing the end of their journey.

"Look, my darling. There it is. Darcy House. Your other home and where we shall stay for a while. Thank goodness, as I am weary of dragging you from place to place."

Lizzy kissed the crown of her sleeping son's head, her softly spoken words apparently unheeded by the oblivious four-month-old infant but clearly not by her husband. Darcy leaned forward slightly in his seat across, furrows rapidly creasing his brow.

"Are you feeling unwell, Elizabeth?"

Lizzy smiled, shaking her head as she met his concerned eyes. "I only meant that I am pleased to be settling in one place for an extended spell. And into a house that is ours. No offense to Lady Catherine's hospitality, but extensive renovations to Rosings will be required ere Anne and Raul have a baby."

Darcy relaxed once again into the plush cushions. "Indeed. Fortunately, they have time. As for renovations, I am confident that Darcy House has been remodeled to my specifications. Alexander will discover a comfortable chamber to sleep in near ours as it should be." His tender gaze rested upon his son, nestled warmly against Lizzy's chest under a thick blanket. "He will have plenty of time to recuperate and grow stronger before we return to Pemberley."

In fact, both mother and child were the picture of health. Lizzy's expressed desire to stay in one place was purely driven by an internal need for familiarity. Darcy House may not have been "home" in the same respect as Pemberley, but it came close.

The object of her musings was now in plain view. The washed white stones and wide sash-paned windows reflected the bright April sunlight, casting a virtual glow around the house where it majestically sat across the grassy park in the middle of Grosvenor Square. All the townhouses fronting the Square were stately, Darcy House not more or less so, but it was the only one with a stunning combination of marble and glass in vast amounts. The wrought iron barriers to the basement quarters and balconies on the upper levels were polished until gleaming, not a hint of rust evident for the Master to see. All debris had been swept away from the gutters and pavement walkways, and a new carpet runner padded the marble steps leading to the vivid blue front door. The windows were open, allowing the fresh breezes of spring to ruffle the curtains and cleanse the interior air, carrying floral fragrances from the lush blooms growing inside the ornate flower boxes underneath each sill.

It was a picture of welcoming perfection, just as Darcy expected.

Mrs. Smyth, the housekeeper of Darcy House, stood in the ground level morning room watching the sedate approach of the rich Darcy coach. She stood with back straight, chin lifted, and hands clasped loosely in front. No overt sign gave away her state of mind except for the persistent spasm behind her left eye that caused the orb to twitch rhythmically. She knew without a doubt that the house was prepared for the arrival of her Master. Her superior expertise and knowledge of Mr. Darcy's expectations allayed the bulk of her trepidation. It should have completely quelled her fears. It always had. But that was before Mrs. Darcy joined the mix.

For five years, Mrs. Smyth had been housekeeper of Darcy House, a position she valued, and it had been bliss. Mr. Darcy was frequently in Town during those years, but usually alone and so reserved that one hardly knew he was present. He rarely hosted any parties and then they were minor affairs with a small number of guests. His demands were few, mainly ones of preserving order and quiet. He was exacting and intense, not in any way foolish or to be trifled with, but since Mrs. Smyth was an excellent, scrupulous manager, they never clashed.

From the day she heard of Mr. Darcy's shocking engagement to the country girl of no family or connections, she had sensed a dark cloud creeping inexorably over her existence. As a city girl born and bred, Mrs. Smyth considered anyone outside the regions of civilized London as suspect and on equal par with the dregs of Whitechapel or Wapping. That Mr. Darcy, a paragon of Society, would marry such a woman was beyond her comprehension. She had assumed that Miss Bingley would someday be Mrs. Darcy, or at least some lady like her. That would have been the correct course, the sensible choice, and Mrs. Smyth saw no logic to his hideous error in judgment, suspecting as many did that there must be some sort of witchcraft or trickery at work from the obviously money-seeking upstart.

Upon her first meeting of Miss Bennet, when Mr. Darcy brought his fiancée and her dowdy father to Darcy House during their engagement, Mrs. Smyth's worst fears were realized. Miss Bennet was plain and drab, dressed in ugly gowns of no style and poor workmanship, with hair and body unadorned in any way. She smiled constantly, vulgarly showing all her teeth, was animated and noisy, and laughed incessantly. Grudgingly, Mrs. Smyth admitted that Miss Bennet carried herself with grace and that her manners were adequate, but those positives were overruled by her improper boldness and teasing informality with Mr. Darcy.

Mr. Darcy was clearly besotted and subtly altered. He smiled too much and laughed aloud. His eyes followed her every move. And worst of all, he welcomed her impertinence and returned her banter! It was frightening to observe and Mrs. Smyth prayed daily that something or someone would intercede and break the spell. Unfortunately, that did not happen and the marriage took place. Mrs. Smyth was relieved when Mr. Darcy informed the staff that, after the wedding, he would immediately be retiring to Pemberley for the winter, not to return until late spring. She rested in the conviction that the naturally inhibited, staid, and domineering Mr. Darcy would shake off the shameful enchantment after months of forced confinement behind the walls and snow-laden landscape of Pemberley. He would recognize his vast mistake, and indeed if it was too late to reverse the blunder, surely he would rectify the damage by grinding the presumptuous nobody down into the submissive, proper wife she should be. Perhaps then, Mrs. Smyth thought, there would be hope for regaining the Darcy reputation and salvaging the future.

That hope was dashed within days of Mrs. Darcy's first season in London. The housekeeper's painful, disgraceful humiliation yet resounded through her mind. The subsequent weeks of bowing to Mrs. Darcy's demands were fresh wounds that gnawed at her serenity.

All of London Society had apparently forgotten the embarrassing background of Elizabeth Darcy, but it did not sway Mrs. Smyth's opinion. She would not forgive. Or relinquish her belief that, although Mrs. Darcy displayed a newfound class and elegance beyond what she had ever imagined possible, there was a lacking propriety and borderline crassness to the Darcy household that had not existed prior. The addition of the boisterous, coarse Dr. Darcy, surely unacceptable if not for the negative influence of Mrs. Darcy, cemented her judgment.

Numerous times after slimly escaping dismissal she had contemplated seeking employment elsewhere. But, in the end, even with the detriments, she was in an esteemed position of power in a prestigious household. Her wage was substantial, her quarters generous, and her freedom liberal. Their tenancy last spring was trying but short, the family then departing to reside the bulk of the year at Pemberley.

So Mrs. Smyth went about her business, blessedly alone in her supremacy. She had almost forgotten the past indignities, but the looming presence not only of Mrs. Darcy and Dr. Darcy but also an infant escalated her distress. Any miniscule hope that matters may have changed, that Mr. Darcy was not as dotty over his wife after a year, were shattered when the orders came through regarding the nursery. Who had ever heard of an infant sleeping within earshot of the master suite? With bells installed to wake if needed? Quarters for a nanny but no mention of a wet nurse! It was unbelievable. Too unbelievable to fully comprehend, so she assumed it was a puzzle and she was missing a piece.

Thus, her dread had risen substantially until the dratted tic occurred with alarming frequency. The arrival of Mr. Darcy's valet and Mrs. Darcy's maid, along with the nanny three hours ago alerted the entire household to the impending appearance of the family. Everyone was on high anticipation, the heightened energy palpable even though they went about their duties with cool efficiency.

Mrs. Smyth waited until the last possible moment, watching the carriage halt and the footman leap down to open the door. She heard the front door of the townhouse open as watchful servants descended the steps to assist with luggage and passengers. Dr. Darcy disembarked first, his skeletal limbs encased in an outlandish foreign outfit of shocking maroon, the toothy smile and piercing blue eyes sweeping over the house sending chills up the housekeeper's spine. She involuntarily backed up a step, but he turned toward the carriage to assist Miss Darcy before spying her staring out the window.

Ah, Miss Darcy. Finally, a true lady of breeding and gentility, Mrs. Smyth thought. She noted the hereditary elegance and nobility apparent in how Miss Darcy moved, in every tilt of her head or lift of her fine-boned hands. Impeccably dressed, hair arranged flawlessly, smile understated, figure tall and gently curved, skin ivory—in all ways the image of a lady.

Next came Mr. Darcy. Mrs. Smyth sighed, her hands clenching involuntarily. Never, not once in even the remotest way, had Mrs. Smyth considered Mr. Darcy as anything other than her employer. For the same reasons that she was so appalled by his choice of bride, she never fancifully or poetically dreamed of him falling in love with his housekeeper. Leave that nonsense to the ridiculous novelists who imagine such a horrid development romantic! She knew her station in life and embraced it fully. Nevertheless, as a woman in her early thirties, she assuredly recognized a handsome man and could readily appreciate the view.

As always, his stature, masculine physique, strongly chiseled facial features, and absorbing sapphire eyes stirred her womanly instincts. It was a purely lustful response, and she knew this, instigated as much by the specimen of prime manhood before her as by her internal urges so tightly controlled. It was rare, but there were those times when she missed her husband. Or rather what he had roused in her. She sighed again, allowing the feelings to wash over her briefly as she gazed upon her master.

As quickly as they came, they disappeared. Mr. Darcy was a man of astounding presence. He wore his authority, eminence, and rank as an aura discernable to all. He was so far above her, a reality that brought no anger or bitterness but instead a sensation of peace. This is how the world was supposed to be—people keeping to where God had placed them in the proper order. Grasping beyond where one was born only brought upset and strife; it disturbed the flow and caused chaos.

The burn of suppressed passionate lust ebbed, replaced by the burn of irritation. She clenched her fists tighter, observing as Mr. Darcy turned toward the carriage, reaching in and grasping onto the extended hand and elbow of his wife. He said something, his face lighting with a smile as Mrs. Darcy came into view. Typically, Mrs. Smyth noted with a grimace, she was laughing. Her dark eyes glittered with mirth, and her full lips curved into a beaming smile displaying her teeth whitely against the crude tan of her skin and ruddiness to her cheeks. The housekeeper swept her eyes over her mistress, admitting grudgingly that she could find no fault with Mrs. Darcy's attire or figure or hairstyle. But the shock of seeing the infant clutched against the woman's chest was stunning.

Mrs. Smyth caught her breath. When the nanny had arrived with the personal servants and not the infant, Mrs. Smyth had been surprised. Fleetingly, she had wondered who was caring for the child, but put the thought aside in the haste of last minute preparations. If asked, she probably would have answered that the wet nurse was caring for the babe, or that it would be swaddled tightly and contained in a carry basket of some sort. Seeing it now with tiny bare feet emerging from the bottom edge of the blanket that Mrs. Darcy held over the body, the round head and pink face pressed against its mother's full bosom was astonishing. Obviously the squalling, probably smelly baby had been held and cared for squarely in the midst of them! The idea was revolting, but then Mrs. Smyth did have to admit honestly that she knew nothing about babies, praise the Maker for that miracle. Nevertheless, it was exceedingly rare, as even she knew, for offspring to be so boldly displayed, let alone carted about.

She shook her head, inhaled deeply, and steeled her spine. "Only three months or so," she murmured aloud, repeating the words again to etch the fact firmly in her mind. With a final sigh, pat of her palms to ensure every hair was secured into the severe bun, and harsh rub to the persistent tic, the housekeeper moved toward the foyer to greet her Master and Mistress.

"Excellent, Georgiana. Remember to casually sweep with your right hand as you rise and grasp onto a few folds, the train will move to the side, and you will be able to back away faultlessly. Small steps though. If your heel snags it will be easier to remedy if you are not off balance from a large stride. Very good. Try it again, Elizabeth. As Georgiana has done."

"Thank goodness the ridiculousness does not extend to the footwear," Lizzy muttered. "If I had to don jewel encrusted shoes with three-inch heels and attached feathers I am certain I would fall on my derriere."

"You shall be marvelous, my dear," Lady Matlock placated, continuing the instruction in her dulcet voice.

The three women stood in the Darcy House ballroom spending their fifth day in a row practicing the choreographed maneuvers required when presented to the Prince Regent at the Court of St. James. Lizzy and Georgiana were granted permission to be presented to the sovereign by Lord Chamberlain, and the ceremony was scheduled for that afternoon. Darcy never doubted the entitlement. As the wife of a wealthy and esteemed landed gentry with a venerated ancestry, an introduction at Court was an expectation.

It was quite probable that the Georgiana of a year prior may have collapsed in fear at the idea of entering St. James's Palace, embarrassing the Darcy name by paralyzing nervousness when the time came. Her limited experiences in social milieus while touring Wales and on Twelfth Night partially paved the way; however, even with that minimal exposure to Society, she seemed to grasp readily the pomp involved. She wore the wide hoop skirts and layers of fabric with natural ease. Not once had she erred in her curtsy, her limber body bending into the deep genuflection and rising dozens of times over without the slightest waver or misstep. She masterfully handled the three-foot train, the yards of lace and braided rouleau edging the delicate satin and tissue gown flowing over the curves of her body fluidly as she walked. It was awe-inspiring to observe her graceful command of the protocol-ridden ceremony and unwieldy costume. Even the laughable extravagance of the court-ordered attire with velvet torque adorned with pearls and three ostrich plumes waving a foot over her head did not seem as amusing on her lithe figure.

Moreover, the lifelong immersion in protocol, ease with aristocracy, and natural elegance of the former Lady Madeline Hamilton, daughter of a Marquess and now the Countess of Matlock, was a soothing balm. For weeks, Lady Matlock prepared Georgiana and Lizzy for their presentation to the Prince Regent and his court.

Lizzy observed her newest sister with a mixture of proud adoration and irritation. She felt ungainly and absurd in the heavy dress. It was a feeling that persisted no matter how often she was assured of her beauty and agility. Her constant muttering and flippant comments did not hide her anxiety from Lady Matlock or Georgiana, both of whom ignored her grumblings and offered gentle encouragements.

"I look nine months pregnant," Lizzy lamented to her husband as he greeted her in their bedchamber an hour later.

"You were stunningly gorgeous when you were nine months pregnant and are stunningly gorgeous now," he replied with conviction.

Lizzy huffed and shook her head. "How am I to ever believe you when you claim I am beautiful upon waking in the morning with my hair a tangled mess?"

"Very well," he laughed. "You are merely pretty and highly desirable when freshly waking beside me. Dressed in such lavish attire, you are stunningly gorgeous. I have qualified my assessment. Does this convince you?"

Lizzy bit her lip, glancing down and blinking furiously as she smoothed invisible wrinkles from the gilded moss-colored crepe falling in leafy overlapping layers over the flexible hoop underneath.

Darcy stepped closer—as close as was possible with the full gown interfering—and gently lifted her chin. "My love, trust me. You are indeed a vision of loveliness. Madame Lanchester is the best modiste in London for Court dress. She would never create a gown that was not flattering to the wearer and perfect for presenting to His Highness. I know it is an unusual cut and weighty, but you truly are beautiful."

And of course it was true. Madame Lanchester was a visionary genius, managing to design gowns that included the abundant arrays of flowers, jewels, rich embroidery, tassels, braided rope, lace, and so on that was requisite, but in an airier pattern that was both lighter in weight and delicate.

For Lizzy, she had gone with rich tones of beige and green that complimented her chocolate hair and bronzed complexion. The bodice was tight, lifting her bosom higher than normal. She further accented the cleavage with a décolletage of starched lace edging a wrapped darker green and beige rope that was then gathered into a knot at the shoulder, puffy sleeves cascading in a veil of satin and crepe to the middle of her upper arm.

The skirt of Chinese crepe as thin as tissue paper was cut into ten hawthorn-leaf shapes, the natural crinkles within the mossy fabric simulating veins. Each "leaf" draped alternately over the petticoat to the floor creating a train of foliage with thin gold braid "branches" connecting. The fawn-colored satin petticoat was adorned along the sides and back with ruffles of blond lace, but the front panel was smooth. The crepe leaves parted just below mid-thigh to reveal a painted garden of flowers and foliage painstakingly detailed with hand-stitched tinseled threads.

The entire ensemble, including the lavish headdress with ostrich feathers and dangling lappets in the same gauzy green crepe, was exquisite.

Odd to be sure, with the hoops a fashion accessory from eras past, but magnificent nevertheless.

Darcy chuckled, indicating his suit with a wave of one hand. "Besides, compared to me in this ghastly outfit, you are understated and almost boring."

"That is absurd and you know it," she retorted acerbically. "You are more handsome than I have ever seen you."

"I daresay I can counter with the identical argument. Do you not also profess my attractiveness upon waking with hair awry and face stubbled? Therefore, your assertion is suspect."

Finally she laughed, if a bit wavering, her voice lifting into her typical teasing tone. "In this case, I confess you have caught me in a falsehood. You are most handsome with hair awry and face stubbled, and unclothed I must add. In this case, you are merely highly attractive. But you are wrong about the outfit being ghastly. Fairly ostentatious, perhaps, but not a total disaster."

Ceremonial court dress for men did not cater to the whims of fashion and fanciful Queens, thus little changed over the decades. But the protocols and requirements were as stringent. Lizzy had been absolutely flabbergasted when Darcy had donned the suit kept protected in the deep recesses of his wardrobe. It was indeed ostentatious but splendid. Tailored in an older military style, the satin lined jacket of midnight blue velvet sported long tails in a curved fashion, reaching to the knees. Both the jacket and matching waistcoat were embellished with thick braids of gold twisted into elaborate patterns along the cuffs, tall collar, and edges. The shirt, breeches, stockings, and shoes were purest white. Polished buckles of gold and inlayed clear rhinestones adorned each shoe and suspender clasp, the buttons similar in extravagance. The total picture was one of baroque excess, fanciful and pretentious in the extreme, and thus, utterly at odds with Darcy's innate reserve. Yet somehow he managed to wear it with an aristocratic comfort, even the lacy cravat floridly tied into a pouf clear down to mid-chest not as ludicrous as one would imagine.

Lizzy shook her head, reaching to toy carefully with the ruffled cravat. "It is extremely unfair actually. You wear this frippery, an antiquated affectation, and look regally urbane and suitable. I am a player in a costume."

He bent, kissing her polished lips gingerly. "Nonsense. You are my wife and dressed as you should be. However, I know this is not your real concern and I want you to know how deeply I appreciate you suffering this agony on my account. It is more than just a duty for me, as you know. To hear your name,

Elizabeth Darcy, called by Lord Chamberlain; to see you standing in Court before the Prince; to know that my excellent wife is formally acknowledged before all in Society on the Court List will be an exalting experience for me. I am honored that you are my wife, Elizabeth, and want the entire breadth of England to witness my good fortune."

"But, Fitzwilliam, that is precisely why I tremble as never in my life! What if I fail you in some way? Stumble or curtsy inadequately or…"

"Elizabeth, if I imagined for one tiny second that you would do any of those things, my pride and confidence would not be so towering. It is distinctly because I am certain of your worthiness and inability to fail at anything you set your mind to that reinforces my belief in your success. Now, come, we cannot delay. His Royal Highness does not yet know it, but he is about to be introduced to two of the most exquisite women in his kingdom."

Lizzy nodded, bravely lifting her chin and smiling. Darcy was not fooled, but he also knew his wife well enough to be sure she would find her inner fortitude and perform brilliantly. He was well aware of her faults, but he equally understood her strengths. At the moment she was a bundle of nerves, and for good reason, but his Lizzy never succumbed to a challenge.

Georgiana and Lady Matlock waited in the foyer with Lord Matlock. Lady Matlock wore an eye-boggling gown in cream satin with uncountable yards of trimmings and appliquéd flowers draped over the wide hip pannier hoops of her youthful presentation. The latter was dressed in his ceremonial garments, elaborate as Darcy's, with the addition of a powdered wig. It wasn't strictly called for, the Prince Regent largely responsible for the decline in the fashion for wigs. But Lord Matlock had his moments of reverting to past norms, such ceremonial appointments one of them. Lizzy groaned, noting how all three of them, along with Darcy, wore their formal vestments with panache.

Two carriages were required, as there was no possible way three women with voluminous skirts could fit into one coach, no matter how spacious. Darcy rode with his wife and sister, Lord and Lady Matlock leading the way to the palace.

The warmth of April was not stifling, but edginess kept the fans fluttering. Lizzy was no longer muttering. In fact she was silent, an unusual state, so Georgiana contributed to the idle chat that passed the time through the crowded London streets.

"Is this the same suit you wore at your levee, William?"

"No, dear. That was a long time ago. I was eighteen, same as you, when presented to His Majesty King George III. Thus I was not at my full growth, at least in the width of my chest. I was to my full height, but far thinner and not as broad. Besides, father ordered my garments. I was merely required to show up for the fitting with no say in the matter. This ensemble is tame compared to his idea of proper dress. It was one of the few times in my life when I actively hated our father."

He said it with humor, all of them laughing, but neither woman doubted his severe annoyance in being asked to wear an outfit so showy while battling his own nerves. He went on to describe his levee with embellished drama, his dry humor easing the tension in the atmosphere. By the time they finally reached the end of Pall Mall and joined the line of waiting carriages on Cleveland Row as they were slowly admitted through the Palace Gates, Lizzy had gotten a grip on her emotions. In fact, she had entered a state of dreamy peace. Everything was crystalline in clarity while also feeling as if seen on the vividly painted surface of a canvas. Almost as if she were observing the events on a successive series of pictures while they happened to someone else.

St. James's Palace sat on what had once been the site of a Norman Era leper hospital for women dedicated to St. James the Less. Thanks to the covetous eye of Henry VIII, who saw the fair fields of Piccadilly as too beautiful to be wasted on dying women, the site was arrogated and a stately manor house was erected along with a lush park. The palace itself was commissioned by Henry, but would not fully become the official Royal residence for some hundred years during the reign of William III in 1698. Even after the disastrous fire in 1809 that destroyed a large portion of the palace and with the current lavish renovations to Buckingham House by John Nash, the Prince's favored architect, St. James's Palace remained as primary residence and administrative center to the monarchy.

The Tudor-style red-brick structure surrounded four enormous courtyards, the northern entrance facing Cleveland Square the main gateway for visitors. The massive gates of black iron flanked by two turreted polygonal towers were open but heavily protected. The dozen soldiers stationed at the gate, wearing brilliant red uniforms and holding wicked shotguns with razor sharp bayonets, assessed each carriage as it passed. The guards meticulously reviewed the necessary documents, ensuring the seal of Lord Chamberlain, and visually searched each vehicle before allowing entry into the courtyard. Additional soldiers lined the walkways and stood by the doors, their eyes unblinking and bodies rigid, each ready to jump into action at the slightest sign of a threat. Servants and palace functionaries kept traffic moving at a steady pace and provided hasty service to the visiting dignitaries. The tri-weekly presentations of debutantes and ladies of Society, known as Court Drawing Rooms, and the Levees for the gentlemen of the Realm followed standard formats that rarely varied. Attention to every conceivable detail and possible variation was expected to be accomplished without mishap or delay.

Lizzy's bizarre serenity kept her from ogling as she might have been tempted to do. Instead, she gazed about the courtyard with calm interest. She noted the minor areas of disrepair amongst the overall impressiveness of the structure, the concentrated grandeur that encompassed everything from the servants to the gleaming windows with their brocade curtains to the sculpted greenery to the scrubbed stones, and the hushed stateliness of the gentry in their opulent garments as they walked with measured enthusiasm into the State Apartments facing the gardens of St. James's Park to the south.

She held to Darcy's forearm as they followed the line of people. He offered support and comfort merely by his steady confidence, but with each step, Lizzy felt her insides relaxing rather than tying up into the tighter knots that she had anticipated. Occasionally, there was a face she recognized, someone who would nod politely or utter brief words of conversation. Darcy, of course, knew everyone, and engaged in casual discourse as they ascended a stairway of tremendous elegance and entered the armory.

The walls of the ancient guardroom were lined with daggers, muskets, and swords. Lizzy's fascination with history was piqued, her pace instinctively declining as she swiveled her head to inspect the collection of ancient weapons. She felt more than heard Darcy's muted chuckle and gazed upward into his serious face. Only a hint of a smile appeared on his lips, but she noted the twinkle in his eyes and also knew why he was laughing at her. They were so akin, she and her spouse, both adoring the study of antiquities. She knew he experienced the same desire to pause and examine the specimens, but of course that was impossible. Here, the Yeoman of the Guard strategically stood to ensure the passageways were kept clear and the traffic flowing. Halting to study as if in a museum was out of the question.

The Tapestry Room was the next chamber. Here, they did stop, and Lizzy would have over an hour to inspect the beautiful weavings and relics of King

Henry VIII. There was nothing to do but wait until called, the order according to rank. The windows were opened to the cooler air without, but the heat from the enormous chandelier hanging from the center of the ceiling and candelabras blazing hundreds of candles added to the generated warmth of pressed bodies. Nevertheless, restrained conversation passed the time. The residuals of her nervousness dissipated as Lizzy noted two points that greatly eased her: the abundance of giddy, blushing, and clearly terrified young ladies who looked near to fainting and thus placed her minor nervousness into perspective; and the reemergence of her inborn spunkiness and wit as she chatted and bantered with the other guests.

Several times, she noted Darcy's proud eyes upon her, his constancy and faith reassuring her further. By the time Georgiana's name was called, Lizzy's only discomfort came from the increasing pressure within her breasts from the need to nurse Alexander.

Georgiana was pale but composed while her dress was properly arranged by Lady Matlock, and she then began the solitary trek down the corridor to the drawing room Presence Chamber. Lady Matlock turned to Lizzy, smiling encouragingly as she silently straightened the flowing skirt and brushed over the fabric. Lizzy again sensed the strange detachment washing over her, her heart beating slightly faster than normal but otherwise her head clear. She did not glance at Darcy as she exited the Tapestry Room, preferring to focus on the next few minutes.

The corridor was short, covered with a rich red carpet runner that stifled any footfalls, reaching Lord Chamberlain just in time to witness Georgiana completing her perfect backward retreat with a final curtsy before turning gracefully and exiting the room. She looked at Lizzy and actually winked! Lizzy nearly burst into laughter but managed to restrain herself at the last moment. Yet something about seeing her shy sister being so impish in such a situation was the final blow to any shreds of nervousness that remained.

She lifted her chin and with a saucy smile handed the printed card with her name etched in fine script upon it to Lord Chamberlain. An assisting gentleman performed a final straighten to her train while in a loud, strong voice Lord Chamberlain declared, "Elizabeth Darcy, née Elizabeth Bennet, wife to Mr. Fitzwilliam Darcy of Pemberley in Derbyshire."

Later, Lizzy would have the oddest recollections of the ethereal moment when she was presented to his Royal Highness the Prince Regent. She vividly remembered the crimson velvet and gold lace covered throne sitting upon the raised dais with a canopy of identical material surmounting. For all her life she would smell sweet violet and primrose and envision the bouquets artistically place about the throne room. She would retain only vague images of the numerous royal attendees and could not recall what His Highness wore, but she sharply saw the bright blue of his eyes that were similar to her husband's and the faintly feminine mouth that lifted in a genuine smile.

He was rather ordinary in appearance, not handsome or remarkable, while also exuding a presence that was unlike anything she had ever experienced at the same time. There was power and majesty that rippled the air about him, an aura of ancient heritage and eminence that awed her. He did not seem as bored as she would have imagined he would be, the ceremony surely excruciatingly tedious from his perspective, and his eyes flickered with polite interest as he watched her execute the proper genuflection. Perhaps he hoped for at least one young lady to topple over, just to bring some excitement to the proceedings! Lizzy did wonder if this were the case as his eyes were distant when she rose, flickering briefly toward a small food-laden table set into an alcove across the room. He did not move a muscle, waiting with regal dignity as she played her part flawlessly, spoke the well-rehearsed words, curtsied to the other royalties flanking the throne, and then swept the train into her right hand as she initiated her smooth retreat.

All in all, the brief seconds before the Prince himself were rather anticlimactic. An attack of hysterical giggles threatened to overwhelm her as she glided back down the short corridor to the Tapestry Room. The sudden rush of relief was unparalleled, her body flushed and head swimming as she entered the room and instantly sought out Darcy. He stood where she had left him, talking with Lord Matlock and Lady Matlock, a ruddy-cheeked Georgiana holding onto his arm. His face was typically composed with only the tiniest of creases wrinkling his brow as indication of his emotions. The second he engaged her eyes he broke out in an atypical grin, his own relief as evident as the exalting pride which lifted his shoulders incrementally higher. He murmured a hasty pardon, crossing to Lizzy with such an expression of joy that for a moment she actually thought he would forget himself and pull her into his embrace. He did nothing of the sort, naturally, stopping short and fluidly raising her gloved fingers to his lips for a firm kiss.

"May we leave now, dearest? I failed to liven the atmosphere by tripping or losing my cap when I bowed, but I may soon incite scandal by leaking all over this ridiculous gown."

Darcy coughed a laugh, grinning sidelong as he offered his arm. "Indeed, let me take my two favorite women home. I have cause to celebrate and I do intend to, especially after the guests depart," he finished in a low voice, his meaning unmistakable. It would not be until the night was long over, warm and satiated in bed with Elizabeth pliantly draped over his body, that it would occur to him that for the first time ever, he had not been self-conscious and flustered while at Court.

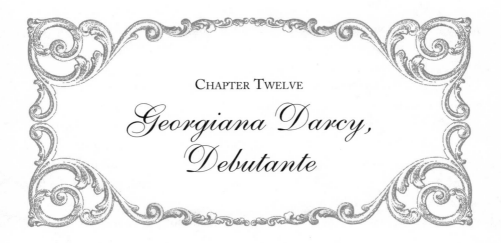

CHAPTER TWELVE

Georgiana Darcy, Debutante

D ARCY'S SECOND SEASON IN London as a married man with a glorious wife and perfect son proved to be a joyous relief from the agonizing years of his bachelorhood and worries of Elizabeth's health that had plagued their first sojourn in Town, but a fresh misery was there as he embarked on the demanding task of chaperoning his debuting sister.

The usual pressure of business matters left languishing for the bulk of the winter, with the residual effects of the Derby mill fire to contend with, kept him busy during the daylight hours. Long hours sequestered with Mr. Daniels, various conferences with purchasers of Pemberley's products, meetings with Duke Grafton and his shipping partners, and sundry new endeavors to diversify and invest the Darcy wealth were a constant drain on his time. Of course, he loved the challenge and excitement of commerce in all its forms, so did not remotely think to bemoan the obligation. Social commitments were chosen wisely due to their infant son's requirements. It was a valid excuse utilized by Darcy to refuse the bulk of offerings extended. Darcy would have been perfectly content to spend each and every night alone with his wife and son with only a handful of intimate gatherings to upset their isolation. His wife, not surprisingly, disagreed with this option, not only for her personal delight in socializing and theatrical entertainments, but also for her keen desire to advance her husband's prestige. Darcy thought it was ridiculous, but Lizzy insisted, so short, well-planned excursions were frequent.

As the previous Season had proven, having a wife gracing his arm at the endless soirees and galas greatly eased his discomfort in social situations. For the most part Darcy discovered that he could enjoy the events to a degree, although it would be common to note him standing apart from the fray in silence or reserved conversation. As was typical from the time he first entered Society as a young man, he warred between a desire to escape to the serene confines of Derbyshire while simultaneously embracing pleasure in the pursuits he enjoyed that could only be found in London, and the diverse intellectual conversation amongst his peers. However, it was less of a struggle now, and he was again surprised to note the increased freedom and joy he felt in all aspects of his life.

In fact, it may have been close to perfection if not for Georgiana.

Oh, not Georgiana specifically, but the emotional trauma involved in her introduction to Society was enormous. Darcy would be forever grateful to Lady Matlock for her invaluable assistance, not certain he would have survived the process otherwise! In general Darcy was not the type of man, or guardian, who apportioned his responsibilities. However, as in the case of debuting at the Court of St. James, the influence and knowledge of Lady Matlock also proved instrumental in acquiring the necessary sponsorship for admission to Almack's Social Club.

Acceptance by the Patronesses of Almack's posed an entirely different set of hurdles.

James Darcy had submitted his son's name for the Season following his eighteenth birthday. Darcy had pleaded with his father to spare him the trauma, but the elder Mr. Darcy was firm. His son would appear at Almack's Club, the concept of rejection unfathomable. Besides, where else would he find an appropriate marriage partner? Fitzwilliam Darcy, heir to Pemberley and the Darcy fortune, was not rejected, and dutifully attended dozens of assemblies over the years, maintaining his yearly subscription as expected. He enjoyed the balls at Almack's as much as he did any others—that is to say not much—but he was wise enough to recognize the importance. In his ceaseless quest to discover the shadowy woman of his dreams, Almack's was the logical place to triumph. Also, as the years unfolded, he came to realize that his participation and cultivation of a positive reputation would aid Georgiana's inclusion when the time came. As much as he personally abhorred a large portion of the game, it was the way of his world.

One never knew the conversations that took place in the upper room where the seven Patronesses gathered to review each applicant. Why some were accepted and others not was often abundantly clear due to some glaring deficiency in the candidate or the family, but at times there seemed to be no logical reason. The power wielded by the Countess of Jersey, the Countess de Lieven, the Marchioness of Londonderry, Lady Cowper, Lady Sefton, the Austrian Princess Esterhazy, and the Baroness Willoughby de Eresby was absolute and irrefutable. Their good opinion once lost was indeed lost forever, and the shame was profound.

Thus it was with tremendous relief when, on the morning following the presentation at Court, the courier arrived to deliver the voucher printed with Georgiana's name endorsed by the Countess de Lieven in her finely scrolled signature. Darcy held the ticket in his hand as he walked to the parlor where his sister and wife relaxed with Alexander, the initial flare of bursting pride steadily waning. Despite a previous vague fear that his sister may be rejected, it was now that his real apprehensions began.

Georgiana took one look at the paper in her brother's hand and launched from her chair with a squeal of delight. Darcy suddenly felt bereft of air. She danced about the room gleefully, receiving hugs from Lizzy, while Darcy thought he might faint. Or cry. For the first time it truly penetrated his mind that his "baby" sister was a woman. It was quite probable that by the end of these months in Town, she could be betrothed and taken away from him.

Why it had never dawned on him in precisely this light, he could not say. But there it suddenly was, and he peered into her radiant face as she chatted exuberantly about dances and handsome suitors, seeing the child of his imagination no longer. His heart constricted with a piercing cold rushing through every cell of his body. Visions of the typical Almack's atmosphere with the unwed of both sexes on the prowl, flirtation blatant and bold, declarations and proposals rampant, rapid courtship the motive, and plotted assignations common caused him to search for the nearest chair!

In her exuberance, Georgiana was oblivious to her brother's distress. His wife noted his reaction and was amused, but also aching for what she knew was a difficult epiphany for the overly protective man.

"Talk to me, love," she whispered to him later that afternoon when he joined her in their bedchamber for Alexander's meal. The four-and-a half-month-old curled his fist around his father's index finger, both hands lying atop the swell of breast currently providing the babe's nourishment.

"Do you have any idea how foolish I feel? I have watched my sister mature with enormous pride these past few years, especially under your tutelage. I have plotted her entrance into Society with a precision Colonel Fitzwilliam would be hard pressed to match. I have even considered the appropriate qualifications for her future husband. Yet for all that, I did not envision her actually with a man." He released a pained snort, shaking his head. "How pathetic is that? But I cannot deny that the image of my sister clasping onto the arm of some stranger is like a knife in my chest."

"If it is any consolation, I honestly do not think this is a picture you will be forced to witness in the near future."

"How can you be so sure? I hesitate to bring it up, but she has been known to fall in love, or what she thought was love, in a hasty manner."

"You know even more than I that the circumstances surrounding Wickham were unique. It is unlikely that the adolescents or other gentlemen haunting Almack's will be quite so devious."

"Perhaps not in the same way or with the personal incentive, but my sister will be highly prized in the marriage market. Which, as much as I abhor the fact, is largely why Almack's exists."

Lizzy laughed, gazing into her husband's worried eyes. "Oh really? Is that why you went? To seek out a prized bride?"

He grimaced, and then chuckled. "You know it was. What else would induce me to suffer the trauma of such a place? Alas, you were never there, so my agony was prolonged."

"Poor Mr. Darcy."

"Yes, and do not forget it," he said, leaning to place a soft nibble on her earlobe before straightening and resuming the gloomy topic. "I may have disdained the game, Elizabeth, but the reality is that every gentlemen and lady attends Almack's not for the dancing. It is to flirt and size up whether a prospective partner is appropriate. Emotions are high with that kind of atmosphere. Desires are encouraged to run free. Everyone is gay and beautiful. It is easy to fall in love there."

"Once again you are underestimating Georgiana. The affair with Wickham wounded her more than I think you know. But it also taught her valuable lessons and matured her in ways not so easily discernable. Oh, do not frown! I think at this point Georgie would be hard pressed to recollect what Wickham even looked like, so her scars are well healed. But the education runs deep. She will not make that mistake again, I can promise you that."

She transferred Alexander to her shoulder for his mid-meal burping. Clearly he was not satiated, his eyes and mouth wide open as he submitted to the necessary pause. Darcy brought his face to the infant's level, instantly and unconsciously creating silly expressions that elicited a sunny smile and moist coo. Darcy still held onto the chubby hand, bestowing kisses and gentle bites.

Lizzy smoothly moved him to her left breast, the feeding recommencing swiftly. Darcy nestled his chin on her shoulder, eyes locked on his nursing son and fingers playing with the mass of springy brown curls. Lizzy continued the conversation as if never interrupted.

"Furthermore, Georgiana, for all her grace and maturity this past year, is young. It isn't that I believe it impossible for her to meet the one intended for her and fall in love. I just think it so unlikely as to be nearly impossible."

"Considering you undoubtedly comprehend the inner meditations of my sister more than I do, I shall accept that assessment. However, I am curious as to how you can be so certain."

"Georgiana has dreams, William. Aspirations. Nothing grand or scandalous, of course. But she wants to enjoy life, travel, and study her music before settling into the routines of domesticity. She talks so often about going abroad, as you know. What I do not think you understand is how vital that is to her. It is precisely because of what Wickham did to her, her extreme foolishness and residuals of guilt over disappointing you, that makes it imperative that she not be hasty."

"But, I never—" he growled, Lizzy stopping his automatic rebuttal with fingertips pressed to his lips.

"Don't say it, love. She knows how you feel. But allow her to hold on to her emotions and the results. Georgiana is wise enough to perceive that she is not wise! If that makes sense."

"No," he retorted sulkily, Lizzy laughing.

"She accepts her limitations, if you will. She is well aware that her experiences are few, that her exposure to the opposite sex is minute and skewed. She refuses to be made a fool of ever again, yet is wise enough to know that it could easily happen due to her naïveté. She sees these events—Almack's, the opera, the ball we shall host, the upcoming summer at Stevenage—as ways to improve her social skills, grow stronger in her convictions, and learn more about life. Your sister is a scholar just like you, my dearest." She kissed the top of his head, Darcy then lifting from his perch on her shoulder to meet her eyes. Lizzy smiled, stroking through his thick hair. "She has vowed only to marry when she can find that one man who will respect her as a near equal and love her unconditionally. You have taught her that, Fitzwilliam. In the meantime, unlike another Darcy whom I love and adore, she intends to have fun with the dancing and, yes, even the flirting! So be prepared."

"I think it shall kill me," he muttered seriously, and then grinned, his voice dropping into a husky timbre. "I do believe this is all too much for me. I need comfort and tender loving from my wife to cope with the stress."

"You know we have an appointment in less than two hours and have yet to begin dressing. Comforting shall have to wait."

"Some comforting can be accomplished in short order if necessary," he retorted, reaching to lift her skirts and commence stroking upward over her bare thigh.

"You are incorrigible," she replied, batting his hand away.

Darcy immediately returned to her leg, adding kisses along her collarbone. "I warned you not to forget my past distress while searching for you, Mrs. Darcy. Your poor husband, who searched for ages while you flittered about the fields of Hertfordshire like a fairy creature delighting in the torment of mortal lovers transfixed by desire, needs to be reassured the wood nymph is his forever."

"Reading Shakespeare again, are we? Spare me the dramatic pathos. You are most assuredly a man who is not suffering from lack of affection." She again batted his seeking hand away, playfully, affecting a severe expression. Darcy chuckled, leaning back into the sofa with hands on his lap and momentarily limiting himself to sensual kisses planted over her bared left shoulder.

Alexander finally attained his stomach's capacity and was handed off to his father for final burping and cuddling. The ritual had not changed in the months since his birth. The big difference now was that he often stayed awake for long periods of time after eating rather than instantly falling into a deep sleep. It was wonderful for Darcy, who still strived to be available for as many meal times as he could manage. As the weeks passed and his son grew with a personality that steadily emerged, Darcy began to rethink his priorities. At Pemberley, where life moved at a slower pace, his hours spent in play and cuddling his son were considerable. However, since traveling away from the homey environs to Kent and Hertfordshire, where dozens of family members reside, and especially since arriving in London, where there were the intense demands upon his time, his availability when Alexander was awake and not being adored by a relative was abbreviated.

The only part of the equation he could control was how he spent his time and this was a gradually dawning realization over those weeks in London.

Always, even as he lamented the numerous business affairs that kept him away from Elizabeth for long hours or weeks when he traveled, he hungered for the stimulation and excitement that commerce provided. The drive to be integrally involved in his estate's running as well as the constantly evolving aspects of industry and politics were too deeply ingrained to be denied. Additionally, he craved physical exercise that required hours at Angelo's fencing or on his horse. He needed the male socialization with his peers at the Jockey Club or White's.

He wisely recognized that being a husband and father did not erase those parts of his life that had ruled for some thirty years, and that fulfilling those fundamental desires kept him balanced and thus a better husband and father. But he also recognized that a portion of his aggressive motivation was a result of the loneliness and emptiness to his life prior to finding Elizabeth. With those holes filled, the urgency for action was not as keen.

Therefore, he started to consider ways to scale his diversities into something more manageable. So far it involved nothing concrete beyond talking to Mr. Daniels, his solicitor, about the best way to consolidate his holdings and streamline matters so his constant attention would not be as vital. It was too soon to see any benefit or make permanent decisions, but he was already surprised at how just broaching the idea eased the burdens weighing upon his heart. He could now hold Alexander and know that as time marched on he would be the kind of father he wanted to be to his children.

Elizabeth rose, moving about the chamber and straightening scattered belongings while Darcy played with the baby. He smiled, kissing the round cheeks and sweet lips, and nuzzling into the squat neck with blowing noises. Alexander arched and wiggled happily, released giggles and babbling vocalizations, and reached purposefully toward his father's face and hair.

Darcy felt that it was only fair for Alexander to be blessed with his wife's thick ringlets since he was burdened with his father's nose, a partial jest that Lizzy persisted in countering. The infant's face had lost all traces of his mother's features, settling into an infantile replica of his father. Of course, the truth was that Darcy thought his child the most handsome infant alive and was immeasurably proud of the pronounced resemblance, even with the prominent nose.

"Here, sweet, your rattle." Darcy repositioned the baby so that he was sitting on his lap and reached into the basket of toys kept by the sofa. He handed Alexander a colorfully painted dried gourd with a slim wooden handle, one of a half dozen rattles in the basket. Alexander instantly grabbed onto the toy and swung the round bulb toward his widely opened mouth. His aim was not the best, the hard object knocking into his nose and causing him to emit a high squeal. He was not to be deterred, however, the rattle again repositioned and the attempt to gnaw on the too-large toy upsetting him far more than the crash into his nose.

"You are supposed to shake it, thusly, Son," Darcy instructed, clasping the fat rattle-wielding wrist and moving it to demonstrate. Alexander watched, fascinated, joyfully bouncing his limbs and laughing, but as soon as Darcy released his wrist the rattle was again drawn toward the yawning mouth. "Everything into the mouth with you. Crazy boy," he said affectionately.

"He likes to eat," Lizzy said. "I have no idea where he gets that desire from." She winked at her spouse, Darcy merely grinning. "However, at this point in time I think it is because he is trying to cut his first teeth."

"Truly? How do you know?"

"Feel his lower gum," she said, picking up two envelopes off the desk and walking back toward the sofa while Darcy did as told.

"I feel hard ridges. Let papa see, Alexander. Now you can open your mouth. Oh, be still, you will get the rattle back in a moment. It looks a bit red, Elizabeth. Will it cause him pain?"

"It can, so I understand. But Mrs. Hanford has a salve that helps. George knew of a formula as well and concocted a liquid that will help if he is uncomfortable. So far he seems unperturbed other than needing to chew on everything in sight. This is also normal, so I am told. Perhaps this smaller rattle that can fit into his mouth will please him." She retrieved a round, disc-shaped silver rattle filled with beads, one side cut out for small hands to grip. Instantly the gourd was discarded for the new, shiny toy. After a few satisfying shakes, the rattle unerringly entered his mouth for serious chewing, Alexander gibbering happily.

Darcy squeezed him tightly and delivered a kiss to the top of his head. "Better now? Cool, hard metal does the trick, yes? I presume teeth are why he has been drooling so copiously lately?" He turned to his wife with raised brow.

"I believe so. Just when Samuel breathes in relief over the absence of regurgitated milk he must contend with saliva stains."

"He will learn to deal with it," Darcy answered with a laugh.

"I have not had the opportunity to share the post with you, what with you distracted with traumatic visions of Georgiana eloping in the darkest hours of the night."

"Hysterical. Is there no end to the misery inflicted upon me by the women in my life?"

"Perhaps this may help, or perhaps not." She waved the envelopes. "One should cheer you although the other will likely educe a groan. Which first?"

"I need cheering, especially since my wife has chosen to deny my fervid need for succoring." He replied with a grin.

"Very well then," she answered, ignoring his remark. "We received a letter from Anne. That is, Mrs. Raul Penaflor Aleman de Vigo, as she made sure to sign it."

"Are they not still in Bath?"

"Yes."

"She is writing letters on her honeymoon?" Darcy shook his head in mock shock, opening the parchment paper handed to him by Lizzy as she sat down beside. "What is wrong with that man? Anne should be far too busy to pen a letter."

"Just because you kept your new wife locked within the bedchamber for several weeks does not mean every gentleman does so. Bath is lovely, so I am told."

"I do not recall you arguing the treatment. In fact, I seem to remember an abundance of satisfied expressions," he said with a leer and arched brow.

Lizzy reddened slightly but laughed. "Just read the letter. You will note that it is not a long letter, so perhaps Dr. Penaflor is not so disappointing in your estimation after all."

"Good for Anne," he murmured, unconsciously bouncing the leg Alexander sat on as he began to read. The baby, of course, immediately forgot the rattle and opted to make a grab for the pretty fluttering paper. Darcy held it away, shushing and absently redirecting the silver chew toy back into the infant's mouth as he continued to read. Alexander, however, chose that moment to notice his feet, dropping the rattle in a concentrated effort to secure the strange, wiggling objects and bring them to his mouth.

Darcy's smile widened as he read. "She sounds so happy," he said softly. "Dr. Penaflor is a good man and I never doubted his love for my cousin. But I know her well, know the tenor of her letters in the past, and this is entirely altered. It is a welcome relief to know she is content, blissful even. No one deserves it more than Anne."

"Let us pray Lady Catherine allows them to resume their blissful happiness once returned to Rosings Park. Frankly, I cannot fathom living in that house with your aunt breathing down my neck."

"It is a large house. And, I am not sure if you noticed, but the suite Anne ordered to be redecorated is on the opposite wing from Lady Catherine's residence."

Lizzy laughed. "Oh indeed! I noticed. Very shrewd of Anne."

"I believe Dr. Penaflor had a say in the matter. He may wish to maintain civility with his mother-in-law, but he is not a fool."

Lizzy sighed, staring dreamily for a moment. "It was a beautiful wedding, even with all the pomp. Anne was lovely in that powder blue dress. A perfect color for her skin tone." Darcy took her hand, smiling. "I admit that I did not expect the ceremony to be charming in any way."

"It was fairly meretricious."

"Yes, but within the pretention it was beautiful. Once Raul and Anne were at the altar you only saw them so radiant and in love. The obscene profusion of flowers and glittering regalia faded in the presence of their joy."

"Aunt Catherine was disappointed that Dr. Penaflor's parents were not outwardly impressed by the flamboyance," he said with an evil chuckle. Alexander suddenly voiced a flood of gibberish, seriously gazing into Darcy's eyes. Darcy laughed, hugging the soft body tightly. "You agree, do you, Alexander? They were enamored by you more than any of the lavish decorations."

He lifted the baby, holding him upright and facing toward him, and commenced an intent, articulate verbal exchange. Lizzy tended to engage in infantile speech when chatting with her son, but Darcy refused to do so. Lizzy forever teased her husband about using five syllable words and complex sentences to a newly born child, but Alexander responded to the erudite commentary with rapt attention.

"Your Aunt Mary's wedding was understated but equally beautiful, wasn't it? Remember the yellow wild flowers that captured your gaze? And your aunt's purple ribbons that so fascinated you? Yes, you do remember, my intelligent boy. Perhaps you shall be musically inclined, unlike your incompetent father, since you hearkened to the organ music and singing. Which reminds me," he said, turning to Lizzy, "Mr. Daniels said the newlyweds are expected home in two days. Did Mrs. Daniels send word?"

"She did," Lizzy answered. "She plans to prepare the house with fresh flowers and linens, stock the cupboards, and so on, before her son and his new wife returned, and wanted to know if Jane and I wished to assist. We made a list of Mary's favorite food items to be purchased and delivered. Mrs. Smyth was not pleased to have Darcy House servants delivering goods, even to Russell Square."

"That is ridiculous. Russell Square is an upscale neighborhood and the house Mr. Daniels purchased is excellent. Did she argue with you?" Darcy asked, his tone abruptly dark and eyes narrowing.

"Of course not. She merely pursed her lips in that disapproving way of hers. I doubt if she concurs that a newly built area, even one near Bedford Square that is primarily inhabited by lawyers and others from the professional class, is 'upscale.'"

"She is walking a thin path, Elizabeth. These continued disrespecting attitudes and veiled insults are annoying me most profoundly. Do you still insist she stays?"

"You know as well as I that she is an excellent housekeeper, William. I can handle it and she truly does not bother me all that much. I find her as amusing as George does, which I know is unkind, but I cannot help it."

Darcy grunted. "Very well. But one toe over the line and she can find employment elsewhere with no recommendation from me."

"Anyway, while I am at Mary's house I will make sure the pianoforte in situated appropriately near the east window as you requested." She smiled warmly at her husband, caressing over his thigh. "She will be absolutely stunned when she sees your gift."

"Our gift," he corrected. "It was only logical. Mary may not be the most talented pianist, but she loves to play so should have an instrument of her own. I just pray Mr. Daniels appreciates her musical ability or he may retaliate by charging me double fees! Now, curiosity is taking hold and I am in an improved humor—although I still may need a few kisses at the least to restore my harmony, so tell me what is in the second envelope."

"A hand-penned invitation to the wedding of Miss Caroline Bingley and the Earl of Blaisdale—"

Darcy groaned.

"—for the fourteenth day of April—"

"I am sure we cannot make it. I am quite certain that is the day you and Alexander will be sitting for your portrait."

Lizzy laughed, nudging him with her shoulder. "You know that is not true. We have our sittings scheduled for this week. And besides, a wedding takes precedence over a portrait painting."

"Not in my opinion! You thought Anne's wedding was garish with Lady Catherine as organizer? Can you even imagine what Caroline Bingley will concoct?" He shuddered. "It is too painful to fathom. Furthermore, how can I stand at her wedding when I so abhor that man? Even Caroline does not deserve that fate."

"I think you are too harsh, William, as we have already discussed. She is very happy! You must believe me when I tell you it is so. Lord Blaisdale for all his faults—and I know you are not exaggerating what you know but rather minimizing for my delicate ears—is quite devoted to her. It is strange, in many respects, but they do seem perfectly suited and loving."

Darcy grunted but did not object. He hated to admit it, but the pairing was logical. He had not forgotten the attention directed toward Caroline at the opera, and as Lord Blaisdale's infatuation for red-haired women was common knowledge, even to Darcy who avoided gossip, he was not surprised. Everyone knew of Blaisdale's disastrous first marriage, most gentlemen sympathetic to his plight despite the Earl's reprehensible behavior, so it was understandable that he would be careful with his second marriage. Caroline was beautiful and well-bred: the perfect Society wife. She, of course, craved wealth and prestige, and would have no expectations for a faithful spouse who loved her.

Darcy had to admit that whenever the two were together they appeared quite content, bordering on affectionate. He now knew how a woman looked upon a man she loved, and vice versa, and recognized the expressions cast between Caroline and Blaisdale as indicative of mutual adoration and desire at the least. Charles was convinced of their regard and thrilled for his sister. And that, of course, was what it came down to, as Lizzy pointed out in the next breath.

"It doesn't matter anyway," she said decisively. "Caroline is your best friend's sister and obliquely related to us, so therefore we will be attending the wedding."

Darcy frowned but said nothing further on the subject, knowing she was correct.

"Look on the bright side, it should be amusing! Perhaps it will cheer you after suffering through Georgiana's debut at Almack's."

"Or it will be two insults within the space of a week that may topple me over the edge to insanity."

"My, you are dramatic. Are you going to be dramatic like your papa, Alexander? Hmmm?" She leaned to retrieve another dropped toy from the floor, stopping to nibble on his fat toes before giving the stuffed hound dog back. One floppy ear went directly into the baby's mouth as she turned her thoughtful gaze upon Darcy. "I have been thinking it may be best if you do not chaperone Georgiana. Wait, hear me out!" She lifted her hand to stay his response. "You can trust Georgie not to do anything foolish. She deserves this time to have fun, and I am not so sure if she will relax with you glowering at anyone who tries to dance with her!"

"I promise I shan't."

"You will try not to, but it will come naturally, my love." She smiled, kissing his cheek. "You will be uncomfortable in the atmosphere and worried for her. Emotion will show on your face to some degree no matter how you strive for nonchalance. There are others who can chaperone, sparing you the torture."

"Who did you have in mind?" He asked suspiciously.

"I was thinking of George or..."

"My Uncle George? Are you serious?" He sputtered. "He would be too busy flirting with every female over the age of five-and-twenty to notice if a gentleman acts inappropriately with my sister!"

"Dramatic again," she countered with a shake of her head and laugh. "Indubitably, George would be pouring on the charm, but he loves Georgie too much to ignore her. You trust him to escort her to Stevenage this summer—"

"I was coerced and taken unawares," he inserted grumpily.

"—so how is this worse? And there is also Richard. He is her guardian, after all, and not so apt to flirt with his heart locked upon Lady Fotherby."

Darcy remained silent, his face set in the expression Lizzy knew meant he was considering. She waited, watching as he kept his focus upon Alexander, bouncing and caressing idly as he frowned and thought her arguments through. Finally, "Very well. I concur that I am overreacting, slightly. I will accompany her this Wednesday for her first appearance. She has requested my presence to ease her nervousness. After that, I will permit Richard and my uncle to alternate if they wish." He glanced up into her eyes, smiling faintly. "I need to learn to let go, yes?"

Lizzy smiled in return, holding his eyes with love and respect, the teasing left unspoken. "Here, let me take our drooling wiggler to Mrs. Hanford so we can begin preparing for the symphony."

When she returned Darcy had doffed his jackets and cravat and was bent over the desk they shared in their smaller Darcy House bedchamber. He was rereading Anne's letter when she approached and slipped her arms around his waist from behind, leaning onto his back and squeezing. He straightened and turned, drawing her gently into his embrace. She draped her arms over his shoulders, twining her fingers into his hair and pulling his head down to meet her upturned lips.

"What were you saying about needing a few kisses to restore your harmony?" She whispered against his lips.

"Hmmm. I believe I said they would suffice if we had no time for more."

Her chuckle was stifled by a passionately seeking mouth. The kisses, or rather one continuous kiss, began tenderly but rapidly smoldered and flamed. Darcy held her firmly against his chest, one hand between her shoulder blades and the other flattened upon her derriere and pressing hard into his pelvis. Heat flared between them, readily felt through the thin layers of clothing.

Yet, despite the ever-present desire to make love to his wife and the instantaneous emergence of his physical response to her passionate touch, Darcy restrained himself. His teasing references to engaging in rushed lovemaking were not untrue or unwelcome, but he comprehended that preparing for a social event took time. He appreciated how carefully Elizabeth fussed over her appearance for these engagements and knew without a doubt that she would stun him with her beauty and perfection. Therefore, he stifled the groan lodged in his throat and pulled away from her lips to commence a languid exploration of her neck with gentle kisses. He moved his hand to the small of her back and slackened the pressure holding her body tightly against his.

"I was thinking," Lizzy whispered huskily, biting his earlobe sharply, "I bathed this morning so do not really need to do so again, and I am sure Marguerite has my garments prepared, and you can remove my day dress as well as she, so... Oh!"

Darcy had uttered not a word. Instead he precipitously lifted her into his arms, moving quickly to the bed. Just that quickly, his solicitude disappeared!

Lizzy laughed breathlessly. "You had to carry me the ten steps to the bed? We couldn't walk?"

"Far speedier this way. Time is of the essence, Mrs. Darcy." He grinned, but was quite serious. He straddled her thighs, hastily discarding his shirt and tossing it onto the floor, and then bent over her supine body with a hand next to each shoulder and arms straight, his body not touching hers. He drew close, his mouth inches from hers. "What is your pleasure, my lover? Shall I kiss and lick your flesh, your writhing and pleading driving me insane with desire until I cannot resist and bury myself deeply here as you lay? Or do you wish to be in control, sending me to places unimaginable with your skillful touch?" As he spoke in a soft whisper he moved his lips along her jaw and face, warm breath stroking her sensitive skin with each word interspersed with feathery kisses.

She was already running her hands over his torso, squeezing and pressing as she arched her back in an effort to contact his body. "I have no preference, Fitzwilliam. Just hurry!"

Darcy smiled, aware she was no longer referring to their evening's agenda and the preparatory requirements. *God, how I rejoice in her response to me!* The power to excite her so easily, so continually, was intoxicating. Of course, his ardor was as swiftly roused, probably even more so, the fire blazing uncontrolled through every nerve and his groin aching with need.

Suddenly it was not about the shortness of time but rather the impatience to be one as they attained pleasure unparalleled. A ragged groan burst forth as he again captured her mouth in a plundering kiss. He kept himself aloft, unerringly using one hand to unclasp the row of peach cloth-covered buttons down the front of her dress.

Lizzy clasped onto his shoulders, abruptly pushing him away as she launched upward from the bed. Darcy was momentarily surprised, but immediately relaxed, sitting back onto his heels. "Impatient, my love?" He asked with a salacious grin and raised brow.

"Together we can accomplish the task quicker."

And they did. Seconds later she was completely nude, garments strewn wildly about the room for probably the thousandth time since their wedding night. She instantly attacked the straining buttons of his trouser fall, eliciting rumbling groans and tensing muscles as she spared several minutes in focused titillation to the newly exposed flesh.

"Oh Lizzy! Please... stop!" He tugged harshly on her pinned hair, not intending to cause her pain but desperate to halt the arousing actions that threatened to send him over the edge without her.

She rose as he bid, running her hands around his hips and over his firm buttocks, holding on as she joined with him in one strong motion. Simultaneously, they expelled loud sighing moans, assuming a familiar rhythm.

Neither spoke, although the room was far from quiet. Time may have been short, but they enjoyed the interlude and did not rush. Attuned to his wife, Darcy knew seconds before she shouted and arched her back, fingertips digging harshly into his shoulder as she shuddered. He released the residual thread of his control, utterly succumbing to the spasms rushing through his body just as she cried out his name.

The dazzling euphoria that blinded their eyes and gripped every muscle lasted a short span of time, but the warm tingling remained long after they collapsed onto the cushioned mattress. Lizzy idly caressed the muscled leg lying across her abdomen as clarity restored and she became aware of the familiar deep, rhythmic exhalations wafting over her bare shoulder. She chuckled, turning to gaze upon the face of her spouse. He was flushed, satisfaction evident in the upward tilt to his lips, but he was also falling into a doze, as he often did after they made love.

"Fitzwilliam," she said with a laugh and nudge to his inert shoulder, "we must leave in less than an hour. No time for a nap."

He garbled unintelligibly, moving only to cup one breast and plant a weak kiss against her upper arm.

She laughed harder, wiggling and twisting until he was rolled onto his back with her leaning on his chest. She inevitably felt invigorated and alive after they loved, especially in the middle of the day. Darcy frequently did as well, but more typically he experienced a period of satiated inertia. He recovered fairly quickly—sometimes recovering very well and desiring a repeat performance—but for that span of time, he was borderline stuporous.

Caught between a laugh and an annoyed grumble, Darcy opened his eyes slowly, peering into the radiant face of his wife. "Go on ahead, darling," he mumbled gratingly, "I'll just rest here for a minute or two." And his eyes slipped closed.

"Oh no you don't!" She exclaimed, leaning to kiss his lips and playfully slap his cheeks. "Samuel will scowl and scold if you force him to hastily dress and shave. You insisted on having your way with me so now you must pay the price."

"Ha!" He said with increased vigor. He opened his eyes, the blue orbs shining and clear, and grinned. "I was prepared to be a gentleman until my lascivious wife threw herself upon me."

"Well," she countered, "You can no longer wail and bemoan your need for comfort amid the stress, now can you?"

Any retort was lost, Lizzy delivering a pert kiss before launching from the bed. She was laughing as she flounced toward her dressing room, turning at the door to blow a kiss his direction. Darcy happily watched her naked figure sway and mince, his lethargy abruptly disappearing in the surging joy that life with Elizabeth brought. With a final chuckle, he too rose from the bed, his step light and gay if a bit more swaggering than his wife's.

❧

Darcy chaperoned his sister for her initial appearance at Almack's Assembly beginning that Wednesday.

Dressed in one of a dozen new gowns designed specifically for her Almack's engagements, Georgiana was a vision of loveliness. Again the mixture of pride and dismay that pierced Darcy's heart was difficult to bear. He knew his sister well enough to recognize the subtle signs of her anxiety and shyness, yet was amazed at her outwardly tranquil expression and lack of fidgeting. It had taken him at least two years to master the reserved aloofness that was now too easily construed as arrogance and disdain, his hands still often betraying his discomfort by twiddling in some manner. Georgiana, on the other hand, was the picture of serenity.

They arrived some half-hour before dancing commenced at eleven o'clock. "You do not wish to be the first to arrive," Darcy explained to Georgiana, "nor should you delay and miss the opportunity to secure a respectable dance partner for the first set." Thus with impeccable timing, they presented their subscription tickets and passed through the widely opened doors, entered the revered interior of the premiere dance assembly in all of England.

For Darcy, entering the spacious and lofty room lit to dazzling proportions by a staggering number of chandeliers and candles brought back painful memories. He glanced about at the crush of young men and women, all in attire richly adorned and fashioned to display their attributes, noting the fathers and mothers and other chaperones peering speculatively at each person of the opposite sex than their ward, and silently sent a prayer heavenward that he had been so blessed to find his Elizabeth.

Georgiana, on the other hand, noted the plush sofas lining the four walls, the profusion of finely dressed handsome men and beautiful women already engaged in gay conversation, the enormous roped-off area for dancing, the soberly uniformed musicians tuning their instruments, and the raised dais upon which the seven Lady Patronesses held court, and her heart soared.

They wove through the tight press nearest the door, but managed less than ten feet into the room before Miss Darcy was hailed by a group of friends. She squeezed Darcy's arm, gazing upward for permission, and at his stiff nod she was gone.

The night passed in a blur for Georgiana. She danced almost every dance and rarely sat down. The introductions to dozens upon dozens of highly eligible bachelors were impossible to remember, and she honestly did not care. She wanted to have fun, leaving thoughts of matrimony or falling in love for another day.

Of course, Darcy did not fully believe this, despite his wife's assurances, and he certainly did not trust the slathering hounds persistently dogging his baby sister's steps with eyes far too bold for his comfort. Five in the morning could not arrive swiftly enough for him!

Georgiana hardly noticed her brother at first, almost forgetting he was there. However, after hours of his stern mien bordering on a scowl with piercing eyes that marked every move she made, his towering attendance hinging on menace in close proximity to wherever she moved within the enormous hall, and his curt retorts to any comments directed his way by anyone of the male sex, she began to seriously yearn for her uncle or cousin! Thankfully, they were all too happy to accompany her for the remaining Wednesdays until they departed in June.

The Season passed without a single offer of marriage made, although that was clearly not due to a lack of interested suitors. Georgiana embraced the lively diversions of dancing and conversation with far greater ease than anyone in her family would have expected, but her characteristic shyness and reticence nonetheless set her apart from the majority of the flirty, bold females, and kept the randy, rambunctious bachelors from pursuing too vigorously. Of course the image of her frightening brother and his surly reputation may have contributed! Whatever the case, she remained unbetrothed and had a marvelous time. Her step along the pathway of affability and confidence furthered considerably, but none of the gentlemen touched her heart specifically.

Darcy's relief was monumental. When the final Almack's Assembly was held and his sister arrived home safely, he physically sensed a cord of coiled tension loosen in his body. Lizzy stood nearby as Georgiana raved on innocently with one eye on her sister and the other on her husband, the tender but humorous smile conveying unmistakably that she knew precisely what he was feeling.

CHAPTER THIRTEEN

A Ball at Grosvenor Square

T HE MATLOCK CARRIAGE SLOWLY rolled through the crowded streets toward the grand Theatre Royal of Drury Lane. It was a spacious carriage, opulent and sturdy, but the five grown occupants in their finery were definitely beginning to feel the effects of close quarters on this sultry evening in late May. The fact that there was nary a hint of breeze added to the discomfort.

"I daresay we could walk to the theatre from here and arrive sooner!" Priscilla Fitzwilliam declared, fan waving steadily.

"The streets of London do seem to congest further with each passing year." Lord Matlock's baritone soothed the sharp ring left by the voice of his daughter-in-law. "Not to mention that Spohr's *Faust* is a special event drawing large crowds. I am curious to see his interpretation of the classic tale."

"As am I," Lady Matlock agreed. "The reports are that it is quite fantastic. A departure from the more familiar Goethe rendering, so I am told."

"I simply adore romantic operas!" Priscilla gushed. "I suppose it is therefore worth this infernal heat and delay. I only pray my curls remain intact." She patted the springy clump of hair strategically escaping from the feathered turban, looking to her husband for verification.

Jonathan, however, was staring at his brother with an amused smirk on his handsome face, noting the involuntary wince even though Richard's attention appeared to be fixed on the passing architecture. "Frankly, all I can dwell upon at the moment is why my brother, who barely tolerates opera in general and abhors German compositions, would insist on accompanying us at all!"

"Do not tease Richard so, Jonathan! I am sure he has his reasons." Lady Matlock leaned over to pat her youngest son's knee.

"I may have no great love for the romantic babblings of the German composers, Jonathan, but I can appreciate opera in a general sense. I am quite fond of Mozart, as you know, since I attended several performances with you and Priscilla over the years."

"Indeed, but Mozart is in a class by himself." Jonathan continued to gaze speculatively at Richard, who ignored him altogether while peering out the window. "You do not even speak German."

"Neither do you very well, yet here you are," Lord Matlock interjected. "It is all about appearances, son."

Lady Matlock laughed. "Perhaps for you, my dear, but some of us do actually enjoy the music and story."

"You speak fluent German, madam, which shall add to the spectacle. I, however, shall be employing all my vast resources of strength to avoid falling asleep and making a fool of myself before all of London society!"

"Do not fear, husband. I shall pinch you if necessary."

"Will you pinch Richard as well, Mother? He will surely require your assistance."

"I suddenly feel as if twenty years has been peeled away and I am again forced to play moderator to my two squabbling boys!"

They all laughed, even a nervous Richard pulling his attention from inner musings to the chatter of his family as they clattered ever so slowly toward the theatre.

The milling crowds along Russell and Catherine Streets were thick, necessitating the driver to halt nearly on the walkway opposite the main entrance. Richard's eyes scanned the press of brightly bejeweled bodies glittering in the glare of gaslight, as always when he searched for Darcy, looking for that one head which seemed to rise above all others. It was Dr. Darcy he found first, momentarily thinking it his cousin until he noted the toothy grin and bellowing laugh almost audible over the cacophony from where he stood yards away. Richard shook his head with a smile and resumed his quest, easily spying Darcy seconds later, where he stood tall and silent behind Elizabeth on the walkway by the right hand corner of the building.

Leaving his parents and illustrious brother to greetings from the gathering luminaries, Colonel Fitzwilliam eased to where Darcy stood, pulling him a pace away. With no preamble, he asked in a hushed whisper, "Anything yet? Have you seen her?"

"Good evening to you as well, Colonel. Beautiful night for the opera, do you agree?"

"Yes, yes! Lovely," Richard waved impatiently, tugging on his coattail in agitation. "Have you—"

"I adore these balmy nights in London," Darcy interrupted pleasantly, gazing toward the clear, star-embellished sky. "So bright and refreshing. Ideal atmosphere for a divine operatic experience, I daresay."

"Darcy, I shall be hard pressed not to injure you in some manner if you do not answer my question!"

Darcy chuckled. "Ah, but I am having entirely too much fun with this to let it go, Cousin. Rest assured, however, that if I had vital news to impart I would have done so. Alas, we only just arrived and have made it no further than this corner. I have been unobtrusively scanning the crowd and see no sign of Lady Fotherby."

"Are you certain she is to appear tonight?" Richard asked with a decidedly plaintive whine.

"So I have been informed by my wife, who is privy to information of this magnitude from sources I have learned to trust. As shall you if your hunt proves successful."

"Do not be vulgar, Darcy."

"No vulgarity intended, merely pointing out the facts so you can be adequately aware of what you are getting yourself into."

"Do you not always say that marriage is the best thing to have ever happened to you?"

"And so it is, my friend. It comes with perquisites unimaginable, one of which happens to be the delights of female gossip, some of it quite entertaining I must confess."

Richard shook his head, laughing low, the playful banter easing his nervousness.

Elizabeth had cautiously probed and discovered that the widowed Lady Fotherby would be making her first public appearance at this specific opera since the death of her husband some seven months prior. All season Colonel Fitzwilliam had quietly attended the various social gatherings his duties allowed, hoping for a glimpse of the woman he loved. But the rumors insisted that she remained sequestered in mourning at the Fotherby estate in Buckinghamshire. Unable to inquire forthrightly, he was left to lament to Darcy, who naturally shared all with his wife.

It had required minimal investigation on Elizabeth's part, as the news of Lady Fotherby's relocation to the London Townhouse now owned by her as a specific inheritance from her husband was a prime topic for tearoom gossip. Richard digested the information with equanimity, only a rapid swallow and the fact that he did not flinch over the news that it a German opera she was to attend signs of his discomposure!

"I would not worry too greatly, Cousin. Even if Elizabeth's intelligence is incorrect, we have secured a positive response to our invitation. Lady Fotherby will be gracing us with her presence at the ball we are hosting in two weeks."

Richard's face beamed. "When did you receive this?"

"Just yesterday. And I expect your undying gratitude and willingness to grant me any favor asked for the remainder of your life as you know how I abhor such extravaganzas."

Richard grunted. "I know full well that Elizabeth bullied you into Darcy House hosting a ball for Georgiana's benefit and as the perfect cap to the season. The painful requirement for you to be charming and gracious for one whole evening has nothing to do with me."

"I do believe that is the Fotherby crest, is it not, dearest?" Elizabeth's voice rose above the din, turning with an innocent twinkle to the two men standing a few feet away. She had not been able to overhear their muted conversation, but she was quite certain of the vein, smiling sweetly at Colonel Fitzwilliam who ignored her faint smirk.

Indeed, the lush carriage indicated, having rounded the corner and creeping toward the curb, bore the coat-of-arms for the Marquess of Fotherby. The occupants could not be seen, but Richard's heart constricted nonetheless.

Darcy leaned close, murmuring into the dazed Colonel's ear, "You would be wise to attach yourself to your parents. I am certain Lady Matlock will consider it her duty to welcome Lady Fotherby, as friend to her mother. Plus, I think she is aware of your infatuation."

"What! How could she—"

"No time! There they are. See, Aunt has noted the carriage. Go! And good luck."

Mechanically, Richard navigated around the bodies to rejoin his family, who were gradually steering toward the main entryway. Clustered knots of society engaged in lively conversation, polite greetings expected and extended. As always the opera, like all such entertainment venues, a cause for amusing discourse and class fraternizing equally as important as the cultural edification. Dignitaries and nobility abounded, Lady Fotherby's inclusion only of minor significance and interest to most. With her renowned husband now passed, she was not nearly as compelling. Except, of course, to those who were either curious gossipmongers by nature or were stimulated by the concept of an unattached and extremely wealthy woman. Richard's eye would not be the only bachelor's speculative gaze to linger upon the beauty of Lady Fotherby, although it is probable that his were the only thoughts of a pure intent.

When she alighted from the carriage Richard's breath caught and the stab of yearning felt in his heart was exquisitely painful. She wore a modest gown of deepest blue, the velvet shimmering in the gaslight and accenting her womanly figure. No jewels or embellishments adorned the austere gown of mourning, nor were her flaxen tresses garnished, but the basic chignon and simple dress only highlighted her natural beauty.

"My dear Lady Fotherby, how delightful it is to see you here. Many of us were concerned for your welfare, distressed over your self-imposed exile, and praying that your grief would soon be relieved."

"Thank you, Lady Matlock. You are kind. Allow me to assure you that I have been well comforted by my children and family. I am quite well indeed. Lord Fotherby would not wish me to wallow in pity and despair."

Lord Matlock nodded, bowing low in greeting. "I believe I can assert that to be a true statement, my Lady. Your husband cared deeply for your well-being and would shudder to think he has caused you undue pain."

Lady Fotherby inclined her head politely, eyes shifting to Richard, who stood silently beside his father. "Colonel Fitzwilliam, I trust you are well?"

"Quite well, my Lady."

"I am surprised to see your son here, Lord Matlock. If I may be indulged to tease just a bit, I seem to recall a young man not overly fond of opera. Of course, tastes do change with time." She smiled winsomely toward Richard, whose knees felt decidedly weak but whose heart was warmed by her presence and favorable demeanor.

Lady Matlock laughed gaily. "You have an excellent memory, Lady Fotherby. And I am afraid little has changed in my son's tastes, but he has learned to oblige his mother's whimsies and is a dutiful son."

"A mother can only hope for such a gift, I believe. Be cheered, Colonel, as I am told this particular offering of *Faust* is an exceptional one."

Richard bowed his head. "I am counting on this allegation, my Lady. I daresay we shall both pray truth in the statement; you so as to find joy in marvelous entertainment, and I so as not to fall asleep."

Her lilting laughter rang out. It was an auspicious beginning. Colonel Fitzwilliam would manage only a short conversation with her during intermission. Her uncle, acting as escort, hovered nearby with a stern frown keeping the worst of the vultures at bay. Still, the brief words shared and casual glances passed were encouraging.

The Darcy Ball offered an improved interaction.

⚜

The ball hosted by the Darcys at Darcy House for their end of the Season extravaganza was anticipated by a number of people for a variety of reasons. Darcy just wanted to get it over with, Mrs. Darcy was eager to display her talents as hostess and advance her husband's celebrity, Georgiana hungered for more dancing and flummery, George simply reveled in the amusement and attention, and Richard prayed to converse with Lady Fotherby.

Every room on the ground and first floors, with the exception of the Master Chambers, was open and aglitter with hundreds of candles and lamps. Sheens of gold and silver erupted from the profusion of metallic ribbons, gilded frames, crystal tableware, enameled vases, marble statues, and polished light holders, harmonizing brilliantly with the opulence of varnished floors, banisters, tables, chairs, and room trimmings fashioned from the finest wood available. The staff had outdone themselves in cleaning, arranging, and preparing, all at the instruction of their Mistress, who overlooked not a single detail.

The guest list of nearly one hundred was modest by typical standards. These final parties of the Season were the ultimate cap, the last chance to make a permanent impression upon Society either as host or attendee. Invitations were coveted, accepted by the dozens, and extended widely. It was not at all unusual for one to visit several glittering houses in one night, the briefest appearance enough to comment upon; conversely, it was the norm to send hundreds of invitations if so bold as to plan a fête during the competitive final weeks, in hopes that a fraction would show up. Glory was attained both in how many invitations one received and in how many personages of importance passed over the threshold.

Lizzy's remaining ignorance in some of the finer machinations of the ton kept her unaware of the fact that by limiting the number of invitations, the Darcy ball instantly ranked as one of the prime tickets in town! Her reasoning was simply the desire to entertain only those people they genuinely enjoyed. Therefore, her first list was smaller still, but fortunately she, as in most matters, asked her husband's opinion. Darcy, naturally, was well aware of all the fine nuances of Society and, despite his marked lack of enthusiasm in hosting a grand soiree of this magnitude, recognized the suggested snub if they ignored too many key members of the London social set. The revised guest list remained modest but was perfectly balanced. The question would not be why the Darcys excluded certain folks, but what those folks had done to deserve the Darcys' censure! Thus, while Lizzy immersed in menus and decorations, Darcy smugly sat back and laughed to himself.

The Darcy Ball resembled more of a Salon atmosphere in the eclectic assortment of guests with their unique personalities. Darcy proudly stood on the bottom step of the foyer stairway, the location elevating his imposing, fashionably attired figure at the juncture of the ballroom and drawing room. He greeted new arrivals with his classic dignified reserve and cordiality while furtively observing Elizabeth as she gracefully glided among the assembled guests. From time to time he could faintly hear her musical laughter, noting with awed contentment how she easily joined conversations with the most diverse of groupings. He did not need to hear her words to tell that she was welcomed by one and all, her dynamic but genteel personality appreciated.

Currently, she stood talking to his great aunt, the Marchioness of Warrow. Darcy smiled briefly, again impressed at the curious rapport she possessed with his flamboyant Aunt Beryl, but then his thoughts were distracted as he greeted the astronomer Sir William Herschel and his wife. The plain truth was that Lizzy thought her husband's notorious relative captivating in her outrageousness. Thrice married and widowed, each husband wealthier than the previous and possessing of a higher title, this younger sister to Darcy's grandfather was one of those English novelties in the same mold as the historic Bess of Hardwick. Well into her seventies, she still radiated a residual beauty and sensual charm that sparkled and left no mystery as to how she once attracted her husbands and numerous lovers.

"Of course, the Duke never could maintain his dignity when sodden with wine!" Lady Warrow declared with a throaty chuckle, Lizzy and the other listeners laughing with her. The fact that the Duke whose story of impropriety she regaled was deceased and unknown to each of them was insignificant; the humor was in how she related the tale with verve and embellishments. Not for the first time, it occurred to Lizzy that George had obviously inherited his flair and abundant humor from his father's sister. "Lord Essenton, my second husband, you know, and dear Sebastian's grandfather"—she lightly patted the arm of the young man standing at attention beside the chair she sat on as if the grandest throne—"smoothly intervened, supporting the soused Duke and escorting him to the terrace for a bracing walk in the January Durham air before he upset any additional trays of food onto Prince Frederick's lap. Luckily his Highness has a marvelous sense of humor and was well past the point of clear-headedness."

"Quite fortunate you both were there, my Lady. Imagine the scandal!"

"Oh, my dear Mr. Gilcrist, such *faux pas* rarely became true scandals; otherwise, no one would ever have the liberty to enjoy themselves! I could shock you endlessly with tales of solecism in the elite. Truly, in my vast years of experience, I have come to believe the poor rural farmer possesses a decorum and sense of etiquette superior to his betters." She smiled slyly, fluttering her fan toward Mr. Gilcrist with the array of jewels covering her delicate gloved hand flashing in the light. "But this must be our secret, sir. We mustn't let on that we know the reality behind the carefully erected façade."

Lord Alvanley laughed boomingly. "Indeed, Lady Warrow, a shocking truth to be sure. Imagine His Highness' consternation if he were to learn of it."

Everyone laughed at that. The exploits of the Prince Regent and his close circle of friends, including Lord Alvanley, were common knowledge.

"Fortunately, not all hope is lost. There are those, my great-nephew a prime example," Lady Warrow smiled at Lizzy, "who remind us rogues of proper behavior. Lessons are being passed on via excellent messengers like my dearly departed brothers, upstanding men all."

"Considering all the accounts I have heard from Mr. Darcy about his grandfather, that is no surprise to me," Lizzy offered.

Lady Warrow laughed. "My dear, the tales I could share! Our father was so rigid and stern I do not think a hurricane would have bent him. No humor whatsoever, poor man. Mother was an outrageous flirt. Surely where I inherited my wicked tendencies, yes, Lord Alvanley?"

He inclined his head, crooked smile devilish. "As you wish, madam."

"I wisely chose husbands with high character and decency. Balance out the ignoble, you see. Propitiously for the aristocratic classes, my offspring, for the most part, have walked paths similar to their sires."

"Thus, England is saved," Lord Alvanley chuckled.

"Mrs. North," Lady Warrow addressed the woman standing beside Lizzy and ignored the Baron's playful slur, "I do not recall if I ever mentioned it, but my Lord Essenton very much resembled your husband. Quite fair and slight of build with a striking pair of gray eyes. You can see the traits in my grandson." She again affectionately touched the arm of the young man. "Not at all dark or blue eyed like most of us Darcys."

Mrs. North smiled and curtseyed in the direction of Lady Warrow's grandson. "Well, Mr. Butler, it is a compliment to be sure, as my husband is a handsome man by all accounts, not just my own."

"Thank you, Mrs. North. I will accept it as such." He inclined his head gracefully, surprising those who had not yet heard him speak with the deep timbre of his voice.

"Mr. Butler," Lizzy addressed the young man, "your lady grandmother was telling me that you compose music?"

"Indeed, Mrs. Darcy. It is a passion of mine to be sure."

"Sebastian is a genius, if I say so myself," Lady Warrow interjected with obvious pride. "His studies at Oxford primarily focus on music, as well as other subjects, all of which he excels in."

"Perhaps, if you feel so inclined, you would be willing to delight us with some of your compositions this evening? I confess I have a poorly discerning ear for music, but my sister, Miss Darcy, is an excellent connoisseur of all types of music. She would adore hearing the fresh arrangements of her cousin, I am sure."

He laughed, bowing. "As long as she is not too harsh a critic, Mrs. Darcy. We artists have fragile egos."

Lizzy opened her mouth to reassure him, but Lady Warrow intervened. "Nonsense, Sebastian! Your music and talent are remarkable. No one could disagree."

"So says the doting grandmother," Lord Alvanley interrupted with a snicker.

"Indeed I do, my Lord Alvanley. And you watch your tongue! I am good friends with your mother, you would do well to remember!" Lord Alvanley bowed in humorous remorse, Lady Warrow's eyes twinkling as she harrumphed. "Besides, you have heard Sebastian play and sing so know the error in your allusions. Rest assured, Mrs. Darcy, anything Mr. Butler plays for your guests would only serve to dazzle them further."

"Well, I daresay the pressure has been increased. I shall need to think cautiously before attending to the task to ensure I adequately dazzle."

Lizzy laughed. "I am not worried, Mr. Butler. And no pressure intended, please. It is a humble request only."

"And one I am happy to grant, Mrs. Darcy. Music truly is my delight and I am horribly arrogant about it and never pass an opportunity to entertain."

"Then this is more than a passing fancy, I presume. Do you wish to advance in your knowledge of music? Apply your gift as a career choice?"

He smiled benignly, a hint of annoyance in his tone when answering. "If you ask my father, Lord Essenton, then the answer is an unequivocal no. He rightly believes that my only job should be learning to be a proper estate manager and future Earl of Essenton."

"I say that is a waste!" Lady Warrow declared firmly. "I doubt my robust son shall be relinquishing his hold on the title anywhere near soon, as he takes after me and not his father, thankfully, so shall live to a ripe old age. Sebastian's talent is far too brilliant to ignore. In fact, we plan to tour the Continent next year after he graduates. No better place to learn the glories of opera than in Austria and abroad."

In another corner of the room, Colonel Fitzwilliam stood with his parents, Gerald and Harriet Vernor, Admiral Ulster, the poets Robert Southey and William Wordsworth, and Lady Jersey. The location was not of his choosing, being at such an angle as to have the foyer and main parlor entryway obscured. Unfortunately, there was no way to relay his distress to his parents, so he employed every ounce of considerable military discipline to calm his impatience while trying to decide if his odds were improved by staying with his mother or wandering about the room. Such was his mental turmoil when Lizzy joined their cluster.

"Lady Jersey," Lizzy curtseyed smoothly toward her exalted guest. "Your presence in our humble home is a true honor."

Lady Jersey inclined her head, face impassive, and voice without emotion. "The honor is mine, Mrs. Darcy, to be sure. I daresay the orchestra Mr. Darcy secured is excellent. I fear I am pressed to sit still for much longer and will need to wrest my Lord husband from his cigar and brandy for a turn about the floor."

"I wish you fortune on that count, Lady Jersey," Lord Matlock said with a chuckle. "The Earl's love of cigars is an established fact."

"Indeed you are correct. Perhaps I can impress upon Mr. Wordsworth to take pity upon me?"

He bowed low. "It would be my greatest pleasure, Countess. Pity would not enter in at all. Shall we?"

The two departed, it now Mr. Southey's turn to chuckle. "I am not quite sure if Lady Jersey fully knows what she has entered into. Mr. Wordsworth is far better at placing words upon parchment than in placing his feet properly upon a dance floor."

"At least she has a willing partner. My Lord husband utilizes no manly diversions to avoid dancing with his Lady wife." Lady Matlock said with a teasing glance to Lord Matlock. "He simply refuses to dance at all."

"Honesty is the cornerstone of a successful marriage, my dear. I honestly abhor dancing and you would honestly abhor your painful feet after I waltzed all over them."

"Admiral, I understand congratulations are in order on your daughter's engagement?"

"Thank you, Mrs. Darcy. Indeed Esther has made an excellent match with Mr. Kemp. We are pleased."

They all noted the sidelong glance directed toward Colonel Fitzwilliam, as well as his faint wince, but only his parents and Lizzy fully knew the cause. Until a few months ago, they had all thought Richard subtly courting his Commanding Officer's daughter. It was a logical match and Lord Matlock was furious when the news reached his ears that his second son had resisted matrimony, once again. Their row was fierce, but it was Lady Matlock who calmed her husband down with sympathetic and oddly knowing gazes at her son. The Colonel trusted Darcy and Lizzy, knew that they would never speak of his romantic woes to his mother. In fact, Lizzy had never said a word to him directly nor shown a clear sign that she knew, Richard only assuming she was aware based on the nature of his cousin's marriage, so he could not imagine how his mother suspected. Yet, not ten minutes later it was further indicated by her comment and sly look that she had some suspicions.

"Elizabeth, I see that the Ambassador and Countess de Lieven have arrived. Richard, you should escort Mrs. Darcy in her hostess duties while Fitzwilliam is engaged with greeting new arrivals. It will give you a change to meet everyone. Surely there will be someone to spark an interest."

Colonel Fitzwilliam was so startled he actually gaped at his innocently smiling mother. Lizzy came to his rescue. "Yes, please do, Colonel. I miss having a handsome man to accompany me. Barging in upon idle chat is exhausting, so your assistance would be appreciated."

Lizzy's charm and witty banter rapidly restored his equilibrium. They continued to wander, pausing for short exchanges with everyone. Twice Lizzy engaged Darcy's eye as they gradually milled through the crowds. The first time he smiled, but shook his head marginally. The second time he again smiled and nodded faintly toward the ballroom, his left brow rising imperceptibly.

"Colonel, let's stroll into the foyer. Perhaps I can rescue my husband and secure a dance."

Darcy was openly relieved. Not only had he missed his wife, but the chore of being "charming and gracious," as Richard had put it, was beginning to wear. He met them as they crossed the threshold, the currently sparsely inhabited foyer offering a vacant pocket for him to corner his beloved spouse and favored cousin.

"Please tell me it is morning already? Or at least that all the invitees have arrived?"

Lizzy laughed, relinquishing Richard's arm for Darcy's and squeezing tight. "The answer to both is no, my love. But the good news is that the flood appears to have fallen to a trickle, so perhaps we can allow the new arrivals to find us."

"Superb. I was beginning to feel like a statue standing conspicuously on the step."

"You did have the vantage point, however. What news to report from your angle?"

He scowled, voice grating. "Georgiana has danced each set, I do believe. She is currently on her second set with Mr. Vesey. I do not like him."

"Well there is a shocking proclamation," Richard said with a laugh, Darcy scowling deeper and adding a glare.

"If that is all you have noticed, then I guess I will share some of my news. Your cousin, Mr. Butler, does indeed compose music as you were told. He has agreed to play for us."

"I hope he has some talent and avoids the morbid tunes that seem so popular among some."

Lizzy was shaking her head. "I do not think so. He seemed a lively, humorous young man. Not somber in the least."

Richard was still smiling at his cousin, Darcy noting the amusement with chagrin. He spoke, eyes riveted to Richard's face, "Lord and Lady Fotherby arrived about twenty minutes ago. They headed toward the dining room."

Richard jerked, eyes widening and mouth falling, speech halting once he found his voice. "Lord... Fotherby! How... What do you mean?"

"William, that is just cruel." Lizzy scolded, although she was fighting not to laugh. "He means the young Lord Fotherby, Richard. No one has learned how to revitalize the dead, despite the fantastical claims in that absurd Frankenstein novel. Did you greet them properly, dearest?"

"Naturally. As abounding in warmth and amiability as I could possibly manage." He smiled gaily at Richard, who grunted in derision. "She is lovely in a gown of pearly white with mere touches of black."

"Ah, a bold statement indeed." Lizzy nodded satisfactorily. "A year will soon be passed. It seems her heart is prepared to move on. Interesting." She did not look at Colonel Fitzwilliam though, instead gazing at Darcy with a mixture of amusement at Richard's predicament and unsettling disquiet at the mere concept of continuing life without her husband. He smiled tenderly, reassuring with a firm squeeze to her hand.

"I deem it only proper for you to welcome the new Lord Fotherby to Darcy House as well, Mistress Darcy. Care to join us, Colonel?"

Richard swallowed and nodded, Darcy pivoting quickly to hide his grin.

The former Lady Simone Halifax, now the widowed Most Honorable Marchioness of Fotherby, stood at the edge of the ballroom dancing area. Numerous guests lined the walls, standing and sitting, dancing partners interchanged and mingled, conversation ebbed and flowed. Lady Fotherby was flanked by her paternal uncle and aunt, Lord and Lady Francis-Nall, and her stepson, the new Lord Fotherby. The sixteen-year-old 9th Marquis of Fotherby, 12th Baron of Armsbury was a slight youth no taller than his stepmother, fair haired with a sallow complexion. He exuded an air of ethereal weakness, his frailty unmistakably a result of a chronic illness that amplified an inherited lack of attractiveness. Appearing far younger than his tender years, he nonetheless held himself with the dignity of his station and gallantly assumed the role of protector to his widowed parent.

Lizzy eased into the assembly as effortlessly as always, Darcy and Colonel Fitzwilliam contributing as fitting to their personalities. That is to say, Darcy offered short sentences and engaged Lord Francis-Nall and Mr. McQuade in a lengthy conversation about the recent races at Ascot, whereas Richard gradually loosened under the carefree chatter and buoyant atmosphere. Never one to remain uncomfortable or tongue-tied for long, he rapidly exchanged his previous anxieties for his native charisma. Of course, it helped that Lady Fotherby was as naturally witty and effervescent as he was and additionally seemed deliberately to steer the dialogue in his direction as often as possible; or at least his heart hoped it was intentional.

"Mrs. Darcy, your home is lovely. I have driven past Darcy House before, but have never been so blessed as to be a guest."

"Thank you, my Lady. I daresay that was not due to any slight intended, but merely because Mr. Darcy has not been fond of entertaining."

Lady Fotherby laughed. "No slight perceived, I assure you. I never knew your husband as well as his esteemed cousin"—she nodded toward Richard with a teasing smile on her lips—"but recognized his reserved nature at a young age. Quite unlike you, Colonel. A notorious flirt, I must say."

"Charm and sporting are taught in the military as tactics for deceiving the enemy. I was merely practicing my profession." Richard quipped with a straight face.

"Indeed, Colonel. Well, you were accomplished, so it surprises me naught that you have risen to such a high rank. We shall see if you have lost your edge and therefore doomed to remain a mere colonel forever."

Richard bowed with a flourish, Lady Fotherby laughing as Lizzy spoke. "Personality is a possession my cousin holds in spades, to the point of irritation from time to time." She offset her words with a playful and affectionate touch to his arm, continuing more seriously. "However, it is his valor and bravery that has earned the notice of his superiors. If it is a subject that interests you, my Lady, Colonel Fitzwilliam is replete with tales both extraordinary and courageous. I cannot say my pride in our country's armed forces was as profound until deeds were extolled by the good Colonel. I am sure he would delight in sharing with you, in his typically captivating way."

Richard's thankfulness at Lizzy's clever manipulation hid his astonishment at her deception. The truth was that he had never once spoken of anything military to Darcy's wife! What tales he told were flippant and spun for humor rather than enlightenment.

His gratefulness increased tenfold when Lady Fotherby replied, "It would be an honor to hear your stories, Colonel Fitzwilliam. You are aware, I am sure, what a strong supporter my late husband was of the King's military. I too shared his passion in the subject. And specifically for the men who sacrifice so much for our great country."

The last was uttered softly and with a penetrating gaze into his eyes. Richard's breath caught and it was as if the entire room faded away for a brief time. Strange how tiny details will suddenly loom large and burn into the consciousness. He noted the color of her eyes, a hazel base with pinpoint flecks of greens and blues; the fine lines at the corners of her eyes which lent an air of maturity to her otherwise youthful face; the multiple lengths of her golden eyelashes; the small mole above her left upper lip; and on it went. The girlish face he remembered so vividly from those bygone days of immature infatuation now melded with and was supplanted by the adult one seen clearly with the steady love of a grown man.

Further conversation flowed, Colonel Fitzwilliam and Lady Fotherby fluently drawn into the general discourse as the topics shifted. None but Lizzy and Darcy noted the oblique if borderline pointed exchanges between the two, although Lord Francis-Nall did frown a time or two. The stiffly hovering Lord Fotherby was finally persuaded by his stepmother to join the bands of adolescents flittering around the room. He resisted, shyness apparent and empathized with by Darcy, but was eventually swayed by the rowdy capture by a couple of friends, sons of other prominent guests.

"Mrs. Darcy, the announcement has been made for the sarabande." Darcy turned to his wife with a staid expression, the twinkle in his vibrant blue eyes only visible to her discerning gaze. "I believe it is incumbent upon us to partake in this particular dance whenever possible. May I have the honor?" His rich voice dropped into an intimate caress.

She took the offered hand with a curtsy and brilliant smile, her own voice a seductive purr. "The honor is mine, Mr. Darcy."

He inclined his head, flashing a bright smile, and squeezing her fingers firmly before leading away.

The handsome couple strolled regally to the line without a backward glance, eyes locked upon the other, and just like that, Richard and Lady Fotherby found themselves alone.

Lady Fotherby wore a wistful smile as she observed the pair. Unconsciously she sighed, murmuring, "They appear so happy together and well matched. Mr. Darcy is particularly gay these days."

"Marriage has brought out his lighter side," Richard said. "He is forever lauding the glories of matrimony."

"Do his acclamations not move you to take the plunge, Colonel?"

He met her eyes with a steady gaze, attempting to discover the reasoning behind the casual remarks while also trying to pour his sentiments into the responses. "In truth, I have begun to rethink my prior adherence to the superior merits of bachelorhood. Perhaps it is the wisdom that comes with age, or seeing others find happiness in marriage, or maybe... other stimulations. But lately, for a few months now, I have seriously altered my attitude."

"How wonderful. I am sure every young lady of eligibility in London will be thrilled to hear the news."

He chuckled. "You are kind, Lady, but this is doubtful. Besides, few of them hold any interest to me."

She feigned shock as she teased, "Why, Colonel, how do you expect to cross from the realm of single man to happily married couple if you limit your choices and remain aloof?"

He paused, speaking concisely in a low tone when answering. "I deem it wiser not to look beyond ladies in near proximity. A man my age knows what he wants." He paused again, waiting, but she merely nodded with a secretive but pleased smile playing about her mouth. Richard could not prevent a wide grin from spreading along with the warmth diffusing through his chest. "May I have the privilege of escorting you in the next dance, Lady Fotherby? I believe it to be a minuet."

For the first time she glanced away, cheeks flushing slightly as she assured they remained isolated. Her voice was apologetic when she replied, "I regret I must decline your kind and welcome offer, Colonel Fitzwilliam. I promised my family I would adhere to their set timetable of mourning my husband for a full year. My recent excursions beyond my home were under the express agreement that I would socialize lightly and not dance." There was a hint of anger to her tone, nothing in her demeanor giving the impression of overwhelming grief at her loss. She shook herself slightly, again meeting Richard's eyes with a sweet smile. "Perhaps another time?"

"Absolutely! The offer will remain extended as long as you wish it to be so."

She smiled wider, boldly holding his gaze as she cocked her head to the side. "Do your duties with your Regiment keep you wholly occupied, Colonel?"

He blinked at the odd change in topic, heart falling although her expression remained open and frankly flirtatious. "To a degree, yes, but I am not without reserves of free time. Why do you ask?"

She shrugged. "No particular reason. I also find that my time is often engaged with the consuming tasks of managing a household, demands of Society, and parenting. The latter, of course, is of tremendous joy to me. In fact, the highlight of each day is when I stroll through The Green Park with my children. The eastern end of Queen's Basin, along the walk there, is our favorite destination and we try to arrive around one in the afternoon each day, as my eldest, Harry, has decided that is lunchtime for the ducks." She smiled, still not averting her eyes. "It is a most refreshing way to spend an afternoon, Colonel. I would highly recommend the diversion as a remedy for stressful duties. And, if one is so fortunate, interesting conversations can be engaged in if friends are encountered by surprise."

Richard soared. Every ounce of steely discipline was called into play to avoid dancing a jig right then. Instead he nodded solemnly. "Yes, I see your point. Thank you for the suggestion, my Lady. I will do my utmost to arrange time to walk."

CHAPTER FOURTEEN

Tales of a Scoundrel

THE DARCYS' SECOND SEASON in London drew to a close with no particular upsets, but two last-minute dramas to deal with.

The invitation hastily given to Georgiana Darcy and Kitty Bennet at the Cole's Masque was indeed a sincere one. Miss Vera Stolesk and Lady Alicia Nash persisted in their desire to have their new friends join in the summertime revelry at the Nash manor north of Stevenage in Hertfordshire. The girls' perseverance brought a shy blush to Georgiana's cheeks while sending Kitty into throes of jubilation. True to Lady Alicia's prediction, her father was amenable to adding two more girls to the mixture. She did wheedle and hyperbolize her desperation, the adorable pout put to good use, but it was a game between father and daughter. Lord Stevenage was not only completely twisted about his only daughter's finger but also delighted to fill the vast corridors of Graceholm Hall with youthful laughter. He spoke with Mr. Darcy personally on the subject, assuring that the girls would be well cared for and chaperoned at all times. George Darcy added his promise to accompany and chaperone, a pledge that did not completely alleviate Darcy's doubts, but between the adult persuasion and the pleading entreaties from Georgiana and Kitty, he could not deny the outing.

Mr. and Mrs. Bennet were consenting to Kitty disappearing to the home of a complete stranger, no persuasion needed at all. Neither Darcy nor Lizzy were surprised. Mrs. Bennet was faint with happiness, quite convinced that Kitty would return betrothed to a rich suitor, while Mr. Bennet merely anticipated the silence that would fall upon Longbourn for two whole months!

Therefore, three days after recuperating from the Darcy Ball, the two elated young ladies embarked upon their adventure with George Darcy playing protector. Sternly spoken admonitions were given, Georgiana undoubtedly the only one who would hearken to any of them, but the embraces and kisses of good-bye were as intensely bestowed as the instructions.

"Be well, my Georgie," Darcy whispered into her ear, disregarding propriety by pulling her into his arms while standing on the street walkway. "Return to me soon. I love you."

"Quit being a mothering hen, William," George interjected with a boisterous laugh and sunny smile. "She will be far too busy to think about a stodgy older brother. And besides, I have promised to watch over them." He winked at Lizzy, who resisted laughing, and boldly met Darcy's scowl and grunt with a cheeky grin.

The adieus were over after that, the carriage disappearing around the corner before Darcy sighed and turned to his wife.

The second drama was far more serious and extremely enlightening, as it concerned George Wickham.

The discussion that took place the day after Georgiana's departure, three days before they were to leave for Pemberley, was the conclusion to a predicament that had initially arisen during the winter. Shortly after their visitors vacated Pemberley after Christmas, Darcy had received a message via the contacts he had in the Newcastle area that Wickham's gambling and erratic behavior were beginning to spiral uncontrollably. There was nothing Darcy could do about the situation other than to instruct his associates to watch for any harm befalling Mrs. Wickham. However, probably before the dispatch made it to the far northern coastal town, Wickham was dishonorably discharged for insubordination. He barely avoided a court martial for drunkenly assaulting a superior officer, so they were informed.

Lizzy was naturally distressed and wrote to her sister immediately. But that letter, like her last several, was never responded to directly. A brief missive from Lydia sent to Mr. and Mrs. Bennet, mere weeks prior to Mary's wedding, droned on and on about "my poor Wickham's misfortunes," but gave no enlightenment as to their future plans. Mary's wedding was clouded by the scandal, Mrs. Bennet seemingly unable, or unwilling, to relent in her vocal lamentation over "dear Lydia's tribulations." Mary handled the drama with her usual aplomb, refusing to allow her mother's morose attitude to affect her happiness, but it served to alleviate her sadness in leaving the comforts of Longbourn for her new life in London. Lizzy and Darcy were strangely relieved and enthusiastic to quit Hertfordshire for the event of Anne de Bourgh's wedding in Kent. Even a fortnight with Lady Catherine no longer seemed as gloomy a prospect!

After that one short message from Lydia, no other word was heard. It was as if the Wickhams had fallen off the face of the earth. Darcy's contacts reported that they moved out of the shabby boarding house they had inhabited after Wickham's discharge, but no one knew where they were headed.

Obviously Darcy and Lizzy discussed the matter, and she was aware of and appreciative of his attempts to locate her sister. But as always when George Wickham's name arose, as infrequently as that occurred, Darcy was closemouthed. Lizzy did not push the subject, knowing that his hesitancy was not due to a wish to secret a part of his life, but due to his protective nature and grievous memories regarding his childhood friend.

That respect for his feelings was shattered, however, when on the day after Georgiana left for Stevenage, he announced to a startled Lizzy that he personally intended to travel north to see if he could ascertain any hints as to the whereabouts of Lydia and Wickham.

"No, William, you will not."

"I beg your pardon?" Darcy glanced up from his desk in shock.

"You will not go traipsing about risking life and limb for my sister. You have already spent far more money than you should in supporting her horrid choice. For this I am eternally grateful for a host of reasons, but enough is enough! I am certain that if there was anyone left who knew their destination upon fleeing Newcastle, he or she would have been uncovered by now. I will not have you frequenting the types of establishments where Wickham entertained and satisfied his aberrant urges. You did that once and it was sufficient for one lifetime."

"I assure you I can take care of myself," he countered with asperity.

"I do not doubt your capabilities, dearest."

Darcy looked away from her humorous smile, gazing out the window in thought as his fingers tapped a rhythm on the polished wooden surface of the desk. Lizzy waited. Finally, he continued, "I have an uncontrollable yearning to wrap my bare hands around that man's neck and squeeze. I have never felt such hatred for another human being, Elizabeth. Never. And it rather frightens me."

"Considering all he has done, I judge your sentiments normal. Yet, that is partially why you cannot go north. I fear you may act upon your inclinations, ridding the world of a worthless scoundrel, but harming your kind heart in the process. Despite some evidence to the contrary, vengeance is not normally in your character."

Darcy released a harsh bark, rising abruptly, and pacing with caged energy before the window. "I am not as certain as you. You know very well, Elizabeth, that I will protect my family at all costs without losing an iota of sleep. It seems, for years now, that Wickham has circled the fringes of my existence. Waiting for another opportunity to strike, to harm those I love, as he has not the courage to attack me directly. I have tried to convince myself that he is merely a pathetic excuse for a man, simply searching for the easy way in life and naturally latching onto the Darcy wealth as the most convenient. But I do not think it is that. Like pieces of a puzzle, it begins to fall into place with the clarity of hindsight."

"What do you mean?"

He paused, fingers again tapping and flicking as he stared sightless out the window. When he finally spoke it was in a low, contemplative voice, "Small, insignificant episodes from my youth. Wickham sidling up to Father and presenting an innocent face when I knew he was not. Pretending to be pious when he hated attending church. Charming, always charming. Using that gift he possessed to great advantage, knowing that I did not possess it myself. His wittiness and dazzling smile enamored everyone. Except my mother," he reflected with sudden wonder. "She could not abide him, now that I think upon it. Said he was too noisy. Hmm."

He shook his head, turning toward Elizabeth. "I will not go so far as to say he consciously plotted to supplant me. I believe it was primarily jealousy. You see, my father and Mr. Wickham had met at Cambridge. Mr. Wickham, the elder, was of modest means, the third son of a country gentleman from Sussex. Their friendship was genuine, but it was Mr. Wickham's intelligence that won him a position in our household. I am absolutely positive that Mr. Wickham never resented the arrangement, recognizing his good fortune in being steward to a grand estate while also working for a man he respected and held affection for. George Wickham, however, thought otherwise."

He sighed, running one broad hand over his face. "He is a born manipu-
lator. Quite impressively skilled at it if one looks at it in that light. I was far
from stupid as a child, but somewhat naïve, as I have told you before. Sheltered.
It was easy to bait me, if one knew how to do it, and Wickham did. He well
understood my nature for adventure, the typical wildness of a boy coupled with
a healthy dose of pride and arrogance." He looked at his wife with a crooked
grin. "Yes, even then, Elizabeth, I confess."

Lizzy laughed softly, nodding.

Darcy continued, the smile gone, "Still, I did not go out of my way to
inflict injury upon my person. I was cautious for the most part, not one who
particularly relished physical pain. Buried deep under the need for excitement
and the desire to push myself physically was a sense of restraint. I was sensible
and serious, as Mrs. Reynolds would always say. But Wickham knew how to
circumvent that. He masterfully, as I now see it, dared and taunted me into
recklessness. Such as climbing that ridiculous tree."

He touched his left rib cage, fingertips absently massaging the palpable
bump. "I never gave you all the details, Elizabeth. Do you know it was
the massive oak in the private garden, the one that grows over the nymph
fountain? I had climbed trees before—what boy doesn't?—but that tree is
enormous. The lowest branch, even now, I can barely touch with my fingers.
At twelve years of age, I needed to scale the statue, stand on a nymph's head,
and jump to the branch."

Lizzy gasped, knowing the scene, and her blood ran cold at the vision of a
young Darcy, or Alexander, performing such a feat.

"Indeed," he agreed with her exclamation. "Utterly foolish. Of course, I
was momentarily filled with conceit as I attained my goal, standing on the limb
in all the glory of a conqueror. Then Wickham said he did not think I had
the nerve to go higher." Darcy closed his eyes in remembered embarrassment.
"Idiot! Headstrong, foolish, imbecilic, cocky. And, as it turned out, incredibly
lucky or protected by God, I know not which. I deftly climbed to the next
limb and then the one above it before slipping. I hit the lowest branch on my
way down, cracking the rib and scraping through my clothes to the skin." He
extended his left arm, one fingertip tracing where the long scar on his inner
forearm remained. "It was that impact and the naiad that saved me, I think.
Or her hair, more precisely, as my arm caught on the upswept end of her
marble tresses, cutting deep, but slowing my descent and flipping me over so

that I landed on the mossy ground rather than the fountain edge. I fainted, or was knocked unconscious, I am not sure which, but when I awoke it was to the gardener bending over me. Wickham had fled the scene, leaving me. The gardener found me accidentally."

Darcy shook his head again, Lizzy spellbound and feeling ill at the story. "He apologized later, saying that he had panicked." Darcy shrugged. "I was young and forgave him. After all, I was not truly hurt all that badly and in the silliness of adolescence such exploits are deemed exciting, worn as a badge of honor while basking in the glow of womanly soothing. But it was just one of many such incidents that I gazed upon years later with discerning eyes and wondered."

"What sort of incidents?" Lizzy spoke in a bare whisper, almost afraid to ask.

Darcy, in all his revelations of his youth, a part of his life that was no longer a mystery to Lizzy, never mentioned George Wickham. She knew that they had been childhood friends, although certainly not on par with his friendship to Gerald Vernor, Albert Hughes, or Richard Fitzwilliam. Yet, in relating their daredevil deeds and boyish capers, he ignored Wickham's existence. She did not press the issue, knowing that memories of Wickham caused him pain and anger. In the end, she had assumed it was not all that important. Now she experienced a shiver of fear, unsure if she was resilient enough to learn the brutal truth about the man her sister was married to.

Darcy obviously wondered the same. He hesitated, studying her closely. Finally, he crossed the thick-carpeted floor, sitting onto the sofa and taking his wife's hands. "I have no proof for the most part, Elizabeth. As a child it was primarily the aforementioned baiting of me, and his false wooing. Falling from that tree was the worse injury I sustained, but there were other times that I could have been wounded due to bizarre accidents or foolish risks. But he acted my friend convincingly with his innate charisma. I confess that we were all taken in by him, me included. I remember wishing I possessed the easy personality of Wickham, and Richard and Gerald for that matter. I tried to emulate them but could never pull it off."

He smiled ruefully, Lizzy reaching to stroke his cheek, her eyes tender. He kissed her fingertips gently, understanding the unspoken words behind the gesture: his wife would never wish for him to be other than who he was, reserved and taciturn with a mellow playfulness and wit seen only by those most intimate.

He continued, holding her eyes, "I do not believe that Wickham was born a villain, but came to use his natural gifts for the negative, all due to an unrelenting resentment. As I wrote in my letter to you, Father assisted with Wickham's education, an education he never would have been capable of under normal circumstances, and Mr. Wickham was grateful. Yet, he continually reminded his son of the disparity in our stations, emphasized their dependence upon and indebtedness to Mr. Darcy. This rankled Wickham, to put it mildly."

He sat back into the sofa, holding tightly to Lizzy's hand as he resumed his narrative. "Again, it is hindsight. Comments he would make, expressions on his face, actions that varied depending on who was present. Subtle aspersions against me, impudent interactions with Georgiana, and inappropriate impertinence to the servants. I increasingly felt uneasy in his presence as we aged, but did not begin to see the full truth of his character until we were older, after mother died. Father was distant, often lost to his grief, so Mr. Wickham assumed more responsibility. He did it gladly, but Wickham resented it. Plus, he interpreted the adults' abstraction as carte blanche. He was bolder, more reckless in conveying his disdain and imperiousness."

He shook his head, eyes locked with Lizzy, but his thoughts looking inward down the passages of time. "Who can ever say with conviction how events may have unfolded if time turned down a separate path? If Mr. Wickham had not rigidly reminded his son of the gap in our stations. If certain comforts and privileges had not been denied. If our parents had not been consumed with other affairs." He shrugged, eyes clearing as he smiled grimly. "However, I do not hold with the opinion that a person is exclusively the product of outside influences, to be pitied or excused for their behavior and choices. Wickham was given opportunities far above most men in his place and he abused them all. During those years, there were numerous thefts about the manor. Trinkets, odd pieces of jewelry, silver utensils, and the like. Nothing of great worth, but losses nonetheless. We never were able to discover the culprit, assumed it was a servant although that seemed unlikely, as they have always been largely trustworthy. I have since come to believe it was Wickham."

"Why?"

"Aside from the fact that it simply fits into his character and that the thefts halted once we left for University is the fact that he always seemed to have money beyond what logic would dictate. Father helped pay for his education at Cambridge, but Wickham should not have been able to... entertain, shall we say, in the manner he did. Even my allowance would not have afforded his extravagant diversions."

The disgust was plain on his face, Darcy being a man whose principles strongly abhorred such "diversions." With tight jaw, furrowed brow, and voice steely, he resumed his narrative, "Long before father's death and the events that unfolded thereafter, I had come to fully understand the character of George Wickham. Those years were an education to me in many ways. A genteel lady such as you, my love, does not require the same education. But trust me, when I said that I knew Wickham was utterly unfit as a clergyman, I know precisely of what I spoke."

His lips pressed tightly together as a shudder ran through his body. Darcy's reverence for the Church was profound, his distress over any profanity extreme. Lizzy squeezed his hands tightly, heart aching as she caressed firmly and waited for him to continue.

He sighed, eyes filled with a flinty hardness. "I am no longer naïve or a fool, Elizabeth. I am well aware of the evil nature of people in our world. It sickens me, but cannot be denied. Is George Wickham evil?" He shrugged. "I suppose that depends on one's definition of the word. But I do know he is not to be trusted and is a scoundrel at the very least. He may not have planned my ruin or death with deliberation, but I am absolutely certain he would have welcomed and reveled in it. And I know his villainy matured because I saw the calculation in how he lied to my father, approached me for his inheritance and for more money, and with Georgiana. And with you."

"William, please…"

"I know I promised you that I would let the past die, forget Wickham's affronts against me and those I love. As long as he was gone and silent I have been able to put it aside—"

Lizzy rose, halting his words. He frowned, watching as she walked toward the window with back to him. "Beloved?"

"And now," she spoke in a tremulous whisper, "because of stupid Lydia you are related to him! How could you bear it? Marrying me knowing he was a part of the bargain? I am so sorry, William!"

He was across the room before the first sentence was finished. Hands grasping her arms and face stern as he whirled her about. "Don't be ridiculous! I would cross hell and back for you, Elizabeth! You know this. As greatly as I despise Wickham, it is a paltry price to pay for the honor and pleasure of being your husband. Do you not see the truth of it, my love? Perhaps I should have shared all with you long ago so you would fully comprehend." He drew her into his embrace, sturdy arms firm about her body, unwavering and secure. "Wickham has been a bane in my life since childhood. He would have continued to be so, I am convinced of it. Do you have any concept of how many 'Lydias' there were before her? Believe me, George Wickham feasted on such innocence, to my eternal disgust, as I witnessed the behavior more times than I can count."

He kissed her crown, breathing deeply of her fragrance. Lizzy held tight, comforted by his strength and steadily beating heart. "Lydia had nothing to do with you, my soul. Wickham may have sensed my regard for you as he knew me well, but months separated those weeks in Hertfordshire and the events at Brighton. He had no clue as to the depth of my love for you, and as we were not together at the time, it is impossible for him to have suspected that his dalliance with Lydia would profoundly affect me. He was absolutely shocked when I showed up in London. No, it was entirely coincidence. And entirely my fault as I have stated before."

Lizzy pulled away from his arms, it now her turn to glare at him sternly. "Now it is you who are being ridiculous!" she snapped. "All you have told me, both today and before, merely clarified Wickham's propensity toward mischief in general. Surely you are not the only one in all his acquaintance to divine his character?"

"No, but I had intimate knowledge and the means to thwart him."

She laughed harshly. "Oh really, William. Be sensible. Even if you had spoken the truth, 'exposed him' as you stated in Lambton, what possible good would it have done? You are only one man and England is a big country. I do not think even you have that much power. You were wise to not risk damaging Georgiana's reputation and your father's good name. Maybe I would have listened and not been so blind, but Lydia would not have. You said yourself that Wickham is a manipulative charmer—"

"Indeed he is!" He brushed his hands angrily through his hair, pivoting on his heels to resume pacing. "I do not trust this disappearance or this past year of quiescence. Elizabeth, he may have been ignorant of my feelings toward you before, but no longer. Furthermore, he knows I have a son."

He stopped abruptly, face thunderous, but eyes inundated with dread. "I will not be a fool who wears blinders and gullibly believes all is well while the fox is loose in the henhouse! He is a blackguard and nothing that has been reported to me this past year has altered my opinion of him. So, yes, I do wish to know what he is up to, not only for Lydia's sake!"

"And if your hands accidentally find themselves around his throat, then so be it? Or if harm befalls you in the search or at his hands, what then? Will it have been worth it?"

They both paused, respirations heavy and audible as they stared at each other from opposite sides of Darcy's large desk.

Lizzy broke the silent tableau first, her voice soft. "I still maintain that vengeance is not a trait near your heart, my dearest. Caution, vigilance, protectiveness, wisdom, and temperance, among a legion of other fine attributes, are the earmark of the man I married. I concur that we should be wary, Wickham not a man to be taken lightly. But I refuse to allow his existence to impinge upon our life and disrupt our happiness. Think how that would please him!"

She smiled, lips lifted in the teasing manner he found utterly delightful.

"And Lydia?" He asked quietly.

Lizzy shook her head, slowly stepping around the desk. "It grieves me, but she is not our primary concern. Besides, all your reports have shown that for all his faults, Wickham seems oddly to care for my sister. And they must be together, or I am sure she would be running back to Longbourn." She was before him now, palms reaching to encompass his face. "I think we need to make a new vow, beloved. You will relinquish your misplaced guilt, but we will not wholly forget the past affairs with Wickham. Heedful, yes, but not aggressively seeking problems where none exist."

"Is this more of the superior wisdom of my wife?"

Lizzy laughed. "If you wish to proclaim it so, then yes."

They were long since returned to Pemberley and enmeshed in the delights of a fine summer before a new communication from Lydia was conveyed to the Bennets. The Wickhams had settled in Exeter of all places, supposedly running an inn. The details were vague, but her tone was cheery and positive. Letters from Lydia to Elizabeth were nonexistent and eventually Lizzy gave up all attempts to communicate directly with her sister. What news she received was via her parents, and that was sporadic as Lydia wrote rarely. Children were never mentioned and this was taken as a merciful development as Darcy shuddered to imagine Wickham as a father. "Perhaps he cannot sire children," Darcy said once to Lizzy. "It would explain how he managed not to compromise any of his numerous bed partners over the years."

As time passed, they found less and less reasons to mention the Wickham name. Darcy harkened to the advice of his wife and let the matter go. Gradually, his guilt faded, but he never surrendered his distrust or wariness.

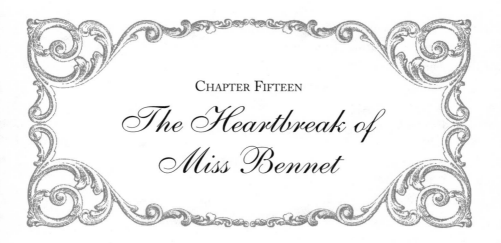

CHAPTER FIFTEEN

The Heartbreak of Miss Bennet

THE TWO MOUNTED MEN galloped to the small rise, reining in their heaving horses as they surveyed the rolling Hertfordshire fields below. The darker of the two gazed without really registering the vista, caught up with internal musings. The other young man turned to his silent companion with a sunny smile.

"Once again I have bested you! Really, Falke, you must try harder." The jest was lost, however, as Falke remained silent. "Very well, then. Tell me what the tyrannical old codger said."

"You know that my father is neither tyrannical nor old, but I thank you for the attempt to lighten my mood." Falke sighed heavily, only then turning to his friend. "He was unmoved by the declarations of my affection. Offered all the rationales that I anticipated, and although I tried to contradict, I really could not do so with great vigor."

"Her connection with the Darcys did not sway his opinion?"

"No. He said that Mr. Darcy, for all his wealth and station, is not a peer of the realm so the strict rules do not apply as forcefully. 'The son of Viscount who will someday inherit the title,' he stated flatly, 'must rise above the petty whims of desire. Honor and duty must prevail.' I hoped that the bewitching Mrs. Darcy, accepted and venerated by all, would soften his attitude. Alas, no."

"I am sorry, my friend. Would that I could help, but you know I am in the same predicament. Luckily, I am not of a romantic nature."

"I never particularly thought myself so either, but a sparkling pair of eyes and dainty dimples changed all that."

"Not to mention a lush figure."

"Don't be vulgar, Nash. Miss Bennet's figure, although enticing, was not the draw and you know it!"

"Of course not. It was her multitudinous accomplishments, keen intelligence, and stellar connections."

Falke glared. "Are you trying to make me angry?"

"Only reminding you of what you already know. You said yourself that you could not argue his reasons. Miss Bennet is a delight, we all agree on that Falke, but for marriage? It was never going to happen, and I think you have always known that."

"I prayed her charms would overrule the deficits. None of those matters bother me, and I would be the one married to her, so why should it disturb my father?"

"Again, you already know the answer to your question. And do not be so sure her 'deficits' would not come to annoy. Can you seriously imagine marriage to a woman of little intelligence and fewer accomplishments? A country girl with no knowledge of what would be required as Lady Gresham? I think you would be bored and disappointed within a year."

"Do you think me so shallow, Nash?"

"Not shallow, but the fact that you are not ranting and raging against your father, or mutinously scurrying off to Gretna Green, means you are unsure of your own heart. I know you well, my friend. You are a stubborn man who does not normally buckle easily."

Falke resumed his gaze of the landscape. In all honesty he knew that the words of both his father and Thomas Nash were right. His affection for Kitty Bennet, although real, was evidently not so intense as to defy his entire family. He envied Darcy who had been master of his own life and able to act on his wishes.

He sighed sadly, eyes closing in true regret, voice mumbled when he spoke. "How shall I ever face her disappointment?"

Nash was surprised. "Have you extended any promises? Surely you were not so foolish!"

"No, no. But she knows of my regard and is not an idiot. She even allowed…" He glanced sheepishly at the other man, swallowing audibly before continuing, "We kissed, in the garden, several times. Nothing else happened!" He added vehemently at the sudden leer on Nash's face. "Miss Bennet is a lady! Halt your insidious thoughts!"

And as he spoke the protective phrases, the memory of how vigorously Miss Bennet had instigated the kisses flashed through his mind and was guiltily squelched. His initial shock at her coquettishness and brazen advance had been rapidly replaced by pleasure in her kisses. Never would he betray her trust in him or harm her reputation, no matter how inappropriate her actions may be in the eyes of some. Falke had only looked upon her zeal as a testament to her attraction to him, a thought that was more than a little satisfying to his ego!

But he knew now that the union was destined to fail ere it had begun, and it broke his heart.

The summer holiday at the Nash country house was passing quite pleasantly for all the guests. Graceholm Hall was a luxurious manor, primarily of Tudor style architecture blended synchronously with Gothic influences, sprawling with numerous wings and hundreds of rooms. Surrounded by acres of rolling green fields, lush gardens, orchid plots, sparse woodlands, and tiny streams, the area was bursting with diversions. Lady Alicia's declaration of guests arriving and departing randomly, and in large numbers, was not at all an exaggeration. The two months the threesome would spend there was probably the longest of any other visitor, most staying for a week or two at most before roaming on to dwell at another friend's home. Such was the way of the aristocracy and wealthy during the languid summer months before the rains and cold of winter prohibited easy travel.

Entertainments of all varieties, both indoor and outdoor, were so plentiful to almost be overwhelming. Long hours in the cool shaded patios or well-ventilated parlors were spent in gay conversation, board and parlor games, and so on. Afternoons picnicking by the river, or strolling through wooded lanes, or horseback riding, or playing lawn games was essential. Evenings and late nights of dancing, attending local theater or musical events, performing dramas and concerts for each other, lively literary readings, and carnivals was the daily cap. These amusements were interspersed with excursions to the horseracing track, markets and fairs, football and other matches, museums, and special functions.

The constant influence of female and male companionship of all ages during that short interval would forever be marked as another ascending step in Georgiana's maturation. Like her brother, she would never be considered a gregarious character. But the months-long barrage of stimulating conversation and activity added to the frivolity and socialization during the Season in London acted as fertilizer to her hidden nature. Lizzy was not at all surprised to see her shy sister-in-law's blossoming. She had recognized instantly the identical sharp wit and extemporaneous humor in Georgiana that her husband possessed. Darcy would eternally present a stoic face to the public; his proclivity for laughter and absurdity a well-kept secret only know to his dearest intimates. Georgiana was similar, but not to the harsh degrees of her brother. The mature Georgiana who returned to Pemberley that fall would never again be the tremulous, blushing, inarticulate creature she previously was.

Yet, as profound as the alterations to Georgiana, they would pale in comparison to how Kitty was affected by her summer stay.

Initially, she was the proverbial child let loose in the candy store! The majority of the recreations were of a type never seen by her or participated in. This fact, however, inhibited her not in the least. Kitty did not seem to comprehend the notion of making a fool of herself, and if a few of the more haughty guests looked askance or quipped with sneering phrases, she was oblivious for the most part. The young men were utterly charmed by her vivacity and most of the young women found her amusing. But it was the attention of Mr. Falke that overrode all else.

Quite simply stated, Kitty was in love.

The mild attraction and playful flirting from the Masque rapidly evolved into full-blown infatuation within days of Mr. Falke's appearance at Gracholm Hall. By the end of a month, Kitty was overwhelmed by emotions unique and never imagined.

"Have you ever been in love, Georgiana?" Kitty's mumbled question was shyly offered as the two walked arm-in-arm along the graveled path between the fragrant rows of orchids.

"Considering the only unattached men I have been exposed to for the past several years are my brother and cousin, it would be unlikely, would it not? I suppose you are referring to Mr. Falke?"

"Yes." She sighed heavily. "Oh Georgiana! He is so wonderful! Unbelievably handsome with stunning dimples! My stomach flutters whenever he smiles at me!"

"I do not think that is adequate proof of true love."

"No, no. Of course it is more than that! He is kind, sympathetic, wise, mature, charming, droll, adorable, sweet…"

"All right!" Georgiana interrupted with a jolly laugh. "I understand now! He is perfection incarnate and you are enchanted. Has your Apollo totally swept you away and declared for your hand?"

"Not as yet, but I am confident he shall."

"How can you be so certain?"

Kitty halted, glancing about to ensure they were alone, leaning nearer to Georgiana and whispering, "He has expressed his affection with the utmost clarity. And last night, when we stole away from the concert, we kissed by the river!"

Georgiana was not nearly as shocked as one would expect. Over a year of observing her brother and his wife in secret clinches had abundantly opened her naïve eyes. Furthermore, the blatant flirting and ardent glances between Kitty and Mr. Falke were noted by all, with widely varying reactions. Georgiana was sincerely happy for her friend and her feminine, romantic sensibilities were stirred.

"Oh, Georgiana! It was divine!" Kitty closed her eyes in remembered delight, her face radiant. "He is divine! I have never imagined how wonderful love can feel!"

"Did he articulate his affection verbally or are you basing all your convictions on the strength of his kisses?"

"Georgiana! You are a tease! And, yes, he did more than just kiss me. He said he wished always to be with me, that I was dear to him, that his greatest desire was to take me to Chapel-en-le-Frith, and more! I am so happy. And Mama will be thrilled!"

Georgiana laughed, steering along the walkway. "Yes, I am sure she shall. Mr. Falke is an excellent gentleman and shall be a fine husband."

Kitty sighed, face yet brilliant with the essence of love, but suddenly introspective. "It is odd, Georgiana."

"What is?"

"For as long as I can recall Mama has spoken of little else but the necessity in securing a worthy husband. I can hardly remember a day when I did not notice men, especially handsome ones, gazing upon them not as individuals, but as prospects. We flirted outrageously, Lydia and I." She chuckled, shaking her head in embarrassment. "I can only imagine how utterly ridiculous we must have appeared! Of course, such coquettishness and charm dazzled Mr. Wickham and earned his love for Lydia. I, however, am thankful for the influence of you and Lizzy. Oh, I know I am not proper! But I do believe I can assert that Mr. Falke loves me for myself. Do you think this is true, Georgiana?" She halted, turning to her silent companion. "Georgiana? Whatever is the matter?"

"It is of no moment, Kitty, truly. Tell me what else Mr. Falke said."

"You pique my curiosity, dear friend. I have noted that whenever Mr. Wickham's name is mentioned a shadow passes over your face. I know Mr. Darcy has a poor opinion of Mr. Wickham, and I once saw Colonel Fitzwilliam grimace with disgust when the name was spoken, but am beginning to suspect you think ill of him as well. Pray, what is the history between you three?"

For a moment Georgiana's heart constricted, the familiar shame and pain of Wickham's betrayal piercing through her soul. Then, to her astonishment, the sensations rapidly dissipated. In that fleeting second as she walked sedately to the stone bench nearby, she realized that she no longer felt hatred or humiliation. In fact, sitting with a jolt of amazement, she could not even conjure a clear picture of his face! Those eyes that she remembered drowning in had no clarity of color. Was he tall? No idea. The tone of his voice? Unknown.

She released a cleansing giggle, lifting a hand to Kitty and pulling her onto the bench beside. "Very well, Kitty, I will tell you." And she did. The only other person she had ever related the entire sordid tale to was Elizabeth. Even William did not know all the false words spoken by Wickham or the foolish actions of his gullible sister; Georgiana needing the comfort he abundantly offered at the time and too ashamed to ever reveal completely. Now she told Kitty, but with nary a trace of the bitterness or mortification generally felt, and none of the tears shed in Elizabeth's arms. It was somewhat like relating a story one had read about, as if the misfortune had struck some other girl in a faraway place. Georgiana actually discovered herself laughing at some of the more ridiculous pronouncements of Wickham's. The whole incident was a million years ago, as far as Georgiana was concerned.

But Kitty listened and was shocked. "I had no idea Mr. Wickham was such a scoundrel! Even Lydia running away with him I thought romantic and daring, an adventure that I envied. What a fool I was! I am beginning to understand the depth of my ignorance of the world."

"And men. Oh Kitty! Are you sure Mr. Falke loves you? I could not bear to see you hurt. Losing someone you love, or even think you love, is horrible. I have seen it, experienced it. Please be sure he cares for you!"

Kitty smiled, patting Georgiana's hand placatingly. "Do not fret so, dear Georgiana. All will be well. Ere the year is complete you shall be dancing at my wedding, I am certain of it!"

Two days later, Mr. Falke and his parents would leave Graceholm Hall and Kitty would never see him again.

Her last conversation with him, her only conversation in the days following her gushing proclamations to Georgiana of love felt and returned, took place the evening before his abrupt departure. His elusiveness in the intervening hours saddened Kitty, her heart of love desiring his presence, but she suspected nothing untoward as the surfeit of social activities frequently conspired to keep the sexes apart. It was not until dinner that she began to suspect something was amiss.

He evaded her gaze from his seat ten guests away, somberly picked at each course, dialogue with those surrounding was minimal, and his father watched him with a stern glare. After the obligatory segregated post-dining amusements, the genders came together and naturally drifted into clusters based on age. Humor was high, as always, few aware of a nervous Mr. Falke and increasingly alarmed Miss Bennet. Just when Kitty thought she would burst into frustrated tears, Mr. Falke eased to her side and with a light touch to her elbow steered her toward the shadowy balcony.

Instantaneously Kitty's spirits lifted. Never remotely fathoming that whatever was disturbing her love could have anything to do with her, she determined to erase his gloom with a repeat performance of passionate kisses. But instead of guiding her to the dimly lit pathways beside the tree-lined edges of the river, he stayed to the wide, moon-bathed lane beyond the parlor balcony. Conscious of the need to be clear of eavesdroppers but within sight of parental eyes, Mr. Falke opened the conversation with words devastating to Kitty.

"Miss Bennet, I regret that I must inform you that I shall be departing Graceholm Hall on the morrow. My father has estate duties to attend to and requires my assistance. I know this is sudden, and pray your understanding."

"Oh! I… that is, will you be returning soon?"

"I fear not."

"Then… Will you visit Meryton? I will be returning home in two weeks and shall wait patiently for your presence. I know my father will adore you and be quite pleased by your attentions."

"I cannot say I shall visit Meryton, Miss Bennet. Do forgive me."

"Anthony, I do not understand! Why are you so formal? I have been 'Kitty' to you for weeks when we are alone. You are worrying me!"

"I am truly sorry, Miss Bennet, but this is for the best."

"What is for the best? You are making no sense!"

"Lower your voice, please!" He hissed, glancing toward the empty balcony and moving further away from the house. "Please, Miss Bennet, control yourself. A scene is improper." He glanced into her face, looking rapidly away from the bewilderment found there. "I have come to realize that our relationship is merely one of friendship. We must endeavor to accept this. It would not have worked out, Miss Bennet, trust me in this."

"But you said you loved me," she whispered. "You kissed me and said you wanted to be with me forever. Were these lies, Anthony? Is that the kind of man you are? Is it?"

"No, God help me, but no!" His mask of rigidity slipped and he clasped her hands, leaning close. "I am sorry, Kitty. But there is no future for us."

"You are being ridiculous, Anthony! Of course we have a future together! We love each other and that is all that matters. Now, stop this playing and let us walk by the river. I know how to cheer you up." She lifted to plant a kiss to his cheek, but he evaded, stepping a pace backward.

"You are mistaken, Miss Bennet. Our time together has been a pleasant diversion and no more. I regret that you assumed otherwise, but I will be leaving tomorrow and…"

"Why? Tell me why, Anthony. I deserve an explanation! I love you! Do you not realize that? You cannot just leave without talking to me!"

He was anguished. He could not tell her the truth: that her family was unacceptable, her wealth inadequate, her station inferior, and her accomplishments insufficient. Better to increase her hatred of him than wound her by insulting all she held dear.

With a monumental effort he stiffened, tightening his face, and chilling his voice. "The explanation is simple, Miss Bennet. I allowed my human desires and failings to overwhelm me. Like a foolish adolescent I indulged in the pleasures to be found in a charming, beautiful woman. I alluded to sentiments I do not feel. I pray that you can someday find it within your heart to forgive me for acting in an ungentlemanly manner, but I do not deserve it. I fear that is all I can offer you."

"Anthony, please..." Kitty sobbed.

"I wish you well, Miss Bennet. Good-bye." He bowed curtly and then turned, briskly striding away and feeling every inch the louse his false words evinced.

Kitty stood stunned, tears flowing down her cheeks, the moments stretching in agonizing clarity as he walked away. "Anthony," she breathed, "please, I... I love you. I... Anthony! No! I love you!"

The stasis broke, her voice rising hysterically, sobs gushing and choking the exclamations, steps stumbling after the heartbreaker she still loved. Kitty was beyond coherent thought, emotions wild as the pain engulfed.

Firm, loving hands reached for her, grasping flailing arms and halting her forward momentum. "Kitty! Be still. Come with me, dear. People are watching." Georgiana pulled gently toward the concealing trees, Kitty weeping and shaking.

~⚜~

The emotions and fate of Mr. Falke remained unknown to Kitty. Her future life would not circle anywhere near his, and she never asked of his situation. Initially, this may have been due largely to anger and pain, but in time her aborted romance with Mr. Falke would follow the identical path to Georgiana's unfortunate liaison with Mr. Wickham. Time heals all wounds, as the old proverb suggests.

However, for the immediate days after the garden theatrics the actions of both Mr. Falke and Miss Bennet were fodder for gossip. The primary deterrent to gleefully provoked scandal was the furious visage of George Darcy. His affection for Miss Kitty was deep and sincere. Much to the amazement of everyone, the perpetually sunny disposition of the good doctor was utterly erased, to be replaced with an expression as stern and dour as ever witnessed on Mr. Fitzwilliam Darcy. For many it was the first time, despite the obvious physical resemblance, that they fully recognized the familial similarity.

Kitty remained locked in her room for two days, appearing finally at the urging of Georgiana and bravely joining the gay entertainments that continued unabated. The sympathy of a few of the girls was genuine and encouraging. For the majority of the other guests her unseemly histrionics only proved their pompous assertions that the lower classes possessed no tact or propriety. Whispers, giggling, and pointing persisted despite Dr. Darcy's frightening glare.

Kitty would learn valuable lessons through her heartache; her maturation swift and agonizing. Georgiana observed her flighty friend's courage and resolve with awe and sadness. Kitty's laugh was not as vibrant, but she did laugh. Her dimples not as deep, but she did smile. Conversation was stilted and laced with melancholy, but plenteous and without obvious bitterness. The long days remaining were torturous for her. But the tears were controlled and only shed when alone. Georgiana fully grasped her friend's anguish and altering spirit, sharing and comforting as best she could manage while silently grieving at her gay friend's metamorphosis.

The wounds were deep and the scars raw. The sultry heat of the Hertfordshire summer would not melt the frozen heart of Kitty Bennet. For months, she would suffer quietly until one day, at a wedding, as snow frosted the ground and winter air froze each breath, the sun would finally shine and thaw her heart.

CHAPTER SIXTEEN

The Dark Peak

THAT DARCY WAS A deep sleeper was a well-established fact. He no longer heard the bell that announced Alexander needing his mother, nor did he note when Lizzy left their bed or returned. Gale force winds and driving sleet battering the windows only served to make him burrow further into the warm mattress. Lizzy was quite convinced that a raging herd of jungle animals could storm the corridors without him flinching. Once Samuel had dropped a tray carrying several glass bottles onto the tiled floor surrounding Darcy's bathing area, creating a noisy crash that echoed through the shut door into their bedchamber. Lizzy woke from her dead sleep and the only reason she did not jump a foot into the air was due to the immobile weight of her husband's leg and arm securing her to the bed. He slept on, his breathing not even effected.

A month or so after their marriage, once she realized just how impenetrable his slumber, she had asked him with concern if he ever worried over a catastrophe happening that he would sleep right through.

"Not at all," he had replied confidently. "Samuel knows how to wake me in the case of an emergency."

"Oh. Is that why the doors are unlocked?" She looked nervously at the doors between their inner sanctum and the dressing rooms and sitting room beyond. Her disquiet over the doors remaining unlocked when they spent a great portion of their time in this room naked and engaged in highly intimate activity was a frequently raised topic. No matter how often Darcy assured her that *no one* would *ever* enter his bedchamber until he personally opened the door or left it standing wide open to be cleaned, she was not completely assuaged.

So he laughed as he always did, brushing aside her trepidation. "I have no reason to lock a door that none would dare enter. Not even Samuel," he said before she verbalized what he knew she was thinking. "Trust me, I will and do respond when necessary."

And he grew secretive as he often did when teasing her.

Several weeks after that conversation, she learned what he meant when he suddenly bolted out of bed one night, grabbing the robe hanging on the bedpost, and was across the room opening the door to the sitting room before Lizzy had fully assimilated that the sound that had woken her was a rapping knock. Why he instantly responded to the bang of the ornamental brass bob striking the plate affixed upon the solid oak was a mystery, but it roused him every time without fail.

This reality was again put to the test one night in early June, shortly after two in the morning. The resounding thud was heard by both of them, but Darcy was robed and reaching for the knob before Lizzy managed to drowsily lift her head from the pillow.

"Yes," he said, his voice firm without any traces of sleep.

"A message from Hasberry, sir," Rothchilde's hushed voice carried to Lizzy, who sat up in bed eagerly.

She heard the rip of a wax seal, the paper being unfolded, and then seconds later Darcy's instructions, "Have the landau prepared. Wake Mrs. Hanford. We will be leaving immediately."

"Yes, sir."

"Thank you," Darcy said, shutting the door and returning to their bed with the opened parchment sheet. "Sleep is over for the night, my love. Bingley writes, in trembling hand I must add, that Jane is laboring." He chuckled, eyes on the words. "He apologizes for disturbing us but the process is moving hastily." He looked at Elizabeth, who was already out of bed and drawing on her robe. "Is it too soon to tease over the fact that she is some weeks earlier than expected and that the labor is apparently of short duration?"

"Yes," she snapped, glaring at his amused expression, "just as it is too soon for me to harass my sister for not taking two days to accomplish the task as it nearly did me." Her eyes clouded. "Too much can yet go wrong."

"Of course you are correct. Forgive me for jesting inappropriately. Get dressed and I will meet you in the foyer." He placed his hands upon her shoulder, squeezing in assurance. "Jane will be fine, Elizabeth. Have no fears."

They arrived to discover Bingley wide-eyed, pale, and pacing the parlor in circles. Unlike Darcy, Bingley had no intention of being anywhere near the birthing room. The thought was unappealing to Jane as well, for many of the obvious reasons but also because Charles was one of those individuals who became physically ill at the sight of blood. Thus, he was doing what most men did in these circumstances: pacing and sweating. Darcy assumed control, distracting the frantic father-to-be with conversation, an adorable six-month old who complaisantly latched onto being woken up in the middle of the night as a time to play, and a generous shot of brandy.

Lizzy rapidly ascended the stairs. Jane had chosen a local midwife to deliver her firstborn, again sticking to traditional methods. She admired Dr. Darcy, knew he was a gifted physician, but her timid nature quailed at the idea of any man, especially one she knew familiarly, witnessing her birth. George understood completely, so was not offended. He did, however, have the midwife's experience verified and sought her out for a frank obstetrical conversation that may have shocked the poor woman to an early grave if not for the extraordinary reputation of Dr. Darcy that was now common knowledge. She saw their consultation with his approval as a badge of honor to increase her renown and her income!

George's "interference" was based on his affection for the Bingleys, and was met with tremendous relief, especially from Charles, who was not handling the whole idea of birth very well. Since the esteemed Dr. Darcy could not deliver his child personally, the next best was a midwife who had passed the formidable doctor's inspection. In truth his fears were the same as every man who loves his wife, but where Darcy possessed rigid control of his emotions for the most part, Bingley was transparent. It was rather comical, but Darcy was sympathetic enough not to point it out.

What Lizzy had said about so many possible complications was absolutely true. But in the end Jane continued the legacy set by Mrs. Bennet with all five of her deliveries. Minutes before eight that morning, after less than twelve hours of labor, Ethan Charles Howard Bingley was born. There were no incidents, no abnormalities, and no untoward aftermath. By the time Charles was ushered into the room an hour later, his wife was sitting serenely in bed—as beautiful as always with only the dusky circles under her eyes and tiny burst blood vessels around her pupils an indication of anything unusual having occurred—with their son bundled in her arms.

Lizzy and Alexander stayed at Hasberry for a week. Darcy returned to Pemberley that day, as it was a busy season for him, but rode over frequently to visit. Alexander was introduced to his new cousin, but the six-month-old wasn't terribly impressed. There was plenty of time to develop a cousinly relationship.

The close proximity of Hasberry to Pemberley was a continual source of joy for the four people involved. Lizzy often commandeered her curricle, taking Alexander for fresh-air drives to visit his aunt for an afternoon. Numerous evenings were spent together, at one house or the other, as the adults dined and played games. Frequently, they were joined by Gerald and Harriet Vernor or Albert and Marilyn Hughes, their nearest neighbors. But the fine weather of summer allowed for dozens of visits with those like the Sitwells who lived a bit farther away. The men gathered for hunts and rides on a weekly basis, the ladies meeting for tea and conversation while the children played. It was a period of gay entertainment from dozens of avenues.

Nevertheless, Pemberley Manor was amazingly quiet that summer. With George and Georgiana away, the upper halls and family rooms seemed surprisingly empty. Alexander was a good-natured child, not disturbing the tranquil atmosphere to any great degree. His moments of temper were exceedingly rare, so loud cries or tantrums were not a common disruption. There were adjustments made to the furniture arrangements in some rooms as he grew more mobile, learning to roll and then creep. Primarily, of course, he was kept to the top floor nursery and bedchambers, as this was where Darcy and Lizzy passed large portions of their day. But it was not at all unusual to find the infant lying on a spread blanket littered with toys and within eyeshot of Darcy as he worked at his desk. Or in the parlor or library with whichever parent was tending him at the time. Mrs. Hanford's services were employed, naturally, both Mr. and Mrs. Darcy busy people. But a large percentage of his waking hours, or even when asleep, Alexander was with a doting parent.

Frequently, he accompanied his father to the stables. Darcy would hold him tightly as they walked among the stalls or watched the grooms and trainers at work. Alexander observed it all with intent eyes, fearlessly touching the enormous animals with his tiny fingers. Parsifal tolerated the oddity only because it was held by his master and did not interrupt the expected treats.

Naturally the groomsmen and stable hands thought he was adorable, fussing over the baby while maintaining a reverential respect for the young heir of Pemberley. He was introduced to the Connemara ponies, although even Darcy was uncomfortable with placing the baby onto one's back as yet. Lizzy glared and sternly reminded him each time they headed out the door that taking Alexander riding was forbidden. Darcy pretended to argue, just for the fun of seeing his wife's eyes flash, but he agreed that it was too soon. The delight in observing Alexander's infantile interest in the environs was enough for the present.

Lizzy welcomed the beautiful weather. She resumed her gardening, the joy of kneeling and digging in the soft earth one that could not be denied. Alexander joined her, usually sitting or sleeping in his well-used perambulator under the shade of a tree. Long walks were essential, both day and evening. Again the baby carriage was utilized, the springs devised by Stan providing for a smoother ride, and there were few Pemberley trails unnavigable. Alexander loved the outdoors, a trait that immeasurably pleased his nature-loving parents. His first touches of grass or dirt or the cool water of the pond were met with the serious gaze they were rapidly growing accustomed too. Alexander examined everything with an intensity that was remarkable. Whether it was a toy or flower or attached appendage, Alexander studied it carefully before deciding what to do with it, that usually entailing trying to eat it. The rescue of any number of inedible objects, some quite disgusting now that he was proficient at escaping his confines, was a fulltime occupation.

She and Darcy carried on their tradition of nightly strolls along the terrace and private garden with Alexander brought along to enjoy the expanse of stars, splashing fountains, and chirping crickets. Darcy happily toted the bright infant in his strong embrace, pointing to the constellations, vegetation, or glimpsed animal as he instructed. Lizzy laughed at his informative dictations, but Alexander listened to every word spoken in his father's resonant timbre as if keenly aware of the meaning.

In this way, the lazy days of summer slipped by with little in the way of drama to intrude. The only lengthy excursion beyond the immediate area was a weeklong trip to the Peaks.

Darcy's yearning to show his wife the one remaining region of Derbyshire that she had yet to fully explore had burned within his soul for ages. Interruptions of a harrowing nature so continually intruded upon his plans that the normally

SHARON LATHAN

non-superstitious man was almost afraid to bring up the subject. But a casual comment by Gerald Vernor restarted the wheels in his mind.

A mutual friend named Mr. Ward Logan owned an estate outside of Castleton, his manor house on the banks of the River Noe in Hope Valley. Darcy and Logan were not close confidants, but did overlap at Cambridge and were friendly enough to play billiards and engage in stimulating discourse from time to time. Over the years since University, chance encounters would occur while in Town or at a Derbyshire function, each man genuinely pleased to pause for a reacquainting conversation. Lizzy had met Mr. and Mrs. Logan at several social events during the past year-and-a-half, first at the Cole's Masque. Only once had Darcy traveled to the Logan estate, Chelmbridge. It was over eight years ago, before Logan was married. He opened his house to a group of Cambridge alumni, the gentlemen spending a week hiking the numerous trails, exploring the caverns, and hunting the wealth of game roaming the rocky moors of the High Peaks.

Thus when Vernor told Darcy that he had seen Logan while on a recent trip to Chesterfield, and that Logan had informed him that he was in town with his wife shopping for a planned summertime trip abroad, Darcy decided it was a sign.

He wrote to Logan, asking if it would be possible for his family to reside at Chelmbridge for a few days early in July while touring the Peaks. Mr. Logan's reply was swift and positive. Darcy was especially pleased with the arrangement, knowing that the comfort and privacy of a house was preferred over a questionable inn. Above all, he insisted on his wife and child being pampered and untroubled. Additionally, Chelmbridge was beautifully located in the valley created by the Noe with uneven hills of green dotted with the gritstone and limestone boulders prevalent in the region. It was nestled on a slight rise above the river, almost precisely upon the dividing line between Hope Valley and the Edale Vale with Mam Tor shadowing. It was an ideal placement with the distance to the main four caverns of the area, and Kinder Scout to the north within an accessible distance.

The plans were set, arrangements made, and their baggage packed without the tiniest upset interfering. Still, Darcy did not breathe freely until the carriage entered the outskirts of Castleton and made the eastern turn toward Peveril Castle. Lizzy was mesmerized by the passing scenery, but not unaware of her husband's foreboding. She shared a look, her lips lifted in the teasing manner that inevitably brightened his spirits.

"Peveril Castle straight ahead," she declared, staring directly into his eyes with laughter held in check. "Our tour of the Dark Peak has official begun."

"Ready for a hard walk, Mrs. Darcy? Your tour involves intense exertion."

Lizzy grinned, accepting his playful challenge. "I bet I shall arrive at the top same time as you, Mr. Darcy."

"We shall see," he said smugly, finally releasing the residual threads of his tension.

As it turned out, he reached the summit of Castle Hill simultaneously with his wife, but that was only because he shortened his stride on the chance he was needed to assist her up the rocky, snaking trail. That, of course, was unnecessary as Lizzy was an excellent walker and climber, navigating the difficult terrain and cresting the hill with relative ease. She did pause, partially to fan her glistening face and inhale deeply several times, but also to appreciate the view.

The impregnable apex flanked by steep cliffs offered an impressive view of the landscape in all directions. The rooftops of Castleton nestled in the sylvan vale below with the blue ribbons of the rivers cutting through the dales. The full breadth of Mam Tor looming to the west, the rugged stone outcroppings bounding the flat pinnacle, and the heights of Hathersage moorland were all stunningly visible. Bravely, they gazed down the sheer precipice into the yawning chasm marking the main entrance to the greatest Peak cavern, Devil's Arse, far below. The panoramic view was truly breathtaking and abundantly worth the strenuous climb even without the Tudor castle sitting in glory upon the knoll.

Built originally in 1080 and later fortified of stone by Henry II from 1155 onward, the once massive keep remained an evocative example of a time long past. Although largely fallen into ruins, the twelfth century gatehouse serving as the entrance to Perevil was intact, opening into a vast courtyard with the sixty-foot gritstone keep dominating the picture.

As with their visit to Bolsover last summer, another ancient castle built by a William Peverel only one hundred years later, Lizzy and Darcy were content to stroll about the grounds and examine the ruins. A brisk breeze blew, tempering the fiercely shining July sun. It was a pleasant way to begin their trip, the adventurous, nature-loving Darcys ready to explore.

The week's agenda was set, Darcy ever the meticulous planner, but of course with Alexander along for the excursion, each day's enterprise could not be as time consuming as they may have wished. They began each day slowly, not leaving the house until after Alexander's morning nap, and maintained a sedate pace, piling into the carriage rather than walking the short distances to the surrounding caves. Mrs. Hanford cared for the infant from the safety of the carriage or shaded locale with Mr. Anders and Watson providing protection while Lizzy and Darcy were away. He was a compliant baby, easy to amuse and keep contained, and handled the rigors of travel and strange environs with amazing composure.

On their first full day in the Peak, they drove to Treak Cliff Cavern, a mine for the beautiful and rare Blue John Stone, a type of bluish-purple mineral found only within the caverns of Derbyshire. Visitors were allowed limited access to the foremost chambers, paying a small fee for a guide to lead the way safely and point to the richly glittering veins of fluorspar. The polished stones were prevalent in the shops of Castleton and Hope, sold as jewelry, ornaments, and utensils, and were even sold in their raw crystallized form from vendors clustered about the mine's trailhead. First mined and fashioned into priceless vessels by the Romans, the unique stone was not rediscovered until the mid-1700s, it now a prime commodity of the Derbyshire region.

Lizzy was awed by her first real cave, the Pemberley cave paling in comparison. Her husband, of course, was not offended by this. He was well aware that the Pemberley cave was dull, only a young boy's imagination seeing it as anything to spark great interest. The humorous aspect of his wife's response to Treak Cliff was that, aside from the Blue John which was remarkable, the cave itself was mundane compared to the others to be visited. Darcy purchased several items made from the multi-colored stone including three pairs of earrings, a necklace, and a hair comb for Lizzy; a carved horse figurine for Alexander's collection; and a set of wine goblets as souvenirs of their visit.

Lizzy's enthusiasm after just one day of hiking steep trails and investigating subterranean cavities was so high that Darcy could barely contain his own zeal to get started the following day. Prior arrangements had been made for their tour of Speedwell Cavern. Darcy vividly remembered the one time he entered the horizontal mouth cut naturally into the sloping hill and descended the 105 steps to the submerged basin. He had no idea what to expect, his jaw dropping at the incredible journey taken and the wonders seen. Therefore, he was excited to share the experience with Elizabeth, knowing she would be as awestruck as he had been.

Hacked by miners searching for lead in the late 1700s, unsuccessfully as it turned out, the narrow entrance at the foot of Winnats Pass was easily reached by a short walk. The carved steps steeply declined, the relatively smooth tunnel a marvel not so much in workmanship, as it was crudely cut, but in the staggering revelation of how difficult the labor must have been. It was cool under the layers of solid rock and dimly lit. Great care was necessary, but the stairs were clear and stable, and they arrived at the gravel and wood landing without mishap.

Darcy was watching Lizzy avidly as they neared the end, thus he saw her momentary confusion as she glanced around, looking for the rocky ground or trail that one would expect. Then he saw her eyes widen in shock as the guide moved unerringly forward and the other people in their small group parted to follow him, allowing her to see that nothing was before them except a line of boats tied to simple wooden posts nailed into the rough wooden dock. They bobbed gently on the canal of dirty water that covered the unseeable rock floor of what was a rounded tunnel gouged horizontally into the solid rock. The "roof" of the small cavern landing was not much higher than a tall man, Darcy's hair brushing the ceiling in places, and the tunnel that could be seen before it disappeared into darkness around a bend, was considerably lower.

He had not worried that Elizabeth would grow frightened, since she had never exhibited a fear of confined places, including the Pemberley cave, but watching her eyes now he began to regret that he had not warned her. She appeared so stunned, looking about with eyes wide and dilated, that he leaned in, his arm pulling her tight to his side.

Yet, just as he was about to whisper that they could leave if she wished, she gazed up at him with the lively exuberance so typically Elizabeth, her voice breathless when she spoke. "We take the boats? Through the tunnel? Oh my word! William, this is incredible! Where do they lead? How do we row? It is so narrow! How far…?"

His laugh stayed her endless questions. "Here I was thinking you were nervous." He kissed her forehead, propelling her gently toward the front boat that was being boarded. "Be patient, Mrs. Darcy. You shall see."

The guide sat in the front, facing forward, with the ten passengers settled onto plank benches. Darcy sat on the outside with Lizzy close to his side, although his caution was probably unnecessary as the boats were inches narrower than the tunnel width, the bottom flat to lend stability, so the likelihood of capsizing was slim. The answer to Lizzy's question of rowing was quickly revealed when the guide grabbed onto a post sticking up from the platform and pulled hard, propelling the boat forward over the water. The speed was faster than one would think, hidden undercurrents from the numerous waterfalls feeding the cavern not only creating a constant echo of rumbling water but aiding the driver's efforts. He used embedded rails and grooves in the rock to grab onto and keep them moving. Spaced lamps swung from hooks in the ceiling, illuminating the passageway and casting ruddy glows onto the striated rock.

It was eerie but beautiful. Dozens of colors wove within the layers of limestone and gritstone, the seeping rivulets of water creating patterns over the encrusted surface. Talking was muted, even the hushed voices carrying strangely and mingling with the echo of moving water. They reached a wider pool, called Halfway House the guide informed them, where they passed another boatload of passengers returning to the dock. Spirits were high, their faces expressing their awe and pleasure as they waved to the newcomers. As they traveled on the one-boat width tunnel, the concept of time passing skewed in the dusky atmosphere, the guide told the story of the past-century's miners searching for the lead they suspected lurked below due to the prevalence of the metal in other parts of the Peaks. It was an endeavor destined to be a financial catastrophe, unfortunately, with tourism being the only recompense.

Finally, they reached the end. A huge pile of rubble formed a beach of sort upon which they disembarked and gathered in a cluster to view the true marvel of Speedwell Cavern. Before them spread a cathedral-like cavern so huge that the ceiling was lost in darkness and so wide that the walls were a vague shadow. The entire area was the site of a vast lake known as the Bottomless Pit due to the fact that decades of excavation with thousands upon thousands of pounds of crumbled rock hewn from the tunnel system had been dumped into the pool without the water level ever changing. No appreciable dent was made, the underground lake seemingly extending to the center of the earth.

They stood on the edge, tossing rocks into the murky water, hearing the plunk as the waving surface was pierced, and wondering when, or if, the rock would finally come to rest upon another. But no one had the answer.

The ride back was quiet, no one wanting to disturb the experience with idle chitchat. It was not until they were again in their carriage heading back to Chelmbridge that Lizzy broke her dazed silence as she tried to describe the environment to Alexander. He, of course, had no idea what she was talking about, but he listened intently nevertheless!

Chelmbridge was a comfortable abode, as Darcy knew it would be. Alexander settled happily into his new surroundings and strange bed, once again proving that he was an unusually accommodating child. Lizzy and Darcy had no comparison, assuming it was fairly normal, a presumption that George found especially amusing. He humorously cautioned them to stop while they were ahead, a jest Darcy frowned at. Yet as they spent more time with the offspring of their friends, they began to realize just how fortunate they were. Not that the Vernor boys or Hughes children were unruly, but they clearly possessed degrees of naughtiness and irritability that Alexander, so far, seemed to lack.

Tonight was a perfect example. Darcy feared Alexander might be weary or especially cranky after three days away from the routine of Pemberley and his familiar surrounds, and being dragged about the rugged countryside in the heat. He was wrong.

The baby ate well of his mashed sweet yams and barley porridge, and then nursed until Lizzy was drained. Darcy assumed care from there, taking Alexander into his temporary nursery for story time while Lizzy relaxed and penned a letter to her sister, Jane. Darcy read from his novel, this time *Rob Roy* by Walter Scott, while Alexander reclined in his arms, sucked on his thumb, and rubbed rhythmically on one ear of his favorite stuffed toy—the hound dog Darcy had purchased so long ago at the shop in Derby, now officially dubbed "Dog" and Alexander's constant companion. He was wide awake tonight, calm and attending to each spoken word. He stared at his father, eyes following the movement of his lips and studying the dramatic expressions Darcy added to the text as he read. Sometimes the babe fell asleep within ten minutes of warm cuddling against his father's strongly beating heart, the musical tones of Darcy's baritone soothing him into a deep slumber. Other times he was alert, babbling and pointing pudgy fingers on the pages opened before him as if reading along with the words.

However the interlude went, Darcy considered it his favorite time of the day. Long after Alexander fell asleep, Darcy would hold him, rocking and embracing. Frequently, time was lost in rapt contemplation of the face he loved so intensely it was a sweet ache. Like his adoration for Elizabeth, the emotions never ceased to uplift his heart and overwhelm him.

Eventually though, it was time to nestle the infant into his cushioned bed, turning his immediate care over to his devoted nanny. Several kisses later, Darcy crossed the hall to the bedchamber suite set aside for the Darcys. Mr. Logan had prepared a spacious set of rooms with a wonderful view of Mam Tor, the chambers airy and elegantly decorated. They were homey, Lizzy and Darcy settling almost as easily as Alexander had.

Darcy had no expectations for romance when he entered the room a half-hour later after washing and undressing, but one glance at his wife revised that opinion. He stopped cold four paces into the room, only able to stare as the blood instantly departed his brain for places further south.

She sat on a chair facing toward him, her long shapely legs crossed at the knees, the top one swinging gracefully. Her arms rested on the chair arms, slim fingers tapping lightly. She was smiling, that sultry smile that alone drove him mad, and her chocolate eyes glittered in the candlelight. She wore the Blue John earrings he bought her, the vivid blue and silver dangling against the ivory expanse of her neck; her thick hair was loosely piled atop her head secured with the Blue John comb, dozens of curly strands falling over her shoulders and framing her face; and the necklace of blue and yellow veined stone hung about her neck, the pendant cradled between her naked breasts. In fact, as he noted immediately upon crossing the threshold, she was completely naked. Except for the jewelry, that is. Not that he noticed them for several seconds, but once he did they added to the eroticism of the spectacle in a profound way that only weakened him further as more blood rushed to his lower regions.

"Enjoying the view, Fitzwilliam?"

"Immensely. Lovely necklace."

"Thank you," she said, running her fingertips seductively over the pendant and brushing the swell of her breasts. "My husband has excellent taste."

"Indeed I do," he murmured huskily, his roving eyes leaving no doubt that he was not referring to the jewels.

Her smile deepened. She stood and paused for effect, knowing full well that her libidinous spouse would appreciate the picture. Then she languidly strolled toward him, her lissome body swaying sensuously, meeting him where he remained rooted in the middle of the room.

He could have moved, his muscles not so weak or paralyzed, but he rather delighted in the visual treat of her slender figure sinuously approaching. She was as svelte as the day they married, but softer with lush, womanly curves in all the right places. Her breasts bounced pleasantly as she walked, the stray wisps of wavy hair buoyantly brushing over her lightly bronzed skin.

She encircled his shoulders and laced her fingers into the hair at the nape of his neck. "And how was that view? As breathtaking as the previous?"

His answer was a lascivious grin and gravelly growl as he drew her firmly against his body. "Any question as to how immensely I admired the view?" The blazing heat emanating from his skin and the aroused length of him pressing into her belly did indeed answer her redundant question.

She chuckled, succumbing rapidly to her own response, especially now that he was already kissing his way down her neck and skillfully caressing her bare flesh. She released the belt holding his robe in place, parting the satiny fabric and sliding her hands over his waist and derriere. She pressed her breasts against his chest, rubbing deliciously over the hair covering his steely muscles, and lifted on her tiptoes to capture an earlobe between her lips.

"I thought it was past time to see if this bed is as sturdy as ours at home." And then she proceeded to lick lightly over his ear.

Darcy groaned. "Are you intending to test the craftsmanship most vigorously, my lover?"

She pulled away, her grin devilish as she peeled the robe off his shoulders and watched it fall to the carpeted floor as her eyes leisurely scanned over the masculine figure exposed. She sighed happily, hands skimming lightly over his broad upper torso and then downward over his flat, solidly muscled abdomen with feathering touches until reaching the juncture of his thighs, the pressure applied there quite firm.

Darcy shuddered, his knees flexing while the rest of his body tensed and arched at the electrifying pleasure. "Elizabeth," he grated, clasping her face in his hands and bending to kiss her.

But she twisted in his arms, leaning backward against him with her arms again draped over his shoulders and playing with his hair. Darcy adjusted speedily, cupping a breast while his mouth busily applied nibbling caresses to her arched neck.

"I am definitely feeling the urge for aggressive, enthusiastic lovemaking and sense the same from you, yes?"

Darcy muttered a harsh *yes* while adjusting his posture and hold upon her body. Some minutes passed before they relocated to the bed, which held up miraculously well through what was assuredly not a gentle interlude but one of crazed passion.

Darcy collapsed beside his panting and still moaning wife, stretching alongside her shivering flesh. Lizzy sluggishly wiggled closer, laying an arm over his heaving chest and kissing his shoulder. It was several minutes before either was capable of coherent speech, but then they began to talk in soft voices about the wonders of the caverns and the delightful holiday they were having thus far. In time, Lizzy propped her head on one hand, the other lazily caressing his body. He, meanwhile, removed the decorative comb and idly played with the long tresses spilling over her back and onto his chest.

Their passion reawakened gradually as the aimless caresses roused the desires perpetually lurking under the surface. Darcy moved first, pulling her onto his body for a long kiss before rotating her onto her back to commence a focused assault. It began slow and gentle as they rolled about the bed, but eventually the heat escalated to inferno magnitude when the need to unite overwhelmed. Darcy grasped her bottom, sliding forward in a measured pace and releasing a long groan of bliss.

"William!" Lizzy gasped, clutching his head to her bosom as spasms of pleasure instantly burst through her body.

"You wanted me," he said, impassioned voice thick and breathless near her mouth, his eyes a steaming azure as he stared at her flushed face. "God, how I love that! Feeling your release while in my arms. Lord, my Lizzy, there is nothing to compare!" He kissed her, hard and deep, lost in the moment and regulation gone as he plunged farther and fiercer with a rapidly accelerating tempo.

Abruptly, he rolled to his back, taking Lizzy with him and maintaining their connection. He grabbed onto the edge of the headboard, arching his entire back and shouting gruffly between the heavenly quakes wracking his body. Lizzy's delirium matched his, again succumbing to the euphoria of amazing lovemaking.

Jests about the solidity of the bed, especially the hardiness of the cherry wood headboard against Darcy's formidable potency and strength were a while in coming. But eventually, they rallied enough to assume their customary sleeping position with Lizzy embraced within her husband's arms, a light coverlet over their love-warmed skin, and sharing a smattering of teases and declarations of eternal adoration. Tradition held with their final whispered words as they fell into satisfied, tranquilized sleep, "*I love you.*"

The next day they changed their tactic, deciding to drive northeast and investigate the stunning vistas and wonders found above ground.

They borrowed the Logans' landau, the top completely folded down, loading it with necessary supplies: a large basket of food and liquids, freshly brushed blankets, and infant requirements. It was a fair day with the sun shining brightly in a brilliant blue sky with streaks of wispy white clouds. A light breeze tempered the heat, although Darcy warned that the wind in the higher elevations could be quite brisk. This only brought a wide smile to Lizzy's face.

Within minutes, they left the sloping, rocky landscape of the Hope Valley, entering the equally sloping and rocky terrain of the Edale Vale. Initially the scenery was unchanged, but as they gradually began to climb toward the higher elevations, the subtle differences were noted. The air was cooler with the gentle breezes augmented by occasional blusters. The rock formations were not just the rubble of gritstone and limestone noted before, but often fashioned into such oddly sculpted statues that were so incredibly beautiful one felt God Himself must have touched them with His hands.

Mr. Anders drove slowly over the rough roads cut into the hills and moors. They were well traveled, but the rugged land did not always yield easily to carriage wheels, even time and traffic not noticeably smoothing the path in places. Darcy held an awake, bouncing, and bonneted Alexander in his arms. They occupied the bench across from his wife and Mrs. Hanford, both women enraptured by the view. Mrs. Hanford, especially, was glowing with an exuberance that shaved ten years off her age. Mrs. Hanford's joy at joining the Darcy household nearly a year ago was primarily due to two factors. One, she was relieved to be dwelling near her extensive family and friends. She was born in Baslow, living there until she married Mr. Hanford when seventeen, whereupon she moved to his tenant's cottage on the Pemberley estate. Never had she traveled away from Derbyshire; it was the only home she knew.

Therefore, her second fount of joy was in being able to continue serving the Darcy family. Proudly, she proclaimed the Hanford association with the esteemed Darcy landowners. She considered it a miracle and the greatest of honors to be granted the chance to not only maintain that connection but to do it in such a personal way.

Mrs. Hanford had contentedly raised six children and was blessed with a dozen grandchildren, so knew that caring for the Darcy baby would be a delight. Mrs. Hanford loved all children, her gift one of easy affinity with youngsters of all ages. Yet, one can't deny that some children are easier to love and tolerate than others! Alexander was a handsome child physically, but his temperament was so carefree and amiable that falling in love with him as an individual was impossible to resist.

Her only unexpected consequence to her employment as nanny was the travel. It had never entered her mind that caring for their son and heir meant she would be accompanying them wherever they went! Of course, many aristocratic families did not travel so extensively with their children, a reality Mrs. Hanford knew to be so even if she did believe to be sad, so if Mr. and Mrs. Darcy had gone on their journeys while leaving Alexander in her care at Pemberley, she would not have been shocked. However, their devotion to Alexander was pronounced and just another of the numerous reasons she respected them and was gratified to be a peripheral part of their family.

When Mrs. Darcy had first asked for her learned opinion on how best to travel with an infant, she was utterly at a loss as to what to say. Finally, she pulled herself together, stammering that she did not possess a "learned opinion" as she had never traveled far with her children, summer or winter.

"That may be so, Mrs. Hanford," Mrs. Darcy said, "but I still trust your instincts in the matter. We have some two months to plan our trip and I am confident that your expertise with infants in general will aid in securing a safe, smooth journey for my son." Then she leaned forward and affectionately squeezed Mrs. Hanford's hand, smiling sincerely. "I am just glad that you will be there to assist us. Between all of us I know it will be well."

And it was then that she fully comprehended that her future would entail more than simply the happiness of helping to raise the future Master of Pemberley and any other children the Darcys were blessed with. So far, she had been fortunate to see the lush landscapes of several counties, breathe the air and walk the fields of Kent and Hertfordshire, gaze upon the tall buildings of London, revel in the finery and jewels of the social elite, explore the wonders of grand parks and busy city streets, and so much more that she had filled two journals already. Now she was ascending the magnificent heights of the Peaks, those famous mountains and moors that were glimpses on the distant horizon all her life but never seen up close. Her exuberance was indeed bubbling, and she felt far more than ten years younger.

The tiny village of Edale was unremarkable. Their carriage rumbled along the road that wound through the narrow gorge created by the Noe, passing the huts known as booths that housed the boothmen, those hardy souls who lived in the rustic dwelling places while tending the wandering livestock that fed off the moor grasses. Edale itself was a collection of stone buildings scattered without symmetrical planning, the bare necessities provided to the local residents and not much else. Naturally there was a pub, but the ramshackle construction was dubious at best, even Darcy's thirst for a cool ale not strong enough to brave the possibility of the place crumbling down when the door slammed behind him! The seventeenth century church sat on a lovely grassy knoll, but was plain and boasted no historical significance, so they chose not to investigate.

They detoured on the road leading to Hayfield, halting at Edale Cross. The medieval stone cross erected some seven-hundred years prior by the Abbots of Basingwerk Abbey to mark the southern boundary of their land was eroded and chipped in places, but astoundingly intact. Re-erected in 1810, the ancient marker was now a local monument and historical artifact proudly preserved and tended to. The cultural significance was intriguing to Darcy and Lizzy, and the Edale Cross area was also a good place to pause for refreshments and casually stroll with the baby.

But they tarried for only a short hiatus, both of them anxious to commence the real point of the day's outing: attaining the plateau of Kinder Scout. They decided on the trails leading from Edale. It was a longer route but a bit less strenuous. Nevertheless, many of the trail portions were steep and nearly invisible amid the thick peat and stones. Hardy folks frequently braved the challenge in order to view the breathtaking vistas from the two thousand foot moor, and Darcy and Lizzy were two such people. Or at least they intended to try.

Leaving a well-fed and sleeping Alexander behind in the care of Mrs. Hanford, Mr. Anders, and Watson, they set out on their adventure. By the end, as the sun was setting to the west and the dimness of twilight illuminated the avenue leading to Chelmbridge, Lizzy was leaning onto her husband's shoulder drowsily holding her eyes open by sheer willpower. But her incredible stamina and walking skills had prevailed, to Darcy's pride and satisfaction. They reached the highest point of Kinder Scout, traversed the craggy heathland, and stood upon the edge of Kinder Downfall with the spray of the waterfall misting their sweaty brows.

Lizzy was not ashamed to admit that she required her strong spouse's assistance over the harsher climbs upon occasion. But for the most part, she accomplished the deed on her own steam and was as proud of herself as Darcy was of her. If she fell asleep less than half an hour after entering the house, without a full meal, and only budged for the subsequent ten hours to dazedly nestle Alexander to her breast, it was worth it. She did not complain about the soreness to her legs or the painful blister on one toe, the memories burned into her brain of the spectacular tableau visualized erasing any discomfort. They did, however, opt to stay at the estate the next day. Or rather Darcy insisted, claiming his own fatigue and desire to fish in the river, go for a horse ride, and picnic on the shaded lawns as the excuse. Lizzy did not believe the fatigue pretext, but a day of rest was a pleasant enough prospect, so she did not argue.

For their final day, they again packed up the landau for what was planned to be a two-part jaunt—the morning for a visit to the grandest of the Peak's caverns, the bizarrely named Devil's Arse, and the afternoon a leisurely drive through the woodlands and moors where the Dark Peak and White Peak merged, and then on to the ancient Roman town of Buxton, now primarily known for her thermal springs and Poole's Cavern.

During the short drive, Mrs. Hanford asked a question that, naturally, launched Darcy into teaching mode.

"Is it true, sir, that thieves live within the depths of the cavern?"

"Indeed, that is what the rumors hold," he answered, smiling at her frightened expression.

Lizzy knew the stories, but the nanny did not, so listened spellbound as Darcy enlightened her. Alexander also seemed to be riveted to the tale, staring at his father from Lizzy's lap.

"It is doubtful that bands of brigands call the inner caves their home in this progressive age," he assured her. "However, in centuries past, it was primarily the baser elements who braved the dark recesses of the Devil's Arse. Some say that it was they who caused such a name to be."

"How do you mean?" she asked, leaning forward unconsciously.

Darcy shrugged. "The name, if you will pardon me, Mrs. Hanford, was given due to the unusual noises that would escape from the mouth. Noises that resembled, forgive me, the passing of wind. Flatulence, you see. Some claim the noises are caused by ghosts who haunt the depths. Others believe the cavern extends to Hades, hence the 'devil' part of the name and why the subterranean river is called the Styx, and that the sounds are of demons. Still others think, more logically, that it may be the echoes from people, the thieving gangs, living below. Of course, the first two are nonsense, so I rather believe the legends of bandits is more probable, or perhaps some scientific explanation yet to be understood."

"So, there is no doubt that thieves dwelt there, at some time?"

"No. Enough evidence exists, especially the wealth of stories. According to legend, and the tales of Samuel Rid, somewhere in the mid-1500s the notorious knave Cock Lorel met with the current King of the Gypsies, whoever that was, at his hideaway in Devil's Arse. Together they devised a secret language that only rogues would understand." He shrugged again. "Probably that is a romantic myth, but the language, thieves' cant or rogues' cant depending upon the source, is verified. More likely it is a compilation of slang words from dozens of underworld guilds. The colorful argot is a common feature of numerous Elizabethan literature and plays. I have a collection of books from the Era, including *Life* by Bampfylde Moore Carew, who claimed to be King of the Beggars."

"There's a title to wear proudly," Lizzy interjected with a laugh.

"Truly," Darcy agreed with a smile. "You are welcome to read them, Mrs. Hanford, as well as anything else in the library, as you know."

"Thank you, sir."

"Today I can promise that we shall see no thieves. We will, however, observe the troglodytes. The cave dwellers, that is. These are normal citizens who chose to live within the upper reaches of the cave. As you shall see, it is quite large. They build small houses under the rock, a whole miniature village, in fact, with barns for their livestock and workshops to ply their trade. Living quite happily and secure, one would imagine."

"How odd," the nanny declared, obviously baffled by the concept.

"I would tend to agree with you, madam. It is not how I would choose to live. But they have done so for centuries, perhaps at one time living in harmony with the thieves!" He laughed, and they joined in. "Now they continue the ancient tradition of making rope for the local mines. The moist atmosphere of the cavern aids the process. Rather ingenious, actually. The poet Charles Cotton wrote in his 'Wonders of the Peake,'

Now to the cave we come, wherein is found,
A new strange thing, a village underground:
Houses and barns for men and beasts behoof,
With walls distinct, under one solid roof.

"Cotton was a devoted Derbyshire gentleman and his poems express his great love for our fair county. I have several compilations of his writings if you appreciate poetry."

Peak Cliff cavern, previously glimpsed from the crest above where Peveril Castle proudly guarded, was easily reached. The gently sloping, picturesque tree and brush-lined pathway leading to the cave followed the river and was a pleasant walk. Dozens of cottages nestled within the trees, residents going about the business of normal life and impervious to the tourists treading past in endless streams. A last curve in the road revealed the massive opening, the effect dazzling to behold.

The yawning portal, entirely natural as this cavern had rarely been used for mining, was a rounded, gaping hole resembling an unpillared arch, easily a hundred feet across and sixty feet high. It cut perpendicularly into the vertical cliff of solid limestone that rose nearly three hundred feet to the bluff above. The floor was predominately level on the right side, swept clean of debris by the people who called this gulf their home, and tapered downward on the leftward side into uneven terraces. The lowest point was where the Peakshole River flowed. The mouth was so wide that one could see a great distance into the interior, the magnitude of just how enormous the cavern was readily discernable. The farthest reaches faded to grey and then inky black as the blaze of day no longer penetrated, but the immediate area was well lighted.

A cluster of small huts covered the area to the right. The flat terraces provided the working surface, the area cluttered with industrious workers and yards of rope strung across the tall posts and wound around big spools. For a fee that they were happy to pay, a local man gave them a tour of the village and demonstrated the art of rope making. Darcy, of course, was especially fascinated.

Alexander and Mrs. Hanford were left outside, sheltered under canopies set up for visitors, while their guide led a small group of adventurous souls deeper into the residential portion of the cave, known as "the vestibule." They passed women and playing children, the activities and mood strangely normal despite the tonnage of solid rock overhead. It was eerie.

They were handed lights and instructed to stay close. The vestibule cavern narrowed toward the back into a low tunnel that required Darcy and several others to stoop in order to pass through, but was fortunately short, before opening into the first of the two largest inner chambers. The Great Cavern, also referred to as Bell House due to its general shape, was dry and cool. The walls were difficult to discern in the dim light, but the floor was littered with loose rocks and fascinating calcifications that glowed in the lamplight hung from the ceiling. Flitches of Bacon, the guide called them, and as absurd as the moniker was, they did rather resemble wavy strips of bacon.

A long walk brought them to a broad river, the fancifully named Styx. Ferrying across the river in tiny boats that required the passenger to lie flat was the only way to reach the next chamber. Darcy had taken the trip once before, during his sojourn with Mr. Logan and his Cambridge friends, so he knew it to be safe if mildly scary. He hesitated, glancing to Lizzy to gauge her opinion. That she was nervous was obvious, but she was not to be deterred.

"I have come this far, William, and I won't turn back." Her voice quavered slightly, but she lifted her chin and bravely stepped into the boat. Darcy chuckled, his heart swelling with pride at her tenacity.

The chamber across the river was larger and far more interesting. Here the walls and ceiling were impossible to see, the breadth of the cave known to be over two hundred feet although one only had the impression of vast space. They cautiously explored, holding tightly to their lights and, in the case of Darcy and Lizzy, tightly to each other. Their feet veered instinctively toward the extremity of the vacuity where the echoing splash of water hinted strongly to what they would see.

Another underground stream, this one shallow, flowed and was fed by an incessant rain of droplets from crevices in the rock high above. It was this natural aperture from whence the cavern's name derived: Roger Rain's House. The combination of moisture in the air, damp rock, nonexistent sunlight, and still air created an environment that was bordering on cold.

Traversing the remaining rock hollows accessible meant crossing the running rivulet numerous times, but the water was shallow. The deeper caves descended gradually as they bored into the earth and were smaller. They were filled with stalactites in all sizes, some enormous and reaching completely to the ground to form natural pillars. Most were intact but many were broken or dislocated from their original placement on the ceiling. There were other oddities such as a huge pile of sand carried in and deposited by the river, the marine exuviae embedded into the strata of the limestone walls, and the three arches so perfectly carved into one rock wall that they appeared hand hewn.

But the crescendo was the spontaneous chorus that broke out. Disembodied voices burst forth from the unseen upper heights of the chasm, lifted in a song that reverberated against the walls. It was beautiful and creepy, pleasurable and astonishing. The mystery was quickly solved once the voices faded, a group of singers descending down a makeshift stairway to stand visible on a sort of chancel where they accepted applause and praise.

Returning to the surface was a relief, even though the enterprise had been thrilling. Both Lizzy and Darcy blinked in the sun that seemed far brighter than it had an hour previously and sucked in huge lungfuls of air.

Lizzy's mien was the common one of impish enthusiasm that Darcy knew meant she had thoroughly enjoyed herself. He had as well, his expression controlled but the wide smile and shimmering eyes revealed his delight in the escapade. Still, Lizzy's first words upon crossing the arched portal echoed his sentiments, "I do not believe I have ever been so happy to see the sun."

They paused on the threshold, gazing back into the abyss. Mrs. Hanford saw them and rose with a still sleeping Alexander in her arms, walking to join them.

Darcy nodded. "I know what you mean. I love adventure, but cave exploration is definitely not on my list of possible hobbies. That takes a special breed of man. But now I have a greater appreciation for the rapidly increasing number of men who are embracing the activity."

"Think how amazing it must be to happen upon a subterranean wonder, knowing that you are the first human eyes to ever behold it. That would be quite exhilarating."

Darcy laughed softly, nudging her hand with his. "You are too busy as a wife and mother to dash off and discover caves, my dear."

She laughed, turning to take Alexander into her arms. "Have no fear. I am abundantly content to care for my husband and son. That is plenty of adventure for me." She kissed the infant's forehead, curly locks tickling her nose, and looked up at her husband with a teasing grin. She opened her mouth to speak, most likely planning a humorous jibe, but the words were never uttered.

A loud cracking sound pierced the air, echoing through the ravine.

Everyone froze, reflexively gazing upward to where the noise originated. A chunk of rock protruding from the face of limestone near the edge of the towering cliff was suddenly and inexplicably breaking away. The clap of severing stone mixed with the high-pitched scrape of rock upon rock and the crunch of crumbling gravel. Time seemed to stop as they stared transfixed at the five-foot boulder directly above their heads that, with a final reverberating boom, disengaged. It started sliding down the flat face, the motion painfully slow in the paralyzed time, but gained speed quickly. The rock's weight and rain of dirt, plants, and gravel caused it to twist in the air, toppling over as the jagged projectile plummeted down the three hundred foot escarpment.

Voices lifted in shouts and screams. People scattered in all directions. Lizzy stood open-mouthed, immobile in stupefied terror, staring at the calamity heading straight for her. Darcy, thankfully, reacted with brisk efficiency. At the second plangent crack, he pivoted, grabbing his wife and child in a crushing embrace, lifting bodily until Lizzy's feet were off the ground, and lunged up the trail away from where the avalanche was destined to land. He whipped his head toward Mrs. Hanford, who also stood rooted to the spot, yelling in a snapping command, "Mrs. Hanford! Move!"

She jolted, but his penetrating order did the trick, she too twirling about. Watson grasped onto her upper arm, hauling hard as they all dashed to safety. Yet, everything was happening so fast. The debris of tiny rocks and dirt showered their shoulders seconds before the rock crashed into the hard-packed ground, sundering down the middle with shards splintering from the edges and flying through the air.

Darcy's wide strides carried them ten feet from the place of impact, almost precisely where they had been standing moments before. Watson and Mrs. Hanford ducked to the left, behind a large tree mere milliseconds before a sharp limestone sliver forcefully speared the trunk inches above Watson's head. Darcy did not look back, plunging headlong with his body curled around his family and his back to the danger. He faltered only once, grunting hoarsely as his step momentarily tottering to the right, but he adroitly recovered and ran until so winded he could barely breathe. Then he ran more, placing a good distance between them and the cavern portal before halting.

The abrupt silence, or relative silence in comparison to the smashing and ripping sounds that still echoed within the cavern recesses, was proof that the immediate danger was past. Nevertheless, he looked behind, making absolutely sure that nothing menacing remained before loosening the bruising grip around Lizzy and settling her to the ground.

She was trembling violently, her eyes wide and pupils dilated. Alexander was awake and equally alarmed, sucking vigorously on a thumb while the other hand was painfully clenched in his mother's hair. Darcy studied them closely, gazing with penetrating intensity into their eyes, and bent to cup Lizzy's cheek.

"Are you hurt? In any way?"

She shook her head, swallowing past the desert in her throat before able to speak. "I'm fine. We are fine."

He scanned over their bodies to verify her claim, and then nodded curtly. His face was grim as he turned to look for Mrs. Hanford and survey the damage.

"William! Oh my God! You are hurt!" She lifted shaking fingertips to the two-inch gash along the underside of his left jawline, the oozing blood that had already soaked into his cravat and collar coating her fingers.

He did not even look at her, shaking his head shortly. "It is nothing. Ah, there is Mrs. Hanford and Watson. They appear uninjured. Stay here," he commanded, glancing at her then as he started to step away. The expression of severe dismay and teary eyes blinking furiously as she tried to remain calm halted him. He sighed, gently clasping her face and bending for a tender, brief kiss. "I am fine, Elizabeth. A scratch only that will easily mend." He wiped the spilled tears from her cheeks. "Now that I know you and Alexander are safe, I must check if anyone needs assistance. Stay here, promise me. I will instruct Watson to take you to the carriage. I will return swiftly." He kissed her again, smiling into her troubled eyes.

She nodded. "Yes. Of course. As you wish. But then we are finding a physician to look at your wound." She spoke firmly, once again in control and exerting her authority, meeting his eyes with a challenge.

He chuckled. "As you wish, Mrs. Darcy." Then he pivoted and strode briskly back to the cave.

Miraculously, no one was severely injured. There were a number of scrapes and abrasion from falling debris or stumbling while running away. Three people suffered cuts similar to Darcy's from launched shards. One man was impaled through the upper arm from a larger piece of rock, a wound messy and extremely painful but not fatal. Another man miscalculated his footing, slipping on a terrace edge, and tumbling down the slope to land in the river gorge. He hit his head hard enough to swoon and develop a huge knot, but aside from a massive headache and the pain from dozens of scrapes, he recovered without defect.

A boy was sent to Castleton to fetch the surgeon. He was a disreputable looking character, but he tended the wounds efficiently enough, so Darcy allowed him to examine his laceration. The wound was not deep, the bleeding clotted long before the surgeon touched it. He cleaned it well, declared that it did not require stitching—not that Darcy would have permitted the scruffy fellow to pierce his skin with a needle—and slathered the slice with an herbal poultice and resin ointment to adhere the skin edges.

The troglodytes rallied together admirably. Moments after the boulder landed, while the sound of impact still shook the air, they were soberly and resourcefully organizing. No one person appeared to be in charge, and few orders were given, but before Darcy or any of the visitors returned to the scene, the cave dwellers had triaged the injured to the main hut and were in the process of rescuing the poor man lying in the riverbed. Children were picking up the smaller rocks and women were sweeping the debris. Several burly men were staring intently at the heavy pieces of stone, clinically discussing where best to discard it, while others were examining the precious ropes and equipment for any damage.

Of all the sights seen that strange morning, in some respects the cool practicality of these hardy people who lived roughly among rock, darkness, and the elements was the oddest.

There was little for any of the gentlemen to do, so the Darcys were finally able to leave the Devil's Arse with relief. The blood-soaked cravat was stowed in a pocket, and Darcy had washed his grimy hands and brushed the dirt off his jacket and out of his hair. The mundane tasks had served to restore his calm for the most part, and he rounded the corner beyond which the carriage waited with his emotions largely under control.

Lizzy, unfortunately, had not been so lucky in finding an outlet for her worry. Alexander had nursed, more for the need to be cuddled than for nourishment, promptly falling back to sleep. This left Lizzy with nothing to do but pace for what felt like hours. She envied the infant's ability to pacify, as she was a bundle of nerves ready to explode! The trauma coupled with visions of her husband bleeding, even though she knew the injury minor, threatened to undo her. When Darcy finally reappeared, walking briskly but composedly, her frayed regulation ripped apart. Tears spilled and she flew across the short distance, barely halting before slamming bodily into him.

As abruptly as the tears fell, she flared irritably. The release of her fear brought on a case of serious pique and she grasped hard onto his upper arm while the other hand lifted his chin so she could examine the dressing.

"He did an adequate job, I suppose," she declared. "I saw him arrive and his appearance did not engender confidence. George would sooner kiss Lady Catherine than dress so disheveled and dirty. Tell me he washed his hands before slathering your face with this?"

Darcy was smiling. "He did, sort of. Do not fear, love. I have sufficient knowledge of how to treat abrasions and lacerations. I have had a few others in my lifetime," he said dryly, Lizzy snorting while she continued to blink her eyes furiously and fuss roughly. "I will send a servant to the apothecary for the necessary ingredients. I doubt it will leave a scar."

He clutched her hands, stopping them from their incessant fidgeting over his garments and person, and brought her fingers to his mouth for a tender kiss. When he spoke, his voice was low, steeped in checked emotion. "We are all well, dearest. But, if you are not too disappointed, I believe I would rather forego the afternoon's agenda and return to Chelmbridge. Not only do I desperately need to change clothing, I also desperately need to hold my family close."

She nodded, smiling as her churlishness evaporated. She leaned into his chest, Darcy embracing and kissing the top of her head. "Indeed, I think I have seen enough caves to last me several years. Take me home, Fitzwilliam."

They would not return "home" for two more days, but the Logans' lovely estate was adequate for the requisite rest, affection, and sweet lovemaking they craved. Mutual agreement meant that Poole's Cavern would be saved for another excursion at a much later date. They ended their holiday staying above ground, leisurely driving over the beautiful and unique landscape of the Peak from Chapel-en-le-Frith down to Buxton and through Tideswell to Hathersage before veering south. They reverted to the favored pastime of touring historical places and churches as they strolled along manicured lawns and easy pathways, pushing a fascinated Alexander in his perambulator.

The last days of peace and delightful entertainment were necessary to erase the fright that cast a pall upon the whole vacation, both of them glad they had not succumbed to their nerves and rushed back to Pemberley immediately. On their first night in the familiar mansion that was in every way their home, after Alexander was tucked into his bed, Darcy pulled his naked wife onto his bared body. He drew her earlobe between his lips, sucking lightly, and then whispered huskily, "Shall we see how our bed compares to the Chelmbridge one in the sturdiness department?"

He grinned, lifting his left brow, Lizzy dissolving in laughter as she nodded a definite affirmative. And with that declaration, and the passion that ensued, the holiday at the Peaks was cemented within their minds as one of tremendous enjoyment only.

CHAPTER SEVENTEEN

Colonel Fitzwilliam's Affairs

RIDING ALONE THROUGH THE ill lit secondary avenues of London as the midnight hour passed was generally considered an unwise option. Colonel Richard Fitzwilliam was a cautious man for the most part, but also one who, after years of war in places that made London's mean streets appear as the golden paved lanes of Heaven, did not frighten easily. Nonetheless, he kept his right hand lightly resting on his thigh near the butt of a loaded pistol. He wore a nondescript suit of dark blue, blending into the shadows as his uniform would not allow. It was essential that his mission not be detected. Finding a balance between stealth while not so obviously trying to evade notice was the key. Fortunately, he was skilled at such tactics, the military thorough in the lessons taught to their officers, as this excursion was of the utmost importance.

He turned down another back alley that led to the main thoroughfare he needed to hastily cross, but which was empty, whereas the broader street would likely not be. Even at this late hour and with the vast majority of the inhabitants of the fine townhouses he passed gone for the summer, the traffic in Town was never sparse. The ring of his mount's hooves on stone blended with the noise echoing from the streets, but he kept his chin down and wide-brimmed hat pulled low just in case attention was drawn. Anonymity was essential. He could not, under any circumstances, encounter someone he knew.

Outwardly calm and vigilant, inside his heart raced. This was the third night in the past two weeks he had embarked on this mission. It was late September, the worst of London's oppressive heat passing as the trees slowly began to color. The afternoon breezes increased, the evenings shortened with impressive sunset displays, migrating birds flurried in droves, and fall blooms emerged as signs of the autumn season ahead. Not surprisingly, it was the first time in many long years that the hardened man of war who had also lived in the busy city for fifteen years noticed his surrounds in such a light. Fleetingly, he wondered if Darcy had experienced the same sort of sentimental, and rather foolish and embarrassing, tendencies as his love blossomed. Not that Richard would ever ask!

Yet, as ridiculous as he felt at times, there was no denying that these past months were the happiest of his life. The "accidental" encounters with Lady Fotherby had continued unabated all summer long. Initial innocent meetings at The Green Park with brief walks gradually lengthening had led to additional "surprise" rendezvous about town, as planned agendas were shared while nonchalantly conversing. It was remarkably easy to arrange. The official social Season was over, but there were always events happening or places to meet casually. However, as amazing as it was to spend time with her in these settings, it was not as fulfilling as it could have been and as they both desperately wished for it to be. Frank or lengthy conversation was impossible.

Her family remained firm on the necessity for her to mourn officially for a year. Although she had not shared her interest in the son of Lord and Lady Matlock, their increasingly frequent chance assignations were notable. Pointed questions had not been asked, but she gleaned from oblique comments and meaningful glances that her father and uncle were suspicious, at the least, and not happy about the development. She was worried about their opinion on the subject, but refused to dwell on it. Rather she delighted in what even at her age and past history was the first love she had ever experienced.

That her emotions toward Richard Fitzwilliam were real and profoundly deep was without doubt. Clearly his devotion was as strong. Two weeks ago while meeting at the British Museum's Roman wing, Lady Fotherby had slipped a folded parchment into his jacket pocket. She was so devious and sly in the transfer that he had not discovered the missive until late that night when preparing for bed!

My Dearest R,

I know this is incredibly forward of me and pray I will not earn your disrespect, but I find that my heart can no longer restrain its need to speak with you in a more intimate setting. Therefore, I beseech you to visit me this Tuesday hence. Come discreetly, I beg of you, at the midnight hour to the rear entrance of my house. My trusted servant will be waiting and escort you in undetected. My only wish is to converse openly and adequately express my feelings. No demands are placed upon you, I promise. I simply yearn for the joy in seeing your face. Yours, S

The agony of waiting through the intervening two days until Tuesday was nearly more than he could bear. He vacillated between unparalleled excitement and intense nervousness. The latter emotion was somewhat embarrassing to admit. The truth was he did not know precisely what she contemplated by "adequately express my feelings" and was unsure what his outlook was on the prospects! Richard was not an innocent and obviously neither was Lady Fotherby. The physical attraction they felt for each other was palpable and the thought of loving her as he wished to with every particle of his body was a joyous imagining that he lived each night in vivid detail.

Yet in every dream, she was his wife.

For the first time in his entire life, the mere notion of intimacy with someone other than the woman he hoped to be wed to before the year was out was an untenable concept. He was more than willing to wait and found the abstaining strangely sweet. Still, as thrilling as the vision of consummating their sacred vows in the proper manner and time, he was only human!

He need not have fretted over the matter, however. It is not that Lady Fotherby—Simone, as she would forever now be to him—was not involved in her own struggle over physical desires; but the simple delight in just sitting together holding hands, talking, and stealing kisses was exalting. They talked until the sun sent its first hazy rays over the horizon, Richard hastily escaping into the few remaining shadows. Embarrassment, hesitation, discomposure, unfamiliarity; it all faded in those hours spent communicating.

He shared his past as he had with few people. Honest tales of his wartime experiences, reminiscences from his youth, blunders and ridiculousness of adolescence, University incidents and education, and so on. She spoke of her arranged marriage to the kindly Lord Fotherby, a man she respected and cared for, but had never loved. Mostly she talked about her sons: Harry who was now seven, and four-year-old Hugh. They were the light of her life, Richard understanding and accepting that his love would never supplant the place they held in her heart, but merely come alongside.

They confessed their mutual infatuation all those years ago, admitting honestly that although real, it was of an immature nature. Perhaps it could have escalated into a deeper love, but no time was spent on worthless regrets. Besides, their current affair possessed all the traits of a silly, juvenile romance in how giddy and delirious they were. Now was all that mattered and by the time the first night waned into the blush of morning, their declarations of love were made and plans for a future together were set in motion. October ten was around the corner and Richard fully intended to make his intentions known and officially ask for permission to court Lady Fotherby no later than October eleventh!

Successfully, he traversed the distance between his house to the grand manor in secret. Miss Hale waited at the servant's door near the kitchen, guiding him through the dark passageways leading to the parlor. She took her seat situated near the doorway, prepared to attentively guard from any unwanted nighttime wanders, while he knocked softly and waited for his love's welcome.

It came quickly, the door opening to reveal her smiling face and seeking hand that grasped his and pulled him into the room. In a heartbeat, Richard yet fumbling to latch the door behind, she was in his arms.

"I missed you so much!" she breathed, raining kisses over his face.

"You just saw me today at the art exhibit," he said with a laugh.

"Yes, but we hardly spoke for all the others demanding my attention. What a bother! Why can they not leave me alone and allow me to gaze upon your face in abstracted contentment?"

"There is little to look at, my dear. You would be bored in minutes."

"Stop that! I weary of you speaking nonsense, Richard Fitzwilliam. Yours is a face I can drown in. Now, come and sit. I have hot tea and your favorite berry tarts. Tell me about your day. You left the exhibit early."

"I really should not have come at all as my duties were overwhelming me, but I could not resist. Speaking with you, however obliquely, stealing a touch of your fingers or perhaps a kiss, has become my intoxicant. I am addicted to you, dearest Simone."

She shook her head, blushing as she poured the tea. "The things you say! Ridiculous."

"Now it is you who are wearying me by not believing the truth of my words, poorly romantic as they are."

"They are beautifully romantic, Richard. Forgive me. I know you speak the truth in your love for me. I suppose I yet have difficulty grasping it fully. It has not been a topic I have allowed myself to dwell on in the past."

He gently clasped her chin in his fingers, lifting to gaze into her eyes. "Are your doubts assaulting you today, my love? Is that why your eyes look sad and tired?"

"Only partially. Actually it is Oliver. I returned from the exhibit to discover the physician here and Oliver suffering an episode. I was furious that he ordered not to send for me. He always thinks more of others than himself, sweet boy."

"Is he better now?"

"Yes, but it was a horrid afternoon. It frightens me so, Richard. The spells occur with increasing frequency and he responds less and less to the treatments. The physicians are confounded. This disease, whatever it is, has no cure or definitive course. All is an unknown while my poor boy suffers."

"You should be sleeping, Simone. Now that I step back from the sweetness of your lips I see your fatigue. I should leave you to your rest."

"No! Please! I... needed to see you. I did rest for a bit once his crisis was over." She cupped his cheek, smiling with the wealth of her love evident. "I, too, am addicted, dearest Richard."

"Well, I am more than pleased to fulfill your requirements, my Lady." And they lost themselves for a time in blissful, but controlled, kisses.

The Fotherby tales of sadness and woe dated back many years prior to Lady Simone Halifax joining the family. Her now deceased husband had been married twice prior to taking his young bride to wife. His first wife, a woman he reportedly had loved deeply although he never spoke of it to Simone, had died along with their only child during the birthing process after a mere five years of marriage. Lord Fotherby had refused to remarry for nearly twenty years. His second wife was thrust upon him by frantic family members fretful about the line's continuation. She was the daughter of a Duke who, despite her impeccable breeding and pedigree, was hiding a chronic illness. None knew of her ailment, the secret hidden carefully behind a stunning dowry and pretty face. Lord Fotherby was furious when the deception was revealed on their wedding night when she was too ill to consummate their marriage.

For fifteen interminable years, they would be married before she finally succumbed to the puzzling disease that defied all medical expertise. In that time, they would rarely speak and even rarer still perform the marital duties necessary to produce an heir, the whole reason for the trumped up marriage in the first place. Nonetheless, three children would be born, two dying in their infancy and a third, Oliver, surviving but clearly stricken with the same malady as his mother.

Lord Fotherby adored his son, worshipped the ground he walked on. It was this overwhelming devotion that prompted him again to take a wife. Left to his own devices, he would not have done so. His heart still belonged to the love of his youth and his physical needs were met by the bevy of mistresses easily accessible to a man of his wealth and power. But Oliver needed a mother. And, as painful as the thought was, Lord Fotherby recognized that he needed another heir.

Well into his sixtieth decade, he was still a vigorous and handsome man, respected throughout the country and fabulously rich. His choices for a third wife were vast, not a father of his class unwilling to give a daughter to Lord Fotherby. In fact, the atmosphere was disgustingly similar to a cattle auction! He had his pick of every available female in all of England. Lady Simone Halifax, daughter to the Earl of Westgate, was not chosen arbitrarily. Physically she was beautiful, but many others were equally so. What drew Lord Fotherby was her innate kindness and empathy balanced with a wit and spunk that he found attractive. He wanted a partner who appealed to him in a sexual way, but who also could take on the various roles necessary for Lady Fotherby and as mother to his son.

Lady Simone was nineteen, over her infatuation with the now departed Second Lieutenant Richard Fitzwilliam, and, although not in love with Lord Fotherby, was in no way against the union. Like all females of her rank she had been raised to comprehend that marriage was rarely a matter of love, but rather a type of business arrangement. If one was so fortunate as to discover affection and admiration then all the better, but it was not anticipated. In this facet, Lady Fotherby would be highly favored. Lord Fotherby was a good man, the best as a matter of fact. Kind, considerate, generous, devoted, humorous, and a gentle lover, he was more than she had ever anticipated in a mate. She genuinely grew to love her stepson Oliver, who was quite like his father in temperament, and her own two sons were a fount of eternal joy.

For nearly twelve years, her life would move on with the typical soirees, Society functions, and duties as mistress of several vast estates. Lord Fotherby was extremely busy and weeks would often go by without her seeing her husband. She held no illusions that he was entirely faithful, this aspect of marriage not expected nor condemned. But he treated her well, made few demands, made his resources lavishly available, and was devoted to their children. Love would never bloom between them, but esteem and fondness were abundant. Heights of passion were never reached, but she knew no different and was satisfied in the tenderness found within the sexual act when he sporadically sought her favors. Life was content and she had no cause to grieve her situation.

Until Colonel Richard Fitzwilliam reentered her life.

Who can adequately describe the vagaries of love? The poets try and do an admirable job. Yet how is it logical to take one look at someone not seen or thought of for years and know instantly that your heart is lost? To Darcy, Richard described that first encounter with Lady Fotherby as taking his breath away. It would be another two years before he would learn that her internal reaction was as strong. Suddenly, she was as an absurd, love-struck teenager in how she would dream of him and look for him at every function attended. When he was spied, her heart would lurch, face flush, and body tingle. It was asinine and she was mortified. But she could no more halt the feelings than halt the sun from rising.

Her guilt during those years over the mental betrayal to her spouse was intense, but he was barely cold in his grave before she was blatantly flirting with the Colonel and pressing into his kiss! Her fingers had throbbed with the warmth of his lips and her spine shivered for hours, no amount of self-chastisement or shame adequate to overrule the sensations. It was pathetic. *She* was pathetic, counting the days until she could throw off the somber colors of mourning and hopefully see him again.

And now he was here, in her arms, returning her love with a checked desire genuine and profound. All traces of guilt were gone. If there was one thing she knew of her late husband, it was that he would have wanted her happiness. He had told her so on his deathbed. Clutching her hand weakly, voice faint, he had thanked her for the years of devotion, for their children, and for her faithfulness and perfection as Lady Fotherby. He assured her once again of the home and riches he had provided for her. Lastly, he had encouraged her to live life fully, find joy and peace. Her tears had been sincere when he passed, knowing that she would miss his smile and warmth and wit, but also knowing that she was young and deserved to move on. Thus, there was no remorse at the passion she now embraced in this man who had, to some degree, always lived in her soul. If it all seemed a bit dreamlike, she was gradually overcoming those doubts as well. It was impossible to cling to uncertainties when gazing into eyes brimming with purest love.

The kiss ended, both recognizing the escalating ardor and needing to withdraw before crossing permanent lines. Simone was nearly virginal in the surprising vibrations that raced through her body when he kissed her. Yet her innocence was not complete and she shivered and suppressed a moan of pure need. Richard smiled and pulled her close, nestling her head against his shoulder, and caressing lightly.

Silence fell for a time, broken by her dulcet tones from within the depths of his neck. "It was important that I see you tonight for another reason as well. I received a letter from my father today. He has invited me to our family estate in Hampshire. It really was more of a command, but he misses the grandchildren and we usually do spend some time there in the summer. I have evaded his requests thus far, but am running out of excuses."

His grip had instinctively tightened, heart falling through the floor. For a frantic moment he experienced a violent stab of fear, a piercing pain followed by a vivid premonition that if she left his presence he would lose her forever. It was irrational and fleeting, but the aftermath lingered and caused him to shudder.

"Simone, must we continue this charade? I love you and you love me! What are a few weeks? Let me come with you and talk to your father now."

She pulled away, staring into his dear face with a sunny smile and touching his cheek. "I thought of this very thing all afternoon, in between caring for Oliver. You are correct. There is no point in waiting any longer."

"Excellent!" He interrupted. "When shall we leave? I can request time away easily..."

Her chuckle and light kiss halted his words. "Let me finish, silly man. My, you are like one of my children running away with yourself so! I do not wish to tarry in our decision to be together any longer than you do. But please allow me to speak with my father first."

He frowned. "This is not the first time I have sensed a hesitation with you on the topic of our marriage, Simone. Do you think your father will be opposed to me?"

"I do not know, Richard, honestly." She rose, hands wringing while pacing before him. "My father has always been obsessed with rank and situation. All four of us girls were auctioned off to the highest bidder." She spoke bitterly. Richard knew from her sharing that she alone of the four daughters was fortunate in her marriage, her siblings wealthy and with titles equal to or above what they possessed prior, but none blessed with a kindly man. "You cannot imagine his glee when the Marquess of Fotherby agreed to marry me."

He bristled, unable to hide his offense at the perceived slight. "I am the son of an Earl. And a colonel in His Majesty's Armed Forces."

"Yes, of course you are right. I am being silly. Worrying for nothing, I am sure." She returned hastily to his side, taking his hands. "I love you, Richard Fitzwilliam. Surely that is all that will truly matter. But please grant me this one concession. I will send for you when the timing is right. And then I will be yours forever. I *will* kiss you under the mistletoe as your wife, Colonel, so be prepared."

"I will be anticipating far more than a kiss, my dear, so you be prepared."

She blushed, again nestling into his shoulder. Warmth returned to his body but could not entirely dissipate the icy chill buried deep inside.

A week passed without word. Busy with his duties, Richard nevertheless marked the passage of each day with growing excitement. Certain that Simone merely needed time to accustom her father to the fact that she planned to remarry so soon after her famous husband's death, he was not concerned at the delay. Instead, he waited semi-patiently, attending to his work with no outward sign of expectation unless one noted how he subtly started every time a messenger arrived. He laughed at himself each time, as it was unlikely that a letter from the Marchioness of Fotherby would be delivered to company barracks! Rather he anticipated that an invitation would be waiting for him at home. Yet, as the week swiftly approached a fortnight with the stack of mail sitting upon his desk devoid of a parchment addressed in her delicate handwriting, his excitement turned to mild disquiet.

But nothing prepared him for the shock he received one morning as he sipped on his coffee and nibbled on a toasted slice of thick bread with cheese melted atop, that day's edition of the *London Times* spread before him. He skimmed through the social page, not particularly interested in what Lady

Whocares had worn to some play at Covent Garden, when his eye was captured. He read the gossipy announcement of the betrothal of the Marquess of Wellson to the widowed Lady Fotherby in utter disbelief, his trance-like gaze returning to the top of the column again and again.

On a windy day in mid-October, after two weeks of pain worse than anything suffered as a result of battle wounds, Colonel Fitzwilliam rode up the long drive toward Pemberley. The mansion beckoned to him with inviting homeness as it always had from the earliest memories of his childhood. No one expected him, the footman Rothchilde hiding his surprise with typical formality.

"Welcome to Pemberley, Colonel," he greeted, as if unexpected visitors were a daily occurrence, taking the offered coat with an impassive expression. "I will inform Miss Darcy that you have arrived."

"Are Mr. and Mrs. Darcy out?"

"They are away at this time, sir. Dr. Darcy is at the hospital in Matlock, but Miss Darcy is in residence."

Richard managed to hide his dismay at that undesirable news. He nodded, heading unerringly for the parlor and liquor cabinet.

"Cousin Richard, what a pleasant surprise."

He turned at the voice, glass of brandy halting midway to his mouth, stunned at the vision before him. It was Georgiana, yet not Georgiana. The woman who was once his child ward strolled gracefully toward him with a beatific smile, blue eyes shimmering with happiness. She wore a gown of rich purple velvet, clinging to her tall, willowy, but curvaceous form with perfection, golden hair piled elegantly atop her regal head, face stunningly beautiful above a slender neck and delicate shoulders. She drew close, raising one fine-boned hand to his cheek as her eyes clouded with concern. "What is it Richard? You look sad."

He would never be able to explain how it happened, but never would he be ashamed at the comfort he sought. With lithe dexterity she captured the glass as it began to fall, gathering his brokenhearted body into her firm, sympathetic embrace, crooning soothingly as she gently rocked the silently weeping man.

They ended up on the settee with him telling her everything as she held tight to one hand. She listened attentively without interjecting once until he had exhausted himself of words.

"I had to come here," he finished, breathing deeply. "Pemberley has always stilled my soul in a way even Rivallain never did. Of course, I was intending to burden your brother with my woes. Forgive me, little mouse, for laying this on your slim shoulders."

He smiled weakly, Georgiana shaking her head slowly. "Do not be ridiculous. This is what friends are for."

"Where are Darcy and Lizzy by the way?"

"They went to the Lake District with the Lathrops, Sitwells, and Vernors. You just missed them as they departed three days ago. They expect to return in a month."

"Were you not invited?"

She laughed. "No, but I would not have wished to spend three weeks with a group of young married couples." She paused, the mournful cast to his face at the reference to marriage too awful to ignore. "Oh, Richard! I am sorry! Is there anything that can be done?"

He stood, walking the gait of an old man to retrieve the forgotten glass of brandy, drinking deeply before answering. "No. She has made her decision apparently and the date is set. A Christmas wedding," he finished bitterly. He drained the drink in one swallow, crashing the glass onto the table's surface. "Why? I keep asking myself why! I know her father is pressuring her into this! It is the only explanation. But it makes no sense! She is an independent woman now. Lord Fotherby made sure of that with a more than adequate jointure to add to her engagement settlement. Seeking her father's permission was merely a formality. One I was more than willing to bow to, as it is only proper, but still just a formality. And to choose Lord Wellson! My God, Georgie! The man is disgusting! Obese, crude, in his late fifties, a reputation of mistresses and illegitimate children scattered all over England. The thought of him with Simone…" He paced furiously and although there was not the slightest hint of humor in the realization, Georgiana could not help but note that he, for the first time in memory, reminded her of her brother when he was dismayed or agitated.

"I waited and waited for her to send word for me to join her," he continued brokenly, voice rising and falling with his anger and pain, "but no word came. Nothing! Then I read about her engagement in the newspaper. In the Society page, for God's sake! She did not even have the decency to write me herself. I couldn't believe it, I just couldn't. In desperation I rode to the estate, but was repelled at the gates, by orders of Lady Fotherby I was told. God, Georgie! How could she be so cold? So unfeeling?"

"Perhaps you misinterpreted her sentiments, dear cousin?"

He shook his head vehemently. "I cannot believe I was so duped! It just cannot be that she would deceive so totally. We talked of marriage, our future together. She said she loved me, over and over! It was in her eyes, Georgie, in her kiss..." He paused, glancing with embarrassment to his innocent cousin whose face remained drawn with sympathy. "Could I have been so blinded by my own desires? I must have, although I still have difficulty countenancing it." He released a harsh, humorless laugh. "My pride does not wish to face that error in judgment, let me tell you. I am not a child to be so led astray!"

"You said yourself that your visits together were few and usually with crowds about. When it comes to affairs of the heart, it is easy to be blinded into believing what one wishes."

He halted his frantic pacing, looking with faint amusement into her mature eyes. "My, quite the expert on love, are we Miss Darcy?"

She blushed, ducking her head. "Little personal knowledge, I am pleased to say. And I do pray I never learn this lesson at the expense of my heart. But you know what William suffered and... Well, I do not suppose I am being a horrid gossip if I reveal what happened to Miss Bennet this summer only to you."

Richard scowled. "Miss Kitty?"

She nodded, it now her turn to launch into another tale of romantic woes. Richard rejoined her on the settee, listening to the story with genuine sadness as he truly cared for Lizzy's sister. Yet, as reprehensible as it was to admit, there was an odd sort of comfort in knowing that others besides himself suffered such heartaches. Additionally, the reminder of Darcy's tangled web on the road to marital happiness was a mild consolation. The chances of his romance turning out as Darcy's did seemed nil; but the hope, however faint, was in the knowledge that there may be peace found after the turmoil.

The following weeks passed in slowness both agonizing with the persistent ache that lived in his heart while also involving moments of tranquility surprising in their intensity.

A leave from his Regiment was granted, only General Tammon guessing that the "family crisis" was more of a personal nature. Richard had fled London with no clear purpose other than to escape the painful memories that seemed to be everywhere he looked and to talk to Darcy. All of their lives, although Darcy tended to be far more secretive than Richard, they had understood each other and innately knew how to cheer each other up.

Affairs of the heart, *l'amour*, were different however.

The Fitzwilliam family was not raised with the staunch religious ethics and morals of the Darcys. That is not to say they did not revere the Church and the tenets taught, but merely held a slightly more liberal interpretation. Richard did not suffer from the same reluctance to engage in or even discuss matters relating to sex as Darcy did. Although far from promiscuous in his romantic encounters over the years, never taking a mistress nor able to claim a huge number of lovers, Richard was quite certain his experience vastly trumped Darcy's prior to marriage. Since it was the one topic they had never talked about, he could not be sure, but if a wager was involved, his bet was that Darcy had been innocent upon his marriage, as unlikely as that may have seemed to most.

So ingrained and natural was this taboo subject that Richard had been only mildly hurt when Darcy retreated and suffered in silent solitude after the rejection by Elizabeth Bennet. It was his mother who put the pieces of that puzzle together, Richard feeling like an absolute imbecile in not figuring it out himself; but Darcy going crazy over a woman had simply not been a concept that ever occurred to him. It was so utterly out of character. Since the resolution of that dilemma and Darcy's happiness in marriage, his cousin had loosened up a bit in expressing emotions and discussing romantic topics. Never, of course, would Darcy follow the often ribald characteristics of some who delighted in boasting about their bedroom antics and prowess, but at least the subject could be broached, as evidenced by his openness in talking about Lady Fotherby. The one area Richard was certain they would agree upon was the sanctity of the marriage state itself and the belief in faithfulness for life; thus, Richard's driving need to seek out his cousin and dearest friend's counsel and comfort. He instinctively knew that Darcy would understand his pain.

So he waited and took whatever comfort and weak joy he could find in the interim.

George Darcy was around from time to time as his duties allowed. Richard divulged bits of the sordid story to the older gentleman, who offered empathetic understanding and wisdom interwoven with jovial amusements to distract. He was very busy, however, between his position at the Matlock hospital and the frequent calls to ill folks in the nearby communities. The fame of Dr. Darcy had spread far and wide. He was unafraid and preferred to get his hands dirty in a way that few physicians of the day would. There was nothing he was hesitant to do, nor were there many ailments or injuries he did not know how to treat. Additionally, when faced with a quandary he was relentless and displayed vigor at odds with his age. He welcomed being summoned at all hours of the day or night, the Pemberley footmen who guarded the house during the sleeping hours working harder than they ever had in answering the bell at the side door and climbing the stairs to waken the doctor. Furthermore, it became necessary to keep a stableboy handy to saddle Dr. Darcy's horse rapidly. A set of rooms in one of the outer buildings had been renovated and given to him as a medical office with constant influxes of bizarre-looking, gleaming devices being delivered along with boxes and boxes of diverse supplies. Darcy encouraged all of it, thrilled beyond measure to have his uncle near and proud of the reputation he earned.

What this meant for Richard was that George was largely away. Therefore, he was left to spend the interminable hours between the oblivion of sleep with Georgiana. The biggest surprise there was how altered the nature of their connection became.

Richard had been astonished upon his Uncle James's death to learn that he was named co-guardian to his eleven-year-old cousin. His relationship with Georgie at the time was fairly close, but between years away at Cambridge, then military training, and the preparations for his first campaign abroad, Second Lieutenant Fitzwilliam spared little thought for his child cousin. For a number of years after James's death, he would encounter Darcy with a combination of pleasure in seeing his serious face after their separations while also examining him closely for any signs of ill health! The idea of what he would do if Darcy died and Georgiana was his to care for was quite beyond his comprehension. Once the war ended and Richard settled with his regiment in London, the relationship with his youngest cousin improved. But how does a man of nearly thirty years truly relate to a shy girl of fifteen? However, the familial affection was strong, the Darcys and Fitzwilliams always truly caring for each other. The more time he spent in Georgiana's company, the more comfortable she became with him and the more she displayed her soft wit, gentle intelligence, and sweet disposition. He began to love her honestly and took his guardian duties more seriously; not that there was much to do in that regard, since her brother was extremely controlling. Additionally, Darcy was as healthy as an ox, so, barring a freak accident, the chances of Colonel Fitzwilliam needing to step up were slim.

Time passed, but in much the same way as Darcy, Richard never really saw Georgiana as anything other than his baby cousin, his little mouse. The horrid manipulation by Wickham had incited him to an anger and urge for violent revenge unlike anything he had experienced even in wartime; but even then, despite recognizing that she could easily have been violated by the evil man, his mind had not taken the leap into considering her a woman capable of romantic feelings and mature intimate relations. Even this past season as he played chaperone at Almack's and other events a number of times, he was more attuned to the ringing command of Darcy to watch her or die, and therefore kept a diligent, piercing eye on the young men revolving around her!

As the nearly three weeks waiting for Darcy's return to Pemberley lapsed largely in Georgiana's company, a measured but profound shift in his thinking occurred. They took long walks in the chilly air, went for extended horseback rides, shopped together in Lambton, dined at each meal, played chess and tennis and a number of other distracting games, performed on their preferred instruments of choice with her teaching him new music, and so on. They sat for hours upon hours in the parlor or library in quiet and sometimes heated conversations as she stunned him further with her possession of a keen grasp of world events and politics, as well as being far more well-read than he was.

The ache of his grief over Lady Fotherby was constant, but ofttimes shoved into some small recess of his being as the pleasure in Georgiana's company grew. They laughed, debated, conversed, and many times simply sat in serene companionship.

One pivotal night, they retired to the music room. Georgiana was playing on the pianoforte while Richard relaxed in a chair and listened. Peace swirled about him as he watched her beautiful face shine as she played and sang one of her own compositions. He offered honest, enthusiastic applause when she completed the piece.

"Bravo, Miss Darcy. Excellently played! I pray you are not weary of me complimenting you, as I will continue to do so. Truly, your talent is too immense to be wasted by entertaining me."

"I in no way deem entertaining you a waste of my time, Cousin. As for any great talent to boast of, I believe I am paltry in comparison to most."

"You do not see your true potential, Georgiana. Trust me. I have heard musical artists at some of the finest establishments in Paris who do not equal you."

Rather than flushing in embarrassment as he expected, her eyes grew dreamy and voice wistful. "Paris. How I would adore to travel there, or Vienna, or Rome, or anywhere to hear such music." She sighed heavily.

"You will in time. Perhaps Lizzy and Darcy can take you there next year since she has never been either. In fact, I make you a promise! If they do not take you, I will. We would have enormous fun together! I could use a reprieve and have not been to the continent since the war."

"Thank you, Richard, but I do not think that would be a good idea."

He was astonished. "Why ever not? I am very good company, as you know, and have been just about everywhere. We would have a marvelous time!"

She smiled sweetly, but there was an odd glint of sadness in her eyes. "You forget, my dear cousin, that I am nineteen now. A woman. It would be inappropriate for you to escort me. The only reason that gossip is not flying even now is due to Uncle George's presence and our relative isolation. Have you not noticed some of the pointed glances our way while strolling through Lambton? It is why I dissembled on traveling to Derby for the day. People would have us betrothed by the time we returned to Pemberley!"

She laughed lightly, turning back to the pianoforte, but Richard was shaken. Assimilating her words and fully examining her, he stared at her as she launched into another delightful concerto. The last vestiges of regarding her as a child were eternally swept away in those moments. No longer would he ever think of her as his little cousin, and the adjustment in his consideration was both wonderful and frightening.

It was wonderful in that he suddenly realized with a heartwarming epiphany that he relished her company. She was a person with numerous admirable traits that complimented him perfectly. After two weeks of almost constant companionship, usually alone, there was no doubt whatsoever that they got on well and shared many of the same ideals. More than once, without completely grasping it, he had recognized the domestic quality to their evenings spent in placid company and reveled in it. Frequently, he now discerned with an alarming shock, he had parted from her for the night with a sadness that had nothing to do with grief over his failed romance with Simone.

The frightening aspect in his abrupt insight was what it potentially portended. Could she be the one he had been waiting for all along? Had these past months only been a divine preparation for the fated future that had been in front of him for years? Were his emotions toward Lady Fotherby as fickle as hers apparently were? Or, was he merely searching desperately for any happiness to ease the pain in his heart? Was the serenity and delight he now felt honest or just a temporary balm? Georgiana was undoubtedly beautiful by anyone's standards, but was he attracted to her in the ways of a husband and lover? Could she ever see him in those roles? Was deep passion necessary and attainable between them, or were friendship and respect and devotion enough?

And worse, what would Darcy say?

The latter was too terrifying to even contemplate, so he left it alone for the time being. In fact, the entire concept was far too enormous to deal with in one sitting. Nonetheless, once opened, the concept could not be tossed aside. Richard Fitzwilliam had serious affairs to contemplate in the weeks ahead.

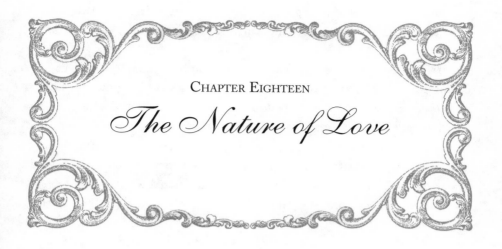

WELL, COLONEL, HAVE YOU reached a decision? You know you are welcome to stay at Pemberley for as long as you wish, but it has been over a month. I would hate to see a troop of soldiers storm the Manor and clap you in chains. A court-martial may be entertaining to observe, but it would be tragic to have you locked up for the next several years. Alexander would miss you."

Richard merely grunted. Darcy smiled, glancing toward his pensive cousin for a moment before returning his attention to Alexander.

They were in the cozily warm parlor on this brisk day in November. Lizzy and Georgiana were upstairs putting the final touches on new ensembles for a dinner party at the Vernors that evening while the gentlemen did nothing. Well, that was not entirely true as Darcy was happily in charge of the baby.

He sat on the sofa across from Richard, far forward with long legs spread wide and bridging the gap between cushioned edge and table, acting as both confining barrier and firm support for the nearly one-year-old's unsteady gait. Walking was a new and marvelous phenomenon, the toddler now preferring the glorious view of the world from above six inches, but still not too graceful with the procedure. The numerous tumbles and near misses from colliding with a sharp piece of furniture when the legs gave out or chubby upper body propelled ahead of the yet uncontrollable lower extremities in no way caused

Alexander to be cautious, but gave his parents shivers of fear. So Darcy did his best to restrain his young son's movements, especially in the cluttered lower level rooms.

At the moment, Alexander was content with the arrangement, happily cooing and babbling as he played with the assortment of brightly colored toys strewn across the once shiny tabletop that had previously graced a gorgeous four-hundred-year-old vase from China. Darcy absently played with the springy curls and stroked the smooth skin, unconsciously prepared to respond to his son as appropriate while carrying on an adult conversation with Richard. It was natural now to slip from serious dialogue uttered with typical resonant tones to the simpler words spoken in a gentle timbre. It made Richard chuckle, but Darcy was barely aware. Nor was he cognizant of the tender expressions, silly faces, and dotty smiles that frequently lit his face when gazing upon or communicating with his firstborn. Furthermore, he only mildly winced when tiny but firm fists grabbed onto trouser cloth and snared a few leg hairs in the process. It was normal and embraced wholeheartedly.

For several weeks now, since the Darcys' return, the still grieving and romantically confused Colonel had watched the domestic interplay between all three Darcys with a heavy heart. There were times, God help him, when he wanted to strangle Darcy for finding such bliss and, as he interpreted it in his pain, shoving the extreme felicity into his face! *Why*, he would mentally rage, *I was perfectly content as a free-from-all-entanglement bachelor until Darcy of all people grew all moony and sentimental! It isn't fair!*

But the petulant child only reared his ugly head infrequently. He was mature enough to recognize that even while winning battles, dashing off to places all over the Continent, rising in his military career, basking in the glory of accolades, and jauntily extolling the virtues of an unencumbered life, he always knew that the lure of home and hearth beckoned. It appeared that domesticity was ingrained into his cells after all and he was not quite sure how pleased he was with the notion.

He sighed, shifting his legs where they stretched on the table. "I appreciate the jest. And you are correct, of course. I cannot evade reality forever." He toed a red and blue striped ball back toward Alexander, who instantly released a silver bell to grab onto the rolling toy as if never seen before, his squeal of glee and bouncing body indicative of his joy. Richard smiled and nodded when Alexander lifted the ball toward him with a gesture of thanks. "It is rather humbling to admit the need for refuge and solace as a child. Somewhat emasculating actually."

"I, of all people, cannot fault you nor tease for that. At least you have not drowned yourself in a brandy bottle, but have managed to act fairly normal. Well, as much as is possible for you, that is."

"What did you just say about not teasing?"

Darcy laughed, bending for the dozenth time to retrieve a toy that tumbled over the table edge and then pausing for a brief nuzzle and kiss.

"Seriously, Darcy, thank you for opening Pemberley to me. I know I did not precisely ask for an invitation, but just knowing that I am always welcome was an immeasurable consolation. Additionally, I cannot thank you enough for keeping the festivities light while I have been here. I was not in the proper frame of mind to play the entertaining funnyman to a host of visitors."

"As to the latter, we keep my uncle around for that express purpose. And it was the wish of both Elizabeth and myself to have a quiet season this year, although I am still shocked that Aunt Madeline did not drag you away for a pointed discussion as she obviously knew something was up to find you here, having not even bothered to make your presence in the region known!" Richard grimaced at that error in good-son judgment. "As to the former, as you said, you are always welcome. My home is yours. Besides, Georgiana was delighted to have you as company while we were gone, and even after we came back for that matter. She seems to have become quite attached to your presence."

Richard glanced swiftly and fearfully to Darcy's face, but he was engaged in a non-verbal communication with Alexander and showed no sign of alluding to anything beyond normal cousinly friendship. "Yes, well, she is a dear friend and soothed me considerably while I waited for you to quit gallivanting about the Lakes."

Darcy had proven true in the special type of brotherly comfort, support, and cheering that Richard had so desperately sought. Initially, Darcy had simply been shocked to the core at the result of Richard's romance. Nearly overwhelmed with remorse at his previous good-natured chafing, he had apologized profusely for his jocosity; but the idea of Richard being unsuccessful had never occurred to him. Of course, the irony in being so confident of Richard's triumph in light of his own fraught path to matrimony was not lost on either of them, and they did share a few laughs over it. In the end, Darcy could offer nothing in the way of a solution—not that Richard anticipated it—only able to be the proverbial shoulder to lean on.

Richard appeared to be handling his broken heart with far better humor and control than Darcy had. Generally, this was attributed, rightfully so, to his inherent optimism and ebullience. He spoke of Lady Fotherby rarely, and only to Darcy. He refused to read any of the London newspapers that were delivered regularly, the fear of seeing her name attached to Lord Wellson's in some Society event too great. Oddly, beyond the official announcement, Lady Fotherby was conspicuously absent. The same could not be said of the popular and exhibitionistic Marquess, who was remarkably at every party or ball or event of import, performing outrageously as usual. Only once was Lady Fotherby mentioned, and that was a saucy jibe as to how his newly betrothed must feel about her intended squiring assorted ladies of dubious character to these functions while she was in apparent seclusion at her father's estate in Hampshire for the holiday season. It was strange.

Darcy was the only one in the family, with the exception of Alexander, who was utterly oblivious to the subtle currents between Georgiana and Richard. No one spoke of it, not even the two individuals who privately wrestled with their emotions. However, there was secret suspicion and speculation that at least some of the Colonel's ability to deal with his gloom was due to the startling alteration in his feelings toward Georgiana.

All Richard knew for certain was that he could not bear to leave without talking to Georgiana about his feelings. It was only the when and how that concerned him. Well, that and the trepidation over what Darcy would do to him when he found out!

"I have already decided, actually, to leave next week," Richard answered the query.

"If you wait a bit longer we can travel together, as we are leaving for London in December. The company would be appreciated and I am not yet that weary of your presence."

Richard chuckled along with Darcy, but then glanced over with a contrite expression on his face as he said, "No offense, my friend, but I would rather not be here when you and Elizabeth celebrate your anniversary. I doubt if you want me dampening your joy."

"You would not—"

"Yes, I would," Richard stated firmly. "But to be blunt, I am actually thinking selfishly."

Darcy nodded and argued no further.

"No point in delaying the inevitable. I suppose when I rode here I had a vague notion of hiding in my room until after the nuptials were past, but what is the point of that? I cannot pretend any longer that I will be able to avoid facing… her… at some point. Not that I travel in the same circles as Lord Wellson, I am pleased to say for a host of reasons." He paused, twirling the dregs in his teacup and staring with mesmerizing intensity. "No, life does move on, Darcy, whether we wish it so or not. You discovered the same, although the woman of your dreams returned to you." His voice was faintly mocking.

"Do not give up all hope, Richard. There is someone else out there for you, I am sure of it. You have taken a large step in admitting you want marriage and family. I think in your case, unlike with me, this was a huge hurdle to overcome."

"Indeed. You always yearned for home and love. Your character and losses placed that desire upon your heart at an exceptionally young age. I, on the other hand, yearned for adventure. Or maybe I merely wished to evade this sort of drama."

Darcy stared at his cousin's cloudy face, trying to decipher the welter of emotions that played over his features. He spoke softly, "Do you hate her? Has your anger turned to bitterness, cousin, or acceptance? Do not allow her actions to scar you so that your heart is stone and unable to love elsewhere."

"Could you have, William? Could you have loved so easily elsewhere if Elizabeth married another?"

Their eyes held for long heartbeats, the contemplative stasis finally broken by Darcy. "No. Never. I am certain of that. But at the risk of incurring your wrath, you know as well as I that we are different in this respect. You just said so yourself." He held up his hand to stay Richard's retort, although oddly none was forthcoming. Richard was honestly interested to hear Darcy's rationale.

"I searched long for love, a particular type of love that I never saw even remotely in anyone until Elizabeth. The odds of me being able to relinquish the totality of my sentiments were unlikely. The odds of finding another woman to love and fill that void, even slightly, were smaller still. You, conversely, barely considered the idea of marriage, let alone passionate love, until a year ago. I am in no way diminishing the force of your convictions and emotions, Cousin. Rather I judge you a man more capable of handling the battles and storms of life. I envy you that trait, always have. Your strength is of a different quality than mine. You are resilient, adaptable, spirited, and sanguine. Doom and gloom simply do not surround you, they never have."

Richard nodded. "Perhaps that means I am incapable of deep love."

"No! I did not mean that!"

Richard chuckled. "Oh, be still, William, I know you didn't. Nor do I think that true of me. You are absolutely correct, actually, annoying as that is to admit to your face. You have a serious streak a hundred miles long whereas I cannot go an hour without joking." He sighed again, deeply, before leaning forward and snatching Alexander away from his perch between his father's legs, the baby hardly blinking as he calmly transferred his interest to the big man's shiny buttons and epaulettes.

"We are different, you and I, in many ways. I know my love for Simone was real and strong. And I know it will hurt for a long while to come. But I also know I can love another. Resilient, as you said." He smirked, Darcy grinning helplessly. "Yet there are dozens of ways in which we are exactly the same. Furthermore, I have changed significantly. I know what I want and it is a family. I want a woman at my side and one of these"—he tickled Alexander, who giggled—"to play with and annoy me at night. And just to be clear, I blame you for every last bit of it and damn you each chance I get!"

"I shall accept responsibility partially, although I believe your mother may have some fault in your corruption. For the record, and I cannot believe I am saying this, the woman who graces your side will be a lucky woman indeed."

"Do you truly mean that?" The sharp tone and piercing glance were not lost on Darcy, but interpreted incorrectly.

"Of course I mean it! I may deny it unless in a court of law, but I do mean it." He smiled to soften his taunt, voice falling into the husky timbre associated with heartfelt emotion. "Lady Fotherby is a fool to choose as she did, Richard. There is no sense in it at all. It is her loss and I pity her idiocy even though I am filled with anger for her hurting you. Elizabeth is merely incensed with no sympathy at all." He chuckled. "You will be a fabulous husband and marvelous father. Any woman will be blessed to be yours."

"Thank you, William. That means the world to me."

Late the following afternoon, Richard successfully sought out Georgiana in the orangery. A light rain had begun to fall again, softly pelting the panes of glass and obscuring what grey daylight feebly shone through, casting the generally bright, almost summery atmosphere of the garden chamber into a gloomy pall. Nonetheless, it was warmer here than anywhere else in the Manor, and the varied blooms and greenery persistently flourished in oblivion to the dormancy in the world without.

The previous night's revelry at the Vernors had extended until daylight was beginning to flirt with the horizon, so the household was even at this late hour in a state of hushed recuperation. Few stirred, Georgiana having not risen until well after noon. She did not bother to dress in more than a simple morning gown and her hair was worn down in a thick, unadorned braid, but Richard thought she never looked lovelier.

"Should I greet with good-morning or good-afternoon?"

Georgiana turned from the roses with a ready smile. "It is nearly close enough for good-evening, so take your pick."

He bowed gallantly, kissing the hand offered, and then tucked it into the crook of his arm. They began to stroll. "How are your feet this afternoon, Colonel?"

"Surviving admirably, Miss Darcy. And yours? I do believe I may have trod upon them a time or two."

"You not even once. Light as air when you dance, kind sir. Pity the same cannot be said for Mr. Simpson or Mr. Dalby." She shuddered dramatically.

Richard tsked sympathetically. "Poor lads. See, you should have reserved all your dances for me and then you would not be suffering so today."

"A girl needs to spread her charms about, so I have been taught. It is the proper way of it, and I am a proper lady so will make the sacrifice. As it is, I danced with you four sets so you are now indelibly part of the Derbyshire rumor mill for some time to come. Horribly irresponsible of me, but I could not resist *your* charms."

"And are my charms and any subsequent rumors involved distasteful, Georgie?"

She flushed slightly, but glanced into his eyes. "You know well that they are not, Richard." He opened his mouth to speak, but she went on quickly, "Did you see William or Lizzy about?"

"No. Mr. Taylor said they have placed orders not to be disturbed until dinner time." He chuckled. "I would have thought after two years of marriage they may have grown bored with languishing in each other's company all day."

Georgiana laughed gaily, slapping at his arm. "You know as well as I that that is unlikely ever to be the case."

"It never bothers you at all? Being ignored while they... focus elsewhere."

"No need to be coy, Cousin. I am not all that innocent! And besides, you forget that I have lived all my life with William's attention often diverted elsewhere, and thus spending days and occasionally weeks rarely seeing him. At least now I know he is not buried unhappily under a mountain of work, but rather buried in a more pleasant manner."

Richard nearly choked at the sly tone of her innuendo, unable to speak as he stared in astonishment at her arch expression. "They will emerge eventually, smiling and rested, glowing ridiculously. No, it warms my heart immeasurably to witness my brother's felicity. The whole world should strive for the same." She paused, releasing Richard's arm to pick a pink camellia, and then turned slowly back toward him. "Forgive me, Richard. That was a thoughtless remark."

"No apology necessary, my dear. And you are correct, of course. The world should strive for happiness and love. The fact that my first foray into the romantic realm failed miserably does not alter that reality. My prayer is that my second attempt shall prove victorious."

She met his eyes, blushing faintly before looking away as she again clasped his arm and began walking. Silence fell for a time, broken by Richard, "Georgiana, you know I am planning to leave tomorrow?" She nodded. "I came here seeking refuge and a sturdy shoulder to cry on, so to speak. However, I never anticipated that I would find both in you. I hope you know how deeply appreciative I am?"

"I do, but you need not thank me, Cousin. I am happy to have been your solace."

"That is the amazing thing, Georgie. Or at least one of the many amazing things." She gazed up at him in question, Richard halting and reaching to lightly stroke her cheek. "I know you offered yourself freely to comfort me with no expectation or hesitation. You are truly a remarkable woman, Georgiana Darcy, a wonderful friend, and very dear to me."

She smiled and laughed, tone teasing. "So you finally admit it? That I am no longer your little mouse?"

"Yes, it is a fact of extreme clarity to me." His voice was muted and a bit shaky. Their eyes locked, both unable to draw away although the reality of what they knew was coming loomed largely between. Surges of emotion raced over their eyes and countenances, too rapid to interpret fully. Richard inhaled deeply, "Georgiana..."

"Richard, I do not think…"

"Please, dear, let me say it. I know it is all too soon, too fast, too real. But I cannot leave without telling you how I feel. I came here broken, despairing, and certain that my life was over as far as love is concerned. I was not looking for anything except escape. Discovering a birth of new emotions for you was most assuredly not on my agenda, but I cannot contradict their blossoming. I have fought it, analyzed it, dissected it, denied it, but the result is the same. I am falling in love with you, Georgiana, as a man does a woman who is astounding and beautiful and kind and generous and, and… so many perfect traits that it would take me hours if not a lifetime to list them all!"

"Richard, please stop!" She pulled away, taking several steps before halting with her back to him.

Silence fell again, Richard gathering his thoughts before resuming. "I have overwhelmed you, haven't I? Forgive me, Georgiana, for being too… enthusiastic. I am not asking for any promises, not that I would not welcome such. But I know the circumstances are… strange, to put it mildly. Just… please, tell me there is hope that your feelings for me may someday be reciprocated, even if it is a faint one."

She turned to him then, face flushed but composed, eyes shining and smile soft. "Richard Fitzwilliam, I have loved you all of my life, you know this. These past weeks have been revealing and surprising. My heart stirs in ways that I do not understand, nor do I think I am quite prepared for."

"Does that mean you are beginning to have feelings of romantic love for me?"

"I do not know! You arrived sad and forlorn, but nonetheless were still just Cousin Richard. My fun-loving guardian whom I have no memory of ever living without. Then, somewhere in the midst, you were a man. Looking at me as a man does. It is all so confusing!"

"You said your heart stirs. Does it stir in the ways of a woman toward a man she loves?"

She stared at him silently for a long while, face pale and eyes slightly wild. Her voice, when she spoke, was hushed to nearly inaudible levels. "Yes. Perhaps. I think so… Oh, Richard! How can this be, between us?"

"It is not so unusual, Georgiana. We have always been close, with a strong bond. This foundation supports a richer emotion. It has taken some time, but I finally grew up in the area of women and love, and am desirous of a committed relationship. And you, my beautiful, dear Georgiana, have matured and flourished right before my eyes."

She sighed. "As much as I appreciate your recognition of my maturity, and as much as I pridefully want to avow it, the truth is that I am yet young and somewhat sheltered despite the eye-opening events of the past two years." She laughed and nodded toward the Master of Pemberley's bedchamber. "Or perhaps it is because of all that has been thrust upon me so radically that I hesitate now. Romance runs amok hereabouts, and it is difficult not to be influenced by it. But, more importantly, I worry for you, my dear friend."

"I know my heart, Georgiana," he stated firmly.

"Are you so sure of that, Richard? Completely? You have been wounded so profoundly by Lady Fotherby. How can your heart honestly be ready to move on so swiftly?"

"I am resilient."

She blinked. "I beg your pardon?"

"Just something Darcy said," he shrugged, smiling weakly.

"Resilient you may be, but you are not fickle. I see the haunting in your eyes at unguarded times. I note how your jaw clenches when the London newspapers are delivered. I know your reluctance to leave Pemberley is partly due to the memories that will assault you in Town and the fear you have of meeting her. I know your heart is not free of her."

"I will not deny any of this, Georgie. My sentiments toward Lady Fotherby were real, and I am not completely past it. But do you not see?" He suddenly crossed the gap between them, taking her hands in his strong ones. "I am not an inconstant man! Love ambushed me to be sure, but I plunged in full force, no faltering. I am not afraid to admit the truth when it is thrust in front of me. I am a man of action, a soldier undaunted by any challenge or situation. And I see it through to the end with total commitment. But in the case of Lady Fotherby, it was not meant to be apparently. Now, it is as if history has repeated itself with you! I am equally startled by the unexpected evolution of my love for you, but I am not afraid or unsure!"

"But I am," she whispered.

"Of what are you afraid, dearest?"

She inhaled, moving to sit on the nearby bench. "I am afraid what we are experiencing is two people drawn by mutual concern, comfort, familiarity, need." She waved her hand vaguely. "And maybe that is enough. I know it is more than some couples ever have. Not all are like my brother and Lizzy, who share a bond of love that is monumental and passionate. Not everyone requires that sort of marriage. But one should not settle."

"We would not be settling, Georgiana. I am positive of that!"

"But you cannot declare that you feel such passion for me. As you did for Simone?"

She looked up at him. He stood tall and firm, face resolute, but he did not readily respond or counter. There was a lingering sadness in the drawn corners of his reddened eyes and the droop in the bend of his lips and the faint grey lines on his cheeks. A wash of intense love and protection deluged her soul. For the first time in her short adult life with any man, even in these past weeks of observing him and trying desperately to make sense of her emotions, she felt an incredible urge to kiss that mouth. To take away his pain and taste of his love. It overwhelmed her, the force of it; but finally it was clear.

She smiled, patting the space beside her. Richard sat, eyes never leaving hers as she took his hands and squeezed firmly.

"I do love you, Richard. I always have and I always will. I am still somewhat confused as to the whole nature of my love for you, but it is immutable, of that I am certain. Furthermore, I am absolutely convinced that this is true of you for me."

"Oh, Georgie!" Tears were welling in his eyes, and she reached to brush a spilled drop away.

"I promise that I will be here for you, waiting. But I want you to leave tomorrow. Go back to London and your regiment. Confront the demons there. You need the time, whether you deem it so or not. You asked for hope, dearest Richard, and I am giving it to you. All I ask in return is that you heal fully, be utterly convinced your heart is all mine before you offer it to me again. You owe this to yourself as well as to me. Can you do this?"

He nodded, too overcome to speak.

"Whatever happens, nothing will alter the bond we have, Cousin. Nothing! All I want is your happiness. If that is me, then we will be marvelous together, I am sure of it. But if not"—she shook her head, reaching to gently cup his face—"I will rejoice in seeing a sincere smile upon your face once again."

She nestled into his chest, Richard embracing fiercely but tenderly. "I love you, Georgiana Darcy."

"And I love you, Richard Fitzwilliam."

Lizzy stood by the window embrasure in their sitting room, staring down onto the muddy drive that not too many hours earlier Colonel Fitzwilliam had ridden south on for his return to London. The door opened behind her, closing with a secure thud, but she did not turn around. Of course it was not necessary, the entrant obvious even if she had not felt his presence and smelt his cologne.

"Alexander is soundly asleep. It took two storybooks to accomplish the task this time. I am beginning to believe reading from picture books is not conducive to influencing somnolence since he insists on pointing to each item until the name is given, often babbling on as he apparently creates his own tale." He stroked over her arms, kissing the top of her head before enfolding in a tight embrace.

"Thank you for attending to him, dearest. I was otherwise engaged."

"Indeed. I thought Georgiana would keep you prisoner all day. Are you going to share with me what is disturbing her? Or is it a female issue that I would rather not be privy to?"

Lizzy laughed, turning to bestow a brief kiss and then grasping his hand and tugging toward the sofa. "It is a female issue, yes, but not of the sort that will make you blush and squirm. Sit and I will remove your boots."

He did, with a loud groan and heavy sigh, eyes closing as his head fell back onto the cushions. "I am exhausted. We had far fewer visitors this year, but the drama swirling about was draining. I thought Richard was doing better, but last night he was clearly agitated. I guess the idea of returning to London was regressing. I tried to get him to talk, but he was unusually taciturn. I feel for him." His voice dropped, eyes opening a slit to look upon his wife where she sat on the ottoman with his feet on her lap, massaging with firm fingers over his soles and calves. "I know it is horrible, but his situation brings up memories that I wish to forget and I confess I am somewhat gladdened to have him gone." Lizzy smiled softly, squeezing his ankles in empathetic understanding. "Mostly though, I am simply torn with grief for him. He is a hardy soul, but I know he is in pain."

"I would not fret too much about Richard. I have it on good authority that he is learning to deal with his broken heart admirably."

He frowned. "What do you mean by that?"

Despite the seriousness of her information, and the honest uncertainty of how he would react, Lizzy could not help but laugh and shake her head. "Fitzwilliam Darcy, you are the most intelligent man I know, and uncannily astute in most matters, but when it comes to interpersonal relationships you are strangely insensate!"

His frown deepened into a faint offended sulk, but he did not argue the assertion. He still did not know what she meant, but before he could inquire for illumination she gave a final sharp stroke to the arch of each foot, causing him to release a throaty moan of pleasure and close his eyes.

"So, do you want me to share what is plaguing Georgiana?" She planted his feet comfortably on the ottoman and moved to sit beside him.

He laced her fingers with his, not opening his eyes. "Please. The conundrum of Colonel Fitzwilliam is out of my hands now, but I may be able to ease my sister's burdens."

"I hate to disappoint you, but the two are intertwined." He glanced at her then, brow arching. Lizzy bit her lip and squeezed the hand lying on his thigh. "William, I do not know how to say this in such a way that might ease your surprise, so I will simply blurt it out. Just try to be calm so we can discuss it." His frown had deepened even further. She swallowed and inhaled. "Richard has declared to Georgiana sentiments of love and wishes for a permanent arrangement with her. Georgiana is yet a bit confused, but I believe her feelings have grown as well and she is not averse to the idea. Nothing was decided definitively, as they both need time, and I am sure Richard would speak to you before asking Georgie to marry him, but it is heading that way."

Of all the reactions she may have anticipated, him merely laying his head back against the cushions, staring up toward the ceiling and face impassive was not one of them. Her voice trailed off, not knowing what to say in light of his odd stoicism. Silence fell for several heartbeats, neither saying a word.

"Georgiana and Richard," he broke the quiet with a muted tone. "Yes, it is all clear now. You are correct, dearest. Completely insensate. I interpreted his agitation as grief over Lady Fotherby, which I largely think is true, and Georgie I thought was just upset about his pain, also largely true. They have always gotten on so well, loved each other sincerely, that the concept of it maturing into something more never occurred to me."

"You... do not seem upset." It was a question as much as a statement, Darcy smiling and turning his head to look at her.

"No, I am not upset. Surprised, indeed so, but it is not a horrible development. I always imagined Georgiana marrying someone with an estate at least equal to Pemberley, perhaps even a title to go with it. I desire the best for my sister, wealth and security being essential; insist on it actually. But love cannot be tossed aside as inconsequential. And Richard is a quality man, as I know.

Honestly, I suppose I would not have preferred to see my sister wed a military man of modest inheritance, but they do not come any better than Colonel Fitzwilliam. You say she is confused? How so?"

"She is young yet and the evolution of her emotions, and Richard's toward her, have happened so abruptly. And under distressing circumstances…"

"Yes," he interrupted. "That concerns me as well. Richard can be impulsive and his heart is wounded, no matter how much he wishes to thrust it aside. Falling in love with Georgiana is not shocking at all, as she is beautiful and perfect in every way, but I do not want to see her hurt by someone who is, however unwittingly, seeking to assuage his own pain. I am glad he left without pushing for an engagement."

"Georgie insisted he return to London and face the past."

"Did she?" He chuckled. "Very wise, my baby sister." He began to laugh louder, shaking his head in resignation. "Yes, I am truly the blind fool in this little drama. All the oblique glances, intimate conversations, and blushes are now flashing through my mind with clarity. Just a couple of days ago Richard was talking about finding love elsewhere, the desire for family and a home of his own, and moving on with his life past the disappointments. He practically nailed me to the wall in declaring his worthiness as husband material! He could have asked permission to court Georgiana right then and it would have been impossible for me to disallow it! Quite crafty, that cousin of mine."

"I doubt if he was purposely attempting to coax you, as I think, from what Georgie says, that he is wise enough to recognize the need for distance and perspective. He would never do anything to cause Georgiana pain."

"No, there is no question of that."

She nestled closer to his side, his arm instantly encircling. "It appeals to you then? The idea of the two of them wed?"

He sighed, nodding slowly. "It will take some getting used to, I confess. An adjustment to my thinking on numerous levels. Her happiness is the prime objective so I would need to know for certain that this is what her heart desires above all else. I am adamant that they not rush, and I will assuredly torture Richard a bit over it. Part of the fun, you see!" He was grinning, his eyes distant. Giggles erupted from Lizzy, Darcy glancing to her amused face. "Yes, Mrs. Darcy? You are entertained?"

"I was recalling a man who raged and stormed when his sister off-handedly mentioned a Lord Gruffudd once upon a time."

"She was only seventeen at that time, may I remind you, and beyond my reach. This scenario is entirely different." He reached to cup her cheek, fingers brushing tenderly. "It is vital that Georgie find the happiness due her, as I have. I want to see Richard content and settled as well, but not at the expense of my sister. I am not taking this lightly, I can assure you. We must all be cautious. And patient."

He leaned in to kiss her, moving slowly and sensuously over her lips. "Now, let us put aside the unsolvable puzzle of lovesick relatives for the moment. If memory serves, we have two special days to celebrate soon."

"We do."

"Alexander's birthday will be a family affair with his own cake being created by Mrs. Langton, that an extravagance if you ask me, but since no one did, I shall remain mute on the subject. But for you, Mrs. Darcy, I have decided that our first anniversary was abbreviated and not the glorious celebration I anticipated. Thus we must doubly lionize this anniversary. Two years of bliss with the most beautiful woman alive."

"And what did you have in mind, Mr. Darcy?" She asked breathlessly, the question partially redundant as he already had her reclining onto the sofa with his hard body pressed onto her now half-clothed flesh.

"Jewels, intimate dinners, dancing, perhaps a picnic in the orangery, more gifts, and long nights of passion before the fire." His husky voice rose from her bared bosom, the stimulating fingers deep under her lacy shift leaving no doubt his intended way to initiate the celebration of their biennial. But he told her anyway, "What I currently have in mind, in case you were unsure, is to wildly, passionately make love to you right here on this sofa. What this will include, for your edification, is…" And he proceeded to descriptively verbalize each move, usually as it was being enacted upon her body.

CHAPTER NINETEEN

Hearts Beat Once Again

COLONEL FITZWILLIAM SPENT THE remaining days of November immersed in his work. There was a great deal to do, stacks of papers having accumulated on his desk and a fresh-faced batch of recruits to whip into shape. All of this was fortuitous, as it allotted him scant time to dwell on the two women who invaded his heart. Nonetheless, as the days passed and December loomed on the horizon, the maddening aspects of his situation escalated.

Georgiana's presence intruded at odd moments throughout his waking day. Her adorable smile, gentle touch, melodic voice raised in song or lively discourse, glowing blue eyes, and lilting laugh pervaded his consciousness and filled his soul with peace and warmth. He missed her in a way that he never had before. Their separation was necessary, but sweetly painful in how he longed for her. That fact alone was gladdening and strengthened his resolve. Absence indeed made the heart grow fonder, and those instances of cheerful contemplation were grasped onto with vigor.

But at night, and even upon unguarded occasions during the day, Simone's memory was equally vibrant and only grew in power. The stimulus was not due to specific places he went, as he rarely ventured beyond his humble house and the Regimental yard and offices. Nor was it mentions of her name in the papers or among his peers, as he still refused to glance at the Society pages and he did not mingle at the Club or other venues where London gossip swirled. She was simply there, in his mind and, to his irritation, his heart with a persistent yearning felt acutely in his body. He heard her voice, saw her smile, envisioned her eyes, and felt the tingles of her touch as surely as if she were standing beside him.

In his dreams she came to his bed with all the erotic and sensual glories that Georgiana did not. This latter distressed him greatly. Was it just lingering feelings of guilt or scruples over falling for someone he had known since infancy? He wished now that he had succumbed to his desires to kiss her that day in the conservatory, but solicitude for her emotions under the bizarre circumstances had stayed him. Was his inability to imagine being with her in an intimate way due to that? Yet, when he tried to force the fantasy, when he purposefully replaced Simone's face and body with Georgiana's, his mind recoiled. Vague qualms raced through his consciousness, inexplicable shame for envisioning her in such a sordid way. Of course this was ludicrous if she was to be his wife! He welcomed dreams of this nature with Georgiana, but they never materialized beyond tender kisses; always melding into Simone's figure and face when the passion ignited beyond his lucid control.

Logic assured him that once Lady Fotherby was completely beyond his reach, his heart and soul would be free to embrace the love he held for Georgiana.

The page finally turned, the dreaded month of December was ushered in, and with it came the arrival of Darcy to Town. His planned journey of approximately three weeks for business had initially been arranged as a family vacation. He and Lizzy thought it would be fun to spend the weeks prior to Christmas in London for the holiday entertainments available and improved shopping choices. They both agreed that this year they preferred a quiet Christmas, opting instead to visit relatives at their residences rather than inviting everyone to Pemberley. However, days before their departure date Alexander developed a mild cold and it was agreed that he should stay home where it was warm and safe.

Darcy arrived in London determined to finish the necessary work. He did, of course, immediately send word to Colonel Fitzwilliam hoping the two could drown their mutual sorrows in vigorous fencing or horseback riding or even darts if that would do the trick. He was not surprised when Richard did not respond.

For his part, Richard was not intentionally being rude. He was considerably swamped with work, his evasion of extracurricular activities not exclusively due to a desire to prevent idle chitchat that may inadvertently lead to a topic he wished to avoid. He knew Darcy would be in Town for several weeks, so figured there would be time later… after… when he would undeniably need his oldest friend's companionship.

Yet, as the days ticked rapidly by and before he found the time to contact Darcy, two events occurred that would forever alter his future.

The first was the murder of Lord Wellson.

Colonel Fitzwilliam got wind of the tale one afternoon, three days before the marriage of Lady Fotherby and Lord Wellson was to occur, while walking through the yard on the way to the stables. A group of privates stood lounging in front of their barracks, unaware of the approaching officer as they were so engrossed in bawdy commentary and laughter.

"Caught him naked as the day he was born, in the act itself!"

"Wonder if he had finished. Seems a shame to take a bullet for the tasty joys of a trollop without the final glory, ya know!"

"What a way to go! Die with a smile on your face!"

"Maybe. Depends on how far it had gone. If the timing was right, then neither of them may have felt any pain."

Richard shook his head, diverting around the rough group and hoping they would not see him as he was in no mood for salutes and genuflecting. His own thoughts were dark today for no reason he could ascertain, and being forced to chastise a rowdy bunch of underlings was not appealing. He was almost past when one of the young men said, "Old rake! Serves him right for carrying on with another man's wife. With the pretty dainty he is engaged to you'd think he'd be willing to keep his stick occupied with her! Weren't enough free bits-of-muslin out there to pluck, so Wellson needs to plow a married woman?"

Richard rounded on the fellows, face grey and tight. "What did you say?"

But he could get nothing coherent out of the men then. They were universally too embarrassed by being caught crudely gossiping and passing around a flask of whiskey by a Commanding Officer.

Heart thudding dangerously, he immediately whirled about and headed toward his office building where newspapers were plentiful. The story was plastered on the front page of every paper.

The notorious Lord Wellson was discovered flagrantly fornicating with the wife of a Fleet Street publisher by the name of Mr. Harris, in the man's own bedroom no less! The man had suspected his wife of dallying with the infamous rogue and came prepared with pistol in hand. It was likely swift and messy, but details of the crime scene were so outrageously exaggerated that the truth would never be fully known. Lady Fotherby's name was dragged into the circulating clamor, the reality that the poor woman was more a victim than any of the others lost to only a few. The scandal was immense and the gossip titillating.

Suddenly Richard could not circumvent hearing her name, and the associated rumors, as they were the prime discussion. Facts of any substance were scarce and so jumbled within the innuendo and blather that deciphering truth was difficult. But one detail that repeated was the news that Lady Fotherby had all this time been in Hampshire at her father's estate. No one had seen or heard from her since well before the betrothal was announced. This was extremely odd, and although most folks used this as a launching point for further vulgar jokes, hidden in the discourse was the sporadic speculation that there was something unnatural about the whole relationship from the outset.

Richard felt truly ill. He could hardly think during the remainder of his day and functioning with any sort of normalcy was nigh on impossible. The new recruits and anyone else who crossed his path suffered the brunt of his foul mood. All the sensibilities of the past weeks that he thought he was successfully dealing with surged forth in a tumultuous spin of emotion. He could not focus onto any one long enough to grasp onto it. The reality that Lord Wellson's death meant she was now a free woman again was not entirely lost on him, but the welter of emotions was so overwhelming and competitive that nothing rational reigned.

As soon as he was able, he left and rode directly to Darcy House. Darcy was waiting, whiskey thrust into Richard's shaking hands before greetings were verbalized. There was some talking as the evening turned into late night, mostly on Richard's part, as Darcy comforted by simply listening, but primarily Richard stared into space as his thoughts swirled.

Two days passed with Richard attempting to perform normally. At times the urge was overwhelming to *do something*, but he had no clue as to what that should be. What was the proper course? She had rejected him, he reasoned, so he certainly owed her nothing. Yet his heart refused to grow cold no matter how he pleaded for it to do so. By the end of those two days, as he rode slowly through the busy streets toward his home, exhausted and sick, the last thing he wanted or expected was to have another shock waiting for him.

My dearest Richard,

How many days and weeks have I contemplated what I would say to you if I was so blessed as to be given the chance! Oh God Richard, I pray you still believe in my love for you! Please, I beg you, do not toss this away as you probably should. I am so afraid that you will do just that and not read what I have to say. I have much to explain, but fear I have no time. As it is, I do not know if my fortunes will prevail long enough for me to finish this letter. I must be hasty.

I need your help, dear one. I am at my father's house in Hampshire, where we have been since my foolish departure from you in September, under lock and heavy guard. My father and my uncle, evil men I now perceive, held me captive, using my children as blackmail to force me to agree to marry Wellson. Never would I have done it! Never! But my sweet Oliver has been so ill and treatment was declined him ere I relented. I know it must sound implausible, like a badly written play, but it is true. I have prayed incessantly for the slightest glimmer of hope, seeking any crack in the vigilance so I could escape and end the sham. It came finally in the news of that horrid man's death! Please forgive me, dear Richard, for possessing no mercy, but I can only exalt in the salvation of his demise. The method matters naught to me, nor do I care about the scandal. I am in a state of utter bliss! Father is furious, somehow in his wicked dementia blaming me. He has gone insane, I am certain of it, and I am extremely fearful. Yet the ensuing chaos has given me an opening. At least I hope.

They are not watching me as closely, so I think I can slip this letter into the outgoing mail. I do not dare trying to escape and I refuse to leave my children in the midst of this madness. Please help me, Richard. Help us. I am not asking for your forgiveness, as I do not deserve it for causing you pain. My only prayer is that your compassion, which you possess in abundance, will draw you to me. There is no one else I can trust. Yours, always, Simone

Richard read the letter through twice in rapid succession. His weariness abruptly faded with the instantaneous rise of his wrath and fear. He noted the date as written on the day of Wellson's murder. Four days ago. For four days she was apparently unable to hide the letter to be sent. For four days she and the children were living in a madhouse suffering God only knew what. It was more than he could bear. But, with the conditioned response of the born military man, he wasted no time on fear or anger.

The first order of business was to enlist aid. No hesitation there, Richard riding fast to the house of his best friend from their Academy days and fellow soldier during numerous campaigns, Colonel Roland Artois. Colonel Artois leaned negligently against the doorframe, casually eating a thickly crusted rye roll, while Richard gave a brief, crisp explanation. Then he grinned, brushed the crumbs off his fingers with a slap, and said, "Sounds like fun. Rescuing a damsel in distress and vexing a Lord. My wife will think me so romantic. We have to include Warren or he will never forgive you."

"My thought exactly. You get him and meet me at the Darcy townhouse." And with nothing further but precise nods, they parted.

If Mr. Travers was taken aback by Colonel Fitzwilliam's curt attitude he did not show it. Fortunately, Mr. Darcy was at home, if in a meeting with his solicitor and shipping partners, but it never crossed the butler's mind to refuse Mr. Darcy's cousin entrance or immediate access to his Master. Darcy strode out of his library office, meeting Richard in the middle of the foyer and without preamble asked, "What has happened?"

"I have no time to explain. I need your carriage and driver, now."

Darcy nodded. "Done." He gestured to Mr. Travers, who waited a distance away, giving the command, and turned back to Richard. "Anything else?"

"My father's physician, Dr. Angless. Can you send word to him to be on the alert? I may need him, I am not sure, but he is one of the best in London."

"I will take care of it personally and have him waiting here. You are going after her."

It wasn't a question and Richard was not at all surprised that Darcy would piece it together. "Yes. She is in Hampshire being held captive. I know," he said, seeing Darcy's raised brow, "it sounds melodramatic and medieval, but she would not lie to me." He said it with conviction, suddenly realizing how true the words were. The clarity in thought was a heady rush, leaving him momentarily breathless at the wonder of how he could ever have doubted her. The guilt at not fighting harder, forcing the truth somehow, threatened to overwhelm him. But just as rapidly he pushed it aside, regaining control, as he needed to do to deal with the present crisis.

The clomping of horses' hooves interrupted further explanation. Richard glanced out the open door to see Artois and Warren in the street. To Darcy he gave instructions to send the driver to the estate in Hampshire as hastily as possible, leaving with a faint smile of thanks.

The three men pushed their horses hard. Fortunately, these were battle-trained mounts prepared for much rougher terrain than the well-maintained roads near London, so the distance was traversed swiftly with the animals breaking out in a minimal sweat. The sprawling estate and ancestral home of the Earl of Wrexham was surrounded by a high iron fence with the gate chained and padlocked. The last time Richard had approached these gates he was met by two stern-faced, armed groundsmen, one of whom had returned with a rebuffing message from Lady Fotherby as well as one from Lord Wrexham with the Earl's official seal ordering him to vacate the premises or face the consequences. This time only one of the groundsmen was on guard, the frightened, wild look in his eyes escalating upon spying the three mounted men in uniforms plastered with medals and officer insignias. He shook his head when the three halted less than a yard from the bars, attempting to speak and glare, but he never had the chance to muster his authority because Richard calmly drew his pistol and with one well-aimed blast he shattered the lock. The chains fell in a metallic clatter to the ground, Colonel Artois spurring his horse forward and kicking the gates open. They rode through in a united front, none of them glancing at the stunned guard.

The drive was circular and short, the house seen from the gates, so there was no doubt that the shot would have been heard. But the soldiers were quick. They flew off their horses before the animals were fully stopped, swords drawn to meet the three footmen descending the entryway steps. Bloodshed was avoided, thankfully, as the servants were no match for the soldiers and they knew it. The orders to prohibit intruders were obliterated the second they laid eyes on the gleaming metal pointed their direction!

Richard warily entered the foyer, eyes keen and reflexes on alert. Warren and Artois followed in a flank position, equally vigilant. Strangely, the initial impression was of echoing emptiness. The footmen had backed away, silently watching from a safe distance. A couple of other servants were noted, frozen with shock and wide-eyed stares. No one spoke or made a single move. The seconds stretched, the warriors rapidly scanning the premises to gain their bearings. Just as Richard turned to signal Warren to remain posted on guard while he and Artois headed upstairs where he assumed Simone and the children would be, an angry voice pierced the air.

"You *will* do as I say, you frigid, ungrateful harpy! Because of your hateful-ness and obstinacy you weren't married last month. None of this would have happened if you were more accommodating!"

Richard whirled to the right, the voice he recognized as Lord Wrexham's reverberating down the long corridor running toward the back of the manor. He sprinted, sword clutched in a white knuckled hand, and unable to hear the murmured response. But the next words left no doubt who he was berating, not that Richard was questioning.

"He wanted you, would have bedded you from the beginning and been content. But, no, not Miss High and Proper! You'll whore for your nobody lover, a soldier with nothing, but not for a nobleman willing to marry you! You, a used slut with that loathsome invalid you call your son!"

"No!"

A murderous Richard burst through the half open door, his pace not slowing as he took in the scene. Lord Wrexham was pacing, his arms gesticu-lating crazily as he continued to rant and swear, impervious to Simone's shouted negation and the fact that she was fast approaching his back with a huge porcelain vase raised over her head. Neither of them noted the noisy entrance of three sword-wielding gentlemen, both too intent upon their individual fury.

"Simone!" Richard shouted.

But it was too late. She started slightly but it was only enough to switch the point of impact from square upon the back of her father's head, as she intended, to his left shoulder. The vase shattered, the sound loud but not drowning the sickening crunch of broken bone. Lord Wrexham yelled in pain and staggered, blood rapidly soaking his shirtsleeve, yet he somehow managed to pivot toward Simone with eyes savagely blazing and right fist raised.

Richard launched forward, leaping over the low table in between, and bowled bodily into the earl. They crashed into the wall and his sword flew out of his hand. He compensated quickly, his fist a blur as it swung upward and made contact with the earl's left temple, the stricken man's eyes glazing and rolling back into his head moments before he bonelessly toppled to the floor.

Richard knelt, checking his pulse to assure he was alive and then peeling back an eyelid to assure he was deeply unconscious. Satisfied on both counts, Richard then turned to Simone.

She stood taut and straight, her eyes glittering with residual anger and gradually dawning happiness. Her cheeks were flushed, hair loose and disheveled, chest heaving with ragged inhalations, and the only thought that went through Richard's mind was that she looked absolutely ravishing!

"You came," she said simply.

"I came," he responded.

And then the stasis broke. They crossed the short space between, arms embracing fiercely and mouths crushing together in a passionate kiss.

Artois nudged Warren, both men smirking as they backed out of the room.

"He always has all the fun," Warren grumbled good-naturedly.

"True. But no one knows the truth but us three, so the tale can be spun to our advantage. At least our wives can think we are the heroes and that should earn us more than a kiss."

⚓

The marriage of Colonel Richard Fitzwilliam and Lady Simone Fotherby took place three weeks after Christmas in the small chapel attached to the Fotherby estate in Buckinghamshire. It was a humble ceremony and reception with the bride wearing an unpretentious pale yellow gown that accented her stunningly youthful blonde coloring and glowing mien. She walked down the aisle preceded by her two sons tossing rose petals and escorted proudly by her stepson, Lord Oliver Fotherby, with eyes only on her earnestly waiting groom. The Colonel wore his most elaborate dress uniform with the wealth of earned medals adorning his chest polished until gleaming, wool tailored to perfection for his stocky physique, and a countenance beaming with transcendent joy.

The intimate gathering of friends and family were unified in their happiness for the couple. How could anyone feel otherwise when the two were so forthright in their giddy elation? The sacred vows were exchanged before the altar with due solemnity only broken for a second when Richard glanced toward Darcy, who winked and grinned. Many in the audience knew of the tortuous road these two had traversed to reach this place as the scandals surrounding Lord Wellson's murder and the formal severing with her father, Lord Wrexham, were now common knowledge. But only a handful knew the full extent of the trauma, and thus rejoiced in the union finally coming to fruition.

Congratulations and blessings were abundant. Darcy was uncharacteristically effusive in his felicitations, saving the best of his teases for after the honeymoon. Lizzy did not hesitate in kissing her cousin smartly on the cheek and hugging his new bride. Dr. George Darcy was as effusive as his nephew and did not reserve his teasing. Raul and Anne Penaflor were genuine in their well wishes while Lady Catherine de Bourgh nodded politely. Lord Matlock was stately, as was Lady Matlock, but the controlled tears in their eyes spoke volumes. Jonathan clapped his brother on the back and offered a lusty "well done" while Priscilla tried not to express her chagrin over the younger brother marrying a woman of higher rank. Lord Montgomery accompanied his wife to her brother's nuptials, although he looked positively bored stiff with the procedure, but Lady Annabella Montgomery was surprisingly moved by her brother's happiness and bestowed a heartfelt kiss and embrace.

Georgiana extended sincere congratulations and wishes for eternal happiness to the couple. Simone embraced her young cousin in true joy and understanding of the circumstances, Richard having divulged his tumultuous emotions during their separation. The groom, however, avoided Georgiana's eyes. His remorse and discomfort were evident, feelings that were ridiculous as Simone and Georgiana genuinely liked each other and neither woman wished for anything but his happiness. It was a strained situation that pained all three of them.

A number of Richard's friends and military associates were present, each delighted to be a part of witnessing the long-time bachelor finally succumb. The Vernors, Sitwells, Hugheses, and Bingleys were in attendance, as were a select group of Lady Fotherby's lifelong friends and her three sisters. Considering the prominence of the bride it was a modest assembly, many in Society shocked and angered to be denied an invitation; but Simone was unfazed. She readily embraced life as wife to an ordinary gentleman, who in her eyes was extraordinary in every possible way.

"So, Cousin, how is matrimony suiting you thus far?"

"I have been married for exactly one hour, Darcy, so aside from wishing desperately that I was alone with my bride, I do not think I can give an explicit accounting of the matrimonial state. Ask me again in a month or so."

"Indeed I will. If you are then ready to quit your bedchamber for an evening with me."

"Remember that I am marrying a woman with children so will undoubtedly not have as much time to dally in my conjugal bed as you probably did."

He grinned at his cousin, Darcy grinning in return.

"Young Lord Fotherby appears healthy at the moment."

"He was slow to recover from the poor medical management administered by Wrexham's quack," Richard said with bitterness. "Simone lost too many hours of sleep worrying over him, another reason her father deserves to be shot for what he did."

Unfortunately, the most Lord Wrexham would suffer as a result of his crime was a left arm that pained him and had limited mobility. It was monumentally unfair, but Simone had no legal recourse, as there was no proof that she was detained against her will unless she chose to launch an extended investigation. Since this would likely be a fruitless effort in light of her father's wealth and influence, it was not worth further scandal that might harm her children. Harry and Hugh were young enough to be innocently unaware of the drama. Oliver's sequelae was serious, his condition critically worsened due to nearly two months of mistreatment. But in the end, that too may have been an odd blessing as Dr. Angless collaborated with the Fotherby family physician, as well as Dr. Darcy putting his superior intellect and unique experience to the mix, and a new plan was devised for the mysterious ailment. Oliver was responding favorably, a great deal of his gaiety and heartiness undoubtedly the result of observing the only mother he had ever known glowing with happiness.

"You a father," Darcy teased, noting the fond smile on Richard's face as he watched Hugh, Harry, and Oliver laughing as they exhaled on a cold window and drew pictures in the vapor. "Who would have thought it?"

"Not I," Richard said with a laugh. "Far too much responsibility for me. Simone must be crazy."

"Maybe," Darcy agreed with a grin. "Do you think you will miss it?" He nodded toward the mass of medals adorning Richard's chest.

"At times I am sure I will. It is hard to fathom no longer being a part of what has been essentially my family and identification for nearly as long as I can remember, but I am prepared to enter a new phase of life and identity as husband, father, and estate manager. I gave the matter intense contemplation, as you know, and it is for the best. I cannot be the husband she deserves if I am encumbered with my professional duties. Nor do I want to run the risk of another war or being deployed. I will not be parted from her, Darcy, not ever again."

Darcy nodded. "I understand completely, my friend."

They paused for a moment to gaze upon their wives where they sat surrounded by children and ladies.

"Have you told Elizabeth of your plans to take her on tour through Europe?"

"I have hinted. I am keeping it tentative at the moment until I finalize some business matters and research travel options. I have never traveled abroad with a family, so concessions must be made. You shall see in due course, Cousin. Life is no longer easy, but well worth the discomfort, I assure you." Richard smiled, a bit foolishly, and Darcy chuckled. "The plans are taking shape and if all is well, then I shall reveal it as a birthday present. By the way, do you think you and Mrs. Fitzwilliam will be able to visit Pemberley for the Summer Festival? We are planning a smaller affair for May this year. I thought I better extend the invitation now, since I will likely not see much of you in the subsequent months."

"Very funny. If you keep this up I am tempted to avoid you purposely for the sake of my sanity! As for the Festival, we will be there… if you think it wise."

Darcy glanced at Richard's suddenly clouded face, noting that his gaze had strayed from divine wife to lovely Georgiana where she stood across the room in animated conversation with Kitty Bennet and a number of others.

"Richard, you need to let your guilt go. How many times must we tell you that Georgiana is perfectly fine? Only you persist in this train of thought. She is young and resilient, much as you are. Her only pain is in your remorse and embarrassment and avoidance of her. She loves you too much to want you to suffer. You need to talk to her, and although this is perhaps not the best venue, you should not embark on your honeymoon with any residual baggage."

Richard nodded, eyes sad but suddenly determined. "You are right. Excuse me please."

He was waylaid on his quest by his wife, a brief moment of whispered declarations of devotion and subtle caresses lightening his spirits. It was a face infused with radiant happiness that greeted Georgiana, who instantly smiled in return.

"Miss Darcy, Miss Bennet," he bowed formally before turning to Kitty. "Miss Bennet, may I steal my cousin away for a stroll on the terrace?"

Arm in arm they walked among the scattered guests enjoying the crisp air, content in the silence of sweet companionship. With each step Richard's irrational guilt disappeared.

It was Georgiana who broke the hush with a softly teasing lilt, "Now, this is not so horrible, is it Richard? Taking a turn with one of your dearest friends?"

He laughed helplessly, gracing her with his beaming face and bright grin.

She halted, reaching gentle fingertips to his cheek. "Ah! There it is! The sincere smile of true happiness that I have longed to rejoice in. The face that I so adore filled with peace. You are a fool, Richard Fitzwilliam, to think that

I would ever wish for anything else for you. But I shall forgive you this one misstep, as long as you promise to be my friend for all of your life."

He blinked stinging tears, swallowing the lump caught in his throat, lowering his head to briefly rest upon her shoulder before again meeting her glorious eyes. He lifted her fingers for a firm kiss, holding her gaze while answering, "All of my life and beyond to eternity, Georgie, my little mouse. That is my promise."

Kitty watched Georgiana and Richard disappear around the corner with a pleased smile on her face. Naturally, she knew the entire tale, she and Georgiana maintaining a constant correspondence over the months. The sadness that Georgiana experienced at what she feared was an estrangement with Richard was profound, and Kitty was thrilled to see the two finally speak. She had no doubt that their relationship's wounds would be repaired, knowing that the affection shared was deep.

She sighed. *Too bad not all relationships can be mended so easily*, she thought. Of course, not all relationships were of an honest nature, a fact that she could not forget no matter how hard she tried. The odd part was that her heart no longer ached for Anthony Falke, and there were even times when she struggled to recall a fine detail of his appearance or character. Yet the damage to her soul remained as bleakly intense as on the day she was rejected so brutally.

Kitty had not shared the events in Stevenage with either parent. Primarily this was due to the painful nature of the ordeal, but also out of mortification. Being rebuffed so vigorously by someone who had professed love and proudly believing oneself a worthy recipient of love, only to have it dashed into a thousand pieces was a staggering abasement.

Torn between the fear of further lies and humiliation, and the conviction that she was deficient in some manner and therefore undeserving of the love she saw portrayed so beautifully in her sisters' marriages, Kitty shrank from any male attention. She resisted attending the various assemblies offered in Meryton and when she was coerced, she danced few sets and generally with boys she knew to be "safe." She had not been particularly keen on accompanying Georgiana to London, even as fond as she was of Colonel Fitzwilliam, but her friend's pleading and misery had won over any misgivings.

Now here she was, a guest at Colonel Fitzwilliam's wedding, surrounded by a sea of men in uniform, and all she could think of was how her mother would shrilly scold her for not taking advantage of a prime marriage market when it was laid on her lap! The thought was actually quite humorous, and she smiled at the mental image of her mother in a nervous tizzy, chuckling under her breath until she realized that her expression had drawn the attention of an adolescent soldier standing several yards away. He bowed in a sort of salute, and to her horror started crossing toward her! Eyes wild, she launched from the chair and made a dash for the doorway.

The last thing she wanted was to make idle conversation with a pimply faced boy cadet. She wove through the press of bodies conversing and laughing, making for an empty corridor to the left. A quick glance behind proved that no one was following or seemed aware of her passage. With a sigh of relief, she opened a random door and noted a darkened room. *Perfect!* She ducked inside and sagged against the latched door, closing her eyes for a silent prayer of thanksgiving.

The room was quite dark and it took her pupils a few minutes to adjust. She realized it was a vast library only because she was standing near a tall shelf of books. All the curtains were drawn, sporadic gaps allowing the muted light of an overcast day in January to pierce for faint illumination. She wended past the shelves and chairs toward the back of the room, no specific destination in mind, and not noting the man leaning casually against the unlit fireplace until she nearly collided with him.

"Oh!" She exclaimed, retreating several paces in alarm. "Forgive me! I did not see you there!"

"Obviously." His voice echoed about the room, resonant tones imbued with traces of latent laughter. "It is understandable, however, so no need to apologize."

For some reason Kitty felt a flair of irritation. "You could have alerted me as to your presence. Then neither of us would be suffering such embarrassment!"

"Why should we be embarrassed? It is a dark room so clearly you did not want to be seen. Seeking privacy, I assumed. As was I."

"Nonetheless, you should have made your presence known."

She could sense his shrug even though the gloom was too great to see more than a vague outline. "It is a large room so I rather hoped you would wander to the far side. I did not wish to intrude upon your solitude, but apparently the intrusion was fated to be for both of us."

"Intrusion was what I was evading, oddly enough," she blurted, biting her lip at the rude slip.

"What sort of intrusion?"

"Unwanted conversation, ironically."

He chuckled, the sound reverberating. "Yes, ironic indeed. Doubly so as I fled here for the same reason."

She cocked her head, straining to see more than an outline of what appeared to be a tall, brawny figure. The voice was indecipherable. Was he young or old? None of the squeak inherent in the truly young, or the tremulousness of the aged, but anywhere in between was possible.

"Who were you avoiding?"

"The dozens of available women from forty years on down who my father deems it his self-appointed duty to parade under my nose at any gathering we attend. Weddings, funerals, all are fair game as far as he is concerned." There was that smoldering laughter again, not a trace of resentment in his words. Kitty realized she was smiling.

"Only forty years on down? How fortunate you are. My mother considers any male not yet in his dotage eligible."

"Is she here now? Pointing out the wealth of handsome and not-so-handsome specimens in uniform? Is that why you scurried away?"

And she did laugh. "No, she is not here, but I was actively imagining her face when I tell her that I did not flirt with and gain the favors of at least one officer. She will be deeply disappointed in me." And for the first time there was no bitterness in the thought.

"I gather that we are both horrid children, severely upsetting to our parents," he said.

"Indeed we are."

"I, for one, have vowed never to force those of the opposite sex upon my children, when they arrive."

"Interesting. Of course, the paradox is that if you do not fulfill the wish of your father, you will never have any offspring to uphold your vow to!"

He laughed aloud, slapping his thigh in mirth. "Excellent! Touché, miss. That, I confess, has never occurred to me! Perhaps I should return to the parlor and see who he has scared up."

"It sounds as though he may have reached the point of desperation with you, so I am not sure you can trust his judgment at this juncture."

"Hmmm... You are undoubtedly correct. I think I am safer here in the dark conversing with a complete stranger. Ah!" And she discerned the slap of his palm against his forehead. "But I forgot that you were seeking solitude and avoiding unwanted conversation. So we now have a dilemma."

"How so?"

"Who should leave? I was here first, so logic would dictate that you depart and face the lurking male hounds. But then I do pride myself on being a gentleman, so decorum dictates that I bow out gracefully and manfully bear the agony. What shall we do?"

"Do you have a coin? We could flip for it, the loser rejoining the assembly and taking their chances."

"Alas, it is too dark." And neither mentioned the simple solution of pulling the drapes.

"Well, we have been talking now for some fifteen minutes, so are no longer *complete* strangers." Kitty offered hesitantly.

"True, true. And the conversation, at least from my perspective, has not been completely unwanted."

"I agree."

Silence fell, Kitty sensing his eyes upon her and feeling the smile. A comfortable quiet settled about them. He shifted from one foot to the other, still leaning against the fireplace and Kitty could now perceive that his arms were crossed over his chest. She paced around a chaise, fingertips brushing over the edges for tactile direction, unconsciously striving to attain an angle that might cast greater clarification upon her partner.

"Are you here as a guest of the bride or groom?"

"The groom. My father is a general in Colonel Fitzwilliam's regiment. I have known him for years, although I cannot say we are close confidants. My brother went to the Academy with him, so is closer in age and relationship. And you?"

"The groom as well. My sister is married to his cousin, Mr. Darcy."

"Ah! So you would be Miss Bennet?"

Kitty nodded, hesitating to speak. For some strange reason, she suddenly felt uneasy, but could not quite place her finger on why.

Then he spoke, "You preferred anonymity, yes?" His voice was soft, almost a caress. "Stay in the shadows, talking with the unseen, unknown individual where it is deemed safe? Why is that, Miss Bennet?"

"I suppose if I never see your face or know who you are than you cannot affect me." The words burst forth, Kitty blushing at her private confession, but he did not seem perturbed.

"Hmmm... Perhaps. Although, in my experience it is the hidden one who is the greater threat. The enemy who lurks in dark places and springs out unawares."

"Is that not, in effect, what you have done?"

He laughed, the sound musical. "From a certain point of view, I suppose that is correct. Although, strictly speaking, you sprung in on me."

"But you were lurking in the dark place."

"Merely because I arrived first. The scenario could have been reversed."

"You are laughing at me," she accused, suppressing a girlish giggle.

"Only a little. In truth I am just pointing out the absurdity in both of our rationales and actions."

"What do you mean?"

Again she felt his shrug. For the first time since entering the library he moved from his languid repose against the mantel, standing straight and even taller than she thought, nearly as tall as Mr. Darcy, and took one stride toward her.

"We hide ourselves away to avoid what we have decided are unpleasant consequences. We seek to be left alone or at least to our own devices without exterior finagling. We weary of the game imposed upon us by well-meaning parents. And we somehow have divined that there is a safety to the dark. Yet, and I can only speak honestly for myself although I am sensing the same from you, we are actually enjoying ourselves. You see? Absurdity."

"I suppose you now want me to congratulate you on your brilliant deductions and acknowledge that I am enjoying myself?"

"Only if you mean it."

Kitty laughed, helpless against the smug, gay inflection obvious in his retort. "I believe, sir, that you are impertinent!"

"I have been accused of worse."

He moved again, but in the dark she lost sight of where he was. "Sir?"

"I believe, Miss Bennet, that it is time for us to dispense with the shadows." He was to her right, not five feet away, and beside the nearest cloaked window. "Are you willing to face the light of day with all its accompanying glories and ugliness?"

"Which are you? The former or the latter?"

"You, Miss Bennet, are a wit and I have decided I like you and that you are in the former category. I will allow you to judge me for yourself. I am brave enough to accept your evaluation."

"Very well then. But I shall be brutally honest."

"Understood." And the curtains were thrust aside, sunlight streaming in and momentarily blinding both of them. Eyes blinked back tears, hands involuntarily rose to shade, but gradually their pupils adjusted. She had suspected that he was a military man, and he was tall, as she had ascertained. Easily in his early thirties if not a bit older, his form trim, but wide in the shoulders and chest. His eyes were deep brown, almost black, with thick lashes framing, and curly hair, black with scattered streaks of grey at the temples.

The seconds stretched as they examined each other unabashedly. Eventually, simultaneously, pleased smiles spread over their faces.

Kitty moved first, extending her fingers and curtsying fluidly. "Miss Katherine Bennet."

He lifted her hand, bowing as he brushed soft lips lightly over her knuckles. "Miss Bennet, a pleasure. I am Major General Artois. Randall Artois."

CHAPTER TWENTY

The Promise of a New Life

WHILE RICHARD DEALT WITH the aftermath of Lady Fotherby's imprisonment and renewed their relationship, Darcy concluded his business in London and hastened home for the Christmas holiday. Anxiousness to share the news of Richard's happiness and engagement—an agreement the reunited lovers formalized less than a day after escaping Hampshire for the plush comfort of the Fotherby townhouse at Mayfair—was matched by an urgency to embrace his wife and son. Christmas was days away and three plus weeks without them was more than he could bear.

Despite his fretfulness, Alexander had recovered rapidly from his cold. Darcy returned to discover a fat, healthy son who greeted him with shrieks of joy and outstretched arms as he toddled across the nursery floor and fell into the strong embrace of his delighted father.

His wife, conversely, greeted him feebly from their bed. Alexander's mild infection had transmitted to Lizzy nastily. She lay under about a dozen quilts, nose red and copiously running, chest rattling with each breath, lips chapped in a feverishly shiny face, and a hacking cough that rendered her weak and winded. It was the first incidence of such an illness with his wife and Darcy was seriously dismayed.

And furious.

But he thrust his anger at not being notified aside, and diligently assumed the task of caring for their son and nursing his wife to health. Luckily the Christmas activities planned were minor and completely arranged, all the presents purchased and wrapped, since Lizzy barely managed to stay awake while Alexander thrilled over his numerous toys. The infant's fascination with the ribbons and paper wrap evinced a weak smile and chuckle that instantly sparked a coughing spell necessitating Darcy carrying her to bed for a hot mist breathing treatment and rest.

Dr. Darcy insisted that it was nothing more than a common cold with chest congestion and minor compared to the influenza Darcy had suffered prior to Alexander's birth, but Darcy was not placated. He fretted, hovered, and enforced every form of therapeutic remedy he could glean from his uncle and the medical books in the library. It took nearly two weeks, but finally Lizzy recovered the greater portion of her natural vigor. Yet she continued to sleep far longer than typical, had a lingering cough, and was frequently weary enough to nap in the afternoons. Attending the Cole's masque was out of the question, the gorgeous gown created for the occasion wrapped and stored for a future engagement.

Even with her steady improvement, Darcy worried over permanent damage to her lungs. To augment her recuperation, Darcy surprised her with a spontaneous gift of three nights basking in the curative waters at Matlock Bath. He was not a great believer in the claims of mineral spas, but even George concurred that it wouldn't hurt.

Leaving Alexander behind for the first time since his birth was difficult, but they said their adieus, smothering him with an abundance of hugs and kisses. They began the short drive to Matlock assuaging their guilt by remembering the medicinal instigation for the short holiday.

However, within a few miles the romantic nature of their destination was secretly beginning to dawn on them!

Matlock village on the east bank of the River Derwent, some eight miles from Pemberley, was a frequent destination, as it was larger than Lambton, thus offering a handful of shops not available in the closer hamlet. And of course Rivallain, home of the Earl of Matlock, was reached via the main thoroughfare over the bridge. Matlock Bath, some miles away and on the western side of the river, nestled high within the thick-forested foothills of the craggy limestone cliffs where the warm thermal springs bubbled, was a novelty for both of them.

Lizzy brightened notably as soon as they began their ascent from the bridge. The sublime beauty of Matlock Dale with dark-blue water flowing briskly amid the blanket of yew, elm, and lime trees clothing the shore from which the humble church's pinnacles reared was impressively picturesque. Even more stunning was the naked limestone brow of High Tor, bursting upward some three-hundred-fifty feet and casting a shadow on the river far below. Centuries of fallen fragments shaped the bed of the river, the current foaming over boulders and rubble in a constantly changing flow, the roar considerable especially now, after recent rains. It was magnificent.

Cut into the gorge in 1815, the new coach road wound through the hills and strips of meadows, giving glimpses of the continually altering terrain below. They passed numerous lodges and bathhouses nestled among the trees, dozens of meandering footpaths through the wood and brush, and the occasional mineral incrustation formed by deposits from the springs that harden and decompose until covered by moss. It was a landscape both familiar due to common Derbyshire vegetation while also utterly unique.

A final bend in the road and opening in the trees revealed the New Bath Hotel. So named simply because it was built in 1802 upon discovery of a newer and warmer spring—many years after the original lodge that was once just the Bath Hotel but was now referred to as the Old Bath Hotel—the massive white wood and brick structure of Regency design sat on a lush five-acre expanse surrounded by trees and sculptured gardens. As modern and prestigious as one could hope for in the lesser-known spa community of Matlock Bath, the hotel had a marvelous reputation for excellence. Plus, and even more important to Darcy than luxury at the moment, was the Roman-style bathing room large enough for swimming. And the waters themselves were reputedly higher in healing properties.

Lizzy smiled, turning to her husband with shining eyes. "It is beautiful, William. Thank you for thinking of this."

He drew her close under his outstretched arm, boldly stealing a brief kiss and caressing over her cheek. "Anything to help you, dearest. I would have gone to Bath if need be, but fortunately, we are close to a spa far more private and less crowded."

He gazed into her eyes, noting the expression of love and joy that momentarily erased all traces of her lingering infirmity, and abruptly the romantic nature of their outing washed over him. By the sudden change in her face—lips parting slightly and half-lidded eyes straying to his mouth—it was clear that the identical thought had occurred to her. Unconsciously, he bent his head, meeting her upturned mouth eagerly. Alas, the kiss was interrupted by the carriage stopping with a jolt.

Darcy frowned and Lizzy giggled. They shared a last, lingering look, communicating their need silently.

Mr. Saxton, the owner, greeted them upon arrival. Darcy's requests, made in advance by Mr. Keith in person and with large quantities of cash exchanged, were explicit. A suite on the first floor with private parlor and additional rooms for their servants, in-room dining when possible, limitless supplies of the curative drinking water, and frequent use of the baths. Fortunately, it was the slow season for tourists, but Mr. Darcy's eminence and wealth were more than adequate to grant the requirements asked for.

The intervening hours between settling in their comfortable and spacious if unadorned chambers and finally meeting in the basement bath were tortuous. Darcy resisted bodily tossing his wife onto the bed and ravishing her only because there were servants in and out. He also insisted she consume a full glass of the mineral water waiting in a large pitcher before they did anything. And of course, he did wish for her to rest and recuperate, thus not too sure how wise it would be to engage immediately in the exhaustive, vigorous session of lovemaking that he desired with a palpable ache. He knew his wife well enough to sense that she was struggling with the same yearning, both of them gripped with emotions akin to the heady days of their honeymoon when touching each other was at times quite all that they thought about! Any residual guilt they secretly harbored at being filled with these sensations while their baby was at home without them vanished under the layers of sexual currents.

Once alone in the Roman style bathing chamber built of heavy masonry and tile in the foundations of the western wing of the hotel, the low arched roof glowing golden and rippling from niched candles surrounding the pool, they were caught up in a flare of raging need. Darcy entered the water first, Lizzy exiting the dressing room moments later wearing a thin shift. She crossed to where he waded in the waist high water, eyes greedily assessing his figure. The vision of his lean physique, with solid, defined muscles wetly glistening in the subdued lighting and black chest hair enhancing his virile masculinity—as well as creating a pathway pointing to the equally delicious and manly lower body only partially obscured by the opaque mineral water—sent her ardor skyward.

She paused at the edge long enough to ask one question, "Is it hot?"

"Only tepid," he replied, arms reaching to assist.

Lizzy nodded, sitting onto the edge and slipping into his ready embrace without hesitation. He pulled her onto his chest, hungry hands roaming everywhere seemingly at once. His voice grated from where bared teeth grazed over her shoulder, "My Lizzy, I desire you so profoundly. I fear I may be unable to be gentle."

"Do not try, Fitzwilliam," she whispered, legs encircling his waist and drawing him firmly against her.

He groaned, any regulation entirely lost as he lowered them both into the water, knees resting onto the last step with Lizzy's bottom on the one above, driving deeply within her all in one smooth motion. "I missed you," he murmured, panting already with the furious pace they mutually craved, "I needed you."

Her response was a quick nod of agreement and then a rough grip to the back of his head, pulling him closer for a pervading kiss that lasted for several minutes until the rising sensations rapidly overtook them and mouths separated to release guttural cries of pleasure.

Long minutes later, as Darcy bobbed gently about the pool with Lizzy slumped against his chest, her head resting on his shoulder, she said, "That was wonderful." Darcy chuckled at the understatement, hands soothingly caressing the water over her back and shoulders. "Correction, it was amazing. Stupendous. Earth shattering. I wonder if the hydropathy experts intended crazed lovemaking as part of their therapy treatment. They should, as I feel incredible." She pulled away until she could see his smiling eyes. "I haven't coughed in quite a while now."

"Well, without founded scientific evidence to determine the definitive cause of your restoration to prime health and eradication of the cough, I suppose it is my duty to ensure that both treatment plans are abundantly administered."

"Indeed, that does appear to be the logical conclusion. So how soon might I anticipate a repeat dose of fantastic loving, Mr. Darcy?"

Darcy chuckled again, that singular deep, throaty chuckle that was more a sensuous growl. "We have another thirty minutes slated for our bath, and if you remove that shift and continue to touch me as you currently are, a second dose is imminent."

Lizzy's laugh was equally sensual, the soaked shift discarded a second later. They made love again, temperately as they floated about the pool, reveling in the blissful water waving over their naked skin and the romantic atmosphere.

It was the mere tip of the iceberg. For the entire sojourn they rarely left their rooms. Darcy had planned a few short excursions, depending on Lizzy's stamina, but few were done. They managed to dress each day, late in the afternoon or evening, for strolls along the secluded pathways. The weather was gloomy, with drizzling rains frequent, so their walks were brief and kept close to the hotel. They were blessed to catch a stunning lunar rainbow on their second night while wandering hand in hand along the trail edging the river during a break in the rain. The combination of moisture in the air, a nearly full moon sitting barely above the horizon, and the darkened sky created a pearly moonbow in a complete arc with a hint of colors visible. They stood for as long as possible, awestruck by the phenomenon, until the encroaching rain misted their faces.

They raced back to the lodge, damp and slightly winded, but exhilarated by the fresh air and breathtaking visual treat. The rush to remove moist clothing to prevent chilling only led to a rapid tumble back into the unmade bed they so recently vacated.

They were utterly insatiable.

"I believe that the moon has turned you into a wild beast," Lizzy teased, her respirations gasping in time with her spouse's. She lay draped across his naked chest, sweat slick on their flushed skin, satisfied and deliriously happy as she tickled over his sensitive rib cage.

He rolled her over, hands clasping her wrists over her head. He grinned wickedly, eyes brazenly scanning over her body, and shook his head slowly. "Perhaps. But personally, I do not think the moon has anything to do with it." And without further ado he lowered his mouth to her bosom, beginning an oral exploration that would eventually have her crying his name in ecstasy.

The exalting pleasure of endless romance with the one person loved more than all others was stronger medicine than the drinking water or calmative baths. Lizzy did sleep for long stretches, but woke refreshed and ready for more romance, often initiating the procedure although Darcy roused swiftly each and every time. Her appetite for both food and her husband increased hourly and daily. It was a pattern of lovemaking, talking, laughing, eating, more love, or maybe sleep, that repeated again and again. Neither could unequivocally assert that they broke any records in those three days, but it assuredly was remarkable. They separated only for their individual toilettes, hastily washing before returning to renewed intimate play and exercise. Darcy did not even bother to shave, Lizzy teasing that the whiskers validated the animalistic transformation. Not that she was complaining one iota!

On their last night, they lay spooned together with Lizzy's back pressed tightly into Darcy's chest. One long, muscular leg twined over hers, keeping her secure and warm. They had napped for several hours after their last wild interlude that had begun while properly dressed and sitting at the dining table when Darcy impulsively hauled her onto his lap to lick the gravy off her bottom lip. That was enough to spark the smoldering fire. The dining chair, thankfully large and sturdy, was utilized efficiently and was miraculously undamaged when they crumbled into a heap of weakened muscles that required approximately fifteen minutes of immobility before staggering together to collapse upon the bed and fall into a deep sleep.

Now they were awake, but content to talk quietly, caress tenderly, and stare out the wide windows at the glowing moon and sparkling stars peeking through the broken clouds. A fire crackled, providing the only illumination. Darcy idly kissed along her sloping neck, rough beard sending delighted shivers over her spine, and ran his fingertips lightly over her flat belly.

"Do you think it possible we created a baby while here, Elizabeth?"

Lizzy smiled, drawing the fingers clasped within her own to her lips for a kiss. "Considering your stored seed after a long abstinence and that we made love, what, a million times?" She laughed. "I imagine it is possible."

"I pray so. I am ready for another child." He paused, cupping her abdomen, and then resumed with conviction. "I believe we have. I feel it."

"Do you now? Clairvoyance, is it?"

"Not precisely, no. But I wish for another baby, one who resembles you this time. And I always get what I want," he finished with smug assurance, grinning as Lizzy laughed and turned in his arms, face radiant with happiness and superb health.

"Arrogant," she teased.

"Indubitably," he agreed, grin widening. "Yet you know it is true that I usually do have my way. And who is it whom continually extols my prowess?"

He lifted his left brow, Lizzy helpless but to laugh and nod. She brushed across his cheek with tender fingertips, encircling his head and embedding her fingers into his mussed hair. "Just in case you are wrong, we have all night and tomorrow morning to work on the project."

"I do so love you, Elizabeth. More than it is possible for me to verbalize."

"I love you as deeply, William, my heart. But do not fret if words fail you, as showing me your adoration conveys the emotion most admirably."

"Are you positive?" He asked with an arched brow and crooked smile. "I could not live with myself if my treasured wife did not adequately comprehend the depth of my sentiments."

"Hmm… Perhaps you should expound upon the subject one more time. Drive the point home, shall we say, so I shan't have any questions."

"Drive the point home? Colorful, my love. I am impressed. Shall I begin by articulating my passion for your silky skin by covering you with moist kisses?" And without waiting for an answer he stretched onto her, his sturdy frame pressing her into the mattress, while his lips nuzzled along her neck, feathering kisses and light flicks of his tongue from her earlobe to fragile collarbone.

At her shoulder he paused, elevating slightly and lifting her arm at the wrist to examine the ivory length as he mused, "Are kisses and nibbles enough to express how I live for the feel of your arms wrapped around me? Can I prove how your beautiful, feminine hands touching me both in tender care and uncontrollable desire heighten my joy?" He brought her inner wrist to his mouth, again kissing and licking, adding suckles and tiny nips to the sensitive area where her pulse raced. He took each finger into his mouth, leisurely sucking, watching her aroused eyes with tremendous satisfaction. A dozen or more intense kisses and he finally traversed the distance, returning to her mouth. His tall, broad-shouldered body again fully covered her svelte one, squeezing so deliciously while he kissed her hungrily.

He moved both large hands to her breasts, palms cupping the fullness that no longer fit completely within his grasp. "Your breasts," he resumed huskily. "Words do fail. None exist to explain how your breasts drive me to insane levels of arousal. It is unfair that one woman should possess breasts so utterly perfect and that I am the man blessed to enjoy them."

"Unfair?" She asked with a laugh.

"Very well, not unfair. I suffer no shame over my incredibly good fortune." And with that declaration he licked over one taut nipple, that taste only the *amuse-bouche* portion of the feast he relished for the subsequent fifteen minutes on her bosom alone.

The declarations and stimulation encompassed every part of her body. When he eventually drove home, as she humorously termed it, burying himself deeply within those secret places that were only and forever his to explore and bring pleasure, their passions were once again surging and raging.

He held her face within the palms of his hands, kissing slowly as his body tirelessly rocked in a measured rhythm. She rose to meet him, her legs wound about his waist and buttocks, the undulant motion controlled and synchronized blissfully. Soft murmurs of love and desire sporadically mixed with the pants and moans. But their faces never parted more than a few inches. Lips nuzzled and kissed, noses brushed cheeks, eyes fluttered open for brief connections, and breath mingled.

Their breathing grew ragged, the tempo quickening as their grips tightened. Darcy clutched her firmly as she did him, fused along every surface. His lidded eyes locked onto her glorious face until the last possible second when the need overwhelmed. He arched his neck, eyes closing as the spasms of intense pleasure rocked their bodies, groaning as he emptied himself thoroughly until finally collapsing into the bend of her neck.

They returned to Pemberley the next day with Lizzy glowing, completely free of cold symptoms, and utterly refreshed. Darcy was invigorated as well, the holiday clearly one highly beneficial to both of them.

The following month passed in a blur. The winter of 1818 was far milder than the previous one. The temperature dropped low enough to freeze the drizzle into light dustings of snow upon occasion, but it never lasted long enough to accumulate before a warmer air current melted it away. When it came to traveling, this was a positive in not being so coldly uncomfortable, but the nearly constant moisture turned the roads into a muddy quagmire. The Darcy coach was sturdy and pulled by strong horses, but the going was slow.

For that reason, they decided to remain in London after Richard and Simone's wedding, keeping their agendas open ended. Darcy attended to business and his favored pursuits while Lizzy and Georgiana shopped and visited with the few friends present in Town prior to the official Season.

Thus, they were in their Darcy House bedchamber on a dreary morning in early February when Lizzy abruptly woke while lying in her husband's arms. She roughly disengaged her limbs from his, her elbow and heels painfully striking his inert flesh a time or two, vaulted out of bed, and barely reached her chamber pot before becoming violently ill.

Trembling and with stomach churning, she shuffled into the bedchamber holding a wet cloth against her forehead. A sleepy, slightly bruised, but anticipatory Darcy sat waiting in the bed for her return. "Are you? That is, do you think?"

Lizzy gingerly laid back down, glaring into her husband's shining eyes from underneath the compress, and answered in a clipped tone, "I cannot be certain, Fitzwilliam, but it certainly seems probable that your wish for another child may be true."

Darcy chuckled, managing to control the overwhelming urge to leap from the bed and dance about the room, nestling his wife close to his warm body. "This is amazing news, my love! I *knew* we conceived while at Matlock Bath! Did I not say so at the time? I could feel it, I just knew! Remember?"

Lizzy smiled faintly at the raging enthusiasm that was rapidly threatening to override his restraint. "Yes, I recall very well, Mr. Darcy. Your rather smug assertions in the ability to impregnate upon demand were abundantly conveyed. How proud you must be."

Darcy laughed harder, kissing with gusto, before pulling away to smooth the hair from her brow with a tender caress. He gently pressed the damp cloth over her pale cheeks, his radiant grin not completely hiding his concern for her well-being. Still, his happiness and pride ruled.

"When, do you think? On our first day, when we made love before the fire with you astride me, and the flames flickered over your skin? That was incredible. Or the time we woke in the darkness of pre-dawn. God, you were unbelievable! I saw stars, Elizabeth, and not because we tumbled to the floor. And that last night. Yes, that may be it! Your eyes were glowing as we finished, and I thought I would never stop shuddering with pleasure and filling you. I was blissfully drained. Or maybe…"

"You forgot to mention the pool, when you tackled me so roughly that I scraped my backside." Her tone was teasing but vaguely surly.

He chuckled, rubbing over the long since healed minor abrasion on her tailbone. "I apologize again, my love"—his tone was low and not the slightest bit remorseful—"but Lord help me, it was worth any pain! I nearly fainted from the heavenly satisfaction."

"Easy for you to say," she grumbled. "It wasn't your bottom bruised."

He threw his head back laughing, Lizzy slapping him on the arm and trying to twist away in irritation. He tightened his grip, however, drawing her closer and kissing her pouting lips. "Is it to begin already, my sweet? The honeyed disposition of early pregnancy? At least now I am prepared for the symptom and can lock my study door while conducting business."

He was grinning broadly, wearing an expression ageless as all men somehow conclude that pregnancy is in greater part a result of their virility, as if the woman has scant to do with the inception.

"Hysterical. Since you apparently are the sole instigator of my condition then I judge it only fair if you must live with the symptomatic consequences!"

"My Lizzy, my beloved wife. I will tolerate anything for you and the blessing of another child growing within. I am so happy! Please tell me you are as well?"

Lizzy smiled softly, reaching to stroke over his stubbly cheeks. "I am only teasing you, William. Of course I am happy! Another child with your eyes and face would please me greatly. Another angel to love and cherish. A sibling for our precious Alexander. Our baby created from our deep love and passion. How could I not be overjoyed?"

"I love you, Elizabeth."

"And I love you, my darling husband." They kissed slowly, reverently, Darcy's strong hand moving to caress over her abdomen in tender awe. Lizzy suddenly giggled, breaking the kiss.

Darcy's brow rose questioningly, luminous jubilation not diminished in the slightest by her oddly placed humor. "Have I amused you, Mrs. Darcy?"

"I was just remembering how wild we were in Matlock. You were an untamed beast and I was as crazed, hence why you felt so certain a baby would be the result. Let us just pray that atmospheric conditions and frenzied lovemaking do not influence personality traits!"

Acknowledgments

MAJOR THANKS TO DEB WERKSMAN, Dominique Raccah, Danielle Jackson, Sarah Ryan, and Susie Benton for continuing to believe in me and being so awesome at what they do. For everyone else at Sourcebooks who does a brilliant job of bringing my books to gorgeous, perfect life: You folks rock!

I can never thank my faithful readers enough for their kindness and support. I hope that each of you knows how incredible you are and how inspiring it is to have satisfied, vocal fans. To my TSBO devotees. Vee, Simone, Esther Ann, Seli, Julie C., Jen, May, Kathy SF, Jeane, Susanne, and Elly, you ladies have been there since the beginning: I love you all.

Huge hugs to my Casablanca sisters for welcoming me in, supporting and encouraging, sharing their wisdom, and for just being totally awesome! Identical warm fuzzies for my local RWA chapter, the Yosemite Romance Writers. You ladies are terrific and darned fun to hang out with.

A special, broad sweeping thank you to the people who individually or collectively provide online resources to writers of history. I certainly would have been lost without you. In that same vein: Thanks to blog/website owners who share their knowledge and time to assist and promote authors. Personally, I can't imagine doing any of this without the Internet. The plethora of sites out there in cyber-land is invaluable.

I can never pass up a chance to thank my wonderful family. My husband

Steve, daughter Emily, and son Kyle are amazing and so supportive. They make it happen for me! Lastly, to my Lord who is faithfully and lovingly continuing to teach me life lessons through all of this, even when I am kicking and screaming! He is forever merciful and gracious, thank goodness.

About the Author

SHARON LATHAN IS A NATIVE Californian currently residing amid the orchards, corn, cotton, and cows in the sunny San Joaquin Valley. Happily married for twenty-four years to her own Mr. Darcy, and mother to two wonderful children, she divides her time between housekeeping tasks, nurturing her family, church activities, and working as a registered nurse in a neonatal ICU. Throw in the cat, dog, and a ton of fish to complete the picture. When not at the hospital or attending to the dreary tasks of homemaking, she is generally found hard at work on her faithful laptop.

For more information about Sharon, the Regency Era, and her bestselling Darcy Saga series, visit her website/blog at: www.sharonlathan.net or www.darcysaga.net. She also invites everyone to join her and the other Sourcebooks romance novelists at: www.casablancaauthors.blogspot.com

Read on for an excerpt of Sharon Lathan's upcoming
novella, featured in the anthology

A Darcy Christmas

Coming soon from Sourcebooks Landmark

Christmas Loneliness

THE SNOWFLAKES DRIFTED SLOWLY downward. They were enormous flakes and floating so delicately on the air that, even in the inky darkness behind the thick glass with only the faint glow of lamplight reflecting, Fitzwilliam Darcy could visualize the minute crystals and unique geometry of each flake. It was mesmerizing and oddly calming to his tumultuous thoughts. He sipped the cocoa that was now lukewarm, watched the snow fall and gather into piles on the panes, and struggled to stir up the Christmas cheer one was supposed to enjoy on Christmas Eve.

It was not working.

He couldn't readily recall the last Christmas that was truly joyous. Surely it was before his mother died, but the memories were faded and supplanted by so many years of forced gaiety. Oh, they exchanged presents and decorated the house and went to church and delighted in a lavish feast. Often they visited Rivallain for the day, the estate of his uncle and aunt, the Earl and Marchioness of Matlock, and once or twice they had dwelt at Darcy House in London for the holiday activities there. But like all festivities since his mother's passing, and now his father's, the celebratory atmosphere was muted.

Of course he strived to celebrate the day for his sister Georgiana's sake, understanding that a child needed the merrymaking. And lauding the birth of their Savior was indeed a commemoration he took very seriously. Yet

SHARON LATHAN

personally, he often felt that the entire season could easily pass by without him noticing or caring.

Darcy had grown so accustomed to the attitude that it hardly registered any longer. Even while plotting and planning for Georgiana and purchasing gifts—that a delight he truly did enjoy—his internal zeal for Christmas was dim. He did not dread the holiday nor was he particularly gloomy over it; he just did not care all that much.

So why was this year so different? Why did he feel a melancholy blanketing his soul? And why did the dreams continue to invade his sleep? Why was *she* persistent in burrowing into his mind and hea…? No! He refused to even think it! This Christmas of 1815 was no different than the previous twenty-seven.

He sighed unconsciously and continued with his rapt contemplation of the falling snow and abstracted sipping of the cooling cocoa.

Georgiana Darcy sat on the sofa near the fire. She had been reading aloud but halted several minutes ago when it became clear that her brother was not listening to her. Now she studied him in perplexity. Georgiana was well aware that Christmas was not exactly a period of crazed jubilation for her brother, but he usually showed some enthusiasm. He never failed to create a special atmosphere for her and showered her with expensive gifts. Since she knew no different, it honestly never occurred to her to yearn for more. Georgiana was a girl quite complacent and content in her life. Her only desire was to please her family, that being primarily her adored older brother. Thus, she was disturbed by his current distraction and somberness.

None would refer to Fitzwilliam Darcy as gregarious or buoyant, but the private man was one of tender humor and affection. That he was overwhelmingly devoted to his sister could be denied by no one, especially Georgiana. She held him in tremendous awe and respect, but also took his love and playful teasing for granted. Yet ever since his return from Town and the sojourn in Hertfordshire with Mr. Bingley, he had been… odd.

She shook her head. It made no sense whatsoever. Naturally it distressed her. Not for her sake but because she loved him too much to think of him as being in pain. Yet, with the overconfidence of youth and the towering admiration of a worshipful younger sister, she shrugged it off. In her mind, her brother was fearless and capable of solving any dilemma.

So she smiled and rose to bid him goodnight. He smiled genuinely in return and held her close for several minutes, wished her sweet dreams and gave a teasing reminder not to wake him at the crack of dawn, and after a tender kiss to her cheek, she retired to her room no longer fretting over her complicated sibling but losing herself in dreams of presents.

Darcy watched her gracefully exit the parlor, his heart surging with happiness as it always did when considering his sister. But as soon as she left, seemingly taking the light and music and laughter with her, the pensiveness drenched him once again. It was late and he felt simultaneously weary and jittery. He stared at the faint light beyond the doorway, imagined the shadowy corridors between this chamber and his suite of cold and empty rooms—*Where did that thought come from?*—and actually shuddered.

Then, just as abruptly as the sadness, he was jolted by a flare of anger. He muttered a harsh curse, strode briskly to the low table where the tea and snacks sat, and placed the drained mug onto the silver tray with a plunk. He squared his shoulders, straightening to his full and considerable height, and marched purposefully from the room.

His thoughts were darker than the illuminated hallways. What was it about Elizabeth Bennet that had bewitched him so? He truly felt as if under a spell that consumed him and made no sense whatsoever. She was so completely unsuitable! She was infatuated by George Wickham, for goodness sake. That spoke volumes. And her family? He shuddered anew.

Oh, but she was beautiful. Indeed, so very beautiful.

He paused outside his dressing room door, one hand on the knob as his throat constricted and heart lurched with longing. He cursed again, a habit that was quite unlike him normally but lately seemed to be occurring frequently, and reached to loosen the cravat that was strangely now choking off his air supply. He pivoted and entered his bedchamber. For tonight, he would manage to undress himself. Facing the calmly professional presence of his valet Samuel while he was in what could only be termed "a mood" was intolerable!

Yet as he resisted slamming the door violently behind him with tremendous restraint, he discovered his steps slowing. He halted in the middle of his room. He gazed at the comforting surroundings, savored the warmth of the crackling fire as it seeped into his chilled skin, and awaited the peaceful relaxation that inevitably washed over him when alone in his sanctuary.

It did not come.

Rather he recalled the dreams that had, in one shape or another, been haunting him nearly from the moment he encountered a vivid pair of brown eyes within the crowd at an obscure dance assembly in Meryton.

He wanted to be angry.

He wanted to be disgusted with himself.

And he wanted to forget her.

At least that is what he told himself. But even now, as he remembered his dreams and remembered their conversations in Hertfordshire, he knew a smile was spreading over his face and heat was flushing through his body.

Some of that, he knew, was due to the nature of many of his dreams. It annoyed him to a degree, and he was embarrassed to a degree. But he logically deduced that it had nothing to do with Miss Elizabeth personally. No, indeed not! It was simply that he had reached the point where needing a woman, a wife, was a physical necessity. Surely that was the primary reason why increasingly erotic musings were causing him to bolt awake in a sweat of unfulfilled desire.

If it was always Elizabeth Darcy—*Bennet!*—who brought him to such a state, well that could be logically explained as well. Right?

Of course! It was because she had enchanted him in some way that he could not comprehend. Her passionate personality, her fire as she argued with him, her intelligence as she countered every last one of his held beliefs, her teasing smile and sparkling eyes as she laughed at him—*At him! Mr. Fitzwilliam Darcy of Pemberley!*—drove him virtually insane until he no longer controlled his faculties. Until his dreams, both day and night, were invaded by her.

Yes, that was it.

And if he was beginning to dream of her as the mother to his children?

Well, that was more troubling.

He again scanned the room, only now he was seeing it as in the recent dreams. Elizabeth curled up in his chair, wearing a soft gown of blue with a baby at her breast. He and Elizabeth reclining on the bed with several children jumping on the mattress as they all laughed. The door to the unused dressing room once belonging to his mother ajar with Elizabeth brushing her incredible hair and smiling at him via the mirror while he held a child in his arms. Elizabeth pregnant and standing before him while he caressed the swell of her belly with his hands. Elizabeth...

He shook his head to clear the strange and disturbing visions that had started in earnest these past two weeks.

Since returning to Pemberley.

Since preparing for Christmas.

He passed a hand over his face.

You are lonely, Darcy, he thought. *Admit it. You want a wife and a family.*

Of course this was not a huge revelation. He had longed for a family of his own for most of his adult life. He had envisioned the silent halls of Pemberley echoing with the noise of childish laughter and running feet. He had desired a relationship as his parents possessed. He had searched endlessly for a woman to love.

Did he love Elizabeth Bennet?

He crawled under the counterpane, the cold linen upon his flesh a sharp contrast to the imaginary fever he felt flowing over his skin while dreaming of her. The flames of passion and tranquil warmth of affection were so incredibly real. Yet, he did not know the answer to his question. Did he love Elizabeth Bennet? Or did he merely desperately crave a connection that presently eluded him? Was he simply weary of searching and being alone?

He no longer knew. But as the tendrils of sleep claimed him, he recognized that his anger and disgust were a sham. The edges of his unconscious mind accepted the love he refused to acknowledge in broad daylight. He reached for the dreams, however they would come to him on this night, Christmas Eve, as an intoxicant that he wanted and required.

"Elizabeth," he whispered as sleep overtook him, not even aware that he had done so.

And eventually the dream came.

This one was different, as they all were, although the essence was the same.

He walked down the main floor corridor toward the parlor with a spring in his step that was utterly inconceivable in his real world but completely normal in this imaginary world. Happy voices, laughter, and singing reverberated down the hall, growing in volume as he neared the gaping portal. He distinguished each one of them, placing names to the individual tones with warm, deep emotion attached. Many of the names would escape him when he woke—this he knew on some level—but in his dream they were dear and intimate.

There was Richard and Georgiana, his Aunt Madeline and Uncle Malcolm, even Jonathan and Priscilla. These were not a surprise. But as he turned the corner and crossed the threshold, his eyes instantly scanned the room and alit upon the one voice dearest of all.

Elizabeth.

He always knew she would be there, somewhere in the midst of those he loved most in the world, belonging there as surely as he did.

She stood next to Richard laughing at some joke his cousin had made. Her ringing laugh, the one he insisted annoyed him while in Hertfordshire but he knew never had, was now the sweetest music. It filled him to bursting with a joy unlike anything he had ever experienced. Even not directed at him, her happiness was a profound balm to his soul, and the smile that had been forming before entering the room grew wider.

Then she noted his presence and turned in his direction, her glorious eyes engaging his. And there quite simply were no words in the English language to describe what passed between or to relate how he felt. Yes indeed, it was magical, and the enchantment feared in his waking moments was wholly understood in this visionary place as the purest form of bonded love.

He accepted it. He relished it. He claimed it. And he returned it wholeheartedly.

He took a step toward her, intending to enfold her into his arms and press her against his heart, but his legs were abruptly engulfed.

"Papa! Papa!"

The dreaming Darcy was not the slightest bit surprised by the chaotic assault of several tiny arms and piping voices. In fact, his spirit soared higher, the missing pieces of his puzzled real life snapping together instantly, into a masterpiece depicting earthly paradise. A booming laugh launched from his mouth and he knelt to administer hugs and kisses to the surging mass of children clamoring to accept his love.

Then Elizabeth was there. His wife. He stood, gazing at her with his entire soul visible in his eyes. She smiled simply, raising one hand to lightly touch his cheek, and said, "Happy Christmas, William."

On some level his rational mind knew it was fantastical, as the number of offspring defied what was physically possible unless Elizabeth had birthed triplets once a year! But of course, dreams have a way of melding reality and allegory. Besides, it was the emotions attached to the fabricating dream that counted. The power of hearing her utter his name, the shortened name only those dear to him used, was so strong. Add to that the intensity of affection from a multitude of quarters and his sleeping mind was soothed as it never was in his waking life.

The dream proceeded as all dreams do. It flipped incoherently from scene to scene, some bizarre in their content and hazy while others were crystalline. The strange mingling of credible specifics—such as Georgiana a grown woman and the heirloom Christmas decorations adorning the Manor—with points impossible—like his parents conversing with Elizabeth—seemed normal within the boundaries of the dream.

It wasn't the details that resonated but the themes of family and love. And as happened every night, he jerked awake before the final consummation of expressing his love to his wife. The ache of need with heart pounding and perspiration rapidly chilling his skin brought on tremors and groans.

He lurched to his feet, crossing the room to stir the smoldering logs. He stared into the flames, his body warming as he tried to make sense of it. The questions flashed through his brain as they did every night. Why her? Was it possible to love in such a way? Was it fated for him as he hoped? Had he childishly imagined his parents possessing such a love? Would he ever have a family of his own? Was he a romantic fool destined to be disappointed?

Did he love Elizabeth Bennet?

And then it dissolved, as it inevitably did. The cold air restored his clarity, the fuzzy sentiments dissipated, his rational intellect reinstated, and logic took over. It was only because he was lonely. It was due to the nature of the Christmas holiday focusing on love and felicity leading to nonsensical musings.

He could not be in love with the lowborn, argumentative, fiery Elizabeth Bennet!

The dreams were nice, pleasant, and passionate, but harmless. *Just enjoy them while they last,* he thought to himself. Why not? They will pass. You will never see Miss Bennet again. God will bring a suitable mate to you. The years will unfold sensibly and composedly. Indeed, serenity will prevail, as it should.

So with that comforting thought conquering the turmoil, his mind calmed and heart beat a regular rhythm. He returned to his bed, his slumber, and his dreams.

Mr. and Mrs. Fitzwilliam Darcy: Two Shall Become One
Sharon Lathan

"Highly entertaining... I felt fully immersed in the time period. Well done!" —*Romance Reader at Heart*

A fascinating portrait of a timeless, consuming love

It's Darcy and Elizabeth's wedding day, and the journey is just beginning as Jane Austen's beloved *Pride and Prejudice* characters embark on the greatest adventure of all: marriage and a life together filled with surprising passion, tender self-discovery, and the simple joys of every day.

As their love story unfolds in this most romantic of Jane Austen sequels, Darcy and Elizabeth each reveal to the other how their relationship blossomed from misunderstanding to perfect understanding and harmony, and a marriage filled with romance, sensuality, and the beauty of a deep, abiding love.

What readers are saying:

"This journey is truly amazing."

"What a wonderful beginning to this truly beautiful marriage."

"Could not stop reading."

"So beautifully written...making me feel as though I was in the room with Lizzy and Darcy...and sharing in all of the touching moments between."

978-1-4022-1523-0 • $14.99 US/ $15.99 CAN/ £7.99 UK

Loving Mr. Darcy: Journeys Beyond Pemberley

SHARON LATHAN

"A romance that transcends time." —*The Romance Studio*

Darcy and Elizabeth embark on the journey of a lifetime

Six months into his marriage to Elizabeth Bennet, Darcy is still head over heels in love, and each day offers more opportunities to surprise and delight his beloved bride. Elizabeth has adapted to being the Mistress of Pemberley, charming everyone she meets and handling her duties with grace and poise. Just when it seems life can't get any better, Elizabeth gets the most wonderful news. The lovers leave the serenity of Pemberley, traveling through the sumptuous landscape of Regency England, experiencing the lavish sights, sounds, and tastes around them. With each day come new discoveries as they become further entwined, body and soul.

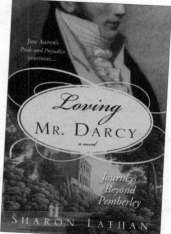

What readers are saying:

"Darcy's passion for love and life with Lizzy is brought to the forefront and captured beautifully."

"Sharon Lathan is a wonderful writer… I believe that Jane Austen herself would love this story as much as I did."

"The historical backdrop of the book is unbelievable—I actually felt like I could see all the places where the Darcys traveled."

"Truly captures the heart of Darcy & Elizabeth! Very well written and totally hot!"

978-1-4022-1741-8 • $14.99 US/ $18.99 CAN/ £7.99 UK

Mr. Darcy Takes a Wife
LINDA BERDOLL
The #1 best-selling Pride and Prejudice sequel

"Wild, bawdy, and utterly enjoyable." —*Booklist*

Hold on to your bonnets!

Every woman wants to be Elizabeth Bennet Darcy—beautiful, gracious, universally admired, strong, daring and outspoken—a thoroughly modern woman in crinolines. And every woman will fall madly in love with Mr. Darcy—tall, dark and handsome, a nobleman and a heartthrob whose virility is matched only by his utter devotion to his wife. Their passion is consuming and idyllic—essentially, they can't keep their hands off each other—through a sweeping tale of adventure and misadventure, human folly and numerous mysteries of parentage. This sexy, epic, hilarious, poignant and romantic sequel to *Pride and Prejudice* goes far beyond Jane Austen.

What readers are saying:

"I couldn't put it down."

"I didn't want it to end!"

"Berdoll does Jane Austen proud! ...A thoroughly delightful and engaging book."

"Delicious fun...I thoroughly enjoyed this book."

"My favorite *Pride and Prejudice* sequel so far."

978-1-4022-0273-5 • $16.95 US/ $19.99 CAN/ £9.99 UK